A panoramic novel of modern China

Pearl Buck gives "a sense of continuity of life in China, the outlook of centuries in the past, the possibilities of the centuries to come. This involves the conflict between tradition and progress. China is finished with one age, she implies, and is ready for a rebirth. But Pearl Buck is enough of the artist not to tell us in specific terms what form that rebirth will take." —*San Francisco Chronicle*

KINFOLK reveals "the full play of a mature and warm mind that has brooded long and thoroughly on Good and Evil."

—*Chicago Sun*

KINFOLK
was originally published by
The John Day Company, Inc.

Pearl S. BUCK

Kinfolk

PUBLISHED BY **POCKET BOOKS** NEW YORK

KINFOLK

John Day edition published 1949

POCKET BOOK edition published June, 1952

9th printing.......................January, 1974

L

Standard Book Number: 671-78268-1.

THE THEATER IN CHINATOWN was crowded to the doors. Every night actors brought from Canton played and sang the old Chinese operas. If Billy Pan, the manager, announced a deficit at the end of the lunar year, businessmen contributed money to cover it. The theater was a bulwark of home for them. Their children went to American schools, spoke the American language, acted like American children. The fathers and mothers were not highly educated people and they could not express to the children what China was, except that it was their own country, which must not be forgotten. But in the theater the children could see for themselves what China was. Here history was played again and ancient heroes came to life before their eyes. It was the only place in Chinatown which could compete with the movies. Parents brought their children early and stayed late. They talked with friends and neighbors, exchanged sweetmeats and gossip, and sat spellbound and dreaming when the curtain went up to show the figures who were contemporary with their ancestors.

The play tonight was *Mu Lan*, the heroine of a thousand years ago, who took her father's place when he fell in battle and so saved her nation from invaders. This was a favorite play, and although it was in the repertory of every company, the citizens of Chinatown never tired of it. It was nearly midnight and they waited with excitement for the curtain to rise on the fifth act. At this moment Billy Pan came to the door and looked over the crowd. He was a stout middle-aged man, dressed in a gray cloth suit, and he was as usual smoking a cigar. His round red face was cheerful and his small eyes twinkled with satisfaction as he glanced about the house. Good business—*Mu Lan* always brought him good business. His shrewd eyes examined the crowd more closely, searching for possible celebrities. It pleased the crowd if he could produce a celebrity after the show. He knew everybody in Chinatown and his eyes slid rapidly from one face to another.

In the tenth row in the middle seat his eyes halted. Dr. Liang Wen Hua! He had seen Dr. Liang only once and then from a platform in uptown New York, when during the war delegates from Chinatown had been invited to come to a celebration of Double Ten. Dr. Liang had made the chief address, and all the delegates had taken pride in the tall handsome figure who was also Chinese. But Dr. Liang had never accepted an invitation to Chinatown. He made the excuse that he could not speak Cantonese, since his native region in China was in the north, near Peking. Yet here he was tonight sitting among the crowd!

The curtain rose and through the darkness Billy Pan edged his way up the narrow aisle. At the tenth row he paused, whispered and waited. The man in the seat next to Dr. Liang came out obediently, and Billy Pan pushed into his place.

"Dr. Liang?" he whispered respectfully.

Dr. Liang turned his head.

"Excuse me, this is Billy Pan, proprietor of theater," Billy Pan whispered in English. "I saw you. Great honor, I am sure! Our theater is very poor. I am sorry you did not tell me you are coming and I would have better show for you, anyway best seat."

Dr. Liang inclined his head. "I am very comfortable, thank you," he said in his low rich voice. "And this is the play I wished to see."

"You not come before, I think?"

"As a professor, I am kept busy."

"You like this play?" Billy Pan persisted.

"I am planning a summer course on the Chinese drama," Dr. Liang replied. "I came to see whether my students might understand this play, as presented by Chinese actors."

"It is too poor," Billy Pan exclaimed.

Dr. Liang smiled. "I suppose American students will not be critical."

Behind them and beside them people were craning their heads. Everybody knew Billy Pan and knew that he would not trouble himself about any ordinary person. Someone recognized Dr. Liang and the name ran along the crowded benches.

"Please," Billy Pan begged. "I ask a great favor of you."

Dr. Liang smiled. "Yes?"

"After the play, will you speak a few words to us from the stage?"

Dr. Liang hesitated.

"Please! It will honor us."

Dr. Liang was gracious. "Very well—but you will have to translate for me. My Chinese is not Cantonese, you know."

"Honored!" Billy Pan exclaimed with fervor.

He rose, sweating and excited, and pushed his way out again and the man whom he had displaced crept back. Now that this man knew by whom he was sitting he felt awkward and humble and he sat as far as possible from the great man.

Dr. Liang did not notice him. His mind was on the gaudy scene upon the stage. In his secret heart he did not enjoy the stylized traditional performance. He had been too long in New York, too often he had gone to Broadway and Radio City. There was something childish about the strutting declaiming actors and the brightly ancient costumes. This sort of thing might be all very well for a country audience before a temple, but certainly it did not suit a modern people. Would he be ashamed if he brought his classes here, or might he explain the drama in terms of the picturesque? He could always tell them that in Shanghai as well as in Peking there was a drama as modern as in New York.

Then it occurred to him that not only the play was difficult. The audience was even more so. Children pattered back and forth and women talked whenever the action dulled for a moment on the stage. Men got up and went out and came back, pausing to greet their friends on the way. It was most unfortunate, he thought, his handsome lips set and his head high, that Chinese like himself were not the sole representatives of his country. It was a great pity that Chinatown had ever been allowed.

The clamor of drums and flutes and violins burst forth in concerted cacophony and the crowd was suddenly silent. The star was coming on. A curtain was drawn back and a brilliant figure dashed upon the stage. It was Mu Lan herself, in the ancient garb of a warrior, and shouts burst from the people. She stalked up and down the stage brandishing the little whip which meant she was on horseback, singing in a high falsetto as she went. From the timbre of the voice Dr. Liang knew that Mu Lan was being played by a young man. The audience, knowing it also, were yet naïvely ready to imagine that she was a beautiful strong young woman.

"I might explain the motif by saying that Mu Lan is the Chinese version of Joan of Arc," Dr. Liang thought.

He was pleased with the idea and his mind played about it. Before he knew it the curtain went down, the hard neon lights flashed on, and Billy Pan stood on the stage waving his arms for attention. Everyone obeyed. People who had been getting up sat down again, and babies began to wail and were hushed. A flood of rapid explosive Cantonese burst from Billy Pan, none of which Dr. Liang could understand. When everyone turned to stare at him, however, he knew that he was being introduced and he rose. The people in the row with him stepped into the aisle to allow him to pass, and he thanked them gravely and walked with dignity up the aisle to the stage and mounted four rickety steps. Billy Pan was waiting for him with a look of devotion, and Dr. Liang smiled slightly. He stood with his hands clasped and he bowed to the audience. Then he began to speak, waiting at the end of each long sentence for Billy Pan to translate.

It was one of his less important speeches, pleasant, courteous, mildly humorous, but the audience was easy to please and laughed heartily and quickly. He was warmed by their pride in him and he took the opportunity to remark that it was the duty of every Chinese to represent his country in the most favorable light to Americans who were, after all, only foreigners. As for himself, he said, he was careful always to behave as though he were, in his own small way, of course, an ambassador. He closed with a reference to Confucius, and was astonished that this did not seem to please the people. They were ignorant, he supposed—very provincial, certainly. He saw them whole, a mass of rather grimy people, small tradesmen and their wives and children, alien and yet somehow building a small commonplace version of China here. Very unfortunate!

He bowed again, smiled, and walked down the steps. Billy Pan followed, and pushing aside the people, he led Dr. Liang out to the street and bawled to a passing taxicab, which swerved and stopped. He opened the door and bowed deeply.

"Thank you, a hundred thanks," he said with fervor. "Come again! Please let me know next time and have dinner with me. There is a good restaurant in next street. I tell him plenty of time to make some good Chinese food, eh? Please! Thank you—thank you—"

He was still bowing when Dr. Liang shut the door firmly and turned to the cab driver.

"Riverside Drive," he said distinctly.

From the darkness of the cab he looked out at Chinatown. The people were going home from the theater, shuffling along the streets. They were waking, he supposed, from the dream world of the past into the dreariness of the present. Yet they did not look dreary. Stopped by a traffic light, he heard their voices laughing and gay, and he saw fathers tenderly carrying little children while mothers led the toddlers. When did they sleep? Shops that were also homes were still lighted and viciously bright neon lamps shone down on windows of chinaware and groceries and lit up long signboards which declared the names of small firms that sold bamboo shoots and dried shrimps and curios. Young men lounged upon the counters and young girls in two's and three's chattered along the sidewalk. It was a lively place, and because it was crude and cheap it was almost worse, Dr. Liang thought, than Americans liked to believe it was, a place of mystery and evil. There was no mystery here, and very little evil. Families lived together closely, and parents struggled with their children to keep to the standards of a country the young had never seen. It was an ordinary place and the people were simple and common. He did not often come here because he found it depressing.

He wished with some annoyance that he had not come tonight, or at least that he had not been recognized. It was gratifying to be known, and yet it made him remember what he habitually tried to forget, that the common people of his country were not in the least like himself.

"Surely you are not a typical Chinese—" how often Americans had cried the words at him!

He always answered them with mild amusement. "I assure you I am a very ordinary Chinese. There are millions like me and better."

He suddenly thought of his eldest son, James, and he sighed. He was profoundly proud of that brilliant boy, the child who had so easily stood at the head of his classes in school and was now at the head of the list of graduates in the medical college.

"A great mind, Dr. Liang," the Chancellor had said only a

few days ago. "A great mind and skillful hands—what a surgeon he will make!"

And now James wanted to waste all his education and go back to China! Who in a war-ruined country could pay the fees of a surgeon?

The cab slowed. "Whereabouts Riverside Drive?" the driver asked.

"Two blocks, and then one to the right, please," Dr. Liang replied.

The streets were quiet with midnight. There was a moon and it shone down on the river. Just ahead was the George Washington Bridge, silvered with light. It was a scene familiar through twenty years of living, but Dr. Liang always felt its beauty. There was nothing more beautiful in the world, perhaps, unless it was the great marble bridge near Peking. But he did not want to be in Peking.

"Here you are," the cabby said.

Dr. Liang stood on the sidewalk and counted his change. The man would expect an exorbitant fee—all American working people expected to earn more than any workingman was worth. He counted out the exact amount and added five per cent to it. His daughter Mary had once been angry with him for that five per cent. "Why don't you ride on the subway?" she had demanded. He had not answered her.

He turned abruptly and entered the apartment house where he lived and stepped into an elevator without speaking. He was very tired and he felt confused and old. His son James was very confusing. The elevator mounted rapidly to the tenth floor and he stepped out. The door to his apartment opened and his wife stood there.

"I have been expecting you for an hour," she said.

He followed her in and she shut the door and yawned loudly. He could see by the slightly dazed look on her plump face that she had been asleep on the couch and her Chinese robe of dark blue silk was wrinkled. He was often ashamed of her, but Americans liked her heartiness and good nature and Chinese feared her temper and her domineering ways. She was an excellent housekeeper, she made him entirely comfortable, and she did not interfere with certain pleasant dreams he had of quite different women whom he met in the pages of Chinese poetry. He was too good a man to allow them to come to life otherwise. He had made Confucian ethics his own and he respected his wife as the mother of his children and the heart of his household. Moreover, she worshiped him, in spite of often scolding him and occasionally flouting him. The problem of her life centered in how to indulge her children and at the same time seem to obey her husband.

"Are the children asleep?" he asked.

"An hour ago," she said, trying to be brisk. "Sit down and rest yourself. I have kept some soup hot."

"My sons might have waited for me," he said in a hurt voice.

"Well, they did not," she said in her practical way. "Now drink your soup and let us get to bed ourselves."

She went into the kitchen and brought out a bowl of soup and a spoon on a tray and a plate of crackers. He crumbled the crackers into the soup and began to eat. "I would have been back earlier except that I was recognized and the crowd would have me address them," he said slowly without looking at her.

"Yes, well—" she said without interest and yawned again.

A crude woman, he thought with distaste, and he did not speak for a while as he ate.

Mrs. Liang sat on a stool and watched him, her eyes bleary with sleep. She perceived simply that he was not pleased with her and she tried to make amends. "It was good of you to speak to those small people," she said. "And I am glad you were not at home. That James of ours did nothing but talk about going back to China." She sighed and scratched her head with her little fingernail. "You must get a good night's sleep—he is going to talk with you in the morning."

"I shall put him off," Dr. Liang declared.

But his appetite failed him and he set the bowl on the table only half empty. He knew that James was not a son to be put off even by his own father. Then he caught sight of Mrs. Liang's mouth wide open in another yawn and he was suddenly angry.

"Come—come," he cried, "get yourself to bed—spare me the sight of you!"

He stalked out of the room and turned out the light at the door. In the darkness she pattered after him humbly, and forgave him. He was a great man, and he was her husband.

Dr. Liang prided himself on his calm. Reared upon Confucian ethics in his early home in China, he had for many years comforted himself for his somewhat arid life in New York by teaching Chinese philosophy in colleges. There, he hoped, crude young Americans might imbibe from him the spiritual nourishment which he liked to think had kept China intact for four thousand years and would, he said confidently in his classroom, weather her through her present difficulties.

He summoned all his calm the next morning, as he faced his son James. The young man, twenty-six years old and last month graduated from a medical college, also faced his father. For months, all during his last year of internship in the medical center, he had been approaching inevitably this hour. He loved and feared his father, and it had taken all his strength to decide that the day had come to tell him finally that he wanted to go back to China. Why it should be this June morning rather than any other, he did not know. He had got up early, full of energy and impatience, to find that the day was clear, that the heat of the past week had broken, and that he felt hungry and well. The duplex apartment in which his family had lived almost as long as he could remember was very pleasant indeed this morning. His father had almost decided last week to put in air conditioning, in order that he could work more comfortably, which always meant more profitably. This morning being cool, he knew he would find his father in the library at his desk, and there he had gone after a hearty breakfast of fruit, bacon and eggs, coffee, and toast. The family always ate American breakfasts, and unless his mother felt inclined to cook, they ate American food altogether. His two sisters could not cook, and his younger brother Peter did not like Chinese food. All the children except himself and Mary had been born in America and were therefore American citizens.

As he listened to his son, Dr. Liang sat quietly in the large brown leather chair where he had written so many of his scholarly works. He was a tall man, for his origins were in the north, that birthplace of so many of China's great men. His sons were tall, too, and he took pleasure in hearing Americans exclaim, "But I thought Chinese were always short!" This cry gave him the opportunity to explain in his deep and gentle voice how unfortunate it was for his people that so many of the Chinese in America were tradesmen from one small region in the province of Kwangtung. They were not at all typical, he went on to say, for their short stature and their dark color were the result of their blood mixture with tribesmen in the hills nearby. The real Chinese, he explained, were tall, as in the north, or fairly tall, as in Central China, and their skin was not dark. He himself had a pallor that was certainly lighter than many Americans owned. He was not fond of exercise and never allowed himself to get sunburned. His sons burned as red brown as any American, for they were good at sports and played tennis brilliantly. He did not encourage his daughters to enlarge their muscles by such activities. Louise, the younger one, disobeyed him frequently, but he liked to think that Mary, the elder, just younger than James, was a true Chinese daughter, obedient and mild and very pretty.

He contemplated his son from behind his spectacles. The lenses were so thick that they magnified his eyes slightly and added force to his gaze.

"It seems unwise to return home at this time," he said. "The country is in great confusion. The Communists are threatening, and as my son your life can scarcely be safe. I would of course commend you to my friends in the government, but they could not guarantee your safety from rebellious students who might revenge themselves on me by killing you."

"I do not want to be under the protection of anyone," James said. "I shall just go." He sat on the sill of the long double window, and gazing toward the river as he spoke, he could see the bridge glittering in the sunlight. It looked at once delicate and strong, a silver cobweb of steel against a misty blue sky.

"But where?" Dr. Liang asked sharply. "Where can you go in China today and not waste yourself?"

James did not answer. He sat motionless, and Dr. Liang saw more strongly than ever the son's resemblance to his mother. Mrs. Liang was a good wife and an exemplary mother. She managed the household well, in spite of imperfect English which she would not improve, but she was stubborn.

"Your education has cost me a great deal of money," Dr. Liang went on. "Fortunately my books on Chinese philosophy have sold well. But suppose they had not?"

James smiled. "I cannot imagine it, Father."

Dr. Liang examined his son's square but very handsome young face. Was this remark made with some jocular meaning? He did not understand American humor, which seemed to saturate his children. But the smile on his son's lips was kindly.

"There is no hospital in China which is up to the standard to which you have been trained," he observed.

"It has been twenty years since you lived there, Father."

"You know very well that I was there ten years ago."

"Only for six months, and you traveled constantly," his son murmured.

"And in all my travels I saw nothing but the most primitive ways of life," Dr. Liang retorted. "The civilization which was kept alive by the great old families such as ours is dying out. When I saw our ancestral halls I wept. My old uncle Tao lives there as a beggar—or very nearly."

"I want to see for myself," James said.

"How do you propose to make your living?" Dr. Liang asked almost harshly. His large beautifully shaped hands, as smooth as a woman's, he kept habitually relaxed in order that there might be no tension in him. The cult of the hands, he often said, was a profound one. Now involuntarily he clenched his hands.

"You need not send me anything, Father," James said.

"Of course I must! I won't have my son going about like a beggar."

"Do you mean I may go?"

"I do not," Dr. Liang exclaimed. "On the contrary, I forbid it."

James stood up. He turned from the window and faced his father. "Please don't say that. I don't want to have to go without your consent."

The moment which both had dreaded for so many years had suddenly come—the moment of open rebellion. Dr. Liang had waked often in the night and dreaded it. He was proud of his elder son, and he told himself and his wife many times that James alone had justified his decision to live abroad. Had they stayed among the wars and confusions of modern China, the boy's brilliant mind, his extraordinary talents, could never have been developed.

There were many other proofs of his wisdom. His children were all well educated; they had this comfortable and even luxurious home. They were healthy and full of energy and able to look after themselves. As for himself, Dr. Liang always said, he felt that Heaven had directed his steps, and that he had been useful in explaining to Americans the real China, the great civilization which today was obscured but which would assuredly shine forth again when peace was established in the world. It was no small mission to bring the East and West together. When times were better again he hoped, he told his American friends, to return to his own country to spend his old age, and there he would expound to his countrymen the glories of the American civilization.

"If you disobey me," Dr. Liang now said, his hands still clenched on his knees, "then I will disown you."

"I shall still be a Liang," James said. "You begot me and you cannot deny that."

Father and son glared at each other without a sign of yielding. "If I cannot deny it, I will forget it," Dr. Liang said loudly.

Outside the door they heard footsteps retreating softly. Dr. Liang rose and strode across the room and threw open the door. No one was there. The spacious rooms were silent. He closed the door again. It was perhaps only the Irish maid Nellie who came every day to clean and to cook. But he had scarcely seated himself again when the door opened impetuously and Mrs. Liang stood there, this morning encased in a long gown of dull purple satin. In spite of her many years here she looked as Chinese as the day she had left her father's house thirty years ago to marry a young student whom she had scarcely seen. Her hair was smoothed back into a neat bun, and her full rosy face was kind but strong-tempered.

"Now what is going on here?" she demanded in the loud voice which her husband detested. Long ago he had learned that the best way to reprove her was by making his own voice especially gentle.

"Our son asks me to allow him to return to our old home." He spoke always in Chinese to his wife, as a reminder that he did not consider her English good enough. His own was pure, with an Oxford accent. He had visited Oxford once for a year's lectures.

"Let him go then," Mrs. Liang exclaimed. She came in and sat down on a large square stool, and her satin gown wrinkled over her breasts and her belly. Dr. Liang looked away.

"You do not understand, mother of my sons." He always called her "mother of my sons" when he wanted to be very

Confucian. "His life would not be safe. I have reproved our Communists so openly here that they will try to kill him if he goes to China."

She sighed loudly at this and plucked from the knot of her hair a gold pin with which she scratched her inner ear. "I told you to stick to Confucius," she complained. "Why should you talk about Communists? No one in America wants to hear about them."

Dr. Liang closed his eyes at this stupidity and at the sight of the hairpin. At one end of it was the earpick and at the other a toothpick. He had besought her to throw this primitive implement away but she had refused. "How then would I pick my teeth and clean my ears?" she had demanded.

"American women do not use these instruments," he had said.

She had stared at him. "How do you know?" she had asked shrewdly.

"Not in public, I mean," he had said hastily.

They had compromised after ten years of argument upon her not using the pin publicly. That is, she did not use it before Americans. Chinese she did not consider the public. She used the earpick now, first on her right ear and then on her left, a busy look on her face. This helped her to think, she often declared.

"I cannot allow you to be killed, my son," she now said to James. "If your father is sure there is danger, then you had better stay here for a year or two longer. That is a good job you are offered in the medical center. They think highly of you there."

Dr. Liang was delighted. She invariably took the children's part against him and he had braced himself for her stand against him now.

He rose. "You see, my son! You can scarcely disobey both parents. Your mother speaks wisely. This is very sensible of you, mother of my sons. Now, please, allow me to do my work. I am in the middle of a very important chapter on Confucius and Communism."

"Do leave the Communists out of your book," Mrs. Liang exclaimed. "Otherwise it can't sell."

"No, no," he said humorously, "you don't understand. It is all in joke."

"But why joke about them?" she asked.

"Come, come, now, let me do my work." He commanded and she retreated protesting. When he turned to speak to his son again, he was gone. James had left the room by the door into the dining room.

Dr. Liang stood irresolute for a moment. Then he sighed, pulled out a large silk handkerchief from the pocket of his expensive dark broadcloth suit, wiped his face and hands, and sat down before his desk.

Outside his father's deeply carpeted study James found his sister Mary. She was a small slight girl who could easily have looked not more than twelve years old except that her dress was that of a twenty-year-old young woman, which she was. Her hands were clenched tightly on her breast and her pretty face was anxious.

"You sent Mother in!" James whispered.

"But to quarrel with Father!" she whispered back. "It's so hopeless."

They tiptoed away hand in hand through the hall and opened the door and went into the lobby outside. James pushed the button for the elevator. "Father always forces a quarrel," he said. "Will you be cold without your coat?"

"No—the sun is warm enough. Jim, why do you let yourself be forced?"

"I don't know." His voice was helpless and his face grim.

The elevator clattered, the gate banged open and they entered. They were silent before the elevator man, although they knew him well and were fond of him. Whatever their division behind their own doors, the Liang family presented a calm front before the people in whose land they were aliens.

"Nice day," the elevator man offered.

"Fine," they answered together.

They left the elevator decorously, side by side. James was tall and Mary came below his shoulder. The elevator man watched them affectionately. "Nice kids, even if they are Chinese!" he told the second elevator man. "You never see them comin' in drunk and havin' to be hauled up like some of the rest of 'em."

The second elevator man scratched his head with his forefinger. "The old Chink is kinda stingy, I notice."

"Don't ask us no favors, though—no dogs to drag out in all kinds of weather."

"Nice family," the other agreed, and yawned.

Out in the sunshine James walked along the street with the long noiseless step that was his inheritance of grace. Mary took two steps to his one. The street was quiet, for it was far uptown. To their left now was the river, spanned by the George Washington Bridge. This bridge had deeply affected their lives. As children it had made them imagine bridges over oceans to China, and it had persuaded them to believe that it was always possible to cross stretches of hardship and unhappiness and set foot on other shores. It had made Peter, by the time he was ten, decide to be an engineer.

"Did Father say you could go?" Mary asked.

"No—and Mother only helped him—not me."

"Oh, and she promised!" Mary cried.

"She said something about staying here for a year or two. You know what she means. She wants me to marry and have a son."

"How can she be so old-fashioned?" Mary moaned. "She might as well have lived her whole life in our village!"

James shrugged his broad shoulders and lifted his hand to push back the lock of strong black hair that the river wind had blown over his forehead. "I'm not thinking only of myself," he said. "I'm thinking of you, too, Mary. If I can't go, they won't let you."

"I suppose you could ask Lili to marry you now," Mary suggested. "That would be a compromise, wouldn't it? Let's sit down, Jim. The wind beats at me and blows the words out of my mouth."

He turned to the benches that stood near the railing above the river and chose an empty one at some distance from the others. A curve in the embankment sheltered them, and the sun poured down upon them.

"You'll think me a coward," he said abruptly. "I've never told Lili that I want to go home."

"I know you haven't," his sister said in her sweet voice. "But I've told her, Jim."

"Mary!" His cry was mingled with reproof and relief. "Without asking me!"

She nodded her head. Putting up her little hand she brushed back the strands of her soft straight black hair which had escaped from the two thick braids wound about her head. "I had to make her see how much it meant to you."

She was too delicately kind to say that Lili Li, to whom he had been secretly engaged for eight days, might not want to live in China.

"What did she say?" Fine tense lines sprang to life in his face. The calm of his outward manner was a habit, worn as separately as a coat which he took off or put on.

"She didn't say anything—she just looked at me," Mary replied. "You know the way she looks."

"I know."

They were silent for a while, gazing out over the river. Ships shone in the sunlight. A man-of-war glittered with flying flags. A yacht, bright with brass, steamed busily toward the harbor. Across the river an enormous sign announced a pleasure park.

James knew very well the way that Lili Li could look. Her great dark eyes were like oval gems of onyx set into the smoothness of her soft face. Her lips were full and rested sweetly together. She painted them, as all girls did, and they looked like a red camellia against the cream of her skin. Silence was her charm. Where other Chinese girls were chattering and restless, in imitation of American girls, Lili was quiet, and every movement was slow and all her slender body was rich with repose. The Li family had come from Shanghai only a year ago, Mr. Li for a gall-bladder operation by American doctors and Mrs. Li to see that Lili, the only child, was educated in American schools. They were wealthy and kindly, and they were frankly glad to be in a country where life was still comfortable. Mr. Li, a prudent man, had years ago sold his silk mills to the Japanese and had deposited his fortune in American banks.

James had fallen in love with Lili at first sight, but she was not easily won. At first she had been shocked at his impetuous proposal, made at the annual New Year's party given by Dr. and Mrs. Liang. She was too sophisticated, as a Shanghai girl, to declare that he should first approach her parents. She compromised between new and old customs by dropping her head, touching her embroidered handkerchief to her lips, and saying that she did not want to marry anybody, not for a long time, because she wanted to finish her education. It took months of constant attendance upon her, buttressed by many courtesies from Dr. Liang to Mr. Li and much advice and practical aid from Mrs. Liang to Mrs. Li on the difficulties of finding a proper place to live and on the strange behavior of American servants, before Mr. and Mrs. Li would advise their daughter to yield even slightly to young Dr. Liang's advances. Mr. Li had meanwhile learned, from sources which seemed naturally open to him in whatever country he was, that Dr. Liang, while not a rich man in the sense of big business, was nevertheless comfortably well off, that he had a high place in society as a scholar and a writer, and that the Li family would gain in prestige by the marriage. Moreover, Dr. James Liang was a brilliant young physician and he would undoubtedly be very rich some day, if he stayed in New York.

Meanwhile Mrs. Li had become anxious, as she grew familiar with American life on the streets of New York, lest Lili be attacked by American ruffians and robbed of her virtue, or, almost worse, lest some American fall in love with her and want to marry her. She was afraid that she and Mr. Li, who were both mild people, might not have the courage to refuse their daughter to an ardent and desperate American. Therefore they had made known their growing approval of the Liang family to Lili, and Lili had accepted James.

Nevertheless she did not wish to let her parents think her the usual old-fashioned obedient Chinese daughter, and so she had told Jim very shyly, after his proposal and her acceptance, that she did not want anybody to know at least for a whole week. To this he had agreed because it gave him time to persuade his father to let him go to China. With that permission he would tell Lili that they would make their home in Peking itself. The Liang ancestral lands and village were only about a hundred *li* south of the city. He was lucky, he told himself, that he would have as his wife a real Chinese girl instead of an American-born Chinese who might be very unhappy even in her own country.

He moved restlessly on the bench beside his sister and then he got up. "When did you tell Lili?" he asked.

"Yesterday. She telephoned to ask me to go to Radio City with her. You know she doesn't dare go alone anywhere."

"That's her mother," James said.

"She's afraid, too," Mary said.

They had discussed Lili's fearfulness before, Mary critically and James with defense. "Inevitably Lili was affected by the war, even in Shanghai," he now said. Mary did not answer. She continued to gaze dreamily across the river at the flashing sign of the amusement park. She had seen that sign all her life but she had never been to the park. Peter and Louise went every summer and came back weary with laughter and half sick with spun sugar and popcorn, both of which she hated. But most of all she hated loud voices and catcalling, whistling young white men. She loathed the touch of their flesh. Her heart was full of dreams about the country she had never seen, yet to which she belonged, where her own people lived. She could believe nothing but good about China, nothing but what was brave about her people. When Madame Chiang had visited America she had been in her first year of high school, and without hope of meeting her. But she had seen her, flashing in and out of hospitals, in and out of great cars, in and out of hotels, and always proud and beautiful. She had made a scrap book of the newspaper photographs.

"I'm going to see Lili now," James said suddenly.

Mary looked at her watch. It was still early. "Hadn't you better telephone first?" she asked. "She may not be up. You know how Mrs. Li is—she plays mah-jongg all night, and Lili stays up—"

"I'll go on the chance," he replied.

"What will you tell her, Jim?" Mary asked. "You can't very well say that you are going—"

"Why not?" he asked.

"But if even Mother wants you to wait?"

"If Lili is willing, we'll be married right away—and we'll go together."

"What if—" Mary broke off and shook her head.

"What if she isn't willing?" Jim asked. "I'll face that—if I must. So long—"

He nodded and walked away, and Mary looked after him thoughtfully. Inside her small neat head her life was planned as carefully as one of the outlines she prepared in her class in child hygiene. She was going to China, too. Jim did not know it yet, but she did. Whether he was married or not, she was going. If he married—well, Lili was helpless and she could help her. Lili knew nothing at all about housekeeping and children. Mrs. Li had always said there were plenty of servants in China and so what was the use of teaching Lili to do things she would never have to do?

Mary watched her brother out of sight, then she rose, shook her skirts, and tripped back to the big apartment house.

She had promised Peter to make shrimp flakes, for no one else would take the trouble, and he loved to eat them while he studied at night. To have the radio turned on full blast, to reach out for handfuls of shrimp flakes while he memorized with such ease the laws of physics—this combination of activities satisfied Peter's whole nature.

Mr. and Mrs. Li had found an apartment on the next street in from the river. It was a sublease from a European motion-picture actress who was at present having one of her wrestling matches with Hollywood. It had been impossible to find an apartment on long lease and next to impossible to get a sublease. Almost any American, at the sight of Mr. Li's fat, kind, yellow face, declared that he had decided not to sublet, after all. Mrs. Liang, who was the interpreter and manager on these occasions, had been filled with fury, but she did not wish to let her new friends know that they were unwelcome in this country of refuge. Besides, she knew that they were not really unwelcome. Shopkeepers would rejoice in Mrs. Li's easy purchases and Mr. Li's ready checkbook. The unwillingness lay in some undefined region which Mrs. Liang preferred not to probe.

Secretly she hated and despised all Americans, but this she kept to herself. Someday when the dreadful discomforts of present China had changed to the solid, pleasantly lazy life of the old normal days, when they had all gone home, and when she had filled her house with servants and once more had nothing to do, she would tell her best friends all that she knew and felt about Americans. It would take a long time and she would not do it until she knew she need never come back to America again. Meanwhile she dared not release herself. She had plodded from agency to agency, had studied the newspapers with her shortsighted eyes, spelling out to herself the advertisements of apartments, and had been rewarded one day by finding this handsome place where the owner had no feeling against Chinese, since she herself was only French.

Julie de Rougemont had laughed a great deal at Mr. Li, who had been only too charmed with her, and within twenty-four hours the Li family was comfortably settled in a highly modern apartment, whose three baths vied with each other in magnificence. Mrs. Li had disliked the mirrored ceiling in the one she used because she did not enjoy looking at herself as she lay in the tub or, did she chance to look up, the sight of herself moving squatly about on the floor, and so she had ordered the mirrors painted, in spite of the lease which insisted that no alterations were to be made. Of the family only Lili seemed to suit the apartment. Lili, slim in her gorgeous and extreme Chinese gowns, matched the modern settees and tables, the blond rugs, the sleek draperies. The French woman had screamed with pleasure at the sight of Lili.

"Ah, what beauty!" she had sighed. "What skin—what hands—and the eyes, *mon Dieu!*"

Mr. and Mrs. Li had looked at their daughter with new respect, but Lili had given no sign of pleasure. Her red mouth, her dark eyes, had remained sweetly unmoved.

At the door of this apartment James now pressed a small button, jeweled with luminous glass. He could hear the soft murmur of voices speaking Chinese. At the sound of the bell they stopped. There was silence, and then after a moment Lili herself opened the door.

"Lili," he cried. "I was hoping you were at home."

Her manner, perfectly decorous, softened. She turned her head and called, "Ma, it is only James."

The rooms came to sudden life. Somewhere Mr. Li coughed and spat heartily and groaned. Mrs. Li shouted in Chinese, "Come in, come in—we are drinking tea. Ha, you—Lili, what's the servant woman's name?"

"Mollie," said Lili.

"Mah-lee," Mrs. Li shouted in English, "more watah, velly hot! Teapot!"

A maid with a scared white face hastened in, fetched the teapot and hurried out again. Mrs. Li looked after her with kindly contempt. "These foreigners," she said confidentially to James, "they are not good servants. They do not understand proper relations. This Mah-lee, she does not ask me how I feel in the morning. She gives me no small attentions. Naturally, I give her no wine money—only her wages. She is discontented, I can see, but why should I pay for what I do not get?"

She looked about and laughed. Then she patted the chair next her. "Sit down," she told James. "How is your mother? And your learned father, is he working? He works too hard!"

James bowed first to Mr. Li and then to Mrs. Li. "Both my parents are well, and you, sir? And you, madame?"

"He," Mrs. Li pointed her chin at Mr. Li, "he coughs a great deal. It is this damp river air."

"I coughed in Shanghai, too," Mr. Li said.

"So you did," Mrs. Li agreed. "It was the damp river air there, also. All rivers are alike, full of water, which is damp."

No one could deny this. The maid brought in the teapot and Lili poured the tea in silence and handed bowls to everybody prettily with both hands.

It was ill luck indeed, James told himself, that he had found Mr. and Mrs. Li both here. It would not occur to them, he knew, to leave him alone with Lili. Why, they would ask themselves, should anyone wish them gone? However long he stayed they would continue to sit in amiable conversation. Nor would Lili move to leave them or to suggest their leaving. She sat gracefully leaning against the back of a green satin chair and looking completely beautiful.

"It is such a nice day," James said helplessly. "I came to see if Lili would take a little walk with me."

Lili looked at her mother and Mrs. Li nodded. "It is bright daylight," she observed. "I see no reason against it. The sunshine will be healthy for you but do not let it burn your face. If you sit down, let it be in the shade."

"I cannot understand these Americans," Mr. Li said in his husky rumbling voice. "They dislike their black people yet they let the sun burn them all as black as white people can get."

"Everybody likes darker people best," Mrs. Li said briskly. "It is only that the white people are rough and like to order others here and there."

"Shall we go?" James asked Lili.

She rose and went to a closet and brought out a pink silk parasol and a black patent-leather handbag.

"Have you money in your purse?" Mr. Li inquired.

"Only about twenty dollars," Lili replied.

"Give her a little more," Mrs. Li coaxed. "She might see a bit of jewelry."

Mr. Li reached into the depths of his loose Chinese robe and pulled out a bulging wallet and peeled off eight ten-dollar notes. "Anything over one hundred American dollars you had better let me look at, lest the foreigners cheat you," he told his daughter in Shanghai dialect.

She took the money, pouting a little. James bowed his farewells and Mrs. Li demanded that he return to eat his midday meal with them.

"Eat with us and I will make a dish myself—say shrimps and cabbage," she said.

"Another day," James replied courteously. "Today I am not very hungry."

He went out with Lili, conscious of her beauty, and they stood side by side as they went down in the elevator, their shoulders barely touching. In the street he scarcely knew how to begin. He was sure that Lili would not speak until he introduced some subject, and whether he should begin to speak at once about going to China he did not know. He looked at her and she turned her head and smiled at him slightly. She wore her hair long on her shoulders in the American fashion, and a fringe curled over her forehead. Under this fringe her eyes, set shallowly beneath her penciled brows, were large and wide open and very black. This pretty face, so flowerlike, comforted James with its calm. In spite of the quiet surface of his own family there were sharp tensions between them all, and the sharper because they were so earnestly hidden until they burst forth in some uncontrollable crisis. Mary, he often felt, for all her helpfulness and adoration for him, was too strong natured and stubborn for a girl. Her smallness was entirely deceiving, for when her will was set she was overpowering. Even their father sometimes shrugged his shoulders and yielded to her tearless determination. She never cried, however angry or hurt she was.

Lili, James felt, was entirely different and therefore adorable. She was soft and yielding and she cried easily. He had seen tears swim into her great eyes when Mr. Li was impatient with her over some trifle. This made him angry and he promised himself that he would always be a patient and kind husband. How could he be otherwise? He longed to take her hand, but she was impeded by the parasol and her handbag.

"Let me hold the parasol," he urged.

She gave it to him, and he reached for her hand and placed it in his arm. "Not in the street!" she exclaimed.

"Here it is quite proper," he assured her. "Where shall we go?"

"To Radio City, please," she replied.

"But I thought you and Mary went there only yesterday?"

"Please, I want to go again today," she pleaded.

He had not the heart to refuse her, and yet it would be impossible to talk if they were watching a picture. She would sit completely absorbed, oblivious to all except the wonder of the story upon the screen, of which, he often discovered, she had comprehended only the more spectacular effects.

"It is either too late or too early," he said playfully. "If we go now we cannot return in time for the midday meal. It is too early for the afternoon picture. Let us just walk along the streets and sit down perhaps on a bench and watch the river. Besides, I want to talk to you, Lili, very seriously."

She did not protest this decision, and he led her to a bench on the river front, and they sat down. He leaned the open parasol on the back of the bench and it shielded them pleasantly from the street. Before them the river spread a sheet of tumbled silver. She looked at the river but he looked at her. He had never kissed her, to his own surprise. It was simply because he did not know what she would think of it. Yet she had seen kisses between men and women on the screen.

"Lili," he said gently.

She turned her long-lashed eyes toward him. The lashes were straight, not curled as were the lashes of American girls, and they were very thick. Her lips did not move.

"Will you let me kiss you?" he asked in the same gentle voice.

She looked to the right and left. No one was near. She opened her bag, took out a paper tissue, wiped the red from her lips, and with an air of patience she put up her face to be kissed. He hesitated, confounded by her performance. Then he could not resist the ready lips and he bent his head and kissed her. Her head pressed against his arm on the back of the bench and she closed her eyes. Her lips were cool and she did not open them. He smelled the gardenia scent of her skin. Then he lifted his swimming head.

"You don't find it strange—to kiss?"

Now that the kiss was over she took a small mirror and a lipstick from her handbag and reddened her lips carefully and examined her hair. Then she shook her head. "Oh, no, James," she said.

Cold horror fell upon him. "You have kissed other men?"

"Only Americans!" she said.

"Americans!" he cried. "But where?"

"In Shanghai," she replied. "Some soldiers and two officers."

"Did they all kiss you?"

"Of course I only allowed the officers more than one time," she said. She was gazing at the river again and he could look at her pure and perfect profile.

"But Lili, you didn't love them!" He pressed her hand to his breast.

"No, not at all," she replied.

"Then why, dear?"

"They asked me, and I said why, and they said for good feeling between Americans and Chinese, and so courteously I did."

He laughed loudly at this, and then silently cursed the men who had taken advantage of her ignorance. "Please promise me you will never kiss any other man but me, Lili. It is not right, you know. Only engaged people and husband and wife should kiss."

She looked at him now with some alarm. "You mean, the officers were bad men?"

"I'm afraid so, dear." He did not want to hurt her, or disillusion her too quickly.

She pondered this for a moment, her face moved with distaste. "They did smell very bad," she said. "And I do promise you, James. For I do not like to kiss very much."

"Only me," he insisted.

She smiled at this and lifted her hand. "Kiss my hand, please, so I don't have so much trouble to take off and on lipstick."

He laughed, detecting in the corners of her long eyes the hint of a sparkle, and he put the delicate scented hand to his lips and then held it while he talked.

"Lili, now that we are alone, I must tell you what I want more than anything in the world after we are married. I want to go back to China, dear, and do my work there in our own country."

There was not a quiver in the narrow hand he held.

"Are you willing for that, Lili?" he asked gently.

"Oh, yes," she said readily. "If my parents agree."

"Do you think they will agree?" he asked anxiously.

"Oh, no," she said in the same ready voice. "I think they will not. We had too much trouble in Shanghai."

"Then, darling," he exclaimed, "what shall we do?"

"I don't know," she said. "Please, James, you think of something else."

"You mean—not go?"

"Yes, please!"

She took his hand and suddenly pressed it to her cheek. "Please stay here," she begged. "Radio City is so nice!"

"But darling, I have work to do," he urged.

"You will have a good job," she reminded him.

She was so lovely in her childlike sweetness that he had not the heart to reproach her. "But China needs us, dear. Think how few hospitals there are! I want someday to make a big hospital where sick people can come and be healed."

"Chinese people are too poor to pay hospitals," she said.

"But in my hospital the rich will help pay for the poor," he urged.

She laughed at this. "Rich people don't want to pay for them," she said shrewdly.

He felt himself caught in some sort of a net, so soft as to be intangible, and yet he was floundering in it. "Lili, answer me straight. Will you come to China with me?"

"If my father says so," she told him.

"Is that a promise, darling?"

"I promise," she said in her sweet ready way.

"We'll live in Peking," he murmured.

"I like Peking," she agreed. "Such nice shops there! Oh, that remembers me—I haven't spent my money." She rose and smiled down at him with the witchery of a child. "Come, please—I want to buy something. A taxi, please!"

He rose and called a cab and she sat down luxuriously.

"Fifth Avenue near the park," she called.

They were put down below Central Park and with the ease of many such trips she went into one expensive shop and then another. At the end of an hour and a half she returned to the first shop she had entered and bought a set of costume jewelry that cost exactly one hundred dollars including the tax. She laughed while she waited for the package. "I was so stupid when I came to New York, James," she confided to him. "I thought I must offer half the price as asked. Now I know with Americans it is not so. You always give them what they want."

He saw the saleswoman gazing at her with admiration and even astonishment at her beauty, and he was proud that she was Chinese—and that she was his. He bent to whisper in her ear, "Only—not kisses!"

She shook her head. "No—only not that."

It was long past noon when he returned her to her parents. Mr. Li was restless with hunger, and he exclaimed at the sight of his daughter. "How long you have been! My belly is thundering."

"What did you buy?" Mrs. Li asked.

It was, James saw, no hour to talk with Mr. Li, and he bade them farewell. Lili followed him to the door. "I will come tonight and ask your father," he said.

"Please do," she said sweetly and shut the door.

At the door of his own home Mary met him, as silent as a little cat. "Will she go?" she demanded in a whisper.

"Yes," James said, "if her father will let her."

"And if he will not?"

"He must," James replied.

"Ha!" Mary cried under her breath.

"Come!" their mother's voice sang at them from the dining room. "Come, eat—the food is hot—don't let the food get cold. Father doesn't like cold food."

"Coming," Mary cried.

"Coming, Mother," James echoed.

There could be no talk or argument at the table. Dr. Liang insisted on perfect calm at his meals. He stood behind his chair in abstracted silence waiting for his family to gather. Mrs. Liang bustled through the rooms calling and compelling. When James and Mary entered the dining room she was hurrying upstairs, her somewhat thick figure toiling its way on half-bound feet. In her childhood her feet had been bound, but when her family discovered that the little boy to whom they had betrothed her years before had grown up into a fastidious and modern young man who swore with ferocity that he would not marry a woman with bound feet, they had hastened to unbind them as far as it was possible. Dr. Liang had never acknowledged that his wife once had bound feet. He had declared to Americans until he believed himself that the custom of binding the feet of young females had died out of China sometime in the last century. "Somewhat earlier than you Westerners stopped binding the waists of your women," he was fond of saying with his charming smile. "I flatter myself," he said next, "that our race was less injured than yours, since important organs were not, luckily for us, located in the feet of our women!" Nothing enraged him more profoundly than to have a luckless missionary, newly home from China, maintain that there was still foot-binding going on in remote villages.

"It is not true," he would say with high dignity. "As a Chinese I know."

He looked up now as his two elder children came in. "Let us sit down," he told them. "I hear your mother screaming on the upper floor, and doubtless Peter and Louise will join us soon."

He began to sup the chicken broth and bean vermicelli with audible satisfaction. Among Americans he would have drunk silently but with his own family it was a pleasure to relax, he declared, and act as a real Chinese.

No one spoke while he ate. Peter came in and sat down. He was a pleasant-looking boy of seventeen, so thin that his long neck was ludicrous. His features were large and unusually strongly marked, and his forehead was high. Dr. Liang found it difficult not to make fun of this son of his, but today because he was displeased with James he felt kindly toward Peter.

"You were working on some physics but a few days ago," he said courteously. "I have not heard the outcome."

"I received a mark of ninety-seven, Father," Peter said. By concentration he could keep his voice down, and he achieved this sentence without a squawk.

"Good son," Dr. Liang exclaimed. "Drink your soup while it is hot."

Mrs. Liang bustled in at this moment, sweating apologies. Louise followed, looking sulky. She was sixteen, taller than Mary, and very pretty. Her short hair was extravagantly curled and she wore a tight red dress and high-heeled black pumps. She had been crying, and Mrs. Liang looked at her crossly as she sat down heavily at her place.

"Think what this girl of ours has been doing!" she said.

Dr. Liang stared at his youngest child. "She has been crying. Why have you scolded her?" Louise was his favorite child and the whole family knew it.

"After all you have said about waist-binding," Mrs. Liang complained. She gulped her soup between sentences, to Dr.

Liang's intense disgust. "She was binding her waist—that's what she was doing! Before the mirror! Her face was all red."

"But why?" Dr. Liang asked, staring at Louise.

"Because why?" Mrs. Liang answered in a loud voice. "Now it is fashionable again, it seems. The Americans are wanting very small waists."

"We are Chinese," Dr. Liang said mildly. He continued to gaze at Louise. "Never forget, my child—we are aliens here. This is not our civilization. We must not forget our sources. Our women are beautiful because they are natural."

The four young people lowered their heads and drank assiduously of the soup in the bowls. Mrs. Liang tipped her bowl, and shouted toward the kitchen, "Neh-lee, Neh-lee!"

The maid Nellie came in quickly, gathered the dishes and brought in bowls of food on a tray. Mrs. Liang watched her sharply while Dr. Liang talked to Louise.

"We should set the example, my child. I often ask Heaven why it is that I am sent here, an exile from my beloved country. Heaven does not answer but my heart makes reply. I have a mission here. My children have a mission, too. We must show this vast new country what it is to be Chinese. Now if you bind your waist, even as the Americans—and can it be true that this vile and harmful practice is again to be adopted?"

"Oh, Father, don't worry," Mary cried out. "Louise won't be uncomfortable for long, you may be sure of that. She loves to eat."

"Shut up," Louise whispered under her breath.

Dr. Liang put down his chopsticks. Mrs. Liang had served a large bowl of rice with vegetables and had set it in front of him. This was his family bowl. When guests were present he used a small bowl, a gentleman's bowl, he laughingly explained. Only peasants used large bowls.

"But I thought most of the people of China were peasants," the guest would reply. Dr. Liang deprecated this with a graceful left hand. He used his left hand for gesturing.

"An unfortunate impression," he always said gently. "Due, I am afraid, to best sellers about China—written by Americans. A very limited point of view, naturally. It is quality that is meaningful in any nation, the articulate few, the scholars. Surely men like myself represent more perfectly than peasants can the spirit of Chinese civilization. Our nation has always been ruled by our intellectuals. Our emperors depended upon wise men."

"Mary!" he now cried sharply, "do not be cruel to your younger sister. Louise, do not be rude to your older sister. The family relationships must be preserved."

"Eh, eh, eat your food, all of you," Mrs. Liang cried impetuously. "When your stomachs are full you will feel better. I made this beef and cabbage myself. Here, father of my sons—"

She reached across the table with her chopsticks in her right hand and picked a tender bit of beef from the dish and put it on Dr. Liang's heap of rice. "Now come—the children will all be good. It will rouse your ulcers to be angry at mealtime."

Like many Chinese intellectuals, as well as rich men, Dr. Liang suffered from the threat of stomach ulcers. Mrs. Liang declared that it was the excessive restraint of his temper which went to his stomach. "You should let your temper out," she sometimes urged her husband in private. "Be angry with the children when you feel like it, but between meals. Slap Mary or twist Peter's ears—it will make you feel better. It is hard on you to have no servants who will bear with a little anger now and then. You felt better when we were in China for that reason. There the ricksha coolie was especially patient —remember? Here you have no way of venting your anger. It stays in your belly and makes boils."

"I hope I am a truly superior man in the Confucian sense, whether I am in China or America," Dr. Liang had replied.

"Confucius died of stomach trouble, too," she had retorted.

This he had not answered, remembering that Confucius himself had said that the superior man must be patient with women, children, and fools.

Now he fell to eating heartily. For so slender a man his appetite was large, and to his wife entirely satisfactory. Nothing gave Mrs. Liang a greater sense of success as a wife than the sight of her husband eating his food with enjoyment. She was irked that her own pleasure was checked by a frame that ran easily to fat, and she was sometimes made melancholy by the sight of her husband's spare and graceful body when he bathed himself. Did he compare her solid shape to the naked outlines of American women? She had long ago refused to go to seashore resorts after one visit to Atlantic City. How could even Dr. Liang keep his virtue in that place? Yet such was American life that he had only to open the page of a magazine, left about carelessly by one of the children, to see even in his own house the pictures of evil females. American women she considered whores without exception when they were young and some although they were middle-aged. Even white-haired dowagers made over Dr. Liang in a manner that could only be called whorish.

She did not believe that her husband, left to himself, could ever be unfaithful to her or to the children. Had she not borne him two handsome sons? Yet the memory of their arranged marriage rankled in her. True, her father had yielded to the extent of allowing them to meet for fifteen minutes, one day, under his own supervision. She had been a tongue-tied girl of eighteen. She could still feel her cheeks burn at that memory. But the tall extremely handsome young man who stood gazing at her then seemed now to have nothing to do with her husband, Dr. Liang. Whether he ever remembered that meeting under the eyes of the watchful old man, she did not know. He had never spoken of it. Even on their wedding night, six months later, he had made no reference to it. Nevertheless he had gone on with the marriage. She had not, she supposed, been too ugly, and in those days she was not fat, although certainly not thin, even then. Her cheeks had been round and red with a high color that tended to grow purple in cold weather. Her plump girlish hands were always chilblained in winter until she came to America.

She had been thoroughly afraid of her husband on her wedding night. He was methodical and almost completely silent. Not until she was sure that there was no more to marriage did she recover her natural and somewhat loud gaiety. By that time she knew she was indispensable to him. She still was, and this kept her fairly careless in mind, except when Dr. Liang began to write poetry, which he sometimes did. These poems were woven about women entirely different from herself and they alarmed her. She searched with jealous eyes their entire acquaintance in New York to discover, if possible, someone who resembled even remotely these ladies of his imagination. Such resemblances were difficult to fasten upon, since his poems were all about ladies who had lived centuries ago in Chinese history. The Fragrant Concubine, for example, was one of his favorites, a delicate lady who when she perspired exuded scent instead of sweat.

"I doubt there was ever this woman," she had exclaimed when Dr. Liang read aloud to some American friends a poem he had written in honor of the Fragrant Concubine.

"She lives in history," Dr. Liang had answered firmly. He looked about the group of earnest American faces. "And in my heart, perhaps," he had added smiling.

Mrs. Liang had quarreled with him that night in her good hearty fashion. "You!" she had cried, scolding and shaking her forefinger at him while he undressed for his bath. "Starting scandal with these Americans!"

He had forgotten the episode and when she saw this she would have been glad to stop there. But some time or other it would happen again and so she went on. "Talking about fragrant concubines!" she stormed.

He had laughed at her. "There was only one," he said, folding his trousers carefully and putting them over the foot of the double brass bed.

"The Americans are so sexy!" she had complained. She spoke in Chinese but the word "sexy" she always used in English. "You should speak to them otherwise."

"You are jealous," he said with pleasure.

"Of a dead woman?" she shrieked.

"Of any woman."

"If you take a woman, I will take a man," she said boldly.

At this he had laughed immoderately. "Come," he said, leaning on the foot of the bed. "You and I will have a race—you for a man, I for a woman! I will buy you a jade ring and bracelet if you win yours first."

She had been properly scandalized at this. "Come to bed, you old man! Stop talking like Americans."

"A little more beef," she said now to her husband as they sat at their family meal. He held out his bowl obediently.

"I shall have to have a nap," he complained.

"It will be good for you," she replied. "You are not too young to sleep a little in the middle of the day."

Around them their four children ate in silence, dipping into the dishes in the middle of the table. Mrs. Liang did not tolerate the presence of the maid Nellie while they ate. All of them enjoyed their food better when they dipped for themselves from the middle dishes, but only the children did so in front of the maid, and not then in the mother's presence. Mrs. Liang had scolded them one day when, coming back from a luncheon in Dr. Liang's honor, she had discovered her four children hunched over the table eating with bowls in their hands, dipping with their chopsticks from the main dishes and chattering with the maid.

"Why shouldn't we act like Chinese since we are Chinese?" James had demanded.

"You in medical school learning about American germs!" Mrs. Liang had cried for the benefit of Nellie.

She had hustled the children from their meal, and waiting until the maid was gone she had presented their iniquity to their father. Dr. Liang had been judicial. "The germ theory is true, of course," he had told his children, "but the immunity of our people to certain germs is very high. Then, too, in one family, there is not much danger. I myself would not care to dip my chopsticks into a bowl with unknown persons even of our own race. But your mother is right. Americans tend to think too little of us, and we should not therefore lend ourselves to their low opinion."

The meal was over; Mrs. Liang produced a box of chocolates which she loved, and Nellie came in and poured hot tea and went away again. Mrs. Liang belched comfortably and Dr. Liang looked at her sadly but in silence. He had eaten too well to reprove her and he rose, yawned, and went to his room to sleep. Mrs. Liang went into the living room and sat down in a deep chair, and, reclining her head she closed her eyes.

In the dining room the four young people were left alone together. Mary folded her arms on the table and leaned on them.

"Are you going to tell Peter and Louise?" she asked.

"What has Jim done now?" Peter asked. He was gobbling chocolates, hunting with his long forefinger for the cream-filled ones.

"He has asked Lili to go back to China with him as soon as they are married, and Lili says she will—if her papa lets her," Mary's mischievous voice echoed Lili's soft Chinese pronunciation, "Baba."

"No kidding!" Peter exclaimed.

"I am going, too," Mary announced.

The three of them turned on her. "Who said?" Louise demanded.

"I say," Mary declared. "I've made up my mind. All this child hygiene—why do you think I have been taking that?"

"So you can be a good mother," Louise said wickedly.

"Oh, shut up!"

Without their parents the four of them were wholly American. Not seeing them, hearing only their voices, none could have heard a difference.

"I think Jim ought to go first and blaze the trail for the rest of us," Peter cried. With excitement his long neck seemed to grow longer.

"How's Jim going?" Louise asked. "It costs oodles of money."

"I've been offered a job," Jim said slowly.

"Oh, where, Jim?"

"In Peking, in the big hospital there."

"Lucky stiff," Peter muttered.

All of them were sick to get to China, all except Louise, and she dared not say she was not. Alone sometimes she was frightened at the thought of China. She loved America. Her days were pure fun, mingled with brief hours of work at high school, and away from her family she lived a life which she concealed from them altogether. She was gay and popular, and she danced well and sang as clearly as a Chinese lark. An American boy had fallen in love with her. No one knew except her best friend Estelle, who was his sister. Romantic Estelle begged them to marry, and Louise spent long hours in exciting conversation. The only trouble was that Philip had not asked Louise to marry him.

"There's a hitch, though," Jim said soberly. "Lili wants her father to agree to her going."

There was a chorus of snorts at this. "Marry her first," Peter advised in a manly voice. "When you're married you can do what you like. Be a Chinese for once—make your wife obey you."

Jim smiled at him and shook his head. "I don't know," he said. "I'm afraid I shan't make a very good Chinese husband, Pete."

"Aw, get tough," Peter urged. "Don't let 'em lick you, Jim. Remember you're our pilot."

James looked around the table at their faces. Peter was

eager; Mary was determined, and Louise looked remote and dreaming. They were all depending on him, their elder brother, the head of the family after their father. The head of the family! When he was that he'd have them all in China where they belonged.

"You can trust me," he said. "I won't give up."

He was somewhat daunted, however, by Lili's air of resolute calm when she arose with undulant grace to meet him that evening, as he entered the elaborate living room of the Li apartment. She put out her hand and took his and led him to the sofa where she had been sitting. On the sofa opposite, Mr. and Mrs. Li sat with some formality and their faces were solemn. When he greeted them they inclined their heads and did not speak and he knew at once that Lili had told them what he had asked. He knew, too, that they had discussed the matter and had decided what their answer would be. Their reserve frightened him. Were they favorable surely they would not have looked so grave. He concealed his fears and sat down beside Lili, accepted the tea she offered him, and declined the suggestion of what she called "viskee-sodah" from the small tray on the table in front of the empty ornate fireplace. They were being very Chinese, he realized, and a mingling of stubbornness and humor with his dismay made him determine to be also as Chinese as he could.

"The night is mild," he announced. "The sky is the color of rain." Because he did not want to speak English tonight he spoke in Mandarin Chinese, native to him but foreign to Mrs. Li's Shanghai-bred tongue.

Nevertheless she answered him in an attempt at the same language. "The river will grow more damp, and it will be bad for our cough."

James drank a little tea and set down the bowl. "There are many varieties of climate in this large country," he remarked. "Would it not be well for you to travel to the West where the air is dry and there is constant sunshine?"

Mrs. Li shook her head. "We cannot leave New York," she sighed. "It is like Shanghai. And where else can we buy fresh ginger and bamboo shoots? In Chinatown the markets are at least as good as in small towns in our own land."

Mr. Li rumbled forth his cough. "The soy sauce is quite good here," he remarked.

Lili said nothing. She sat in repose, her exquisite hands crossed on the lap of her apple-green satin robe. She wore a white gardenia in her hair and green jade earrings. The scent of the gardenia wrapped her in fragrant air, and stole into the young man's heart. He grew impatient with the slow preambles of Chinese courtesy and he suddenly cast them aside. Leaning forward he addressed himself to Mr. Li in English.

"Sir, I think Lili has told you that I have asked her to marry me very soon and go with me to China. I have come to ask your permission."

Mrs. Li rose immediately. "Come, child," she said to Lili in her Shanghai dialect. "We shall leave this matter to the two men."

Lili obeyed, and Mr. Li maintained a grave silence while they left the room together. When they were gone he rose and went to the door and closed it. He wore tonight Chinese robes which covered his portly figure and gave him great dignity. James had seen him until now only in the new Western clothes he had bought when he first came to America, and although they were expensive and of excellent quality, they did not suit his shoulders rounded from a lifetime in comfortable Chinese garments and they revealed too harshly his hanging belly. The thinness of his legs, too, was concealed now by the long and richly brocaded satin robes of a dull blue. When he returned he sat down beside James and put out his plump tapering fingers and began to talk in Chinese.

"What I am about to say has nothing to do with you." His Mandarin was stilted but intelligible. Every businessman was compelled to know Mandarin, wherever his home in China. "I am very willing for you to marry Lili. It will be a weight off my mind. But you ask me to allow you to take my daughter back to the country from which we have escaped. Now, do not mistake me. I hate this foreign country and I love our country. But I tell you, times are very bad in China. Even without my gall bladder I found business hard. Only a few of us have money, and since the Americans always want to have fifty-one per cent and we Chinese are determined to keep fifty-one per cent, business stands still. This is why I took the opportunity to come to this country and get my gall bladder cut out. When I go to the operation next month, it would comfort me to think my daughter is married safely to a good young man with ability, such as you are. Then I can die without distress."

James broke in. "Sir, it is not necessary for you to die. I understand those things and—"

Mr. Li put up his pale soft hand and stopped him. "You are not cutting me open," he said gently. "Were you holding the knife I would not think of death."

James quivered with inspiration and anxiety. "Sir, if you can trust me to perform the operation—"

Mr. Li looked instantly alarmed. "No—no—" he exclaimed. "Americans are used to cutting. Besides, you are young and I am an important man."

He sighed and rubbed his belly with the palm of his hand. "Yet I wish—no, it cannot be. The doctor has been chosen and I have already paid out some money. In the night, I will tell you, I am afraid."

"Don't be afraid, sir," James urged. "The surgeons here are excellent."

To this Mr. Li replied in a mournful voice, "A Chinese does not willfully kill. But Americans think nothing of it. You did not see their soldiers in Shanghai. They rode about in their small cars and killed anyone in their way. On one street in one day near our house they killed seven people without stopping to find out what they had done. Why should they spare a single old Chinese like me? And, more than that, I have inquired and found that even though I die I must pay them. What injustice is this? Yet I am helpless. I cannot cut open my own belly. If the doctors were Chinese they would not expect to be paid for killing me, as you know. They might expect to be sued. But here it seems doctors cannot commit murder, whomever they kill. I have inquired and I have been told that even the President of America would have to pay his doctor were he killed. As you know, we would never consent to such extortion."

Mr. Li's earnest soft voice flowed on and on. He spoke little before his wife and daughter, and when he was alone with a man all this talk came flowing out of him. He felt very near to this handsome young Chinese. He had lost his only son in childhood and he felt he was getting back a son again, one stronger and healthier and better in every way than the poor little boy whose mother had smothered him to death with too much love. Little Ah Fah had died of a dose of opium which Mrs. Li had commanded for a stomachache he had developed after eating too many sweet rice cakes. A zealous but ignorant nursemaid had doubled the dose. Mr. Li had felt himself so confounded and overwhelmed by women that after his son's death he had withdrawn from life. His sexual impulses, never strong, had left him completely, and he refused the concubine whom Mrs. Li had proposed for him as atonement for her carelessness. Her grief, however, had touched his heart, and at last he turned to her. Outside his enormous and richly decorated house in the French Concession of Shanghai he had been an astute and successful businessman, but at home he was subdued, indulgent, and almost totally silent.

James did not attempt to contradict anything Mr. Li now said. He realized that it was somehow a relief to the older man to pour out all his fears and prejudices and he sat, half smiling, listening, seeming to agree, waiting for the end when he supposed Mr. Li would give his consent.

"Now," Mr. Li said, "here is what I ask. Do not go back to China for a few years. Later, certainly! I do not wish to be buried here and if I die, as I expect to do, under the foreign knife, my body is to be placed in a metal coffin. The coffin is to be filled with lime and sealed and placed in storage. I do not wish to be buried in this American earth. When the affairs of our country are improved enough for you to take my daughter's mother, my daughter, and I hope my grandchildren back to Shanghai, my body must go with the family. The house in Shanghai is yours. It is very large, and it is completely furnished, on the eastern side Chinese, on the western side foreign. The garden is very large indeed, at least ten foreign acres, fifty Chinese *mou*, and there is a very old pine tree in the center of the rock garden. Under the pine tree is a space which I prepared for my grave when I made the garden twenty years ago. The family cemetery is in our village outside Soochow, but I wish to lie for a generation or so among my grandchildren. Later, when you want to be buried there yourself you can have me moved to the family place. By that time I shall be used to being dead and it will not matter. After a hundred years we are all dust."

James stirred. "Sir, I want to work——"

Mr. Li put up his hand again. "It is not necessary," he said gently. "I have money enough to support at least five generations. I saw perfectly what the Japanese intended to do. Anyone could see what would happen when the foreigners stopped what they called their first world war. I sold my mills when the Japanese reached Manchuria. By then of course war was inevitable. All my fortune is in banks here in New York. I do not mind telling you that I am one of the largest depositors in three banks in this city."

Mr. Li smiled dimly and put up his hand again when he saw that once more James was about to speak.

"Wait—this is not all. I will settle everything on you, as my son, on the day I go under the foreign knife. I can trust you. You will take care of an old father and mother. Yes, you will be my real son. I ask only one return—that you will take my name when you marry my daughter; it is an old custom with us, you know, when a man has no son."

He looked shrewdly at the grave young man who suddenly pressed his lips together and hurried on. "The surname Li is honorable. It is among the Hundred Names. And your father has another son. I am not robbing him. Now then, everything is clear between us. Certainly I give my permission for the wedding. Let it be at once. Say two weeks from today? That gives time for new clothes and the guests to be chosen and so on. It gives me nearly a month before my death. With luck I even hope that before I die my daughter may conceive. Well, that would be very good luck, and that is perhaps too much to ask. Still—" Mr. Li pursed his lips and smiled.

James had no heart to break the old man's dreams, and yet it must be done. Trained as a surgeon, he went swiftly to the task. "I do not believe you will die, sir," he said, "and it is better if you do not take it for granted. The mind must help the body to live—we doctors know that. But, sir, please do not ask me to change the plan I have made for my life. I am surnamed Liang, and I must remain what I am born. I thank you deeply and I will be to you as a son, whatever my name."

Mr. Li winced and tears filled his eyes. James looking away from his face saw the fat white hands lying on the satin lap begin to tremble. He looked away from the hands and went on. "I am glad that you want Lili and our children to live in our own country. So far we are agreed. I have grown up here and it is not good for us. We are exiles, however kind the people. But even that is not why I want to go home. I have a hope—

fantastic, perhaps—that I can do some good for my own people."

"The times are so bad," Mr. Li's voice was a wail.

"I know—and that is why I feel I must go back," James said.

He could not tell Mr. Li what it was that made his purpose hard in his heart. He had never said even to Mary that in some deeply repressed corner of his being he grieved that his own father had chosen to live in exile during the years of their country's hardship. He knew all the arguments, that a scholar could not work in the midst of turmoil and war. He believed these arguments were true. He knew that his father's delicately balanced mind needed safety and quiet and security in order to do its work. But he had long ago determined that he would work where he was most needed, in the midst of turmoil, even in war. He would not allow his mind to be delicate nor his heart remote.

Mr. Li came to the attack again, not harshly or boldly but with pleading. "Lili has been gently reared. She grew very nervous and ill during the bombing of Shanghai. Perhaps she has not told you how nearly she was killed?"

"No!" James cried in a low voice of horror.

Mr. Li nodded. "She was shopping in Wing On's department store. I had told her she could buy a sable coat. The Russians sent in very good furs to us. She was trying it on when the bomb fell. Luckily she had gone to the stairs, where there was a window, to see the fur by the daylight. Thus she was able to run down the stairs, and escape before the whole building collapsed," Mr. Li sighed. "Unfortunately she threw off the coat, thinking it would be too heavy. Otherwise she would have kept that, too."

James did not speak. He continued to look steadfastly at Mr. Li, his face very grave.

Mr. Li went on. "For this reason she is easily frightened, and perhaps will be so all her life. Now maybe Shanghai is better, but we cannot be sure of this. All sorts of disaster still threaten. What if the Communists win? Who can know Heaven's will? For that reason, even as you say you will not accept our name, I must say that Lili shall not go to China now."

This was Mr. Li's ultimatum and James knew it. He knew also that by Chinese reasoning, had he been willing to yield and change his surname, Mr. Li might have made compromise and allowed him to take Lili to China. If one does not give, one cannot expect to receive. He felt the soft implacable net of the reciprocity of Chinese life spread about his feet, and his heart grew firm. He had lived in freedom and he stood alone. He got up, thrust his hands into his pockets, and squared his shoulders. "I shall be sorry to leave my wife here in America to wait alone until China is fit for her to live in. But my work must come first."

Sweat broke out on Mr. Li's pale face. "You are too foreign," he said. A dull ferocity flamed in his face. His lips turned slowly blue. "With a Chinese, family comes first."

James looked down steadfastly into the upturned face. With understanding and sympathy the younger man looked at the older, and still he could not yield. More than his own life was held in this moment. He had lived for all the years of his adolescence and young manhood in the presence of a dream, and the dream was his country, in peril and need, and himself, devoted to her rescue. He could not give up his dream, for then he would die. And it was worse for a young man to die than an old one. Mr. Li, James told himself hardily, had never done China any good. He was one of those who had lived for his own family. To family how often China had been sacrificed and by how many!

He felt his soul blaze into solitary fire. "Whatever I am, I am first myself," he told Mr. Li as he turned and left the room and walking down the hall went out of the house.

He could not go home. The night air was soft and the streets were quiet. He glanced at his watch and saw that it was eleven o'clock. There was all night yet to face. He walked slowly, hatless, his hands in his pockets, down the streets and across to the river. There the bridge was, the George Washington Bridge. The name meant something. He had grown up with American heroes. George Washington was more living to him than Confucius. Confucius was a preacher or maybe a teacher, like his father, but George Washington was a doer and the creator of a new nation. The bridge stretched across the enormous span of the river. Mists were rising in soft swirls from the chilled water, and the farther end of the bridge was hidden. It reached from the near shore endlessly into the distance, into the future, and his rich imagination made it a symbol. He would cross the bridge of his dreams, even though he walked alone.

. . . But in the night, alone in his bed, Lili crept out of his heart and into his mind. He lay in the darkness thinking of her, loving her with all the strength of his young repressed manhood. He had grown up among American boys and girls, seeing their horseplay of sex, and not sharing in it. The knowledge that he was not of their race had been barrier enough, but the delicacy of his soul was the real barrier. He did not want to kiss any girl, to fumble breasts and dance thigh to thigh. It was not sin, but it was not pleasure. More than once a girl had made him feel that she did not mind his being Chinese. It was not enough and he had pretended he did not understand her. He would marry his own kind and they would glory in being Chinese. His pride had been fulfilled in Lili. When she came fresh from China he saw that she was more beautiful than any girl he had ever seen in America. All his restraints tumbled in this night and he determined that he would not give her up. He would go to China and he would take her with him.

When he got up from restless sleep he looked fresh and strong with determination. He bathed; he shaved; he dressed himself carefully in his new gray pin-striped suit and he put on a wine-red tie. When he came to the breakfast table only Mary and Peter were there, and Peter was studying while he ate and did not look up. But Mary cried out at the sight of him. "My, you're handsome this morning! Did Baba say yes?"

James grinned and sat down to a heaping bowl of oatmeal. "Baba said no, and I'm going over there this morning to take Lili by force."

"I wish you luck," Mary said. She was suddenly grave, and she whispered under her breath, "Oh, how I wish you luck!"

He pretended he did not hear her while he poured cream and heaped sugar into the bowl.

For a moment when the door opened into the Li apartment he thought that Lili had been forbidden to see him. Mollie the maid looked distressed. She shut the door softly and glanced up the stairs. "They had some sort of a row here," she whispered. "When I got in this morning—" She shook her head.

Then Lili herself interrupted them. She came to the head of

the stairs, looking exquisite and pale in a blue silk gown and little black slippers, and walked slowly down. Mollie disappeared and James went forward and took Lili in his arms. She crumpled against his shoulder and began to sob softly.

"You made Baba so angry," she wept.

He was distressed by her weeping, and he led her along in his arms until they were in the small music room off the hall. Here he shut the door and sat down with her on a love seat. "Lili darling, don't cry," he coaxed. He pulled out the fresh new handkerchief he had put into his breast pocket and wiped her eyes, holding her face up by his hand under her chin as though she were a child. Her lips were pale this morning and they quivered, and he kissed them. She did not open her eyes and large tears rolled out from under her lashes.

"Was he very angry with you, dear?" he asked tenderly. He drew her head to his shoulder again.

"Baba says I mustn't marry you," she sobbed. "He says he will find me another husband."

James felt his heart knock at his ribs. "He can't do that, darling—not if you don't want him to—"

She dabbed at her eyes with her own handkerchief, a small scrap of silk and lace. "You must help me," she murmured.

He was trembling with fear and love. "I will, darling, of course. But you must be brave, too, Lili. If we stick together, no one can force us apart."

Her tears rolled again. "Baba can," she said faintly.

"No, Lili—not even he."

Despair all but overwhelmed him. She was so yielding, so soft, so trained to obedience. What if he could not put strength into her soul? Ah, but he must! Somehow he must inspire her to see what the bridge meant and when she saw she would be strong enough to walk beside him, wherever it led them.

"Listen to me, darling." He brushed away the soft curls of her hair from her ear. "You have such pretty ears, Lili!" He kissed the small ear she turned to him. "Think while I talk, dear. Try to understand how I feel. Our people are good—our people are wonderful. China is great. She is not really weak. She is only in distress. All the great strength is simply waiting until we come to her help. She has lived in an old, old world and she needs to be born into the new one. I am a doctor and I think naturally in terms of birth—of bringing forth life—"

She was looking at him with wide blank eyes. "But if Baba won't give us any money how will we live in China?"

He laughed at this. "I will work and make money."

To his shocked surprise she grew angry at this and she stamped her little foot on his. It did not hurt him, and yet the dig of her heel wounded his heart. "You talk only silly," she exclaimed. "In China you cannot work. There is no money."

"The hospital will pay me," he retorted.

"A little money," she said scornfully. "How much? Maybe in one month what I paid yesterday for my necklace. Baba is right."

His arms grew cold around her. "Do you mean you don't want to marry me?"

She wept again loudly and she threw her arms about his neck. "I do—I do—but please, here, in New York, I like it so much!"

He said gravely, "I must go."

His arms dropped and she put them back again. "No, you must love me, please!"

In her distraction she was so beautiful, so helpless that he held her again, while his heart broke. So they sat a long time, and he did not know what thoughts went on in her mind.

It was she who spoke first after a while. She wiped her eyes and swallowed her sobs and said in her soft voice, "There is only one way, James. You must go first, without me. When Baba lets me, I will come."

"You mean—go without being married?"

She nodded. "It is the only way," she said. "Baba will not make me marry another man right away now if I cry every day. Maybe he won't die. Then—after you make money—buy a house maybe—or just even rent a nice house—"

He sat staring at her and she did not look at him. She twisted her little wet handkerchief into knots and then untwisted it and spread it on her knee, pulling the lace edge, doing everything, he thought, to avoid his eyes.

"This is what you want me to do, is it, Lili?" he asked at last.

She lifted her eyes to his. "Not what I want—" she whispered.

He was very gentle, very tender. "Then, dear, couldn't you come with me—run away, maybe?"

She shook her head positively. "I—can't," she said in a small sweet voice. "Oh, no!"

"You really are sending me away—alone?"

She began to cry. "It is you who want to go alone—if you stay here everything is all right. I am not troubling—it is you—you—"

He did not try to comfort her. He sat listening; he saw the tears on her cheeks and felt her little hands pressing his. The palms were hot. When her sobbing died and she fell silent he saw her peeping at him from under her wet lashes. She even tried to smile. But he would not allow himself either love or pity.

"Perhaps you are right," he said. "It is I who want to go— even alone."

And he rose and went away, refusing at the door, in his one backward look, the appeal of her startled eyes, her hands suddenly outstretched.

2

THE OCEAN WAS NOT THE RIVER. No bridge could cross it. James stood for hours every day, staring down into the clear green water that foamed into white waves where the prow of the ship clove its way westward. He was lonely and still he wanted to be alone. There were few passengers—two solitary old Chinese who he suspected were Cantonese going home to die, a hard-bitten American businessman, a Standard Oil executive, a journalist, two or three missionaries and their wives. Only the missionaries spoke to him every morning when they passed, and he did not encourage them.

The ocean was not the river. It changed from day to day, from hour to hour. Under a gray sky it was green. Under rain it was gray. In sunshine it was pure royal blue, and under the moon it was a tender silver. The moon was what he could not endure. The moon made him think of Lili. Long ago he had forgiven her. She was mild and sweet, an affectionate child, sad with fear that her father would die while she was away. It had ended like that by the time he left New York. She was afraid her father would die, and she had begged him to wait until the operation was over. He had not waited because he was afraid old Mr. Li might die indeed, and then he would not have the heart to leave Lili.

"It is better for me to go," he had told her. "If he dies, then you will have the courage to come to me."

He stretched out in his steamer chair, lying very still, his eyes closed. He was in mid-ocean, days lay behind him, days waited ahead. His body ached with loneliness, defrauded of marriage. It seemed to him now that he had left his father's house in a confusion of suffering. He had not tried to persuade Lili again and he had seen her only once more, the last night before he went away. It was too late then to change anything, even had there been a change in her. He had already sent cables accepting the job at the hospital in Peking, announcing that he would come alone and therefore would not need one of the resident doctor's houses, would gladly accept two rooms in the men's dormitory, and that he was leaving at once. Passports and visas were rushed through with the help of governments. It suddenly became important for Dr. James Liang to reach China. He was to bring with him supplies of drugs, especially the new streptomycin samples for use in tuberculosis. Three-fourths of the students in government universities had tuberculosis from bad food and poor housing after the war.

There had been no change in Lili. She had allowed him to hold her in his arms; she had wept a little; she had let him kiss her, and she told him her father was sure he was going to die and had willed her all his money and the Shanghai house. Her heart was numb and he could not respond. Too much was ahead; his dream, broken, was somehow coming true in a solitary fashion, without her. The dream was older than his love for her and the dream must go on. "Good-by, darling," he kept whispering to her. "Good-by—good-by—"

The anguish of saying good-by to Lili had served this poor purpose, however—it had dimmed the pain of all other farewells. He had clasped his father's hand, put his arms about his mother, kissed Louise, and held Peter's hand for a long moment with no feeling anywhere in him. Only when Mary crept into his arms and clung to him had he felt a spark of sorrow. She had whispered fiercely into his ear, "You are to send for me—don't forget, Jim! The very first minute!" Her bright black eyes had kept up their demand until the train carried him out of sight.

He sighed. The wind gathering out of the ocean twilight was growing cold and he got up, folded his steamer rug, picked up the books he had not read, and went below to his cabin. No one shared it with him for the ship was half empty. He lay down on the bunk and crossed his hands behind his head, and then into his solitude came again the last moments of his leave-taking of Lili. This had become the habit of his brain, he thought impatiently, and his soul was weary. He tried consciously to push out of his mind Lili's face, the scent of her person, the childish softness of her flesh, the sound of her voice. He tried to think of his father and mother, of his life in

America, the hospital, of plans when he landed in his own country, as new and foreign to him as though he had no Chinese blood in his veins. But his brain went the dreary round that his heart determined. Love was unassuaged.

He set his teeth and listened to the rhythm of the sea, beating against the ship. He opened his eyes and stared at the gray wash of the waves over the porthole. To lie like this in a ship and feel himself tossed upon vast waters was humbling enough. The ship was a midget upon the ocean and he but a mite upon the ship, and why should he think himself important in this vastness of his own country? Four thousand years China had lived without him and she would live thousands more after he was gone. She would never miss him. He began to curse himself for a fool and to think his father was a wise man. He might have lived comfortably in a huge modern city; he might have married Lili and inherited her father's wealth, and with leisure he might have pursued his way in research which could do for China infinitely more than his meager life. Had he thrown everything away?

The door opened and the cabin boy put in his head. He was a young Chinese, and he had been overjoyed when he found that James could speak his native Mandarin.

"You, sir, must get up and eat your evening meal."

"I am not hungry," James replied.

"But they are having very good meat," the boy urged. "Also there is rice."

"Even meat and rice," James said smiling.

The boy came in and closed the door behind him. "I am too bold, but you are ill, sir?"

"No—not ill," James replied. The boy was young and slender, an ordinary lad with nothing to recommend him. Some time in his youth he should have had his tonsils taken out, and certainly an orthodontist could have done something for his profile. But his teeth were white and clean and his skin was smooth and his eyes were bright. Above his high round forehead his black hair stood up in a brush. He wore the long blue cotton gown of all cabin boys and he had not buttoned the collar.

"Your heart is sick," the boy said shrewdly. "Have you left your family somewhere?"

"They are in America," James said.

"But you are not American."

"No, yet I grew up there."

The boy's eyes sparkled. "America is very good," he announced. "Americans are funny. They get angry quickly. Then they hit you. But they give you money afterward."

"I have not seen this aspect of Americans," James said.

"I know many Americans," the boy went on. He was enjoying a chance to make conversation. "They come and go on this ship. At night they take young women behind the lifeboats and kiss them."

"Do you watch them?" James asked. While he talked he need not think.

"I watch them," the boy admitted. "Only thus can I know them."

"How did you come to be on this ship?" James asked.

"My uncle is the cook," the boy replied.

"Yet by your tongue you come from Anhwei, which is far from the sea."

"We are Anhwei people, but in a famine we went to Shanghai to beg, and my uncle stayed and did not go back to the land. At first he pulled a ricksha, then he got a job with a foreigner to pull his private ricksha and be coolie, and then he worked well and went into the house as number three boy and then he became number one boy and he learned cooking and when the cook died, he was cook. When the war came the foreign master went away, and my uncle came on this ship."

"And will you always stay on this ship?" James asked.

The boy opened the door and looked up and down the corridor.

"No steward," he said in a low voice, and his face crinkled with silent laughter. He closed the door.

"Sit down," James said.

The boy sat down on the edge of the couch against the outer wall of the cabin. He pulled up his sleeves from his hands and prepared himself for more enjoyable conversation. "Only you can speak our language on this ship except my uncle. My uncle is very tired all the time and he will not talk much. If I talk too much please tell me."

"Talk as much as you please," James said. "I know no one else on the ship."

The boy considered. Then he looked at James half mischievously. "What shall I talk? I have many things in my life."

James laughed for the first time in days. "What do you think about when you are alone?"

The boy smiled delightedly. "My home," he said.

"Then tell me about your home."

The boy cleared his throat and pulled up his sleeves again. "We live in a small place," he began. "It is the Three-mile Village of the Wangs. Our family name is Wang. I am the middle son and so I have no good place in the family. Two brothers are older than I, three are younger. What happens to me is not important." He laughed at himself and went on. "This is good, because my father and mother do not care what I do. So I can do anything."

"But what do you want most to do?" James asked. This was the first time he had ever talked with what he thought of as a real Chinese—that is, someone who belonged to the earth of China.

The boy scratched his scalp with his little fingernail, and looked thoughtful. "What I want is too foolish," he said shyly.

"What most people want seems foolish," James said to encourage him. He was somewhat astonished to see that he had unwittingly uttered a truth, and it led him to another. "The important thing is to know what one wants."

"I would like to become a ship steward," Young Wang said earnestly. "This is foolish for no one in our family has been in ships except my uncle and me. We do not know anything about ships. We are farmers."

"Why do you want to live on ships?" James asked.

"To come and go across wide waters."

"What makes you want to come and go?" James pursued this boy's mind with rising interest.

Young Wang crossed his legs. "It is this way," he began again. "My heart goes up when I cross the sea. China is good and America is good. I can buy better rice in China but the oranges in America are sweet. More ships, more fun for everybody. Also it is good business. I can get rich quick."

James laughed. "You don't want to go to school?" he asked.

Wang shook his head. "In old times learning was good business," he said affably. "Now on ships is a better way for riches."

Out in the corridor a dinner gong sounded loudly and Young Wang leaped to his feet. "The chief steward will let out his rage at me," he exclaimed and darted to the door.

There he paused for a moment. "Meat and rice are very good today," he cried and disappeared.

James laughed and got out of the bunk. He was suddenly hungry. Meat and rice were very good.

He was proud of the skyline of Shanghai. This astonished him. In spite of the photographs and stories from friends he had not believed that there were such tall buildings in China. The long flat approach to the city had not been reassuring. For hours the ship had steamed slowly between mudbanks in a river of mud that fanned wide into the green ocean.

"No bath this morning, please," Young Wang had said cheerfully soon after dawn. "Only river water."

So as soon as he was dressed he had gone on deck. No shore was in sight and the ocean had changed to a muddy brown. It was his first glimpse of the soil of China, washed by the river from a thousand miles of land. Later the land itself had stolen almost imperceptibly to the horizon in the long barren mudbanks. These gave way to flat green fields and a few squat farmhouses, some low-built warehouses, a mill, a village, a town. He went below and ate his breakfast quickly and came back to stand again at the rail. There was nothing beautiful in the landscape except the brilliant blue sky, which today was cloudless. Had it been gray, the dun of land and water and sky would have frightened him.

Then suddenly at midmorning against this bright sky a new skyline had broken. He saw high buildings massed together and he perceived with a pleasurable shock that it was Shanghai and that it was as modern, from this distance, as he had been told it was by patriotic countrymen. "China is not all ignorant peasants and thatch-roofed villages," they had said impatiently. "We have our modern cities, too. One city is more important than a thousand villages."

He felt relief. The homecoming was not to be too strange. He did not step from his father's comfortable apartment into a mud-walled hut.

Someone was at his elbow and he turned. It was Young Wang, his face sparkling and his eyes shining. "Very nice day," he remarked.

"You are going ashore?" James asked.

"By and by," Young Wang replied. "You go to hotel?"

"Yes," James replied.

Young Wang stayed until the last possible moment and then rushed downstairs to his duties. Meanwhile the Bund loomed toward the ship. It was really quite beautiful. The street was wide and paved, and a park was green at one end.

As the ship edged to the pier, James looked down into a crowd of his own people. Their brown faces were upturned, curious, gay, patient. Here and there a white face was lifted startlingly clear against the universal brown. It was a reversal of New York where the crowd was white, and the brown face startling. He had grown up immunizing himself to the stares of white people as he walked along the streets, but here it would be comforting to belong to the crowd. In a few minutes he would be lost in it, and no one would look at him twice. Here was where he belonged.

He felt an exhilaration which was very nearly happiness. His country would not be strange to him. Why had Lili and her family ever left it and why did they not want to come back? Perhaps they had left too soon after the war. At the thought of Lili, constant in his mind, he went below to finish his packing. The sooner he reached his hotel the sooner he might find a letter from her, sent airmail, to be waiting for him.

But when he reached his hotel, an hour later, there was no letter. An indolent clerk in a dirty white gown ruffled some envelopes.

"Let me see, please," James said.

The clerk pushed the envelopes toward him and flung out a clatter of words in Shanghai dialect to his assistant who laughed. James could not understand and he pretended not to hear. He looked at each envelope slowly. There was no letter from Lili but there was a square envelope of heavy pink paper and upon it was scrawled in large vinelike letters his name. On the back in the same loose combination of tendrils he saw the name Thelma Barnabas, Rue du Consulat. He tore open the envelope and took out a single pink sheet and the black letters flung themselves at him.

Dear Dr. Liang:
  With what enthusiasm do the intellectuals of Shanghai await the arrival of the son of the great Liang Wen Hua! Dare I hope you will gather with us at *my* house? I have had the temerity to invite our small, but, I think, dis-

tinguished circle. We dine at seven tonight. A car will call for you half an hour before.

Yours in expectation,
Thelma Barnabas

This strange epistle James turned over once or twice and then thrust into his pocket. There was no elevator in the hotel and he mounted a flight of dirty marble stairs, a bellboy with his bags leading the way. They reached the door at the end of a winding carpetless hallway. The boy struggled with a door, flung it open, and went in. James went into a large shabby room whose tall windows were hung with Chinese silk curtains of a faded rose. A soiled Peking carpet was on the floor and upon the double brass bed was a cover of dingy embroidery. Once the room had been handsome, but negligence had given it a look of decay. Upon one wall, however, was a framed water color of misty hills, which he liked at once.

He tipped the boy and closed the door. The telephone jangled and when he lifted the receiver he heard a woman's voice, dominating, ardent, gushing, "Dr. James Liang?"

"Yes."

"Oh, Dr. Liang—how wonderful! Welcome to poor old war-torn Shanghai! What an honor to have the distinguished—have you got my letter?"

"I have," James replied, disliking the voice very much.

"You will come?" The voice was persuading, coaxing, compelling.

James hesitated. "I've only just—"

The voice broke in. "Oh, but you must! You don't know us but we know you—you're Liang Wen Hua's son! We'll have to introduce ourselves—a little group of pure intellectuals—it's so important these days, don't you think, when everything is so materialistic! Surely you've heard of the Dialectic Society? That's our group—of course I'm only honorary, not being Chinese, but the poor things do need a place to meet and my house is theirs. I tell Charles—he's my husband—that it's the least we can do—the intellectuals are really starving—and they're so important. But you know—your wonderful father is international honorary president—"

He did know but he had forgotten. Liang Wen Hua was the honorary president of many intellectual groups. The Dialectic Society of China was, as Mrs. Barnabas said, a small group of men and women, educated abroad or in modern schools here. They wrote articles and essays and edited a thin weekly in English, where they published their writings and criticized what they wrote. His father had once been one of them.

"I will come," James said.

"Oh, wonderful," Mrs. Barnabas sang. "I'll send the car for you at six-thirty."

It was a diversion, at least, James told himself. The air of Shanghai seemed flat to him even though he recognized its cause. It was absurd that a bit of paper bearing Lili's words to him would have changed the entire city, but so it was. He went to the window and gazed into a street which might have belonged to any modern city except that the people were polyglot. Watching that restless moving throng he caught its restlessness. He must get out in it and move with it. Where were these thousands of persons going? Each, of necessity, must be on his own errand, and yet they were flowing in two concentrated opposing currents. Well, he had his private errand, too. He would go and see Lili's home, the house which might have been his, had he been willing to obey Mr. Li. He knew where it was, and he locked his door and went downstairs.

Outside the open door of the hotel lobby he stepped into one of the pedicycles which had taken the place of old-fashioned rickshas on the streets of Shanghai. A thin lackadaisical man, still young, grunted at the directions James gave him and pedaled dangerously into the traffic of streetcars, wheelbarrows, busses, cars, and carriages. Far more dangerous than vehicles were these thousands of people who came and went upon the streets. They spilled over the sidewalks and flowed among the traffic in a dark stream, cursed by drivers and cursing in return. The streets were a continuing brawl. Most of the people looked poor and their faces were strained and anxious, but among them were also the well dressed and complacent, winding their way unobtrusively among the others.

The pedicycle rider flung a hand toward a building as they went on and James leaned forward to catch what he said. He heard the two words Wing On, and remembered what Mr. Li had told him. The building had been rebuilt and it was a thriving department store again. Lili ought to see it, he thought. Then she would forget the horror of the day when it had nearly carried her to death in its destruction. There was little sign of that now. He craned to look at the great ornate structure, cheaply built and yet somehow effective in the strange hybrid design an architect had given it.

The driver stopped before a gate, sweating and mopping his face. "The Li Palace," he announced loudly. James got out and bade the man wait. He would not stay long. It *was* a palace, he supposed. He could see nothing except the high gray brick wall, topped by green dust-laden trees. A row of broken glass was set into the cement which covered the ridge of the wall. The driver beat upon the gate with his closed fists and a uniformed gatekeeper opened it.

James spoke in his best Chinese. "I am a friend of the Li family, who are now in New York. I should like just to look at the home where they used to live."

But the gatekeeper was surly. Whether he spoke only Shanghai dialect or whether he had orders to let no one enter, who could tell? He growled a refusal. James looked over his shoulder and saw an immense square brick house surrounded by deep verandas, set in a green lawn and palm trees. Then the gate shut in his face. There was nothing to do but go back to the hotel.

He was awakened by the raucous telephone and still half asleep he took up the receiver. The clerk's voice purred in his ear. "Cah donstaahs waiting you."

"Coming!" James cried.

Six-thirty—impossible! But so it was. He leaped up, and realized that he had slept all afternoon, needing sleep upon solid earth after the interrupting rise and fall of the ship. He felt rested, and before the mirror, brushing his stiff black hair into its usual pompadour, he saw that fatigue had faded from his eyes. He looked forward with mild interest to the evening, expecting amusement, at least.

Yet where had Mrs. Barnabas hidden this car during the war? A White Russian chauffeur held the door for him and he stepped into cushioned comfort. A silver vase of roses, attached to the seat, scented the stillness. For when the doors were closed no noise penetrated their insulation. The jabber and chatter of the streets, the wails of beggars, were shut away. Even the smooth monotone of the engine could not be heard. Between him and the chauffeur was a wall of glass and he had not the courage to lift the speaking tube at his right hand and ask who Mrs. Barnabas was and how she had this princely car.

In silence he was carried through the summer evening, through the crowds who stared at him with hatred in their eyes, as he soon perceived. They were asking who he was and how came he to be riding in such splendor and alone. He looked away from them and wished that the Russian did not honk the horn so loudly and constantly and he longed for darkness to hide him.

Before darkness fell, however, the car paused at a great gate which swung open to receive it, and he was carried up a broad driveway between high magnolia trees to a great house of gray brick, as solid as a bank. At white marble steps under a wide porte-cochere the car stopped, and the door was opened by a Chinese manservant in a red silk robe tied with a wide soft girdle of crushed blue satin.

"This way, please," he told James and led the way into a huge hall filled with heavy Chinese tables and chairs of blackwood.

"Oh, Dr. Liang!"

James heard the rushing dominating voice of the telephone, and he saw his hostess. His first impression was of a tall slender brilliant bird. Her middle-aged face was negligible. Small-boned, highly colored, it was merely a spot upon which to focus for a moment. Above it was a brilliant turban of cloth of gold, the same fabric that made her high-necked, semi-Chinese costume. She held out thin jeweled hands to clutch his and he felt her hot and tenacious fingers dragging him toward an open door.

"Come in—come in—we're all here waiting—"

"I'm afraid I slept—"

"And why shouldn't you sleep—why shouldn't the son of Liang Wen Hua do whatever he likes—"

They were in an enormous glittering room. Thirty or forty men and women, most of them Chinese, were sitting or lounging on low chairs, divans, and hassocks upholstered in brocades. A stout tall American, bald-headed and red-faced, was mixing cocktails.

"My husband, Barny—" his hostess announced, "and the others—the Dialectic Society of China—"

He was introduced to one after another, always as the son

of his father, and he met cold eyes, cynical eyes, coy eyes, careless eyes, envious eyes, and when it was over he sat down on the end of an overcrowded sofa.

Mr. Barnabas strode toward him. "Hello, Dr. Liang. Glad to welcome you home to China—have a Martini—I'm the only person in Shanghai who can make 'em taste like New York—"

James accepted the glass and held it without tasting its contents. He felt overwhelmed, drowned in color and noise, as everyone began to talk exactly as though he were not there. Mrs. Barnabas was smiling coquettishly at a handsome young Chinese. She laid her brightly ringed hand on his for a moment. Mr. Barnabas stood gazing at this and at everything, swaying a little on his black patent-leather toes, smiling vacantly as he sipped his cocktail. Then he sat down on the floor beside James, his long legs tangling.

"Well, how does it seem to be home?" he asked.

"I cannot realize it yet," James replied.

"You won't find it so different from New York," Mr. Barnabas said proudly. "This bunch now—every one of 'em talks English. Don't know any Chinese myself—don't have to. Mrs. Barny, now, goes in for art and literature and so on, but I'm just a plain businessman. Course I like her to have a good time."

"What is your business, sir?" James asked.

"Export—furs, racing ponies—I get 'em from Manchuria—native oils, tungsten, anything."

"The war did not hurt your business?"

Mr. Barnabas laughed. "Not a bit! I made a deal, of course. The Japs let me alone. I didn't like them, mind you—rather have the Chinese any time—but what I say is you can always make a deal."

"Dr. Liang!" Mrs. Barnabas sang her high notes. "Please come here—"

She patted a seat beside her on the divan. James rose and sat down beside her. She turned her small, pale-green eyes upon him.

"Now you really must settle this for the whole Dialectic Society. We've debated so often—do be the judge!"

"The question?" James asked smiling. How absurd this woman was!

"Do you think that Robert Browning's work improved or deteriorated after his marriage to Elizabeth Barrett? Now wait

—let me say it—of course *hers* improved—really, she had written nothing—she caught the flame from his lighted torch! But he was the true genius, don't you think—and the real inner meaning of the question is—does the true genius flower alone out of its own solitary power, or can it—must it—have the sunshine of great love—or great suffering, or something on that order?"

She was serious! Listening and gazing into the little crimson birdlike face James let laughter subside in amazement. He looked at the faces about him, all turned to him, waiting. He longed to cry out at them, "Do you really discuss such things —even here, even now?" But he had not the heart to hurt them.

"I am only a scientist," he said modestly. "I fear I have no opinion on Browning—or genius—"

There was a moment's silence. Mrs. Barnabas cried out. "Oh, we can't believe that—when your father's such a genius!" But her outcry was drowned in a rising tide of voices, all subdued, all working together to cover and conceal what he had said. He found himself alone again and was glad when a moment later a resplendent servant announced dinner.

At the long table, however, in the privacy of the many guests, while Mrs. Barnabas talked with a pale and elongated young man who had been introduced as the Chinese Shelley, James entered into conversation with a rather pretty young woman who sat at his right. She spoke to him first and in English. "Shall you stay in Shanghai, Dr. Liang?"

"No, I am going to Peking, to the medical center there."

"Ah, Peking!" she breathed. "It is quite nice there now. Everybody has money."

"Indeed?" James could not decide what this young woman was. Chinese, certainly, but what else?

"While the war was going on, everybody had jobs. It was not too bad."

"You were there?"

"Yes." The young woman had a pretty mouth, small and red. "I sing also. I gave some concerts there—for the Europeans. Of course I studied in Paris. My name is Hellene Ho."

"What do all these other people do?" James asked bluntly.

Hellene pointed with her little finger. "He is essayist; he is poet; he is novelist; she is costume designer; she is artist; she is sculptor—"

"They can't live by these things," James suggested.

Hellene laughed brightly. "Oh, no, certainly they cannot. They live by other ways—some teaching, some selling things, some just borrowing money from Mrs. Barnabas."

"Why does she—"

"Why she does?" Hellene broke in. "Really she is rather kind, but otherwise she gets some attentions to herself. Nobody cares too much to come and see her, and Mr. Barnabas is just merchant prince. If she can say she is patroness of young Chinese thought leaders, she can invite some important guests, like you, Dr. Liang! Can you come only to see Mrs. Barnabas which you don't know? Naturally you come to meet Dialectic Society, don't you?"

The profuse and rich meal went on, course after course. Mrs. Barnabas neglected him except to ask an occasional bright question. "Isn't that brilliant father of yours coming home to stay? But of course he's doing such wonderful things for America, isn't he!"

James met these remarks with calm. After the dinner was over he took his leave early. Mr. Barnabas had disappeared and the Dialectic Society looked sleepy and overstuffed. Only Mrs. Barnabas still glittered.

"Do, do come again, you dangerous young man," she sighed as James shook her hand.

"Dangerous?" he repeated blankly.

"So handsome!" Mrs. Barnabas sang. "All the charm of the East and yet something wonderful—electric—from the West."

James ground his teeth in silence, bowed, and went quietly away. The scarlet-robed menservants were pouring liqueurs and nobody saw him go.

In three or four days he was wholly impatient with Shanghai. Behind the façade of the Bund the city was crowded, dirty and noisy. His hotel looked rich and comfortable on the surface but he found his bathroom grimy and he doubted the freshness of his sheets. The towels were gray and scanty. When he spoke to his room boy of these matters, the fellow grinned. He had soon learned that James could not understand his Shanghai dialect, and spoke to him as if he were a foreigner. "Allee samee wartime, now," he said, and made no effort to change towels or sheets.

Two or three Chinese businessmen, heads of local guilds, sent their cards and came to call upon him, and on the third night they combined in a feast of welcome at a restaurant. There were a few good dishes, sharks' fins in chicken broth, a sweet pudding of glutenous rice, a river carp broiled whole, but the rest of the food was mediocre. Nothing was as it had been, they declared. The country was sinking to ruin. Prices were impossible to pay and no one had any pride left. After the small feast the sons of the merchants gathered around him and asked him eagerly how they could get to America. Here there was nothing to do, they told him. Schools were no good; there were no jobs. He thought as he looked at them, listening, that all of them were too pale and thin. When the main dishes had been brought in by a dirty waiter they had eaten ravenously.

"I came back because I believe that I can do something useful here," he said.

They looked at one another with blank eyes. "There is nothing you can do," they declared. "There is nothing anybody can do."

Defeat was the smell of the city. In his hotel a few sullen American businessmen loitered over whisky sodas, waiting for old times to begin again. They would wait and then go home. In New York a Chinese delegate to the United Nations had said to him, "I would not say this before Americans, but I tell you—do not be shocked at what you see in China. You will not be proud of your country. Your father is wiser than you."

"But my father is very proud of our country and he has taught us to be so, too," he had retorted.

The delegate had smiled and gone his way. It was a familiar smile, one which James had often seen when he spoke of his father to a Chinese. He had not been sure what it meant. Now he began to understand.

On the sixth day he had explored the city enough to know that he never wanted to see it again. It was a mongrel of the lowest breeding. Scum from everywhere in the world had come together to produce this hateful spawn. Nobody looked to see whether faces were white or black or brown because all were there, sometimes in a single face. Was this what came about when races met and mingled? Rich and poor were equally hateful. The ladies of the rich, lingering in the hotel lobby at night, displayed their filmy nylons imported from America, their brocades from India, their diamonds and emeralds and sables, and all the talk was of how much they had paid for such baubles. Their tongues ran to millions of American dollars and if much of this was bombast and he could reduce millions to thousands, still it was foul. For on the streets when he rose restless at dawn there were scavengers going about picking up the dead. These were the beggars and the refugees who had starved during the night. Their bodies were heaped into carts and dragged away before the sun rose.

In this world Lili had been born and reared. The thought came to him like a blow across the heart. This explained her sweet, almost childish indifference. All the rich women had it. The women, the young girls, all of them had her gentle, cool selfishness. Selfishness—he could not avoid the word. But who could avoid it in Shanghai? Here was a little island of tight luxury set in a vast sea of utter misery. To step off the island was to be drowned in the sea.

On the afternoon of the sixth day there was still no letter from Lili, but there was one from Mary. He seized it from the clerk's dirty hand and went up to his room to be alone and found his door open, although he had left it locked. He went in and there sat Young Wang in the easiest chair. He wore an ordinary blue cotton jacket and trousers and he had a bundle tied in a square of faded blue cotton cloth. On his head he wore a sailor's cap of white duck, stiff and clean. He rose when James came in and laughed.

"This big turnip that I am, I feared you had already gone to Peking."

"I have not been able to get a railway ticket yet," James said. He longed to read his letter. Now that he had news of Lili in his hand it was unbearable not to know what it was, for surely Mary would tell of her.

"You must stay night and day at the station or you can get no ticket," Young Wang said. He laughed again. "Of course you cannot do this, master, but I can do it for you and me together."

James looked at him. The round good-humored face was sly and twinkling. "Good it would be for you if you would hire me as your servant," Young Wang said. "Good for me, too."

"But the ship?" James felt a stealing desire to have this healthy young peasant between himself and whatever was to come.

"The ship is gone to Manila," Young Wang said cheerfully. "My uncle gave me a big fight. He smokes opium, very lazy, and every morning I have his work and mine, too. I am a better cook than he is now, but he takes cook cash, not me. So yesterday I told him this is new China, and old people cannot rule young people. He hit me with the coal shovel. I am more strong than he is, young and not smoking opium. I pushed him once and he fell down and went to sleep. But this is very bad, too, and I think it is better I am not there when he wakes up, because his face is lost too much." Young Wang laughed heartily and in spite of himself James smiled.

Young Wang's face glistened with sweat and he wiped it on the tail of his jacket. "As to wages," he went on, "I will take whatever you give me. Suppose you pay for my food, some clothes, one bed, then never mind. Maybe some dollars at feast day. Just now I have cash. But better you give me dollars for railway tickets. You go second class, good enough, first class too much. I will buy fourth-class ticket for me and sit by you as servant in second class."

James listened to this arrangement of his life and yielded. He took out his wallet and handed Young Wang a roll of dollars. Young Wang received it reverently and counted each bill aloud in a hushed voice. "You are very rich, master," he said gently. "I leave my things here while I take so much money." He put his bundle under the table in a far corner, smiled, and let himself out of the door without noise.

James felt vaguely comforted by this new alliance, even though the fellow was only a servant. He needed the comfort a few minutes later. As his eyes hurried over the pages of Mary's careful neat handwriting he began to grow frightened. There was no mention of Lili. Then at the very end, squeezed against the corner, he saw her name. "Mr. Li did not die," Mary wrote. "Sometimes I wish he had. Jim, you mustn't mind. Lili is going everywhere with Ting. Nothing has been announced."

That was all. Ting, the son of a Chinese official in America, was a handsome gay young student at Yale. James had known him for years, for they had gone to the same preparatory school. Mr. Ting was kind enough, a harried gray-haired man, somehow holding his post through many changes in government. But Charlie Ting was an idler and a wastrel. In Chinatown he had to pay cash even though he was an official's son.

He had once married secretly an American hat-check girl at the Waldorf and it had cost his father five thousand dollars to make her willing to divorce Charlie—or Ting, as the Americans always called him.

Mary's letter dropped to the floor and he seized sheets of the coarse hotel paper and his fountain pen and began to pour out his demanding heart to Lili. The thought of Ting, who had slept with a dozen girls, daring to touch her soft hand sickened him with rage. He wrote for an hour and a half, and then laid down his pen and gathered up the sheets and read them over half aloud, trying to imagine her face when they reached her. Would his words touch her heart? He grew gloomy. What power had words in the living flashing presence of Ting? He dropped the sheets on the table and laid his head upon his arms. He would not allow himself the folly of tears, but he sat in grim silence, his face hidden. Outside the open window he heard a brawl rise suddenly and end in the dull sound of a thudding club, but he did not get up to see what it was. The city was full of such brawls. There were too many starving people, and policemen treated them as criminals. Perhaps they were. There was no line between starvation and crime. He felt himself torn in the division of reality. The world, the whole world, was divided into two parts, the island of the rich and the ocean of the poor. Where would he live? He still had his feet on the island, but he was facing the rough dark waters. He must go back—or else he must leap. Lili, his gentle love, could never follow him if he took that leap. She was a flower, a delicate thing, whose roots must grow in the loam of plenty. There was still time for him to go back to America. A cable, his hand on the telephone, a few words, and he could tell her he was coming. The letter was no use. Either he must go back—or take the reckless leap.

The door opened and Young Wang came in and closed it carefully. James lifted his head. Young Wang's jacket was torn, the buttons ripped from their moorings, and he had lost his sailor's cap. But in his hand he held an envelope. He came to the table and shook out the contents. They were railroad tickets.

"I spend too much money, master," Young Wang said solemnly. "But I think it is good to spend it so. To get a ticket honestly we must wait many days. This way I bought two tickets from a man privately inside the station."

"Why are your clothes torn?" James exclaimed.

"Other men also wish to buy," Young Wang said, grinning. "Never mind—I fix my coat."

He got down on his hands and knees, found his bundle, and opened it. From a small paper box he took six safety pins. "Foreign ladies drop pins on the floor and I pick them up," he said. "In my village no one can buy them, and I take them home to my mother. But now I use them to keep my skin from leaking out." He pinned his jacket neatly together, and James watched him.

"What day are the tickets for?" he asked.

"Tomorrow morning, six o'clock. But I think it better if we go now, master. Many people will wait at the station and jump in the train. We must jump first, or tickets will be no good. Tickets are only for the train conductor, not for passengers."

"Let's get ready and go," James said. He tore the letter into small bits and dropped them into a huge brass cuspidor that stood by the table.

This is not to say that he could forget Lili. In the night at the station he sat upon a rail seat that rose out of a sleeping mass of people on the floor, leaning against baskets and bundles, and thought of nothing but Lili. Part of the time he thought of her with bitter clearness and when he dozed into exhaustion he dreamed of himself successful and famous and somehow drawing her to him again. Ting would never be anything, but he, James Liang, would certainly be something, and surely there would come the day when Lili would see what she was doing. He woke to gaze down into Young Wang's bland and peaceful face as he slept back to back with a stout old man. Young Wang had chosen this wide back against which to lean and had almost at once gone to sleep. The day had been warm, but toward evening it had begun to rain and inside the cement-floored station the night air was now almost chill. Once in two or three hours a train whistle blew and the crowd staggered to their feet and seized their bundles and pressed through the gates, only to come surging back and fall upon the floor to sleep again. Each time Young Wang had gone to see whether by any chance the train north was making an unscheduled departure. "Sometimes people too many, train sneaks away," he explained to James. The last time he had come back dawn was beginning to break and he would not let himself fall asleep again. He yawned ferociously, smiled at James, and announced that he had just bribed the stationmaster to tell him when the train was really going north.

In something less than an hour the stationmaster sauntered by, looking neither to right nor to left, and Young Wang seized all the baggage he could carry and James rose to follow him. From somewhere two coolies appeared and silently tied the rest of the suitcases together and followed behind.

Outside on the platform the air was misty and cool and the electric lights were feeble. There was no train in sight. A few anxious souls were asleep even on the platform and they still slept. But Young Wang peered into the distance. "Train comes," he announced in a tense whisper. Nothing could be seen but his eyes pierced beyond sight.

"How do you know?" James asked.

"Feel the earth under my feet," Young Wang answered.

In a quarter of an hour the train pulled into the station and the crowd pressed through the gates and began climbing into doors and windows alike. But Young Wang was ahead of them all. Yelling and pushing with sharp elbows, he commandeered two seats, heaped them with baggage and sat on top of them. James, caught like driftwood on a wave, heard him roaring at the top of his lungs that his master was a Big Man from America. When he came into sight, Young Wang climbed down, smiled, and showed him a pleasant enough corner by the window.

"Bags must stay here," he said. "If no bags, then seat will be gone soon."

The aisles were full and men and children sat even on the baggage racks overhead. The noise on the roof meant that those who had not found places inside were on top of the car. The engine gave a series of jerks, people screamed, a few fell off, the train started northward, and James found that for a full hour he had not had time to think of Lili.

If the day was long and hideous, the night was less so only because from exhaustion he fell into a daze of unconsciousness which was not sleep. He dreamed that he was held in some prison full of writhing people who had nothing to do with him and yet he was one of them. He woke to gaze out of the dusty windows at a dull landscape whose colors he did not see.

On the morning of the second day Young Wang broke a window pane. Fresh cool air rushed in and James felt his brain cleared suddenly. He had been sitting in deep depression, unwashed, for there was no water on the train. When he had struggled to the lavatory he had found it occupied by two women, their bedding, and three children, and he had retreated again. When the train stopped Young Wang had allowed him out only with great anxiety, and had begged him not to leave the side of the train, because no one knew how quickly the train might go. Then Young Wang, rearranging his possessions to allow him to lie on top of them, had thrust a heavy oiled paper umbrella he had bought from a vendor through the cracked glass of the window.

Now James leaned toward the hole and breathed in the air. He had been poisoned by the fetid atmosphere within the car. He drank in the freshness of the morning and saw to his surprise that the land was not dim and colorless. Instead it was brilliantly green and against the vivid hue men and women in blue garments worked in the fields. Small brick-walled villages studded the level plains and on the horizon were violet-colored hills.

"Forgive, forgive!" a gentle trembling voice said. An old gentleman in a crumpled silk robe pushed past him, put his head through the opened window and was violently sick in a deprecating courteous fashion.

James waited, pinned beneath him, and at last the man stepped back, smiling with desperate calm. "I am too coarse," he said. "But I have been trying for hours not to soil the train."

"Do you have pain in you?" James asked.

"No pain, thank you," he replied. "The train rolls me inside. It is a pity we must travel in such ways. A sedan chair is more healthy. The speed is too much nowadays." He sighed and returned to his place on the floor. It was impossible not to like this old man. He had spread a quilt neatly under him and he drew it about him so that he need not touch the persons on either side of him. One was a soldier who slept with his mouth open and smelled of garlic and wine and the other was a young woman who suckled two children, an infant and a boy of three.

James turned his face again to the landscape. The old gentleman had been very careful and neat and there was no vomit on the window.

The train was many hours late. Long ago they should have

reached Nanking, and only now were the purple hills looming into view. Young Wang sat up when he saw them, and began to fasten bundles together again. Somehow or other he had accumulated several more than he had brought on the train. At various places when the train stopped he had bought packages of tea, of dried fish, of fried brown bean curd, or larded cakes. Each town had its specialty and vendors brought them to the train. Since there was no food served, anything to eat was valuable and Young Wang had stored up enough for himself and James, and what was left he would give to his family as presents at some distant day. He prudently bought nothing that was fresh except at midnight two large bowls of hot soup, one of which he had given to his master. At Nanking the train stopped, and they must take a ferry and cross the river to take a north-bound train again on the other side.

"You get ready, please," he bade James with authority. "Here is one big fight for the ferry first."

When the train slid loudly into the station the baggage was slung about his person like armor and he plunged relentlessly into the crowd, creating a space in which James followed him with a doggedness that was almost ruthless. By this means they reached the ferry in time to find a place that was not on the edge of the boat.

"Too many people drown," Young Wang told James over his shoulder. "Push, push, splash!"

So it happened that when they were on the ferry James saw the unlucky old gentleman, clawing his way on at the last moment, gain a tiny space as the ferry left the banks. In mid-river there was indeed a splash. A few voices cried out that the old man had fallen in the water. The ferry continued on its way, but with a shout James leaped through the crowd. He fell heavily. Young Wang had clutched his ankles and would not be shaken off.

"Let go, you fool!" James shouted. But nothing would loose the hands locked at his feet. Scores of hands reached out to prevent him when he tried to drag himself to the edge of the ferry. "Too late, too late!" they cried. "It is destiny! The current has taken that old head far away."

It was indeed too late. The river swirled with a hundred wicked crosscurrents and had James plunged it would have been to search in vain for the quiet old man. He stood dazed for a moment, speechless with a terrible silent anger. Then he turned on Young Wang.

"Let go!" he roared. The brown hands unlocked, but Young Wang stood between him and the water. James turned his back on him and Young Wang reached out and unseen he took hold of the end of his coat and held it until they reached the shore.

On the northern shore James turned and looked back at Nanking, the capital of his country. It lay hidden behind a high gray wall, centuries old. Beyond it he could see the double crest of Purple Mountain, where Sun Yat-sen's tomb had been built. He knew from scores of photographs how the tomb looked. Some day when he had discovered his own country he would go there and look at the tomb of the man who had lived too long, or died too soon—he did not know which.

When the train reached Peking he was in a fever of weariness. He had been traveling for days and he realized that he had become utterly dependent on Young Wang. The sprightly young man had provided him with food and hot tea at intervals, had night and morning fetched him hot water in a tin basin wherewith to wash, had pushed soldiers and women and callous men off the seats he had pre-empted for himself and his master, had fanned away flies, had again broken a window pane, and had made life somehow endurable.

3

MARY READ ALOUD A LETTER from James at the noon meal. The family was still in New York, although summer had deepened and Dr. Liang was beginning to feel the heat. He sat delicately languid and listened to the letter, dated two weeks earlier and from Peking.

"I shall not crystallize my impressions of our country," James wrote. "They are too mixed. But I have found this old city reassuring. Even the Japanese respected its ancient beauty. This is not to say that I have seen much of it. I took up my duties at the hospital the day after I arrived, and when night comes I am too weary to sight-see. My view is also somewhat biased by the fact that I see only sick people. Trachoma is frightful. So is tuberculosis. I operate on the eyes but can do nothing for the lungs. Ulcers, gangrene—"

"Spare us, Mary," Dr. Liang said gently. "We are trying to eat—and it is very hot."

Mary folded the letter and put it in her pocket.

"You can read it to me when we are alone," Mrs. Liang said briskly. "Liang, eat some of the beef and peppers! You know you like this dish."

She dipped her chopsticks into the bowl and picked out a bit of meat and laid it on his plate. He ignored it and ate some rice from his bowl, a mouthful or two. Then he began to talk gently and slowly, each word made clear, as he did when he lectured. "I am happy to hear that Peking is untouched. I hope to spend my old age there, in a quiet lane, in an old house with a garden. I shall be paterfamilias—let us say, grand-paterfamilias. I seem to see myself at the head of our family table and about me are my children, married and living with me under one great roof in the old style, my grandchildren running about my courts. Ah, happy old age!"

He smiled, and Mrs. Liang, who had been listening with lively interest, broke in, "Liang, I tell you, don't count on it! Children nowadays are unreliable. Suppose they don't want to live under one roof with us?"

Dr. Liang shook his head gently. "I am a reasonably pleasant person, I believe?" He looked at his children's faces with a touching trust. "I am not obnoxious, am I? Not repulsive?"

"Of course not, Pa," Louise exclaimed. She was looking very pretty today. Heat flushed her usually pale face and her eyes, set shallowly under flying brows, were dark and humid. She had a secretive reserve except toward her father. The whole family knew that Dr. Liang loved Louise better than any of the other children, and they accepted it as natural, since she was the youngest.

"You will come and live with me, Little Lou?" Dr. Liang went on, half playfully, half pathetically. "Ma, we will have at least one child with us. We must find a very nice husband for her, some nice young professor, a scholar with whom I can discuss the dreams of Chuangtse and the poetry of Li Po, the charming drunkard."

Dr. Liang liked to tease his children affectionately with threats of finding husbands and wives for them in the old fashion of Chinese parents. Actually he had declared that while he would introduce suitable young persons to his sons and daughters he would not force his choice upon any of them. He was too modern and he loved them too well.

The mention of marriage roused Mrs. Liang's curiosity. "Does James say anything about Lili?" she asked Mary.

"Nothing," Mary replied.

"Then he must have heard," Mrs. Liang exclaimed.

"I told him," Mary said.

Dr. Liang was vexed at this. He spoke with sharpness. "Now, Mary, that was very premature. I was talking with Mr. Li only yesterday and he said that Lili has not made up her mind. Besides Charles Ting there are three other young men who have approached her. It is quite possible that in the midst of so much rivalry she will turn from them all and still choose James."

Mrs. Liang sniffed. "Liang, I must tell you—at first I thought it would be very nice to enjoy some money from the Li family. Your salary as a professor is not large, and at present your writing is not very useful to us. With conditions bad in our country, the Americans are naturally not interested in us. So I thought it might be necessary some day to have a rich daughter-in-law. But now I don't like this Lili. I think she would divorce James quickly when she likes. I suggest rather a better type of girl, who is more faithful, someone like Sonia Pan."

Peter groaned loudly. "Sonia Pan! She's ugly."

Mrs. Liang would not yield. "Ugly girls can be fixed now. It is not like before. And she is very good. She does not waste money."

"It would be no use for her to waste money on herself," Louise murmured.

Dr. Liang coughed. "I am sure Ma is right. Sonia is a very good girl. But the Pan family is not quite—after all, Ma—a Chinatown family, you know—"

"Billy Pan is a good businessman," Mrs. Liang argued.

"That is not everything," Dr. Liang said gently.

"Sonia would be good for a daughter-in-law," Mrs. Liang persisted. "She would live in Peking very well with us and she would not be too modern. Lili would not like old-fashioned ways. She would want to live in her own house. Sonia would listen to me."

Mary interposed. "Father, I think it is no use to talk of Sonia when James has never thought of her."

"Quite right, my dear," Dr. Liang said gratefully. "Let us also think of something else. What do you say to a little vacation for all of us? I am feeling the heat. I long for mountains. My spirit always soars when I am in the mountains. Sometimes I wish we could move to the country to live."

"It would be too inconvenient," Mrs. Liang said. "You would be lonely, Liang. Who would be there to listen to you talk? And it is too hard to buy the food for you. When you feel like country you can always go to Central Park."

She rose and began to collect the dishes. Yet as always her heart relented toward her husband. It was true that New York was hot. Certainly it was not so hot as Shanghai was in the summer, but he forgot that. He had forgotten so much about China. It would be no great expense to go to some small place in the mountains to the north. She pattered back into the living room to tell him so. But he was asleep, stretched out on the long sofa, breathing deeply and calmly.

She gazed at him for a moment and wondered if he looked

thinner and decided he did not. When they were first married he had been very thin and tall and to her surprise he wept when anything was hard. His mother said he had always wept easily and therefore he must be shielded from distress. It was, she had said, his scholarly temperament. Mrs. Liang, then a ruddy strong young woman, had listened and she did not understand her young husband, but evidently he was some sort of treasure. She still did not understand him, but he was still her treasure. She would not wake him.

So turning away she mounted the stairs slowly to find Mary and then she felt sleepy also and yawned. After all, she was not so young as she had been. The house was very quiet. The children must have gone outside, perhaps to the park. The letter from James could wait. She opened the door of her bedroom softly and then closed it. The room looked cool and pleasant and she took off her silk robe and folded it carefully across a chair. Then she lay down on the bed; her jaw fell, and she was instantly asleep.

On a bench by the river, Mary, Peter, and Louise discussed this first long letter from James. He had sent a cable announcing his arrival in Peking, and they had awaited the letter with impatience. By it they would judge whether China was what they hoped it was or feared it was not. On the whole, the letter was favorable. The journey northward, James wrote, was something to experience rather than talk about. He was inclined sometimes to think that the worst they had heard from Chinese who had fled to New York was not bad enough. Filth and poverty were everywhere. The train was something that could not be imagined and the callousness to death had frightened him. It was not only that an old man had been swept from the ferry, or that the dead lay in the streets of Shanghai. There was some sort of cruelty here toward the helpless—he was not ready yet to define it. The animals were wretched, even the donkeys and mules carried loads far too heavy and these loads were laid on raw sores on the beasts' backs. Yet he supposed that animals must share the miseries of men, and men staggered under dreadful burdens.

Mary had been reading the letter aloud solemnly to the two on either side of her. Now she paused and the letter fell to her lap. She gazed at the bridge, shimmering in the afternoon heat. The water in the river was as smooth as oil. "This helps me to understand something about our mother," she said. "She is cruel to animals, too, though she is kind enough to people. How she hates the little dogs that women make pets of here!"

"They are pretty silly, though," Peter said.

"She doesn't like to see animals treated as human beings," Louise suggested.

"It's more than that," Mary said soberly. She took up the letter again and read on.

When James had reached Peking, he wrote, he had gone straight to the hospital and had found two comfortable rooms ready for him. It was like stepping back into New York. The hospital was very fine and luxurious, built by Americans with American money. The Japanese had left it alone, or very nearly, and the equipment, while not of the latest, was still very good. The view from his windows was superb. The city roofs were delicately shaped and old courtyards were rich with ancient trees. Over the city wall in the distance were the bare outlines of mountains. He had been here only a week and so he had not taken time to do any sight-seeing, but Peking was the way he had dreamed China looked. The streets were wide and the gates were massive and beautiful. Everything had been built with the outlook of centuries in the past and centuries yet to come. The city seemed indestructible. It made him proud to be a Chinese. He had gone to see the marble bridge because their father had told him it was even more beautiful than the George Washington Bridge. It was impossible to compare them. This bridge in Peking was made of marble and stone and there were sculptured lions on it. It was true that the mounting curve was matchless.

The three, reading, lifted their eyes again to the curve of steel beyond where they sat. It soared against the sky, as modern as the century in which they lived. They could not imagine a bridge of marble with sculptured lions.

Peking, James wrote, made him want to send for them all. People told him that the winters were cold and that in the early spring yellow dust floated over the city, borne by bitter winds from the northern desert. Summer was the perfect season. He was really very happy. Something deep in his soul was being satisfied. He worked hard but he did not tire as he had in New York. He felt relaxed. Nobody hurried and yet more work was done, he believed, than he had ever seen done before. People moved at an even, steady pace, their minds at ease. They seemed ready for any fate. They were sturdy and self-confident. He was beginning to understand Americans better than he had even when he was with them. He felt now that Americans suffered from submerged feelings of guilt, as though they knew they were not as good as they wanted to be or wanted people to think they were. But here in Peking people did not care what other people thought, and so they could be only as good as they wanted to be. Life flowed, like a river.

"It sounds like heaven," Mary said, and her eyes dreamed.

Neither Peter nor Louise answered.

She read on. "I feel that if Lili saw this place she would be willing to come to me," James wrote. "Houses are not hard to find. We could live very happily—she would not need to work. She could live as idly as a lily, indeed, and being so beautiful who would blame her?"

Mary stopped here. What James commissioned her to do in the next few sentences was only for her eyes. But Peter gave a yelp. He rose and straightened the fold in his trousers carefully. "Tell Jim he is way back in the past so far as that young woman is concerned. She's been tentatively engaged to three men since she was tentatively engaged to him."

"Don't talk so," Mary commanded him.

"Ting told me," Peter retorted. "Ting says he is going to get his dad to put pressure on old Li. It's the only way to pin Lili down."

"What pressure?" Mary asked.

"Ting says old Li was really a collaborator with the Japs and his dad has the proof. He skipped out just in time to avoid getting put in jail—or coughing up a couple of million to put into certain outstretched hands."

Both girls stared at him. "Really?" Louise murmured. She enjoyed gossip.

"Tell Jim unless he can put on pressure, too, he had just better forget the whole business," Peter said. He set his straw hat at an angle. " 'By, kids! I promised Ting to meet him. We're going to run out to the beach with a couple of girls."

His sisters did not speak. They watched him thoughtfully as he sauntered to the street, hailed a taxi, and disappeared.

"Do you think we ought to tell Mother what he does?" Louise asked.

"She can't do anything," Mary said. "He needs to go away from America. I wish Jim would send for him."

"Peter doesn't know enough to be of any use anywhere," Louise yawned. "I'm going home to sleep—Estelle wants me to go to a dance with them tonight."

"Where?" Mary asked.

"Some roof or other," Louise answered indifferently. She hid from her shrewd elder sister the excitement of her heart. Tonight she would dance with Philip. Estelle was making it a party of four.

Alone on the bench, Mary read again the letter from beginning to end, trying to imagine scene by scene what it contained. But she had no experience to feed her imagination with reality, and at last she rose and walked home. The house was quiet and in the living room her father still slept, his face handsome and full of peace. She tiptoed into his study and took the receiver from the telephone and dialed.

"Oh, please, is Lili there?" she asked, when she heard Mollie's voice.

"I'll call her, miss," Mollie's stolid voice answered. She listened and heard Mollie's heavy footsteps, Lili's little cry of surprise, Lili's high heels tripping over bare floors, and then Lili's sweet voice that sounded falsetto over the wires.

"Yes, ye-es?" That was Lili.

"Lili, this is Mary. I've had a letter from Jim. Shall I bring it over?"

There was a pause, and Lili laughed. "Oh, lovelee!" she trilled. "But Mary, just now I am so busy."

"Then when?" Mary asked firmly.

"Oh ye-es, let me see, Mary—shall I call you?"

Mary's ready temper flew from her heart. "Don't trouble— you don't want to hear it, Lili. Why don't you say so?"

"But I do, very much!"

"You do not."

"Ye-es, Mary, please come over now—with the letter, please!"

"You are busy," Mary said cruelly.

"Ye-es—never mind. You come now, please. I don't do anything else. I just wait for you."

The pretty voice was pleading. Mary longed to refuse, but she dared not. She must do what she could for James.

"All right," she said shortly. "I'm on my way now."

She put up the telephone and went at once, letting herself out of the house silently. She did not want anyone to know where she was, for she did not want anyone to know what happened—whatever it was to be.

Lili was lying on a couch in her bedroom and there Mollie led Mary. "She says to tell you she's got only a little while, being as she's promised to go to a tea," Mollie said at the door.

"I shan't need but a little while," Mary said.

There was no hint of haste in Lili's calm manner. She put out her soft hand to Mary. "You know, I'm glad you told me about Jim's letter. I feel so bad here—about Jim." She held her hand on her left breast. She had taken off her Chinese gown and lay in a delicate lace-trimmed American slip. American dress she considered ugly, but she wore American underwear with joy. Her bare shoulders and arms were exquisite ivory. Mary looked away from them. It seemed in some strange fashion a desecration that she should be here in this intimate room and James so far away.

Lili continued in the same plaintive tone. "Every day I wish to write a letter to Jim."

"It would make him very happy," Mary murmured. She sat down in a pink satin chair and felt hot and plain. She brushed back her hair with her hands and wiped her temples with her handkerchief.

"Oh, what can I tell him?" Lili asked. "Everything is not sure. Maybe many years before he is ready for me!"

"He is ready for you now," Mary said. She unfolded the letter and began to read it slowly and clearly. Lili listened, her head leaned on her hand, her great eyes earnest and a tender smile about her mouth. She did not speak. When Mary had finished she lay back and closed her eyes. Then she felt under the satin pillow and found a lace handkerchief with which she slowly wiped her eyes. "I long to go to Peking," she said in a heartbroken voice.

"Then why don't you?" Mary asked. She wondered if she had misjudged the beautiful girl. It was so hard to understand the girls who came from China. One knew the blood was the same, but to have grown up in America and in China made two different beings. Lili was so soft, she yielded everywhere—until one knew she had really yielded nowhere.

"I cannot just go to Peking," Lili said without opening her eyes. Her beautiful lips trembled. "I have to think about many things."

"If you loved James you would think only of him," Mary said.

Lili shook her head. She touched the wisp of lace to her lips. "You talk just like American," she complained. "I am Chinese. I cannot just think about one man."

At this Mary lost her temper. "I can see that," she said bitterly. "I guess anybody can see that. You think of a lot of men."

Tears rolled down Lili's cheeks. She opened her eyes and gazed at Mary through wet lashes. "You don't understand," she whispered. "You are so American!"

"I'll tell James you can't just think of him," Mary said.

Lili gave a soft scream. "Please don't tell him this! He is American, too, and he can't understand."

"What shall I tell him, then?" Mary asked. "I've got to tell him something, Lili. He loves you—and you're being too cruel."

Lili was silent for a moment. Then she looked sidewise at Mary. "Tell him—tell him—I write very soon!" She clapped her hands and laughed. Then she got up from the couch. "I have to go with Baba and Ma to tea at the Consulate, but I don't want to go a bit. I much rather sit here with you and listen to the letter all over again. But I must go—they tell me to."

She smiled lovingly at Mary, and as firmly as though Lili had laid her hands upon her, Mary felt herself pushed from the room.

4

IN HIS ROOM at the end of a hot day James read Mary's letter. She confessed that she was writing too quickly after she had seen Lili. She ought to have waited for a few days until her anger was cooled. "But you know how hard it is for me to wait," she said, "especially when it has to do with you, Jim. Lili did not say she would not marry you or that she was going to marry anyone else. She just said she had many things to consider. I don't know whether she is hard or soft. Somehow she does manage to get her way."

James folded the letter. It was a long letter covering many pages, and Mary had put into it family news and scraps of gossip about their friends and she had mailed it before the family went to the mountains. By now they would be in the cool green hills of Vermont. He thought with homesickness of the clear streams of cold water running over round brown stones, and the winds fragrant with pines. Yet when he was there he had not thought of it as home. Home, then, had been China. By what contrary whims of the soul was he always to feel homesickness wherever he was? Were Lili here, he thought restlessly, then his heart would be settled.

He no longer thought of going back to America. Lili must come to him. He knew now that here was where he must stay. He was a doctor first, and he was already entangled in the needs of the people who came to the hospital in terror and desperation. No one came for foreign medicine, as it was called, unless death were the alternative, and each day's work was the saving of creatures already committed to death. He handled bodies bruised with the pinching fingers of old wives and punctured with the needles of old-fashioned doctors. Many of his gangrene cases began as poison from unsterilized needles thrust into shoulders and limbs and breasts to exorcise devils. He tried to teach health while he healed, but the dark eyes of the sick were dull and unheeding. He began to dream of health education in schools, among the young. Yet how could he do more than he was doing? A dozen operations in a day were routine. The hospital was understaffed. American doctors had not yet returned and the Chinese doctors trained abroad were constantly being tempted to easier jobs. It took courage to operate when the death of an already dying person might mean a lawsuit, if he were a rich general or a millionaire. Only the poor were grateful and only the poor did not want revenge.

In his growing anger against his rich patients he found himself turning to the poor who came to the clinics and crowded the charity wards. His first quarrel with the hospital came over the question of the charity wards which were daily squeezed smaller to provide more private rooms. When he saw beds touching one another and pallets on the floors he went to the office of his superiors and opened the door abruptly.

"Dr. Peng!" he began and stopped.

The handsome delicate-featured Dr. Peng Chenyu was seated at his carved desk, and leaning over him was the pretty head nurse. They were talking in earnest tones, the man smiling, the girl coquettish. Then they saw James standing square and frank as an American in the open doorway.

The girl stepped back and slipped from the room by a side door. Dr. Peng spoke in his high smooth voice. "Dr. Liang," he said in English, "please be so kind as to knock before you enter."

James spoke in Chinese. He rarely used English. It disgusted him that every little student nurse and interne tried to chatter in English. "That this was a private office I did not know, Dr. Peng," he said. "I come to complain. The wards are being reduced until now my patients are lying on the floor."

Dr. Peng smiled and lifted a small object from his desk. It was the nude figure of a woman and it was made of white jade. "Do you know what this is?" he asked, still in English. He came from Shanghai and he did not speak Mandarin well.

"A naked woman," James said bluntly.

"Much more interesting than that," Dr. Peng said delicately. His voice had the cadences of poetry. "It is the figure that native doctors use to diagnose the ills of an old-fashioned woman patient. She will not show herself to a man—as you have doubtless discovered—but she puts her pretty fingertip somewhere on this jade figure, to show where her pain is." Dr. Peng laughed silently. "What amuses me is how lovingly the Chinese doctors carve these little figures, or have them carved, and how precious is the material! Do sit down, Dr. Liang."

"I have no time," James said. "I have come to complain about the wards."

Dr. Peng held the little figure in his palm. "As to our wards," he said gently, "we regret very much that they are too few."

"This pandering to the rich disgusts me," James said. "Every few days I find workmen putting up walls about a section of the ward to make a new private room for a general or an official."

"It is not pandering," Dr. Peng said. Virtue shone in his narrow brilliantly black eyes. "It is necessity. Charity patients do not pay. Generals and officials and millionaires pay very well. I daresay you would complain, Dr. Liang, if your salary were curtailed—an excellent salary it is, too. You are worth it, of course. But the rich people pay for it. Do not forget that our grants from America ceased last year. We have to find our own salaries as well as support the hospital."

James glared into the handsome smooth face. Then he turned and went out, slamming the door slightly. What Peng had said was true. The hospital was expensive beyond all proportion to the lives of the people. Only the rich could afford to lie under these massive roofs, only the rich could afford to walk the marble-floored halls and use the tiled baths. There was no place for the poor except in the crowded wards.

He went back to the clinic and patients pressed toward him. "Doctor—doctor—good doctor," they wailed at him when he came into the room. At first their urgency had confused him and had even made him angry. But now he knew they could not help crying out to him. They had endured so much and there were so many of them. "I am here," he said quietly. "I will not go away until I have seen each one of you." Only when they found that they could trust his word did they become quiet.

"Please forgive us," an old man said gently. "Usually the doctors do not like to see so many sick and poor waiting for them and they choose only a few of us and the rest of us must go away again."

James had found that this was so. What angered and discouraged him most profoundly was the callousness of his own colleagues to the ills of people who came to them for healing. The selfishness of the rich he had soon come to take for granted, but what he could not take for granted, as the weeks went on, was the heartlessness of doctors and nurses. Not all of them, he granted grudgingly—Dr. Liu Chen was an honor to any hospital, and he learned always to call upon one or another of three nurses. The kindness of these three he could trust, Rose Mei, Kitty Sen, and Marie Yang. All nurses had foreign names and used them carefully, just as they spent half a week's salary on permanent waves at the hands of a White Russian hairdresser in what had once been the Legation Quarter.

Much of his private thought went into angry pondering over this callousness of his fellows. Dr. Kang, for example, with whom he often operated, was a delightful friend, an enthusiastic companion on the rare evenings when they were free to go to a famous restaurant or to sit in the deserted palace gardens or even to ride outside the city walls to sleep for the night in some cool old temple. Kang was a learned man, and not only a graduate of Johns Hopkins. He knew Chinese literature as well as Western and he had a famous collection of musical instruments from many places in the world. He was the friend of a great actor, and one day in August he took James to his friend's house, and James met the pleasant round-faced man who had a genius for making himself look like a beautiful woman. The whole afternoon was a dream out of history. The house was huge, room opened into room and court led to court. In an outdoor pavilion they had sat and had eaten the cream-filled Tibetan sweetmeats which the actor loved and dreaded. "My career depends upon my figure," he said with a rueful merriment, "and my cook, alas, is superb. Only while the Japanese were here could I eat and let myself grow fat. Also I grew a moustache and beard. Now that they are gone I must return to my roles."

He touched the strings of a flat harp and sang in his high falsetto which gave so perfectly the illusion that it was a woman's young voice. The air was tender with sweetness and mild sadness. The atmosphere of age and mellow living and thinking suffused the evening.

Every chair, every table, the scrolls upon the walls, the tiles of the floors, the lattices of the windows, the carvings of the outdoor pavilion in which they had sat, the shrubs and rocks of the garden courts—all were exquisite and planned with a sophisticated sense of beauty. Kang had seemed entirely at home there as he had discussed with his friend the detail of a song, the finesse of a gesture. James had listened, feeling himself unlearned and crude because he had spent his life in the West. He began that night to blame his father for taking him away so young into the foreign world.

In the hospital the next day he was shocked afresh by Kang's arrogance and his complete indifference to suffering. He was an excellent surgeon, one of the best that James had ever seen at work. His thin strong hands were all fine bone and smooth sinew. Any patient might be grateful for those hands working in his vitals with such speed and accuracy. But once the task was over whether the patient lived or died was none of Kang's concern. He seldom inquired. He often refused altogether to operate on an old woman, on a poor man, or on a frightened child. Crying children especially annoyed him.

"Take the child away," he had ordered Rose one day.

"But it is mastoid, Doctor," she urged. "The boy will die."

Kang shrugged his shoulders and washed his hands thoroughly at the spotless basin. Rose took the child to James and told him the story. James operated and the child lived.

There was no use in talking to Kang but James did it. "That mastoid case," he had said the next evening. They were on their way to a wedding. One of the older doctors was taking a young wife. Kang was pulling on his white gloves. He never wore Chinese clothes and his black dinner suit was as immaculate as it would have been were he in New York.

"What mastoid?" he asked. He frowned at the red tea flower in his buttonhole. It looked somewhat faded, but this was not the season for the flowers.

"That boy who was brought from his village yesterday morning," James said. For the first time since he had come he wore his tuxedo and it was not well pressed. Young Wang had left him at Peking to return to his village home and the hospital servant was green and untrained in Western ways.

Dr. Kang had looked impatient. "My dear Liang, surely I can choose my own cases."

"But the boy would have died," James remonstrated.

"Thousands—millions, I might say—must die," Dr. Kang had retorted. "When you have been here a year or two longer you will understand that common sense alone compels you to take the long view. What are we? A handful of doctors in a nation as medieval as Europe in the sixteenth century. We cannot possibly save everyone from dying. We would be the first dead, did we try!"

It was true. James did not reply. He followed Kang into the wide hall which ran through the doctor's house and stepped into the carriage which stood waiting at the gate.

The wedding was to be at the Peking Hotel. Modern weddings were seldom in homes, as the old-fashioned ones still were, and now streams of fashionably dressed people were being driven in horse carriages and motorcars toward the hotel. Dr. Su, the groom, had been three times married and twice divorced. His first wife still lived in the remote ancestral homestead somewhere in Szechuan, but nobody had ever seen her, nor did he ever speak of her. Two sons, now grown, were internes at the hospital but they also never spoke of the small silent illiterate woman who was their mother. Tonight they stood near their father when James entered the lobby of the hotel. Dr. Su, in Western evening dress and white gloves, welcomed his guests pleasantly, and a uniformed servant offered cocktails and tea. Dr. Su had been married so often that he did not take the event with any embarrassment and he chatted with his colleagues and friends.

"Dr. Liang—Jim," he said affectionately in English. "Come along, man—choose your drink. Tea? You are so old-fashioned."

James smiled. "Such tea seems rather a novelty to me," he said. He liked Dr. Su, who was his senior surgeon, and he spoke to him in English as a courtesy. He had never heard Dr. Su speak Chinese except to a servant.

The great lobby, fragrant with lilies, was soon filled with guests. The men were in Western clothes for the most part, and the women in graceful close-fitting Chinese dress. Here and there a military officer's uniform shone resplendently and swords clanked. There were a few elderly men in rich Chinese gowns, enough to show that Dr. Su had his grateful patients everywhere.

In the midst of the talk the music, subdued until now, broke into the Mendelssohn Wedding March and Dr. Su's elder son, a shy, grave young man, touched his father's arm. "Pa," he said, "they are waiting for you."

Dr. Su looked startled, then he laughed. "I'd forgotten," he said frankly. He wiped his lips with a spotless white silk handkerchief, for he had been eating butterfly shrimps with his cocktails. He cleared his throat, looked dignified, and walked beside his son toward the ballroom where the guests were already assembling. He turned into a side entrance, and a few minutes later the audience saw his tall slender figure appear on the stage followed now by both sons and Dr. Kang, who was his best man.

Well-to-do modern people had many foreign weddings and there was nothing new about this one. Only the servants of the guests saw anything strange about it and they clustered about the door, gazing in the same open-mouthed astonishment with which they stared at Hollywood motion pictures. They fell back for the bride and her bridesmaids. Her father walked beside her looking hot and ill at ease. He was a retired warlord, and having taken off his uniform permanently immediately after the war, he wore now a heavy brocaded silvery satin robe and a black velvet jacket. Since he no longer troubled to hold in his large belly with a military belt, his figure was pyramid-shaped and his shaven head sat like a melon upon it. The shining figure of his daughter was tiny against his mass. Her satin gown, her train, her lace veil were shell pink instead of white and she wore diamonds in her ears, about her neck, and on her arms. Upon her finger she wore a huge diamond solitaire. Dr. Su was a prudent man and each time he had divorced his former wives he had recovered this ring.

His face did not change as he watched his young bride come up the aisle, nor did she lift her eyes. She was walking with painful intent to the march, but Dr. Su noticed that she missed the beat. He was a little annoyed at this, for she was supposed to be a fairly brilliant pianist. He had heard her play Chopin concertos with dash and execution. He himself was a good violinist, although he made the excuse that his surgery made it necessary for him to keep the ends of his fingers sensitive and therefore he could not practice as much as he wished. One reason he had chosen this little creature among scores like her was that she might accompany him upon the piano when he played for guests at his frequent dinner parties.

He looked somewhat critically at the little figure coming up the aisle followed by the train of girls in dresses of all colors. He did not know her very well, but that perhaps did not matter. He had known his second wife very well, and they had quarreled bitterly. They had been lovers before their marriage and after it. His third wife had taken an American as a lover, and that he could not tolerate, especially when he saw the tall boy in uniform. He was too handsome, too easy, too romantic looking, and Dr. Su knew that never again would he be able to hold his wife's attention.

His first wife he scarcely remembered. That wedding had been different indeed. He had been in haste and impatience to get to America. It was the first time, and America then had seemed wonderful and perfect and his home hatefully old-fashioned. But his mother would not let him go until he had consented to marry the girl to whom his parents had engaged him so long ago, so much a part of his childhood that it was nothing to him. The wedding had been the traditional one, the bride in red satin from head to foot, a veil of beads hanging over her face. The feasting had gone on for three days. When he saw her alone for the first night he had found her a pretty little thing, speechless with shyness. He had never been able to persuade her to say anything to him. A month of this silent marriage and his mother let him go. His first son was born while he was in Baltimore. His second son had been born after his return. Then he had left home, never to go back until his parents were killed during a harvesttime by angry tenant farmers. They had not hurt the timid woman who hid in a dry well nor the two little boys whom she clutched. But after that he had brought his sons away with him and their mother lived on in the old home with his eldest uncle who took over the lands.

The wedding ceremony was half through before he realized he had paid no heed to it.

"Where is the ring?" the officiating Presbyterian minister asked. "Here, sir," the eldest son whispered. He took it from his pocket and gave it to the best man who gave it to the groom. Dr. Su put it on the delicate third finger where the solitaire shone so bravely, and thus he was married again.

The wedding music blared from the horns and trumpets of the hired hotel band and the procession marched gaily down the aisle. In the lobby Dr. Su took his stand under a huge bell of red paper roses and prepared to receive the congratulations of his friends. He was now a rich man, thanks to his father-in-law. The dining-room doors were thrown open and the smell of fine feast foods streamed out upon the summer air.

James went forward to shake hands with Dr. Su. He had been moved against his will by the wedding and the music. So he supposed would it have been had Lili been ready to marry him. Half curiously he looked at the face of the bride. It was painted and powdered into an exquisite mask, as lifeless as the face of a movie star. He bowed and turned away.

"I say," Dr. Kang called at the door, "aren't you staying for the feast? Everything is first rate here."

"Thank you, I have duties at the hospital," James said, and he went out into the street. A cluster of ricksha men seized their vehicles at the sight of him and he climbed into the nearest one. The puller was a youngish man and since the night was hot he wore no jacket. His smooth brown back rippled with the undercurrent of muscles and he ran without effort. But he was too thin and the shape of his skeleton was clear, a fine firm structure, the bones strong and delicate. He wore his hair long enough to fall almost to his neck and it flowed behind him in the breeze. His profile when he turned it was clean and large.

"Where is your home?" James asked when the fellow slowed to a walk near the hospital.

"In a village a hundred *li* from here," the man replied.

"Why are you here?" James asked.

The man turned his head and smiled and showed white perfect teeth. "There are too many of us on the land," he said frankly. "My father owns very little and he rents as much as he can. But the landlord lives abroad and his old uncle does as he likes with the rents."

"What village is yours?" James asked with sudden curiosity.

"The village of Anming," the man said.

"Anming," James repeated. "That is my village, too."

The man laughed. "Then I will not ask you for wine

money," he declared. They were at the hospital gate now and he set down the poles of the ricksha.

"Because we come from the same village I must give you wine money," James declared in turn. He could not tell this fellow that the absent landlord was his own father!

The man made a feint of politeness but his eyes glistened when James poured silver into his palm. "I wish our landlord were like you, elder brother," he said smiling, and with such thanks he took up his ricksha and darted away into the street and out of sight.

James went slowly up the stairs of the doctors' house and to his own two rooms. Something familiar struck his eyes. Upon the handle of the door hung an imitation panama hat. Young Wang's, without a doubt! The fellow had a weakness for hats. He went in and found Young Wang in his white cotton underwear, mopping the floors. He had taken off his outer clothes, and had laid his jacket across the bed.

Young Wang grinned at him from his knees and his white teeth flashed. "Master, this floor!" he exclaimed. "How many days since it was washed?"

"How do I know?" James replied, smiling back at him.

Young Wang got up, darted forward and took his hat. He held it in both hands and admired it. "What did you pay for this fine hat, master?"

"I bought it in America," James said.

"Everything is better there than here," Young Wang said, and he put the hat reverently into the closet. Then he wrung out the cloth, emptied the pail out the window and put it under the bed.

James sat down in the wicker easy chair. The room seemed pleasantly cool after the street. Young Wang had drawn the shutters and had laid out fresh towels. He pattered about the room now dusting everywhere with a damp cloth.

"Peking is a great city full of big dust," he said cheerfully.

James watched him without speaking. Within his mind, always preoccupied with his work and not given to much sorting of thought, he felt that he had come to a dividing place. He would have to become one person or another. Either he must join the league of his fellow doctors and live oblivious of his countrymen, or he must take some sort of plunge which he could not define. The surface life was safe enough and quite pleasant. He need not give up his professional standards. His colleagues were good and careful and sometimes superlative doctors. But except for Liu Chen they were not more than that. They worked the full day, they did their duty to the hospital. No one could complain that when Dr. Kang decided to take a case he was less than competent. Dr. Su, who was more human and therefore more likable, even went further sometimes than his duty. But it would have occurred to none of them, and perhaps not even to Liu Chen, to go beyond the demands of his profession.

"You are thinner," Young Wang said, staring at him as he whisked his cloth about the legs of the table. "You must think of your body." He reached the mirror and he paused to stare at himself with humorous eyes. He laughed and pointed a finger at his own image. "That big turnip there," he said. "Anybody can tell he comes from the country!"

"How did you find your village?" James asked.

Young Wang accepted the invitation to converse. He threw the duster over his shoulder and squatted on his heels.

"Sit on a chair," James said.

"I do not dare," Young Wang replied politely, and began at once smoothly and coolly to tell his tale. "When I returned to my village I found it was under water. The rains have been too heavy and the nearest dike of the river overflowed. I had first to hire a boat in the small city nearby and I went to my village. It was nearly gone. The houses had crumbled and only the treetops stood above the water except at one place where the land rises a few feet. Upon this small island my village crowded itself. We are all Wangs and of us there are a hundred and five hearts. Thanks to the gods, the waters had risen slowly and so our men had been able to move food and bedding and some small benches for the old to sit on. Also we have some bamboo mats which we have spread upon willow poles for shelter."

Young Wang laughed as though the predicament were amusing. Then he looked rueful and shook his head. "It is very hard on old people and small children," he sighed. "Several small ones have fallen into the water and have been swept away. Three old people have died and there has been no place to bury them and so we let them down into the water. This is very bad because now they cannot lie with our ancestors and so all the old people are afraid to die. This is bad, too, for death is natural to the old and they should find comfort in it."

James listened with growing horror. "Does no one come from the city to help you?" he demanded.

Young Wang raised his eyebrows at the question. "Who comes to help?" he asked. "People have enough trouble for themselves. Ours is not the only village. There are many like us."

"The mayor of the city should help," James declared. "Or the governor of the province should at least take notice."

"No one takes notice of the folk," Young Wang said. "Those governors and officials are high people and they have their own affairs."

He sighed loudly, rose from his heels, and whirled his duster over the mirror, glancing at himself with some admiration as he did so.

James watched this. How deep was Young Wang's grief for his family? He seemed callous and even gay, and yet surely he had feeling. "Did you leave your family on that island?" he asked.

"My parents I took to the city and also my brothers and sisters." Young Wang picked up a fountain pen from the table and pulled the top from it cautiously. "I found rooms in an inn for them. But it costs very much money and so I came back to work for you, master. Before this, wages were nothing to me, but now I ask that you give me three months' in advance, and then I will go back to them at the end of the month and pay for what I owe and if the waters have sunk down, I will help them to move again to the village."

"But you said there was no house," James reminded him.

"Oh, the house is never mind," Young Wang replied. "A few days' labor will put up a mud house again. I will carry some thatch from the city markets and we have willow trees for poles."

He tested the pen on a bit of paper. "This is one of those self-come ink pens," he said. "I wish very much someday to have one. But still why should I have it when I cannot write my own name?"

These last words Young Wang said with more sorrow than he had said anything and a flush of shame rose from his neck and spread over his face. He covered the pen again and laid it on the table. "Shall I bring you some night food?" he asked.

"No," James replied. "I must return to the hospital and see how my patients are before they sleep. I will eat later in the dining hall downstairs."

"They give you good food here?" Young Wang asked wistfully.

"Excellent.'"

"Do the servants eat what is left?"

"I will see that you get your food," James replied. He knew that doctors often had their private servants. They were fed, probably at the hospital kitchens.

Young Wang immediately looked cheerful. "With my belly certain of fullness three times each day, I fear no god or man," he declared.

"That is good," James replied. He went away to his patients and left Young Wang standing before the mirror, arranging the belt about his thin waist.

5

JAMES LIANG WAS NOT A MAN who put his thoughts easily into words. He had learned to distrust words as gestures and flourishes of the mind, more especially of his father's mind. As a child and a boy he had sat through long evenings in the big comfortable living room and had listened to his father and his friends, elegant and educated in the cultures of England and Europe. Whatever they discussed, and they discussed everything, was spun into a web of words which yet had no substance. By the end of an evening instead of conclusion and conviction the web had dissolved into a mist, and the mist itself dissolved in the silence of the room when they had gone. His father, so genial and brilliant with his guests, came back from the door silent and empty. If the boy James asked a question he was impatient. "It is time for sleep," he always said shortly.

In this distrust of words James had turned to his American schoolmates, who spun no webs either of thoughts or of words. A hard-hitting fist was more honored than a graceful phrase, and a fact was always more valuable than an idea. Action instead of feeling was what he had learned outside his home, and action he preferred when his father yielded often to the inexplicable melancholy of the exile. From this melancholy his father's only escape again was in words. A mood, caught from a gray sky over the river and a chill autumn wind, was translated into an essay of tragedy. James was grown before he understood that nothing his father wrote was from conviction. All was from feeling, transient enough. Therefore the young man had learned also to distrust feeling.

Thus, he had nothing with which to understand his own melancholy as the summer ripened in the ancient city. That he was not happy he knew. That he was lonely he knew very well. He tried to believe that this was because of Lili but his too honest heart told him that it was not. He came to putting it in words only in the few brief letters which he wrote to his sister Mary, among the dutiful ones he wrote his father and mother.

"I may as well tell you that there is too much here that is rotten," he wrote to Mary. "I suppose this is partly because we are an old people and much dead wood has not been cut away. There is decay here—I cannot find out just where, but I see it in Su and Kang and Peng and others. It is even in the nurses. But also it is in the cooks and the orderlies. Money sticks to every hand. Well, it sticks to many hands in America, too, but here there is no pretense about it. Maybe pretense is not good. Anyway, I somehow feel I have no home in the world."

In this letter he said nothing about Lili, and reading it in the solitude of her own room Mary rejoiced. Then she read the letter again slowly. It had come to her at a moment when she herself was restless. The summer in the Vermont mountains had filled her with health and energy which as yet had no purpose. She had no lover. She had rejected with some disgust a young Chinese journalist who had pursued her. To accept an American would have been to violate the profound love of her country which was the true passion of her heart. She had quarreled all summer with Louise when she found that this younger sister moped when the mail was delayed. It had not taken too long to discover that Louise read a letter from Estelle almost as eagerly as she read the less frequent ones from Philip.

Mary had taken Louise for a walk when she discovered this, and upon a path fragrant with pine trees in the sun she had faced her sister. "Louise, don't be a fool." Thus their talk had begun.

Louise had blushed. Both girls stood still, and by chance it was Louise who stood in the sunshine. Mary looked at her intently and severely. "So you blush!" she cried.

Louise tossed her curled hair. "No, I don't blush."

"Your face is red," Mary said. "I can see something in your eyes. Do you think Philip will marry a Chinese girl? You are silly, Louise. His father and mother will not allow it."

"Who talked about marriage?" Louise asked. She began to walk on quickly. Mary had waited a moment, watching the slender figure of her sister in its pale yellow dress. Then she had followed with impetuous steps.

"I hope you are not thinking of anything else, Louise," she said. She seized her sister's hand. "Louise, do not forget—we are not American. Although we have never seen our own country, yet we are Chinese. We cannot behave like American girls."

Louise pulled her hand away. "Let me alone," she cried, and suddenly she began to run down the path and Mary had not pursued her. She sat down on a log and sitting alone she had tried to think what she should do, whether she should tell her parents, whether even she should write to James.

In the end after the family had come back to the city she had talked to Peter, but he had been scornful. "It doesn't matter what Louise does," he had said in his young and lordly fashion. "I tell you Louise is already spoiled."

Mary's heart had stopped. "Peter, what do you mean?" she had demanded.

Peter had laughed at her look. "Perhaps they have not slept together, if that is what scares you. Mary, you are very old-fashioned. No, but if Philip wanted Louise she would go to him."

"Doesn't Philip want her?"

Peter shook his head.

"You mean you have talked with him about Louise?" Mary cried.

Peter looked unwilling. Mary and he breakfasted early and usually alone, and they were talking in the dining room before their parents had come down. "I saw him kiss her one day," he said at last.

"No!" Mary whispered. "Did Louise let him?"

Peter grinned. "She helped."

Mary was silent for a moment. As plainly as though she had been in Peter's place she saw the tall young American with Louise in his arms. "I shall tell Pa," she said.

Peter shrugged his shoulders. "You have always had too much courage," he said. He had risen from the table at that, and had gone away to his own affairs. He had only two weeks left him before college and nothing else was important to him.

When Dr. Liang came down ten minutes later he found his elder daughter looking very pretty but preoccupied. He wondered if she were thinking about some young man. Her mar-

riage was the subject of frequent conversation between him
and Mrs. Liang and he intended as soon as he saw a suitable
young man to make the proper preliminary approaches. Now,
observing his daughter's pretty face and figure, it occurred to
him that he ought not to delay too long.

"Good morning, Pa," Mary said.

"Good morning," he replied. He sat down and sipped the
glass of orange juice at his plate.

"Pa!" Mary said suddenly.

He liked to be calm in the mornings and he heard with
some distaste the hint of determination in her voice.

"Yes?" he replied mildly. They spoke in English.

"Pa, I don't want to tell you this at breakfast because I
know you like quiet, but I must tell you before Ma comes
down. Louise is in love with Philip."

Dr. Liang looked surprised. Nellie came in and set his oatmeal before him and he spread sugar on it in a thin even coat.
When she had gone out he asked, "Who is Philip?"

"You know, Pa—he is Estelle's brother—Estelle Morgan."

Dr. Liang looked shocked. "An American!"

"Yes, Pa. Don't pretend you don't know, please, Pa! She
has let him kiss her."

Dr. Liang suddenly had no appetite. He pushed the dish of
oatmeal away. "Mary, do you know of what you accuse your
sister?"

"That's why I thought you ought to know. Shall we tell
Ma?"

"Tell me what?" Mrs. Liang demanded briskly. She came
into the room at this moment, her full eyelids still a little
swollen with sleep. "Eh, Liang—what is the matter? Is the
oatmeal burned again?"

"No—it is something even worse," he said angrily.

Mary looked at one parent and then the other. The matter
was now in her father's hands.

"Who has done something?" Mrs. Liang demanded. She sat
down, yawned, and poured herself some tea from the pot on
the table.

"Your youngest daughter," he said severely.

"Louise is also your daughter," Mrs. Liang put in.

"She has allowed an American man to become—familiar."

"Oh, Pa, I didn't say that," Mary cried.

"It is the same thing," he said in a lofty voice. He looked at his wife. "I always said that you allowed that girl too much of her own way," he said solemnly. "She comes and goes as if she were not Chinese. She has no breeding. She is not respectful. Now she insults even our ancestors."

"Oh, Pa," Mary said softly. Whenever her father became very Chinese she knew he was really angry.

"Do not interrupt me," he replied. "And leave the room, if you please. This is for your mother and me to discuss alone."

He waited until Mary had closed the door and then he began to speak in Chinese. His voice, usually mellifluous and deep, was now high and harsh. He pointed his long forefinger at his wife. "You," he said, "you! I told you, when we first came here, to watch the girls."

Mrs. Liang turned pale and began to cry. "How can I watch them?" she asked.

"You have not taught them respect," he retorted. "They do not obey you. You should tell them what they must do and what they must not do. I have said to you many times we are Chinese. Therefore we must behave as Chinese. What is not suitable for us in China is not suitable here."

Mrs. Liang continued to sob but not too loudly lest Nellie the maid hear her. She did not know that Nellie had already heard her and was now standing at the door with her ear against it. When she heard nothing but Chinese she looked peevish and when she heard Mrs. Liang's sobs her lips framed the words, "Poor thing!" Then after a moment, still hearing nothing but Chinese, she went back to her dishes again.

"You have no proper feeling for me as your husband," Dr. Liang went on severely. "What will people say when they hear that our daughters behave like wantons? They will say that our Confucian ways cannot withstand the ways of barbarians."

As long as he spoke of Louise Mrs. Liang had only continued to sob but now when he blamed her she wiped her eyes and puckered her lips. "Why then did you come to America, Liang?" she demanded. "At home it was easy to watch the girls. I could have hired amahs to go with them everywhere. How can I go about with them here? Am I an amah? And if I hired two white amahs could they be trusted?"

Dr. Liang pushed back his chair. Their quarrels proceeded always in the same way. He attacked his wife with scolding words until she reached the point of real anger and then he grew majestic and uttered a final sentence. This he did now. "When Louise comes downstairs, send her to my study," he commanded.

He refused to finish his meal and he walked with dignity out of the room and across the hall to his study and closed the door. Once alone he allowed himself to be as disturbed as he felt. He sat down in his easy chair and cracked his finger joints one after the other and stared at a rubbing of Confucius that hung on the wall. This rubbing he had not valued for a number of years because he had bought it for a dollar in an old shop in Nanking. Since it was paper and could be folded up small he had brought it with other trifles to America to use sometime as a gift. But only a few years ago he had seen one exactly like it in an exhibition and it had been reprinted in a great popular magazine. Then he found his own copy and had it framed in imitation bamboo. When visitors came into his study he pointed to it gracefully. "There is my inspiration," he said.

Now he looked at Confucius with some irritation. This morning the rubbing merely seemed to be that of a foolishly complacent old man swaddled in too many robes. He turned away from it, closed his eyes, and let his anger against Louise swell to a point where it would be properly explosive. There he maintained it by force of will while he read again his morning portion of the Analects.

Meanwhile Louise had tripped downstairs barefoot, still wearing her nightgown over which she had thrown a pink satin bed jacket. She peeped into the dining room and saw her mother sitting alone at the table. So she came in.

"Oh, Ma," she said. "I was afraid Pa was here. I am so hungry but I didn't want to get up. I thought maybe Nellie would bring me up a tray."

"Your pa wants to see you," her mother said coldly.

Louise took a bit of toast and nibbled it. "Why, what have I done?" she asked pertly.

Mrs. Liang frowned and pursed her lips. "*Pei!*" she exploded softly. "Think what it is you have done that you do not want him to know!"

Louise looked alarmed. "Who told him?" she demanded.

"Never mind."

"It was Mary!" Louise exclaimed.

"Never mind!"

"Oh, Ma!" Louise wailed.

In his study Dr. Liang heard the duet and he rose and opened the door suddenly. Both women looked at him, but he stared only at his daughter. "Go upstairs and put on your clothes. Then come to my study," he commanded.

"Isn't she to eat something first?" Mrs. Liang demanded. The presence of one of the children always gave her courage.

"No," Dr. Liang said and shut the door.

Mother and daughter looked at one another. Then Mrs. Liang spoke. "Go upstairs," she said softly. "I will fetch you a tray and you can eat while you dress."

"Scrambled eggs, please," Louise whispered.

Dr. Liang, listening, heard only the hurrying footsteps of his daughter on the stairs. He leaned back, mollified. He was still obeyed.

Upstairs Louise did not go to her own room. Instead she opened the door of Mary's room. Mary was at her desk, writing to James, and she saw her younger sister standing with her back to the door, the wide satin skirt of her nightgown whirled around her, and her pretty face pink with anger.

"Mary, what did you say to Pa?" Louise demanded in a loud whisper.

"Peter told me you let Philip kiss you," Mary said gravely.

"Did you have to tell Pa?" Louise demanded.

"Yes."

Louise stared at her sister. Something adamant in that soft little face confounded her and she suddenly began to cry. "I hate you!" she sobbed, still whispering, and she opened the door and whirled out.

Mary sat for a long moment, then took up her pen again and wrote, "I think the only thing that can keep Louise from being a fool is for me to bring her to China. If the ocean is between her and Philip perhaps we can guard her."

When she had finished her letter she sat quite thoughtfully for a long time. Then she got up and began to tidy the small drawers at the top of her bureau.

In something over half an hour she paused in this task, and opening the door of her room she heard the unmistakable sounds of a stick beating upon something soft. Then she heard screams—Louise's voice—and almost at once her mother's loud shouts. She ran downstairs swiftly and opened the door of her father's study. He had his malacca cane in one hand,

and with the other he held Louise by the hair. He had bent
her back, but he held her head firmly while with his right
hand he lifted the cane and struck it upon her shoulders. Mrs.
Liang was vainly trying to put herself between the cane and
the girl.

"My father?" Mary said distinctly.

Dr. Liang's face was twisted and purple. But at the sight of
his elder daughter he looked dazed and threw down the cane
and pushed Louise away from him.

"Take her out of my sight," he gasped. "I never want to see
her again."

Louise lay on the floor where she fell, sobbing aloud, and
Mrs. Liang sat down in a chair. Sweat was pouring down her
cheeks and she lifted the edge of her coat to wipe it away.

"Father," Mary said again. The intense quiet of her voice
seemed to bring silence and order into the room. "What you
have done is not right."

Dr. Liang had thrown himself into his leather armchair. His
hands trembled and his face was ashen. "She is no longer my
daughter," he said. He looked with contempt upon Louise
where she still lay weeping, her face buried in her arms.

"The American girls kiss boys and think nothing of it,"
Mary pleaded. "Remember that she has been here all her life.
You brought us here, Pa. We can't remember any other
country."

"It is not only the kiss," Mrs. Liang said heavily. "There is
more than the kiss." She spoke in Chinese but "kiss" she said
in English.

"What has she done?" Mary asked. Her heart began to beat
hard. Had Peter lied to her? Did he know?

"Don't repeat it!" Dr. Liang shouted.

Mrs. Liang groaned aloud. "Eh-yah! I could not—"

Louise suddenly stopped weeping. She was listening. But
she did not move and she lay, a figure of young sorrow, upon
the floor.

Dr. Liang's face began to work in strange grimaces. "Everything for which I have striven is now destroyed," he said in a
strangled voice. "I am about to be disgraced by my own
daughter. My enemies will laugh at me. My students will de-
ride the teachings of Confucius because my own daughter has
derided them."

Mary was sorry for them all. She stood with pity warm in

her dark eyes. She understood her father's pride and her mother's bewilderment. And she understood very well Louise, who in eagerness to make herself beloved had confounded herself more than any.

"Pa," Mary said gently. "I have thought of something. Let me take her back to China."

"Two girls!" Mrs. Liang exclaimed.

Mary still spoke to her father. "Pa, James is your oldest son. Let him help you. I was about to ask you anyway if you would let me go and keep his house for him until he marries. Let me go and let me take Louise with me."

Louise turned her face. "I don't want to go!" she muttered.

"Be silent!" Dr. Liang cried. All his rage choked him again. "You! Do you dare to speak?"

"I won't go—I won't go!" Louise wailed.

Dr. Liang's jaw tightened and two small muscles stood out on his cheeks. Had he not loved his younger daughter with so much pride he would not have been so bitterly angry now. He wanted to beat her again, but he dared not before Mary. Yet the wound of his proud heart was too severe. He could not restrain himself and he cried out, "If you do not want to go, then I say you shall go! We will have no peace until you are gone!"

"Liang!" his wife cried. "You cannot send two girls alone across the ocean! How will it be when they get to Shanghai? Since the war everything is bad there."

"Peter shall go with them," Dr. Liang cried. "Let them all go!" He slapped his outspread hands upon the desk, and then to the horror of his family he began to weep silently, without covering his face. They could not bear it. Mary stooped to her sister. "Come—get up," she said. "We must leave Pa alone."

Louise, seeing her father's face, obeyed and the two girls went out. When the door closed behind them Mrs. Liang rose and went to her husband. She stood behind him where she could not see his face and she put out her two hands and with the tips of her fingers she began to rub his temples rhythmically. He sighed and leaned his head back against her breast.

After a while she spoke. "You must not blame them too much," she said. "They are like plants growing in a foreign soil. If they bear strange flowers, it is the soil that is evil."

"You know that I cannot—go back," he said listlessly.

"I know that," she said patiently.

"I cannot do my work there," he went on. "What place is there for a scholar—for any civilized being—in the midst of chaos and war?"

"None," she agreed. This they had talked about often.

"While chaos has raged in my own country, I have kept its spirit alive here in a foreign land," he said in a heartbroken voice.

"Everyone knows you are a great man," she said sadly.

He pulled away from her suddenly. "I suppose you wish you could go with the children," he said. "You will be lonely here only with me."

She stood motionless while she spoke, her hands at her bosom. "Liang—would you not go just for a little while?"

He pushed aside the sheaf of manuscript on his desk. "How can I? I have classes about to begin. Besides—how can I earn my living in China—unless I become an official?"

"You could become an official," she said.

"No, I cannot," he said loudly. "I can do a great many things for the sake of peace and our ancient civilization—but I cannot do that."

She waited another long moment. She turned her head and looked out the window at all the things she hated. She hated living high in the air like this, as though they were birds nesting in a cliff. As a girl she had lived in houses low and close to the earth, where she could step through the open door and feel earth under her feet. She hated high buildings and tall chimneys and bustling streets. But her love for him was still greater than her hatred of these things, although she did not understand him even in the least part of his being. She had come from a simple, goodhearted merchant family in a small town. His family had been gentry for ten generations. She had been chosen for him because her health and vigor, his mother had said, would strengthen his overdelicate youth and renew the family's vitality. She had loved him from their wedding night.

"If you cannot go, I will stay with you," she said, "and I will not be lonely."

Upstairs in her room Mary faced Louise. She tried not to be excitable or angry, but she found it difficult to be calm. Her father's Confucian teaching of calm under all circumstances had become her conscience. Now, feeling her cheeks hot and her eyes burning, she nevertheless tried to keep her voice gentle.

"Louise, what have you done?" she demanded.

Louise sat down on the edge of the bed. She twisted a curl of her hair around her forefinger and pouted her red lips. She feared Mary more than any member of the family, not because this elder sister was harsh, but because she had an honesty which was not to be corrupted. Did Mary believe that something should be told she would tell it, at whatever cost to anyone, and Louise was not prepared to put herself into such danger.

"You had better tell me so that I can help you," Mary said.

"I don't want your help," Louise pouted.

"Nevertheless I must help you," Mary said in the same steadfast voice. "What did you tell Pa that made him so angry?"

Tears came into Louise's eyes. Her courage was not deeply rooted and now it began to fade. What had seemed only a sweet exciting secret when she was with Estelle had become a frightful thing when she was besieged by her family. Chastity for a woman, seemingly so lightly considered by her schoolmates, returned to what she had been taught by her Chinese family—the test of all that woman was.

"What did you tell Pa?" Mary insisted. Her voice, in spite of herself, became stern.

"I told him—I told him—" Thus truth began to trickle from her with her tears.

"Go on," Mary commanded.

"When he said—when he said—he would never consent to—to an American son-in-law—" she began now to cry in good earnest.

"You said—" Mary prompted her relentlessly.

"I said it was too late!" The words came out of Louise in one burst.

"You haven't married Philip secretly!" Mary cried.

Louise shook her head, and then she said in a very small voice, "No. But I can never marry anybody else—because—because—"

She could not finish but now Mary knew. She sat quite still, gazing at Louise, who turned and flung herself face down on the bed and sobbed aloud. There had been many times when

Louise had lain there sobbing for some small trouble and always Mary had gone to her to soothe and comfort her, as the elder sister. But now she did not move. She felt sick and she did not want to touch Louise. It had never occurred to her to imagine that Louise would have let Philip—she could not put the thought into words, even in her own mind. That Louise could be silly, could allow Philip perhaps to kiss her and fondle her, that she could dream of his marriage to her, all was believable. But not this—

She rose, not able to endure her own sickness, and she went to the closet and took out a dress for the street. Without speaking, while Louise sobbed on, Mary changed into this blue dress and brushed her hair and touched her lips with red. It was not often she painted her lips, but now they felt pale and dry. Her face in the mirror was pale and her eyes looked strange. Louise looked sidewise at her in the midst of her weeping. "Where are you going?" she asked.

"Outdoors," Mary said. "I want to be alone."

Louise broke into a fresh wail. "Aren't you going to help me?"

Mary's hand was on the door, but she paused. "Yes, I will help you, but just now I don't know how. I shall have to think."

She went out and closed the door softly, and softly she crept down the stairs. In her father's study she heard her parents' voices murmuring and she tiptoed past the door and out into the hall. The elevator man was talkative and she could scarcely force herself to answer his questions. "Yes, thank you," she said, "my brother in China is quite well. Yes, he likes it there. Of course, after all it is our home. Yes, some day doubtless we will all return to China. Yes, of course we do like it here—but it is not our country."

She was out in the street at last. It was hot and dusty with the late summer lingering into autumn and people looked tired. She walked slowly toward the river, biting her lips and trembling as she went. She longed exceedingly for James. Yet how could this ever be put into a letter? And what could she do indeed? Her parents, she knew, were worse than useless. They would be utterly bewildered. In old China Louise would have been put to death. But old China was gone. Young Chinese women since the war—well, there had been plenty of American GI babies with Chinese mothers. That would be no argument with her parents. In a strange mixed fashion, for all her father's modernity, he still belonged to the old China because for him China was something Confucius had made, and Confucius would have said that certainly Louise ought to die, because she had dishonored the family. Her father would not say Louise had to die, but he would make up his mind never to forgive her.

Mary sat down on a bench by the river and lifted her eyes toward the bridge. It shimmered a beaten silver, and in the haze of noonday the arch lifted high above reality and the distant end was miragelike. James seemed lost to her, as though he were in another world. China was another world, a better one than this, she ardently believed. She felt profoundly lonely without her brother, the only person in the family with whom she could communicate. She had never, as Louise had, thrown herself into her school life. Around her was always the cloak of indifference, of being Chinese, and on guard alike against hostility or too lavish adoration, she had maintained herself separate. Only James had crossed that barrier and with him alone had she found friendship and companionship. Since he had gone, she had scarcely spoken to anyone beyond the casual talk of small necessities.

Now her pent-up heart demanded frankness, and as she sat there, a small solitary figure, resolutely ignoring the tentative eyes of curious men as they strolled past and yet feeling them with a sort of subdued anger, residual from her disgust with Louise, she began to think of Philip. There was Philip. He, too, had been responsible, and he ought to know what he had done to their family. A Chinese girl was part of her family until she married and became part of another family, and nothing could separate her. What had happened to her brought its weight upon them all. She ought to go and talk to Philip. If James were here he would talk to him, without doubt or hesitation, but James was not here, and Peter was too young, and so she must do it, for obviously her father could not. Her father could be angry and he could even beat Louise but he would not lower himself to talk to Philip. He would say and perhaps rightly that Louise was to blame because the woman is always to blame.

She sighed and then got up and crossed the street to a drugstore. There at the pay telephone she called Estelle Morgan. A maid answered. Miss Estelle was not back yet from the seashore. Was Philip there? Mr. Philip was just leaving for an appointment at his father's office. Could she speak to him, then? It was urgent. A moment later Philip's fresh tenor voice came over the wires.

"Hello?"

She knew him a little, not much. She had seen him two or three times when he came for Louise, but usually Louise met him outside. She remembered him as tall, and somewhat too slender for his height, and she remembered that his face looked too young and perhaps too fine-featured for a man.

"Philip Morgan?"

"Yes."

"This is Mary Liang. Could you—may I—talk with you for a few minutes? Not over the telephone, I mean. It's—it's quite important."

A second pause, then two and three before he answered. "Yes, of course, Mary. Only it just happens that I have to meet my father. He's waiting at the office for me."

"If I got into a taxi, could you wait for me and we could drive downtown together?"

There was a second's pause again, then two, then three.

"All right, Mary."

He hung up the receiver and she flew to the door and caught a passing taxi and gave the address while she slammed the door.

In ten minutes she drew up before the quiet house in Sutton Place, and then she saw Philip come out of the door. He smiled in answer to the doorman's greeting, and she caught a fleet look of surprise on that doorman's face when he opened the taxi and saw her there.

"Hello, Mary," Philip said. He sat down beside her.

"Hello," she replied, and felt his wary diffident mood.

"Stays hot, doesn't it?" he asked, trying to be casual.

"Yes," she replied. Then she took her heart in her hands. She had only a few minutes. But she needed only a few minutes to find out all she needed to know.

"Philip," she began impetuously, "I have to hurry because I know you haven't much time. But I must tell you that my father has found out about you and Louise. He is very angry. He has told her that she must go to China right away. She doesn't want to go. I think you know why. But I want to know how you feel. I mean—what I want to say is—if you are in love with Louise—"

Her face burned scarlet and she turned her head away. The taxi was racing downtown. She wished it would go more slowly. There had to be time. A light changed to red and the taxi stopped. She forced herself to look at Philip. His pale face had turned even more pale.

"I'm not in love—with anybody," he said.

"Then why did you—" she began, and could not go on.

His eyes were downcast and he had dropped his head so that she could not look at him. His profile was gentle and his lips were trembling. She could see how Louise had come to love him. He was not coarse and big-nosed as so many Americans were, and his skin was smooth and delicate, his hair and eyes were brown. She felt rather sorry for him.

"I don't know how it happened," he stammered. "Gosh, I like Louise awfully. We were all having too good a time, I guess. It was pretty late. I'm afraid I was a little tight—"

"When was it?" she asked in a faint voice.

"Only a couple of weeks ago—" he muttered. "We were all at a roadhouse. I'm awfully sorry. I could kick myself. The funny thing is—I guess it was the first time for both of us. We were both—scared."

The light changed and the taxi jerked them forward. He caught her arm and she shrank from his touch. She would have got out before the light changed, because now she knew everything she had to know. No, there was one more thing.

"I suppose your family wouldn't want you to marry—a Chinese girl, even if you did want to?"

"My mother wouldn't like it," Philip said huskily. "My dad is more—broadminded. Of course we all like Louise awfully. She's pretty and smart and all that."

There was no sign whatever of love in his voice or his eyes. She stopped feeling sorry for him and she grew angry enough to want to defend her sister. "I suppose you don't know what you have done to our family," she said bitterly. "It is easy for you Americans, but for us—it just spoils her chances of a good marriage—I mean, it would have to be told. And it would always be between her and her husband."

"Gosh," he said miserably, "I'm sorry."

She wanted to wound him and she did not know how. "If

it had been in the old times in China you'd both be killed," she went on.

"Gosh," he said again. "I guess we ought to be glad it's not old times."

To her surprise when he said this she wanted to cry. Her throat grew tight and her eyes filled with tears. He did not know what he had done and nothing could make him know because he had nothing with which to understand what he had done. It had simply been, with him, an evening's drunkenness, then something more of fun, and now something he was vaguely sorry for. In her fury she imagined that he would have taken it more seriously had Louise not been Chinese, though it was a hundred times more serious for that very reason. But he would not understand that either—or care.

She leaned forward and tapped on the glass. "Let me out," she called to the driver. "I want to get out right here." The taxi drew up to the curb and she got out without saying goodby and slammed the door. She saw Philip's face, startled and concerned, looking at her through the glass as the cab darted away.

6

ON A WARM SEPTEMBER AFTERNOON James was washing his hands after a leg amputation. His patient was a man, young and strong, and he would live easily. James was not concerned about his recovery. He was deeply concerned, however, over the growing number of such wounds, all gun-inflicted and all reaching him too late to save legs and arms. Seven men had died because the wounds were in the body trunk. Last night when he had gone to see his patient he had asked him bluntly where he got so deep a wound in his lower thigh.

The man was the son of a farmer to the north of the city and he spoke with a burr at the end of every noun. "Bandits keep pressing us," he said and turned away his head.

"Bandits?" James asked.

"Bandits is what we used to call them and it is what we still call them," the man said. His eyes were bitter.

"Where are they?" James asked.

"In our own village," the man said bitterly. "They do not come from outside any more. They are among our own. Look you, please! I am surnamed Hwang. My whole village is Hwang. But this man who put his bullet into me is also surnamed Hwang."

James interrupted. "You mean he is a Com—"

"Hush!" the man said. "Do not say the word. Call them bandits. Eh, they are everywhere! The hungry, the ones who will not work, the ones who hate their work, the tenants on the farm—they turn into—bandits." He sighed. "The times are evil. Such a good gun he had! I have a cheap thing made by the Japs. I took it away from a Jap. But I am only Hwang the Honest. That's what I am called. The bandit Hwang has a fine American gun. I saw it in his house one day. When I saw it, I knew he was a—bandit. I needed not to look into his eyes."

"Where did he get such a gun?" James had asked. Yes, the wound had been very deep.

"These guns come from America," the man had said. "They give them to our soldiers and then—the bandits get them."

"How?" James had asked sternly.

"There are many ways," the man had said listlessly.

James knew he must ask no more questions, and he went away. How many things he did not understand! Now the operation was safely over and the man would get well, and perhaps then he would talk. Actually the man had talked a good deal while he was under ether. The nurse Rose had been his assistant today and he had caught her nervous glance, when the man began to mutter.

"Bandits—bandits—my brother—"

"A little more ether," James said to the anesthetist.

"His heart is already weak," Rose reminded them. She held the man's wrist between her thumb and finger.

So they let him mutter, "Starve—my brother—no—no—Communists—"

No one paid heed to this last word which had burst from the man's mouth like a bullet from a gun.

Remembering it James wondered if he himself were naïve. He was aware, only half-consciously, of some profound though secret struggle going on among the people. Yet, since no one spoke of it he did not think of it. The day's work absorbed him, and he disliked political quarrels. The true scientist, he believed, would have nothing to do with politics. He must keep himself whole. Yet perhaps he had accepted too easily his father's belief in government, whatever it was.

"Heaven chooses a ruler," his father had been wont to declare. "Only when that ruler forsakes wisdom does Heaven put him aside." From these high-sounding words Dr. Liang Wen Hua was apt to descend to this remark, to his children. "Whatever we have in the way of a government it is better than Communism. Do you think you could enjoy our personal luxuries under those Red devils?"

At this moment, while James was so thinking, the door opened and a hand thrust itself in, holding an envelope. James recognized the hand. It was that of Young Wang who, always terrified of seeing cutting and bleeding, would on no account put his head into a room where by any chance an operation might be going on. James went to the door and took the envelope.

"An electric letter—from your father," Young Wang's voice said huskily through the door.

James had long since stopped wondering how Young Wang knew everything before he did. The envelope was sealed. Besides, Young Wang could not read nor write. Perhaps the clerk had told the messenger who brought the cablegram. James opened the message. It was indeed from his father. Even in a cablegram his father could not resist the careful phrase. "The other children joining you in our homeland. Sailing today. Explanation to follow by airmail." He looked at the date. They had sailed yesterday.

The other children, Mary, Peter, Louise! He was shocked by the imminence. What had happened? Mary he would have welcomed—but all three of them, so young, so unprepared! He was profoundly distressed. What would he do with them? He was only himself beginning to be reconciled, or rather resigned to not being reconciled, to what life was here. Peter! What could he do with Peter, who was more American than any American? It was too late to cable back in protest. That was like his father, too, to inform only after he had acted.

"Bad news?" Dr. Liu Chen asked. He had come in also to wash, having today taken the place of an anesthetist who had died a week ago of cholera. There was just enough cholera in the city to worry the doctors but nothing like an epidemic. Still, it was more than the city had suffered in many years. The war had left dregs everywhere and old diseases had been stirred up again. People were afraid of plague once more in the north.

"Not exactly," James said. Had it been one of the other doctors he would not have gone on, but Liu was comfortable and kind. Above all, he was modest. He had been educated at a small college in the United States and afterward he had taken his internship at a settlement hospital which no one knew when he mentioned it. He was modest but he was not humble. He carried himself with pleasant composure and when he went to a party that any of the doctors gave, he was friendly and never pretended to anything. He himself gave no parties. Several times he had invited James to dine with him, and they went always to a restaurant and never to a hotel.

"I have strange news from my father," James went on. "He tells me he is sending my two sisters and my brother to me, and I cannot imagine why, since they are all in school."

Dr. Liu, very clean and smelling of soap, was now carefully sharpening a small scalpel on a fine oiled stone. "Perhaps he wishes them to learn something of their own civilization," he suggested. He spoke, as always, in Chinese. His English was not very good, for he came from a part of the country where the people confused two or three consonants and he found that by doing so in English he often said what he did not mean.

"Perhaps," James said. Being much troubled he went on again, as he stood watching the hairline edge on the scalpel. "The question is where shall I put them. I shall have to find a house somewhere."

"That is not too difficult, provided you do not want what is called a modern house," Dr. Liu said. He placed the scalpel carefully into the sterilizer and turned on the electricity. This made him think of something. "I have invented a sterilizer to be used with charcoal," he said. His square ugly face lit with enthusiasm as he spoke.

Long ago Liu Chen had given up improving his looks. He was above middle height, his frame was strong, for he came of peasant stock, and his cheekbones were high and his eyes small. He would still have been a peasant had it not been for a missionary who had taught him to read and then had helped him go to school. Liu Chen had a good mind which held tenaciously everything he poured into it, but nothing was learned easily. He took great care to learn exactly, therefore, for he knew that whatever his mind had seized could never be changed. He was somewhat too slow to be a first-rate surgeon, but he made up for this by taking a deep personal interest in his patients. Rose or Marie often met him in the night, especially just before dawn in those hours when the sick die easily. He would be prowling through the wide corridors on his way to a room or a ward, to see for himself how his patients did. He looked apologetic when he met a nurse, for his presence seemed to accuse them. Indeed, Marie, who was mischievous, had once teased him.

"You think no one knows anything except yourself," she said, scolding him.

Liu Chen had smiled bashfully. "It is not that."

"Then what is it?" she had demanded, standing before him with her hands on her hips.

"I am only afraid I did something wrong," he answered. "Something you would not know about."

Standing beside his patient he did not speak. He watched intently, listening to the breathing and touching the skin to see if it were dry or moist, and then with the lightest pressure he would feel the pulse and catch the heartbeat. If all were well, he would steal away. But sometimes he would shout for the nurse and call for oxygen and stimulants to pull back a still living creature from death. The patient did not know what had happened, but he would open his weary dull eyes and see the doctor standing there, gaunt and silent, and he would feel safe. Then he would himself take the turn for life. This was especially true with children, for Dr. Liu loved all children. Whether he had any of his own no one knew, for he never spoke of his family. No one even knew where he lived. James perceived only that this strange uncouth man was different from the other doctors. In some ways he was less skilled, and yet he had a living spirit in him which he was able to impart to the sick and which was better than cold skill.

"I would like to see your sterilizer," James said now.

Liu Chen turned away and pretended to adjust something on the handle of the door of the instrument case. "Some day," he said. "Meanwhile, can I help you to find a house? I know one in the hutung two streets to the north of here. It is large, but it is cheap because it is haunted."

"Haunted?"

"Yes—by weasels," Liu Chen replied. He had adjusted the handle and he closed the door firmly. He answered James's smile with his own. "You, of course, will not mind weasels. But they are akin to foxes among our people, and while I also do not fear them, I remember that my old grandmother in our village would have burned a house down rather than live in it, were it haunted by weasels." His face took on a curious apologetic look that was yet very much in earnest. "You know, I would not say this before our friends, the other doctors, but I sometimes wonder if there is not more to these old beliefs of the folk than we think? Certainly there is something mischievous about weasels. They steal into a house by the hundreds once people grow afraid of them."

James laughed. "I will go with you to see the house this evening," he promised.

So it was arranged and he could only spend the rest of the day at his usual work, wondering and waiting for the letter which his father had promised, and which since it came by air would reach him before he had to go to Shanghai to meet his sisters and brother. The cable had put out of his mind the talk with the wounded man, and in the afternoon after his hours were over he met Liu Chen at the stone lions that guarded the hospital gate and they walked briskly along the street, unheeding of the cries of ricksha pullers beseeching them to ride. One such fellow persisted in running after them. He was a tall lean hound of a man, and he fell into cursing when neither James nor Liu Chen turned to hire him. "You!" he shouted after them. "You ought not to use your legs and rob us of our wages! Such as you make Communists of us!"

The two men did not turn but they heard this and James remembered then the man whose leg he had taken off in the morning. "Do you know anything about the Communists?" he asked Liu Chen.

"No," Liu Chen said shortly. "Nobody knows anything about them." He quickened his pace and turned a corner and they walked down a quiet lane between high brick walls. "This is the hutung," he said. "The gate is yonder."

They went fifty feet farther and reached a plain wooden gate made double and hanging upon heavy iron hinges. It stood ajar and Liu Chen pushed it open. They stepped over a high lintel and into a deserted court where the weeds grew high between the stones. Once inside Liu Chen closed the door safely. Then he pulled his handkerchief from his pocket and wiped his face and his bare head. "Eh!" he said in a low voice. "You must not ask a man in broad daylight what he knows about the Communists. It made my sweat pour out."

"You mean—" James said.

"I do mean that, indeed," Liu Chen said quickly. "Come, let us see the house. It is too big for you, but you can shut away some of the courts. Or I might rent a little one for myself."

"That would be pleasant," James said.

Liu Chen laughed loudly. "If your sisters are pretty!"

James did not laugh and neither did he answer. For the first time it seemed to him that Liu Chen was coarse, because of his peasant origin. Almost at once Liu Chen saw that he had offended. "No—no," he said quickly. "I was only joking."

"Have you wife and children?" James asked.

Liu Chen shook his head somewhat moodily. "No, I have no wife. Look at me, and you see a man spoiled. I cannot take a peasant woman because I am too good for her. But I am too much peasant for any of these new women, do you see? Even though I have been to America, in their dainty noses I still smell of the ox. What would they do in my father's house? My mother cannot read a word and she is like any country woman. Well, I do not go home much because they grieve that they have no grandson. I am caught between old and new—I have no home and perhaps I am to have none."

"I cannot believe that," James said. "It seems to me that you are the best of both kinds of people."

This praise moved Liu Chen. His square face grew red and his eyes glistened. "You are too kind," he said and he coughed as though he were choking. "Come," he said. "We must see the house."

This house had been a very handsome one when it was built and the strong old brick walls and the stout beams held. But the paint was peeling from the wood and the lime had blistered. The stone floors were covered with a coat of sand blown there by many windstorms. There were none of the things to which Mary and Louise and Peter were accustomed, or to which James himself was used—no bathroom, no heating of any kind, no electricity, no running water. There was a well; there were four large courts which held some good trees and a terrace with ancient peonies still living; there were twelve large rooms, three to each court and connected with outdoor passageways whose balustrades were finely carved. In the windows there were delicate lattices and behind the lattices the paper had been replaced with glass most of which was still not broken. Everywhere were the footsteps of weasels in the sand and the long trailing marks of their brushes. In the dust upon the lintels were their marks and there were bones of mice and chickens and birds which they had eaten and bits of fur and skin and feathers.

James stared about him and Liu Chen watched him. "It looks too bad, does it not?" Liu said. "Still, a few servants hired to clean, and you will see a different house. You can buy a foreign stove at the thieves' market and a carpenter will make some beds and tables and the tailor some bedding. A charcoal stove and a cook—and he will buy some earthenware pots—you will see how easily it can all be done, and how cheaply. But perhaps you have plenty of money."

"I have not," James said quickly. His father must send him money, and yet how well he knew his father would often forget! Peter must go to college and so must Louise. Mary could teach somewhere. Between them they could pay the daily bills, and what their father sent could be used to make their life better. "I will take the house," he told Liu Chen, "and mind you, if you want a room, you shall have it. I can see you would be very useful to us. After all, we are too much like foreigners here in our own country. Our father let us grow up in America."

Liu Chen turned red again. His skin was thin and clear and easily flushed, although it was dark. "No, no," he said, "do not feel you must be polite. And please call me Chen."

"I am not polite—I mean it," James said.

"Then wait and see whether the others like me," Chen said modestly.

By now they had reached the inner court. It was quiet here and strangely peaceful. The deserted house encircled them and under their feet the weeds grew high and sun-browned between the stones. A great twisted pine stood against the house, its branches so thick and widespreading that their weight had bowed the trunk and the tree looked like an old man carrying too heavy a burden. The sun had shone upon the pine all day and the needles were fragrant and the walls held the fragrance, for no wind could reach here. Chen threw himself on the wild grass under the tree and James sat down beside him. Twilight was still an hour away.

"You asked me about the Communists," Chen said abruptly. "They have taken my own village which is three hundred miles to the northwest. Therefore I do know something about them."

"Is your house safe?" James asked.

"Yes, for we are poor enough to be safe. My parents owned no land. They were tenants before the Communists came. Now they are landowners. Their landlord was the usual sort, short-tempered, greedy, but not more than many others. When the Communists came they did not kill him, for the people pleaded for him. They only strung him up by the thumbs and gave him a good beating and then allowed him as much land as he could work himself—no more. To my parents they gave a small farm. Now we are the landowners!" Chen laughed dryly.

James laughed. "I suppose you like the Communists."

Chen sat up and wrapped his arms about his knees. His spiky black hair stood up on his forehead and his thick eyebrows drew down. "No," he said, "no! Had I been only a peasant still, nothing more than the son of my father, I daresay I would have been happy enough, but I am something more. I am a doctor."

"Do they want doctors?" James asked.

"They want them very much. They want them too much. They have offered me a great deal. But they cannot offer me enough." These words Chen spoke in short sentences and his eyes were bitter. He tugged at a clump of grass between two stones and it came up root and all. Ants scurried out, terrified by the sudden light of day. "You know, there is very much that makes me angry at the hospital. I say this because I see it makes you angry, too. You don't understand why our fellow doctors are so cold, do you?"

"No," James said quietly. "That puzzles me very much. Kang, for instance, a superb doctor, but not caring whether people live or die. I say to myself, what is the use of being a doctor in that case?"

They were speaking Chinese, not the old slow involved speech of the past, but the quick terse tongue of the modern, energized by the languages of the West.

"So I say also," Chen said solemnly. "And I am very angry with Kang and Su and Peng and all those men. They have no feeling for our own people. You cannot understand it, Liang, but I can. I have seen old scholars like them, too. There is so much you cannot understand. I can understand you because I was also in America, but I was there only for a few years. You will have to learn to know our people. You must begin with the simple ones. Yet most of us are simple."

Chen cleared his throat and made his voice somewhat louder, almost as though he were about to begin an argument. "Liang, listen to me! These new men, Kang and Su and Peng and their like, they are not really very new. Their learning is new, but the men behave like the old ones. In my village there was an old scholar. Now why do I call him a scholar? He went up for the Imperial Examinations five times and after the first degree, he failed every time. Yet each time he came back more lordly than before. He could dine with no one except our landlord. The two of them went together. And when the local magistrate came to the village to examine the crops, then the three of them dined together. They were too good for the rest of us. And later when a warlord took our region, then there were four of them to dine together. And they were all too good for the rest of us, who were only the people. Scholar, landlord, magistrate, warlord—there you have the tyrants of the people. And we have them still. To go to a college in America does not change a man's heart. It only gives him a new weapon, sharper than the old, to use against the people—if that be his heart."

Chen spoke with deep passion and James was astounded. He had not heard Chen speak often in the gatherings which the doctors had together sometimes, and if he did speak it was only to make a joke at something or to point out some small foolish thing, such as a dog creeping under the table and trying not to be seen while it waited to snatch a bone. "Brothers," he had said once when this happened at a feast of browned duck in a restaurant, "it is very hard on this poor dog that we are all dainty moderns and do not throw duck bones on the floor. For his sake let us this one time return to the ways of our ancestors." With these words Chen had thrown the head of the duck, which he had been chewing, down upon the floor. The dog rushed for it and Kang had given it a kick that sent it howling away, but still clenching the duck head between its teeth. "Liu, don't be a fool," Kang had said in a surly voice. Chen had not spoken again all evening and no one had heeded his silence. Now all these words poured out of him.

"I cannot understand why you are not a Communist," James said quietly. His heart was altogether with what Chen had said, but he wished to try him further.

Chen twisted an end of the pine branch near him and sniffed the scent loudly into his nostrils. "This pine must be five hundred years old," he said. "Did you know, Liang, that our ancestors rewarded such trees with a title? Indeed it was so, exactly as though the tree were a human. They called them Duke this or Lord that. Well, so trees ought to be given praise to endure for five hundred years in this world! So you say I should be a Communist? I cannot be. I will tell you why.

They wanted me to dip my hand in blood and swear something. Swear what? Nothing much—loyalty, brotherhood, eternal faith—all the usual oaths of a gang. But I have sworn my loyalties to all humanity and not to any part of it. I told them so and they wanted to shoot me. So I left by night. Now you see why I have no home." Chen laughed too loudly and got to his feet. "Come, let us settle the matter of this house! Its owner lives next door—a good old man who smokes opium, and he will give you a quick bargain for cash."

Chen walked away and James followed, surprised and interested in spite of his vague distrust. The fellow was confused and angry with life. There was no knowing what such a man could or would do before he was settled. But it was impossible not to like him. Walking slightly behind him James looked at his square shoulders and thick neck and upright jet-black hair. Chen walked with his hands in his pockets and these pockets belonged to a suit which he had devised for himself. The trousers were Western, but the dark blue material being cheap the garment had shrunk when washed so that his strong thighs seemed about to burst the seams. The coat was somewhat like a uniform except that it was bare of any ornament, and it buttoned in the front straight from hem to collar. The buttons were of ordinary white bone. There were many pockets on both sides, each of which held something and this gave thickness to Liu Chen's thin but big frame.

They went out of the gate and down the length of the wall to another gate. Here Chen went in, and addressing a shabby manservant who sat on his heels against the wall, he asked for the master.

"The master is asleep but the old mistress is awake and it is she who decides what is to be done," the man said without getting up. Clearly everything in this house was badly managed.

"Then we will see the mistress," Chen said.

Still without getting up the man bawled to a woman servant who thrust her head out of the gate of the inner court, wiped her wet hands on her apron, and came out.

"What do you gentlemen want?" she demanded. "My mistress will not come out just to look at you."

The man grinned and hooked his thumb over his shoulder at her. "Do not get yourself into talk with this old rot," he told Chen. "Her tongue is tougher than any man's."

The woman pretended to box his ears and he dodged. "Eh—eh?" he cried. "It is not I who ask anything of you. You have nothing left that I want!"

"You turtle!" the woman screamed at him. Then she laughed and looked sidewise at the visitors and forced herself to be sober. "What did you say you wanted?" she asked.

Chen had watched this byplay with a grin on his face. "We want to inquire about the rent of the house next door. Of course the house is worthless because of the weasels, but my friend here is brave and he may take it if it costs little enough."

The woman pursed her mouth but something gleamed in her eye. "There are not so many weasels as there were. My mistress hired an exorcist last month and since then the weasels are afraid."

"We saw weasel marks plainly enough," Chen said bluntly. "If the price is too high we do not want to wait."

"Now then," the woman said hastily. "Why do all you foreign Chinese have such high tempers? You are no better than the Western people. Stay here and I will ask my mistress."

In something less than a quarter of an hour an old woman came to the gate of the inner courtyard and leaning on a carved stick she peered through. She was very old indeed, and her scanty hair, though still black, had dropped away and someone, perhaps the loud-voiced woman, had painted her scalp with black ink to look like hair. Against this intense blackness the old lady's face was like chalk. Indeed, her whole body, tiny and bent, seemed very nearly dust. Out of this tortured frame her voice came forth shrill and piping. "You want to rent the weasel house?" she asked.

"Yes, madam," James said.

"Then you must give me one hundred taels a month," she said.

So old was she that still she counted money in taels! James looked at Chen who turned on his heel and marched to the gate without answer and James, seeing this, followed him. At the gate the penetrating old voice caught them like a hook. "How much will you give me?" it inquired.

"Twenty," Chen said.

The old lady's eyes were small and black and something quivered in them like points of steel. "But the weasels are very few," she objected. "Give me fifty and I will send for the exorcist again."

"I do not fear the weasels. Twenty-five," James said firmly.

"Twenty-five," the old lady wailed. "But will it be cash?"

"Cash," James agreed. "Tomorrow."

"Cash tomorrow," the old lady echoed and began to cough until her skeleton shook in every bone. She went away coughing and the manservant rose. "If she is ill tomorrow I am here," he said heartily. "I am like a son to the old pair."

"Have they no sons?" Chen asked with some sympathy.

"They have two sons somewhere," the man said shrugging his shoulders. "But what are sons nowadays? They are no longer filial—not if they go to foreign schools. That is why the old man keeps himself asleep with opium. He does not want to see these new times, he says. Old Lady smokes, too, but there is not always enough for both of them."

Chen listened to this attentively. Then he said somewhat coldly, "We will come tomorrow at this time with the money."

"I will not give it to any hand but the old lady's," James said, "and I want a paper saying it has been received." He had seen the opium smokers who came to the hospital to be cured. There was neither heart nor soul left in them.

They walked toward the hospital somewhat solemnly, thinking of that strange lost household, whose sons came home no more.

"In these times the old are piteous, too," Chen said suddenly. "Doubtless that old pair had thought their sons would care for them as they had taken care of their own parents. Doubtless they dreamed of grandchildren running about. Oh, it wasn't all perfect in the old days—don't mistake me! Old people grew tiresome and plenty of sons wanted to be rid of them. But duty would not allow it. Well, it was called duty but actually it was pride and shame. If a man's parents were not cared for and happy it was his shame. If they were cared for and happy it was his pride. Now pride and shame have gone to other matters and so the old are lost."

"What other matters?" James asked. He was not so much curious for the answer as to hear what Chen would say. He was beginning to feel a warm sort of love for this honest, thinking fellow.

Chen shook his head. "How do I know? I can't understand. It seems to be getting rich, getting a pretty modern woman for a new wife, living in a house with electricity and running water—stupid things."

He sighed loudly. "Well, here is the hospital gate again. We part here, do we not? Shall we meet tomorrow here at the same time in the afternoon? Or do you need me any more?"

He was so eager, so anxious to come that James said very heartily, "Come with me, please. I dare not face the ghostly old lady alone."

Chen laughed and so they parted, and James went back to his room. There Young Wang waited for him impatiently, for he had promised the gateman to have a feast with him tonight.

"Here you are, master," he exclaimed. "I thought you had fallen down a well somewhere or that you had been beset by thieves."

"No, I have rented a house."

Young Wang's jaw dropped. "A house!"

"Yes. Tomorrow you will go with me to see it. It will have to be cleaned."

"I shall have to hire servants under me," Young Wang exclaimed. "It would give me no face were I the only servant in a whole house."

James saw himself already beset with household difficulties. "Tomorrow," he said, "when we have seen the house we will decide on such matters."

The next afternoon he and Young Wang went together to the stone lions and James was glad to see the strong square-shouldered figure of Chen waiting for him there. It seemed natural enough today to call him Chen.

"Have you the money?" Chen asked at once. He nodded to Young Wang, who grinned.

"I have it and a little more with which to buy a good lock for the door."

"We must not buy any furniture until the house is clean and the carpenters and plasterers have done their work," Chen said briskly. "There is no use in giving them places to sit down and rest themselves."

They walked away quickly, again setting up a roar of anger among the waiting rickshas, and were soon at the gate of their landlord.

The gate was open and the manservant and woman servant were both waiting for them, wearing clean garments. Young

Wang took a dislike to them at once. "These are wild people," he told James in a low voice, but James only smiled.

After they had entered the house Young Wang was even more distressed when he saw the master and mistress. For today the old gentleman had somehow been persuaded to get up and he appeared wrapped in an old soiled gray satin robe that was now much too large for him, and although his hair had been brushed and his face washed, nothing could hide the dreadful ashen color of his skin that was stretched over his fleshless frame. Beside him and a little behind was the old mistress. Young Wang pulled at James's sleeve. "Master, this is very evil," he whispered. "A landlord who eats opium is like a leech fastened to your belly!"

"Perhaps I can cure him some day," James replied. He had set his heart upon the house and he was not inclined to listen to Young Wang's fears.

"Where is the document of rental?" Chen asked.

"Here," the manservant said and pulled from his sleeve a small scroll which he unrolled; it was handwritten in shaky letters and James read it with difficulty. But Chen read it over his shoulder easily and quickly and he pointed out two places which did not please him.

"The rent is not to be paid two months in advance," he said. "One month is sufficient."

The old gentleman's jaw fell ajar but he nodded and the brush and the ink block were fetched and with much trembling preparation he made the change.

"Now," Chen said, "you are not to say that you take no responsibility for the house. We will make the repairs but if it is found that a beam is rotten or the foundation yields, that is to be your business."

Once more in silence the old man made the change.

"I will add one more thing myself," Chen said, looking very stern. And bending he wrote in a fluent style this sentence, "The landlord agrees never to ask for the rent in advance."

"Good, good," Young Wang murmured.

"Now for the seal," Chen said.

The manservant brought out the red family seal from the table drawer and he stamped it upon the paper, and James wrote his own name beneath it and Chen wrote his as a witness, and so now the money could be given over. James gave it to the old gentleman, who, not having spoken one word all the time, put out his two hands together like a bowl and received it. When he felt the money in his hands he clenched them together and rose and hurried out of the room blindly, his robes dragging after him. The old lady went after him and then the woman servant and there was only the manservant left to see them away. It was so sad a sight that James felt depressed by it and Chen sighed. "These are among the many lost," he said gently, and they went once again to look at the house that now belonged to James.

Only Young Wang was not sad. He took lively interest in the house and discovered a cistern beyond the well, and he found a good drain, stone lined though very ancient, which could carry the household waste water through the back wall to a creek that ran behind the house. Nor was he afraid of the weasels. He took a fallen tree branch and clubbed one long lank fellow to death where it hid behind a door. "Some big female cats will chase these devils away," he exclaimed. "Leave it to me, master. Cats are better than exorcists. But they must be big ones who will fight, or the weasels will suck even their blood."

So in the days that followed, under Young Wang's interest this house became a shelter again for human beings. He it was who harried carpenters and plasterers and cleaning women until the place was new again and its stale odor of the past was gone. He it was who went to the thieves' market at dawn and bought tables and chairs and pots and bowls and kitchen ladles of beaten iron and cauldrons for the brick stoves in the kitchen. James and Chen together went to old furniture shops and bought heavy blackwood tables for the main rooms and they bought Western beds.

"My sisters will never be able to sleep on boards, however good Chinese they become," he told Chen. "And I myself—I prefer American springs under me."

He indulged himself and bought a few fine scrolls for the wall and an old piano that some Westerner had left behind when he went away before the war. "It is a palace," Chen said proudly, and did not notice that James did not reply. In such indulgence James took no great pleasure. If he had been preparing a home for Lili, he thought solemnly, how different it might have been! But then, none of this would have been good enough.

The days drew on and the expected letter from his father did not arrive. James was not surprised. He could imagine, as well as though he were in that New York apartment, how his father rose each morning contemplating the writing of the letter, how after contemplation he postponed, and how meanwhile he went to his classes on Chinese literature and came home exhausted, how he refreshed himself with a short nap, some tea which in private he liked to drink with cream and sugar, although publicly he declared these things only spoiled good tea, and how after reading a little while to refresh his spirit it was too late to write a letter that day.

From his mother, however, James did receive a letter. Like most of her letters, it was so rich with piety and good purpose that he was not able to discern from it what had happened. That it concerned Louise, that she had been foolish and led away by the Americans, that she was after all very young and much prettier than Mary, who had never had American young men admirers, and he must not therefore be too harsh a judge of Louise, who was growing up pretty even to Americans, and this was very difficult and a family problem, and she had been trying to persuade his pa to come to China, too, and they could all be happy again together in a house somewhere in Peking, only of course Pa felt he could not leave his work just now and perhaps in another year or two—so his mother wrote. She had not at all approved the sudden way in which Mary had taken Louise away and Peter, too, just about to enter college to become a great engineer, but the ocean was always there and they could come back if they did not like China nowadays. Only Louise of course had better stay long enough to fall in love with a nice young Chinese. It was the elder brother's duty to take the father's place and if James, her dear son, knew any nice young men, Chinese of course, and could arrange a marriage for Louise, undoubtedly that would be the solution, although he must not misunderstand and think that Louise had to get married. Luckily there was nothing like that, but still there might have been and they must all be thankful. Such was the gist of his mother's letter and James read it over thoughtfully three times and gathered that Louise was somehow a new problem.

Without much enlightenment therefore he asked for a week's vacation and with Young Wang at his heels he waited one day on the familiar dock in Shanghai for the steamship.

The house was ready. He had found work for Mary in the children's annex of the hospital and he had registered Peter in the college now receiving a fresh life under the leadership of a famous Chinese scholar. For Louise he had planned nothing because he knew nothing. She could always enter a girls' school. There was also a Catholic convent, kept by six sisters, two of them Chinese and four of them French. He must talk with Mary before deciding for Louise.

The day was windy and gray and the waterside was black. Small boats were pushing about scavenging in the filthy river. Each had its family of man and woman and children and a grandparent or two, and these looked cold and unhappy. He was sorry that the three who were coming to him must see the Bund on such a day. The tall modern buildings looked forbidding and alien, as though they did not belong there. They lifted their heads too high above the boats and the crowded streets.

Even Young Wang seemed subdued. He had left a small underservant in charge of the house with his old mother for amah. Young Wang was proving a stern headboy. He did not allow Little Dog the least latitude for laziness, and the boy was beginning to look harried. Young Wang himself, dressed in a clean uniform of the semi-official sort in which he delighted, stood now just behind his master. He would have preferred no women in the household, for a man was easier to serve. His master's sisters were Chinese, but they had been in America so long that he feared they had the tedious and fussy ways of American ladies in houses. He felt somewhat diminished and in low spirits when he thought of this. Either he was headboy or he was not, he told himself. He would take orders only from his master. So far as he was concerned there was no mistress. When his master married a wife there would be a rightful mistress. This point was clear in his mind by the time the yelling coolies were lassoing the ship, and he felt better and the grin returned to his face.

James saw them at once. They stood apart from both Chinese and Americans in a small close knot of three. Peter was between the two girls and he was holding his hat with both hands. A fresh autumn wind had sprung up with the dawn and was increasing as the skies grew dark toward noon. This wind blew into the air like a red flag the scarf Louise wore and fluttered her curled hair. Mary had wrapped her blue scarf tightly about her head. He saw their faces quite clearly and he felt concern and yet a sort of warm pleasure that here at last was something of his own.

He would not acknowledge that these months had been lonely but now he knew they had been. He did not know why. He was surrounded with people from morning until night and his work was satisfying and yet discouraging—satisfying because everything done for the crowds of sick amounted to much, and yet discouraging because he was always conscious of the millions beyond all aid. Underneath satisfaction and discontent was the feeling that he was living on the surface of his country and that he had put down no roots into it. He was still alien, and he wanted to lose this feeling of being alien. He wanted to plunge deep into the earth and the waters of his people, and he did not know how. He wanted to belong here so profoundly that he could never go away again. He could not live airily the rootless surface existence of the other doctors. Chen of course was the exception to them. He had grown very fond of Chen and he had begged him to come and share the house with them, but Chen had until now refused. When James had spoken again he had said, "Let us wait and see. It may be that your sisters and brother will not like me and then it will be difficult for both of us if they want me to go away again."

"How foolish you are," James had replied.

"No, I am only shy," Chen had said and had roared out his great laugh. This laugh, James now knew, did in reality cover a very tender shyness, and so he had said no more.

But it was not only doctors who were living unrooted upon the surface of the life here. James discovered that there were many others who also lived thus, young men and women who had lived and studied in France and England as well as in America, and even some who had studied in Russia. But these who had studied in Russia were different from the others. They had not, at least the ones he knew in Peking, allied themselves with the Communists, but they talked in words of force. The people, they declared, should be "forced" to change their medieval ways of thinking and feeling and behaving. What this force was to be they did not say, nor did they know how it was to be applied. James, listening to much talk at their gatherings, had gradually withdrawn from them all and he devoted himself entirely to his work in the hospital. Yet he knew that though he spent his whole life in this work, it would not reach below the surface. Suppose that he had four hundred patients a month, that would be fewer than five thousand persons a year, and if he lived his life out, that would not be half a million people and what were so few among the hundreds of millions? Somehow he must live in larger and deeper ways, which he had not yet discovered.

Meanwhile here was the family responsibility thrust upon him by his father and he must meet it first. There was a shout from the wharf coolies; they threw out the great knots of woven rope and the ship ground against the dock. The gangplank was lowered, and he waited and then felt Mary's warm arms about him and Louise's hands in his, and Peter thrust his arm through his brother's.

"You're looking well, Jim," Mary said breathlessly. "A little thin, maybe."

"Shanghai is some place," Peter said.

Only Louise said nothing. James saw that she was very much thinner and that she looked as though she had been crying. He had taken rooms at the best of the few good hotels, and he had ordered a good luncheon for this midday and now he was glad that he had done so, for the rain began to fall in earnest and shivering ricksha coolies crowded under the roof of the dock, and the miserable scavenger boats tried to hide themselves under the piers. Louise looked at them and looked away.

"Young Wang!" James called. "You take care of the baggage, please!"

Young Wang appeared smiling. "I will do it, master. And please, here is the carriage."

He had hired a carriage whose cushions had been newly covered with khaki and whose horse was something less starved than others. The driver was huddled under an oilcloth on his high seat but when he saw his customers he jumped down and took away the old newspapers which he had spread over the cushions.

It seemed even a little cozy inside the carriage, especially when the big oilcloth apron smelling of tung oil had been fastened to hooks in the umbrella top and the horse trotted away from the dock.

"Well," James said, smiling on them all. "This is nice."

They smiled at him wanly, or so he thought.

"Louise was seasick," Mary said.

"So were you," Peter said.

"Not much, really," Mary retorted. "You are too proud of yourself, Peter."

The long sea voyage had worn down their tempers a little. "I wish I could have ordered a good day for you," James said, trying to be cheerful. Still, he told himself, it was well enough to go through the streets behind this oilcloth curtain. Chinese people seemed always unprotected against rain and snow. Their cotton garments melted like wet paper, and while in the sunshine they looked gay enough all of them were miserable in rain. And the Bund lasted for so short a distance. Too soon the streets became crowded and disheveled. The hotel entrance was pleasant and a smart doorman received them. Their rooms, taken for a day and a night, had made inroads upon his funds but James was grateful for temporary comfort. The lobby was warm and lined with palms, and sheltered at least from the weather. Well-dressed Chinese and a few foreigners sat upon the imitation-leather chairs. It was not too different from what they were used to, James thought. Upstairs the rooms were clean. He had taken two, one for himself and Peter and one for the girls, with a connecting bath.

"What measly towels!" Louise said when she looked in.

"I believe they are made in the factories here," James said.

"Why is it we can't do anything as well as other people?" Louise muttered.

"Now, Louise," Mary said, "don't begin by being disgusted with everything."

"We'd better have some food," James said. "We'll all feel better. Then we can go to a movie this afternoon, if you like. That sounds like New York, doesn't it? Let's get ready."

He wanted very much an hour alone with Mary but he knew that there would be no chance for this. In his room with Peter he did not know whether to ask questions or not. He began tentatively enough as he watched his younger brother brush his hair carefully before the mirror.

"It's a great surprise, all this," he said. "Ma's letter didn't make anything very plain, either, and I haven't heard from Pa."

"It's a big fuss about nothing, if you ask me," Peter grunted. He took out a cigarette rather ostentatiously. He had not smoked when James was at home, because this doctor brother had objected to his smoking before he had stopped growing. Now he wanted James to know that he did as he liked and expected to continue doing so. James understood and said nothing.

"Louise made Pa angry," Peter went on. "I never thought he really meant to ship us off, though. He threatens so many things he never does. But there was no question about this. He went himself and bought the tickets and he wouldn't pay for any tuition for us. I want to turn right around and go back, of course. I can make up the few weeks that I am missing at college. I'm still going to be an engineer."

James smiled. "Better stay a few months anyway, now you're here," he said. "Half a year doesn't matter at your age. And I've fixed up rather a nice house in Peking for us all. It's a fine old city—makes you proud."

"Is it better than Shanghai?"

"I think so anyway."

There seemed nothing to say for a few minutes. Then James returned to the effort. "So you don't know really what Louise did?"

"Oh, I know," Peter said. "She's in love with Philip Morgan, and Phil doesn't want to marry her. That's about it. I know Phil. He doesn't want to marry anybody now. When he does he will probably marry some debutante."

He was careful not to say that Philip probably did not want to marry a Chinese. He thought of himself as an American. Now something occurred to him. "Say, I heard something interesting on the ship. We had a fellow on board from Hollywood. He's coming out here to shoot some pictures. It's a story about a GI—sort of a Chinese Madame Butterfly story, he said, only the GI doesn't go away. He takes his gal home. He said that while they don't want stories about white men and Negroes getting married they don't mind Chinese any more. Pretty good, isn't it?"

James smiled. He could not speak, watching this brother of his. Peter was utterly and completely foreign. He had nothing to help him here, no shred of knowledge, no hour of experience, to help him endure being Chinese. For it would be a matter of endurance. Peter had never absorbed either atmosphere or ideas from their father, and now James realized, though grudgingly, that the atmosphere of ancient Chinese philosophy which his father had so persistently built around them had helped only him and Mary. Even after they understood its artificiality, and then perhaps its uselessness in these swift modern times, it had become a part of them, thinly spun, indeed, but there, nevertheless, its mild silvery thread running through the structure of their beings. But Peter and Louise had absorbed none of it. Instead they had come to despise it, and they were never deceived for an instant by its unreality. Nor did they understand or care that once it had been a reality.

"So Louise was sent here to get over a love affair," James said.

"Something like that," Peter said briskly. He got up, bored by Louise. "Jim, if I stay for this autumn will you promise to make Pa let me go home in time for midyears?"

"If you won't call it home," Jim replied. "This is home, you know."

"Oh well—you know what I mean," Peter said. He stood restlessly, his hands jingling some change in his pockets. "I don't want to waste time, even if I have plenty of it."

"I think you ought to go back at midyears," James said, getting to his feet. "There is no good place here to get engineering. The country needs fellows like you—needs them now, if this eternal quarrel would ever end between the government and the Communists. We're all held up by that. But maybe by the time you're through, it will be settled one way or the other." He paused. "Of course there's always the chance you may not want to go back. Something steals into you. I don't want to go back—though there's much I don't like here, I can tell you."

"I know I'll want to go back," Peter said. "Come on, let's eat."

It was the end of talk, and they joined Mary and Louise in the hall and went downstairs to a hearty lunch of barley broth, boiled beef, cabbage and potatoes and a cornstarch pudding. It was the standard hotel meal for foreigners.

But it was quite pleasant in the motion-picture theater. The building had been designed by an American and the seats were still new enough not to have their upholstery torn and the springs exposed. The air was thick with the smell of Chinese food, for everybody seemed to be munching something, but they grew used to that. It was still raining when they came in and it was pleasant to get under shelter. The picture was

American, too. It was a Western, and after it was finished there was an old Harold Lloyd comedy, so old that to the four young people sitting together it was new, and they laughed at it. When they came out it was nearly dark and again the hotel seemed shelter. Young Wang had brought their baggage and when they came in he served tea with small cakes and sandwiches from the hotel kitchen. These tasted good and they began talking as they ate. James told them about the house in Peking, which perhaps sounded better than it was as he told of it, and Peter heard about the college and Mary about the hospital. Louise, James said, could make up her mind about what she wanted to do when she got there. Maybe she would just want to keep house for them for a few weeks until she saw everything. None of them talked about America. They did not unpack very much because they were to take the train before noon the next day. The trains were better now and they did not need to go more than an hour before theirs started. Young Wang would go early and spend a little money.

They parted, brothers and sisters, with a warm family feeling. It was good to be together. Before he went to bed James sent a cablegram to his parents. "Children arrived safely. All well. We go north tomorrow. Love and respect. James."

He lay awake long after Peter was breathing in deep even waves of sleep. He had wanted to get Mary away and ask her about Lili, but he had not dared to leave Louise alone. There was something desperate in her face.

7

LONG AGO MRS. LIANG had learned not to open envelopes addressed to her husband. Therefore she did not open the yellow envelope which she hoped brought news of the children's safe arrival. It came after luncheon when Dr. Liang was taking a nap in his study, and she tiptoed to the door and listened. She could hear him breathing heavily, and she sighed and went back to the living room and sat down by the window. She held the envelope in her hand, for she was not willing for one moment to lay it down. There was so much she wanted to know which of course it would not tell her. There was so much she wanted to know which indeed no one could tell her, because only someone like herself would perceive it. For example, what was it like now really to live again in Peking? She loved Peking. To herself she called it by the old name of Peking, as most Chinese did, although before foreigners she was careful to say Peiping, to show that she was a modern woman and loyal to the present government.

Still, she had not at all liked Madame Chiang Kai-shek when she came here to New York. She and Dr. Liang had sent a large bouquet of chrysanthemums to Madame Chiang, yellow ones, costing one dollar apiece, but Madame Chiang had not even acknowledged them. Some secretary had merely scrawled a note of receipt. When later among other Chinese they had gone to a reception Liang had taken Madame's hand very warmly, but she herself had not touched Madame Chiang. She had bowed a little and said in Chinese, "Eh-eh, you've come, have you?" exactly as in her old-fashioned home her mother had greeted guests whom she did not like. Madame Chiang's face had not changed. The Americans thought her beautiful but in China there were many women more beautiful.

"Eh, why do I think about Madame Chiang?" Mrs. Liang asked herself now.

Outside in the park the leaves were beginning to fall and this meant that winter would soon come. She dreaded the long cold American winters. It was cold in Peking, too, but the days were always sunny. Even when there came down a snowstorm from the north, it passed quickly. Peking in the snow! Nothing was more beautiful. And how the bright red berries of Indian bamboo used to shine through the whiteness of the snow! She wiped her eyes quietly. That home in Peking, set so firmly upon the earth that no wind could shake it, was still her dearest memory. When the winds blew here the tall building trembled and she was always afraid, although she had learned not to show it because Liang grew so angry with her. Liang was often angry with her and for many things she did not blame him. He is not very happy here, too, she thought. No one is happy away from the earth and waters of his own home. Then why did Liang stay here?

There was the Li family, also. Why did they stay here? Lili was becoming quite famous now among the Americans. They had taken her up as a fad and only the other day in a picture magazine she had seen Lili's face, looking at her from a full page. "Chinese Beauty," was written underneath, and then there had been a story about her which said she was considered the most beautiful girl in China. But none of the story was true. There were many girls in China more beautiful than Lili. James was lucky not to marry her. Still, if he had married, he would be here and all the children would be here, and the house would not be so quiet. When the children were here she had so much to say, but now she could not think of anything to say to Liang.

Suddenly she heard him cough. Then she heard his step, and she ran to the door again and opened it softly. He was awake but he looked unwell and pale. "Liang, here is an electric letter from the children," she said. Now that they were alone she had returned to speaking Chinese altogether, unless some foreigner came to visit them. Her English was slipping from her.

"Give it to me," he said.

She stood waiting while he tore open the envelope with his thumbnail and took out the inner sheet. He did not read it aloud. She waited.

"They have arrived safely and they are well. James sends this word," he said finally.

A misty happiness filled her body. "So they are safe," she murmured.

"Of course." He stooped and pulled on his slippers. "You are always so fearful."

"But the ocean is terrible," she pleaded.

"Not in the great modern ships," he replied. "You always behave as though there were nothing but old-fashioned junks."

She understood that his nap had left him feeling heavy and uncomfortable and so she said, "I will fetch you some hot tea and then it will be good for you to take a short walk in the park. You have to make a talk tonight before American ladies."

"I don't see why I am always compelled to make these talks," he grumbled.

She hastened to agree with him. "Nor do I, Liang. Why do you not refuse? It is so foolish for you to waste your time. How can women understand the things you talk about?"

She hoped to comfort him but instead she made him very angry. "Not all women are like you," he said coldly. "There are even some women who appreciate the subject to which I have devoted my life."

"I am always wrong," she said and turned and went away to the kitchen. Had the children been here she would have answered him with some temper of her own but indeed she had none now. Well, a woman without children had no courage before a man. In the kitchen alone, for she kept the maid now only half a day, she filled the kettle and lit the gas stove. Secretly she was afraid of the suddenness of the gas lighting, but she forced herself to light the match and hold it to the burner.

She made the tea and took it into the study. Liang sat before his desk, drowsing over some notes, and he did not speak when she poured the tea into the bowl and set it on the table, and so she tiptoed away to sit by the window again in the living room. The wind was beginning to rise. She saw the leaves falling faster in the park below, and the building seemed to sway in a slow whirling motion. Certainly she heard it creak. A look of terror came over her face and she clutched the edge of the window sill with both hands.

In his own way Dr. Liang also was suffering. His philosophy had not deserted him, nor did he feel that he had done anything wrong. Therefore he could not understand why his usual buoyancy had left him and why he felt dry and sad. The house was quiet, but he liked quiet. He had done a great deal of work since the children went and so much indeed that he had made entirely new notes for his course in contemporary Chinese literature. The children's mother was of course somewhat depressed. That was inevitable. She was the mother type rather than the wife type. He had come to this conclusion long ago. In his own way Dr. Liang thought a great deal about women. No woman could have persuaded him from the path of rectitude and he was a man genuinely chaste. But he thought about women, nevertheless, and he analyzed many women in his mind, without any thought of their relation to him. Indeed he wanted nothing of them, for himself. They were merely interesting specimens of the human race. Confucius had thought little of women, and he had long pondered this aspect of the master's mind. There must have been a reason for this contempt. Perhaps the master had endured a willful wife, and had taken his revenge in private by writing down his wishful hope that women were beneath the notice of men. "Women, children and fools," he had said, although recently Dr. Liang had been inclined to believe that Confucius was partly wrong in this classification, for he was becoming convinced that not all women were fools.

There was, for example, Violet Sung. Beautiful in the most truly exotic fashion, cultivated, even learned, Violet had come from Paris a few months ago to take New York by storm. She was besieged by suitors of every nationality, and she would marry none of them. Marriage, she said in her quiet profound way of speaking, was not for women like her. The rumor now, however, was that she had accepted the love of a handsome middle-aged Englishman whose business interests kept him half the year in New York. If this were true, then it was an affair of the utmost good taste. Violet and Ranald Grahame were seen together often but not too often, and they seldom arrived together at any public place and never went away together.

Yet Dr. Liang was inclined to believe the rumor if only because of the bitter gossip raging among the Chinese. Not, of course, among the commonplace Chinese of Chinatown, who were only tradesmen, but among Chinese society, the rich émigrés. Chinese men were especially bitter, as if they felt that Violet had rejected each of them individually when she accepted an Englishman. Dr. Liang had philosophy enough to enjoy this jealousy and to acknowledge half humorously that he had some of it himself. He would have been thoroughly alarmed had Violet pursued him, for he knew that he was not capable of a violent love affair, nor indeed did he desire it. He was not the physical type. Nevertheless, he enjoyed the deference that Violet had always shown him in public, and before others he indulged in a little domineering flirtation, being so much older than she and besides a very famous man. Once he had found himself alone with her by accident when they arrived not quite late enough at a late party, to which Mrs. Liang had not been invited, and he had been afraid of Violet Sung and entirely correct in his behavior. He had asked her formally where her ancestral home was in China. This question she had evaded somewhat, saying that she came from Shanghai, and that her ancestral home she believed was somewhere in Chekiang, although her father had long lived in Paris. Looking at her after other guests came and remembering her evasiveness, it occurred to him that she might be the daughter of a Frenchwoman and a Chinese. Yes, she had the look of foreign blood, very subtly subdued. It was more original to be Chinese than French. And of course the strong Chinese blood always predominated.

Thus Violet Sung made a very interesting type for a philosopher to study. Someday he might work up a lecture on the difference between the mother type and the Violet type, and whether a man should have both types in his life, and if so, how such a relationship could be harmonious with the demands of modern life. In old-fashioned China, of course, all had been well arranged. The first wife was the mother. Thereafter a man took as concubine the other type. But this apparently offended the newer civilization of the Americans, who were not so naturalistic as the older peoples of Asia, or for that matter, of Europe. A formula here had yet to be found. The present number of illegitimate children which he understood to be very large—he must look up the annual number, if he went on with the lecture—was proof of the necessity for man even here of the two types of women.

At this moment Dr. Liang felt the need of an audience.

There was no one in the house except Mrs. Liang and although he had no respect for her intelligence his thoughts flowed more clearly when he spoke them aloud.

He rose and went rather impetuously into the living room. "Eh," he said, "I want to talk to you." So absorbed was he that he did not notice that her face was ashen or that she was clutching the window sill in a strange way. When she saw him she let go and leaned back in her chair. "A big storm is coming," she muttered, but he did not hear her.

He sat down on the chair opposite her, and leaning forward with his elbows on his knees he linked together loosely his large, exquisitely shaped hands. "I want to ask you a question as a good mother," he said. "Do you prefer the Western way of having concubines outside the family in secret or our old-fashioned way of bringing them into the family and allowing all the children to be born under one roof?"

Mrs. Liang was smitten with fear. Was he thinking of taking a concubine now that the children were gone? Her lips went dry and she stared at him. "What thoughts have you?" she demanded.

But he did not see her fear. He was entirely absorbed in the thread of the lecture that was developing in him rapidly. "I want to know what you think," he insisted.

She collected her terrified thoughts. They had been distracted enough by the storm but now here was this distraction also in the house! She began to speak, and her rather thick lips quivered. "Of course our way is better," she faltered. "Otherwise the man's seed is sown wild and the children have no name. Why should children suffer for what their father does?"

Why indeed? Her heart yearned over her own. Of course if Liang wanted another woman he must bring her into this house. It would be shameful for him to descend to the sort of thing that foreigners did. Yet could she endure another woman here? No! if she came, let her come. She herself would ask for enough money to buy a ticket home and she would go to her children. She was about to rise with dignity from her chair and tell Liang that in this case she wanted to go to the children.

He gave her no time either to rise or to speak. Instead he himself rose briskly. "Thank you," he said with unusual courtesy. "I wanted to know what you would think—the mother type—" he murmured.

He hastened back to his study and closed the door firmly and at once sat down and began to write fluently at his desk. He wrote for two hours, and when he had finished he felt pleased with himself and very hungry. He came out of his study to find that Mrs. Liang had his supper on the table. She said she did not wish to eat and she served him in silence. The meal was good. She had heated chicken broth and dropped noodles into it, and she had mixed shelled shrimp and salted turnip tops with eggs into an omelet and she had made rice congee. This with salted fish made him a meal. He ate it with enjoyment, although he missed the tinge of garlic with which she would have seasoned the food had he not been going out that night. Long ago he had impressed on her that she must never put garlic in his food when he was going out to lecture to American ladies. They disliked the odor, and he could not sufficiently protect himself from their eagerness in pressing about him after his lecture was over. He drank two cups of tea in silence while he reviewed what he was going to say. Mrs. Liang was accustomed to this silence before he went into public life and she did not break it. When he rose she went into the hall and held his coat and hat ready for him.

"Do not stay up for me," he told her kindly and he went out without waiting for her answer.

After he had gone she stood uncertainly for a moment and then she went upstairs to her room and took out a sheet of paper and began to write to the children.

"My precious ones," she began after the formal opening. How fortunate she was in having learned to read and write! Well, she must thank Liang for that, for it was only because he had insisted that she had been taught. Even so, she knew she often made mistakes in the radicals of certain characters. But the children could always read her letters.

"I am in deep trouble," she wrote. "Your pa is thinking of taking another woman into our house. This is too much for me here in America. In China the houses are big and there are many servants and we could live separately. But here how could I bear to cook her food and pour her tea? If he decides to do this thing I will ask for ticket money—"

She paused. The house was certainly swaying in the storm. She felt slightly sick and quickly she took up her pen again.

"I am very lonely here. Your pa has gone away to talk to American ladies. I ought not to complain for he earns one hundred American dollars when he does so. But tonight there is a big wind from the ocean side, and I feel the house shaking. Your pa says this is impossible since it is built of iron. Yet I feel it shaking, whatever he says, and I think Heaven is not pleased with these high houses. We are meant to live down upon the earth——"

She meandered on in a long incoherent letter, telling her children everything that came into her mind.

Dr. Liang after an hour and twenty minutes was closing his lecture. The auditorium of the exclusive club was filled with women, all sitting in silence. Lights placed skillfully above and below threw Dr. Liang's tall slender figure into splendid relief. "As for me," he said with a slight half smile, "as a Chinese man and a Confucian I prefer the mother type. She is perhaps the true Chinese woman. My own wife is that type, and she and I have sent our children back to China to renew the bond with their mother earth. I want them to be Chinese in the most profound sense, children of the earth—and children of the dawn!"

He ended, his voice reverent, his head high, and he bowed. There was a moment's silence and then waves of applause brought him back to bow again and again. He did not know exactly what "children of the dawn" meant but the phrase had come to him and he was pleased with it.

8

THE HOUSE IN PEKING which had seemed pleasantly ready when James left it last now looked bare and crudely furnished as he led his sisters and Peter into it. Little Dog and his mother had done their best. They had swept the floors and had wiped away the dust and the kitchen stove was ready to light. Upon a small earthenware charcoal stove a kettle was boiling for tea. Chen had been there also and he had brought two green porcelain pots, each holding a small gnarled pine tree. Upon the table in the middle room of the first court, which was to be the living room, he had placed a round white bowl of small yellow chrysanthemums, of the sort which could be bought at the market for a few pennies.

James glanced at the faces of the three as they stood at the wide door of this room, now open to the court. Louise looked about her with resentful eyes. Peter was smiling tolerantly. Only Mary looked with interest at what she saw. "It's a fine big room," she said.

"We are now about to live as our ancestors did," James said. "We can see for ourselves how valuable modern gadgets are and whether happiness is dependent upon them. There is no running water, but the hot-water coolies will pour boiling hot water into the tin tub in the room I have set aside as the bathroom, and Little Dog will temper it with cold water drawn from the well. The stove in the kitchen is of brick and it burns twists of grass. Little Dog's mother will cook our food there. For light at night I have allowed kerosene lamps instead of the bean-oil lamps or candles which we really should use. And I have bought American beds in the thieves' market. I thought that there perhaps we could improve upon our ancestors."

"It can all be made lovely," Mary murmured.

"With the lattices we don't need curtains," James went on, "and upon these stone floors we can lay carpets in winter if we like. There are fine carpets made here in Peking."

"It is lovely already," Mary said.

"But the walls!" Louise cried suddenly. "I hate these walls all around the courts—we can't see from the windows!"

"We can always walk out of the gate," James said. "The gate will not be locked. Our ancestors liked walls. You'll find that everybody here still has walls."

"Where is my room?" Peter asked.

"We can divide the rooms as we like," James replied. "But I thought you and I would share this left part of the house, Peter, and the girls will take the rooms on the right. By the way, Mary, if you or Louise see something like a rat, it is only a weasel. I think they are all gone, but in case they aren't they will not stay long after we move in."

"Weasels?" Louise shrieked. "I never heard of them in houses!"

"You will hear of many things here," James said, "some pleasant and some not."

He had not yet made up his mind how he would treat Louise. Until now she had only been the pretty and spoiled little sister in whom he had a sentimental interest. Now suddenly she had become a woman without any of the lingering years between childhood and womanhood. She was a flower which had not been given time to bloom. The bud had been forced. For Mary had told him at last exactly what had happened. In the hours together in their cabin on the ship she had got from Louise the full story. It had been easy indeed, for Louise spent many evenings in tears, and when she found that Mary was not disposed to scold her, tears had led quickly to confidence, often repeated. Mary had told James everything on the train, while Louise and Peter were in the dining car and James had decided that he was not hungry. James had taken a second-class compartment for the four of them, feeling that the crowded open car was too much to bear so soon after America. While the train swayed and shook over the landscape of small farms and barking dogs and shrieking geese, whose blue-clad peasants stood watching the cars rush past, Mary told James.

"Louise thought Philip would marry her. I excuse her that much," she said at last.

James had listened amazed and angry with Louise. Strangely, he thought, he could not blame Philip. Americans were not taught as Chinese were. When Louise was willing, it could not be imagined that Philip would not accept.

"Louise was a fool," he said. Outside the window the hills of central China were flattening into the long levels of the north.

"It was first Estelle's foolishness," Mary said. She was watching her brother's face. James must not be too hard on Louise now. The little sister had suffered from her parents. "Estelle persuaded Louise too much," Mary went on. "I think she made Louise forget she is Chinese. Such things they can do, but we cannot."

"Philip wouldn't marry a Chinese," James said brusquely.

"Anyway, don't talk to Louise," Mary begged. "Pa talked so loud, and Ma cried and cried."

So James allowed no sign to escape him to let Louise know that now he knew what she had done. But in his heart he agreed that his father had been wise to send her at once thousands of miles away. So young a wound would heal. It would be difficult to marry her now to a man who would forgive her. Yet marriage, it seemed to him, was the only possibility. Louise would not be satisfied to return to girlhood and innocence, even if she could. Everything in her had been forced. A green fruit had been ripened by unseasonable heat.

Yet it seemed to him, after thought, that he must be firm with Louise. She must be treated as a grown woman although as a girl, too, who needed to be watched and restricted. He wished very much that he could arrange a marriage for her in the old-fashioned Chinese way, and transfer to a husband the responsibility for this pretty creature who was no longer a virgin. Only a husband could suffice, even if Louise would scarcely agree to being married off summarily.

He pondered this again while he changed his clothes and arranged his possessions in his new room. Through the open door he heard Peter walking about, flinging down his suitcases, moving chairs and tables. Peter too would not be too easy to look after, but what to do with Louise must be his first care. The thought of Chen came into his mind. If Chen should fall in love with Louise it would be excellent indeed. Certainly he must be careful that none of the doctors who were already married, some to old-fashioned wives whom they kept in the country, grew interested in Louise. There was much looseness in what was called modern society in Peking. Men and women came together and separated. They married and divorced with no more effort than a notice put in the newspapers. There was something about Louise that repelled him and made it hard for him to be affectionate with her in his old brotherly fashion. She looked young and yet experienced. Mary looked the virgin she was, and of the two, Louise now seemed older.

The four came together at their night meal, for they had reached Peking in the late afternoon. Now that the lamps were lit, the rooms looked softened and more homelike. When Young Wang had ordered Little Dog to bring in the dishes of hot food for him to arrange upon the table, they sat down with good appetite. Even Louise looked less sullen, although she was ready at once to complain.

"There are no closets in our rooms," she said. "Where shall I hang my dresses?"

"I'll have some built," James said. "But if you wear Chinese things you won't need anything but the shelves in the wall cupboard. Our ancestors kept their clothes folded."

"I shall wear Chinese clothes entirely now," Mary said.

"Not I," Louise retorted.

"It's quiet here," Peter said suddenly. "You'd never know you were in a city."

"That's the beauty of the walls," James said.

After the meal was over he had to go to the hospital. He had already been away his full week, and he wanted to see his patients, and though he was reluctant to leave the three, yet he must go. They were still at the table, cracking dried lichee nuts and drinking tea, when he rose and stood behind his chair. "If you need me Young Wang can come and fetch me," he told them. "Tomorrow we will talk over everything and decide what each one is to do. You do not begin work until the first of the month, Mary. You ought to start college, Peter—classes opened last week. But perhaps you all want a few days in which to see the city."

"We are not babies," Mary said smiling. "We can look after ourselves. And don't feel you have to apologize to us for China, Jim."

He smiled back at her, thankful for her common sense. It was true that, quite without knowing it, he had been fearful lest they dislike everything here, because it was not what they were used to having in America. Mary with her shrewd eyes had understood his fears.

At the hospital he found Chen, in whose care he had left his sick. Chen had been zealous, but in spite of all his care of the patients, a woman had died. She had come into the hospital after birth with puerperal fever, as so many women came. She had seemed better when James left, but the fever had taken a turn for the worse, and she had died quickly the next day.

"Though I was with her, I could do nothing," Chen mourned. "The fever ate her up. Now she leaves the newborn child. What shall we do with him?"

"Where is he now?" James asked.

"I have him in the children's ward but he cannot stay there too long—you know how crowded it is, and the nurses are impatient with too many crying at once."

"I will have my sister Mary come over tomorrow," James said.

They went the rounds together and Rose and Marie pattered after them. These two nurses had attached themselves to the two doctors whom they liked best and with Kitty, who was a relief nurse, these made a solid core of five in the hospital. They took no part in the social life of the other doctors and nurses and maintained a rigid front toward gossip and love affairs. Had there been only Rose and Marie, this gossip would have reached them and they would have been accused of living with the two doctors they now followed. But the three nurses together made such gossip impossible.

His other patients were not dangerously ill and when the rounds were over James was loath to part from Chen. He wanted to talk with him. At least he wanted to get on terms of being able to talk with him and even to get his advice, perhaps, about Louise. He would not of course tell even Chen what had really happened. He would merely say that the girl was in the midst of an unhappy love affair, unhappy because her love was not returned, and that it was necessary to take her mind away from her own trouble. But before he said anything Chen must meet Louise. "Come home with me, Chen," he said abruptly. "You are the first one I wish them to meet."

Chen blushed savagely. "I never know how to talk to young women," he mumbled, "especially ones who have just come from America."

"Oh, come," James urged. "You will find my sisters very easy. Louise is supposed to be quite pretty and she talks readily enough to any man. She'll help you."

After a little more reluctance which James saw only covered Chen's curiosity and real desire to come, the two set off on foot through the quiet streets. The hutung was very near and in a few minutes they had reached it. He pushed open the door and was delighted at what he saw. Peter and his sisters were sitting in the large central court under the light of three paper lanterns which Young Wang had strung to the great pine tree. Little Dog had brought out a teapot and some chairs, and Young Wang was squatting on his heels playing a flute. It was just as he would have liked Chen to see them. He was pleased that Louise sat most clearly in the light and that she looked soft and very pretty. He glanced at Chen and saw his gaze already turned to her. He introduced them quickly.

"Liu Chen, my elder sister Mary, my younger sister Louise, my brother Peter. Liu Chen is my best friend, as I have told you, and now let us call each other by our first names. Chen, be at home here."

Little Dog ran to fetch more chairs and his mother fetched bowls and some small cakes and a dish of watermelon seeds, and Young Wang retiring behind the pine tree continued to play softly his gently winding airs. It was very pleasant. In a little while they were laughing, for not one of them except Chen could crack watermelon seeds properly, and he was compelled to teach them. It was the first time that James had seen Louise laugh since he had met her in Shanghai. Now with a fat black seed between her white teeth she opened her red lips to show Chen that she could crack it, and Chen began to tell her how to do it. But she was laughing so much she could not.

By the time the evening was over they were all gay, for Chen revealed that he knew sleight of hand. "I had an uncle who was a traveling juggler," he confessed. "You see, the land cannot support everybody, and since we were not scholars, we had to work. But my uncle would not work, and since he had long thin hands without any bones, my grandfather feared he might become a pickpocket and disgrace an honest family. So he apprenticed him to a juggler, and my uncle grew very clever."

Young Wang stopped his flute playing, and he sat on the

outside of the circle on a piece of broken brick, and behind him stood Little Dog and his mother, and they all watched Liu Chen and laughed continually at what he could do. He took bowls of water out of the air and he swallowed lighted cigarettes and made Louise's earrings disappear.

When all had laughed until they were weary, and the moon was high in the sky Chen slapped his knees. "It is nearly midnight and Jim and I must go early to work." He rose and tightened the girdle which he wore always about his waist instead of a belt.

"I have tried to persuade Chen to come and live with us," James said.

"Oh, yes," Louise cried eagerly. "That would be fun."

"There is plenty of room," Mary said, "and we'll all live more cheaply, several together."

"I'd like it," Peter said politely. He was not quite sure, now that he had stopped laughing, what Liu Chen was. A doctor? But he spoke no English apparently. All evening, while they had slipped in and out of English, he had steadily spoken only Chinese.

"Now you see how welcome you are," James said. "Come, Chen, promise us."

Chen looked about on them, his eyes glistening in the moonlight and a half smile upon his lips. His eyes fell last on Louise. "Well, well, I will think about it," he said. "Perhaps it is too soon," he said, laughing again. "I have bad table manners and when I sleep I snore loudly."

"Never mind!" Mary said.

The end of it was that in less than a week Chen moved into the house, taking the far end room beyond Peter's. To Little Dog Young Wang said, "Now there is somebody in the house who knows what must be done. He is no foreigner like the others." And he slapped Little Dog lightly on both ears, to show him that he, like Liu Chen, would stand no nonsense under this roof.

Mrs. Liang's letter reached her children only after a month. She had not understood that extra stamps were needed for airmail and so it had been carried across the ocean by an ordinary steamship, had waited the pleasure of a clerk in the Shanghai post office who had just got himself married and was in no haste about his work, and had reached the hospital in mid-autumn.

The autumn was unusually mild. There had been no high winds and therefore little dust, and the camel caravans had not yet come in for the winter to stir up the streets with their huge flopping feet. Since it was the first really peaceful year since the Japanese had withdrawn, the chrysanthemums were large and fine. Gardeners in private houses and in commercial gardens had vied with each other to produce the sort of flowers that they had before the war. Mary had gone drunk with pleasure in them. Chrysanthemum vendors had learned that if they came to the gate early in the morning before she went to the hospital or late after she came back, they were sure of a sale. She had bought dozens of pots. The court was lined with them, and they stood against the walls of the house inside the rooms. In her own room the window was a bower with her favorites, whose curled scarlet petals were lined with gold.

She was very happy. She loved the house, and she missed nothing of what she had had in New York. The closeness of this house to the earth, its snugness under the heavy roof, the privacy of the court, the shade under the great leaning pine, all was as she liked it. Especially she liked the simplicity of life in such a house. There was no machinery to vex by breaking down when it was most needed. Little Dog's mother and Little Dog himself were excellent servants, provided one made certain of a few rules of cleanliness. Little Dog must not wash his clothes in the dishpan, and Little Dog's mother must not wash the rice bowls by running her fingers around them in a pail of cold water. They obeyed her with smiling tolerance, or she thought they did. She explained to them earnestly about germs, and argued with Chen when he simply said everything must be eaten hot.

"I am sure that Little Dog understands, and I have told Young Wang to watch the other two."

"Young Wang is a good fellow," Chen said, "but I trust my own intelligence rather than his. I prefer to eat my food hot, especially as there is still some cholera in the city."

Chen and Mary argued over many things. Both were stubborn and neither yielded to the other. Louise always took Chen's side, whatever the argument. It seemed sometimes that she did not love her elder sister, and Mary more than once went away with tears in her eyes, which she was too proud to show. After she had so left them one day, Louise said to Chen, "Mary has never let me feel free. It was really her fault, I believe, that Pa made us come here."

Chen by now knew that she had been in love with an American and that her parents had sent her away. James had told him this, and Chen had listened, his heart beating rather fast and his blood feeling hot in his veins. He was angry that an American should look at a Chinese girl, but he felt sorry for Louise. She was very young, and too pretty for her own good. He discussed with James at some length the problem of beauty in a woman, and whether it was her fault that her strength was not equal to her temptations. "This strength," Chen said, "might actually be greater than that of an ugly woman, but the ugly woman is praised for a self-control which may in fact be very slight indeed."

"I hope you are not sorry that you have come to Peking?" Chen now said to Louise. He was surprised and somewhat alarmed at the tenderness he felt was in his voice, and hearing it he became bashful.

"I don't like it here as well as I do in New York," Louise said.

"But you have a very gay time, don't you?" Chen urged. He knew how eagerly James hoped that this younger sister would want to stay here, and how much he hoped, indeed, that she would find a husband.

Louise pouted and shrugged her shoulders. "There is nothing very gay in Peking," she said.

"There are the palaces," Chen reminded her. They had spent several Sunday afternoons, all of them together, visiting the Forbidden City, and they had been invited on some picnics by Dr. Su and Dr. Kang to go outside the city walls and see the Summer Palace and the fine old monasteries in the hills.

"What I mean is that there is nothing here like Radio City," Louise said with contempt in her large black eyes.

Chen was speaking in Chinese but she spoke English always.

"I was never in New York," Chen said somewhat humbly.

"Then you never saw the best of America," Louise retorted.

"Perhaps," Chen said thoughtfully. He continued to look at Louise.

"Why are you staring at me?" she demanded.

"Because you are very pretty," Chen said. This truth came

out of him so suddenly that he was astonished and then ashamed and he turned red.

Louise laughed. "Have you only just found it out?" she asked.

"Yes," Chen said abruptly. He felt much distressed that he had spoken so coarsely and without saying anything more he went away.

Ever since that day, now some two weeks ago, he had been troubled by his conscience. Should he not tell James that he was beginning to think often of Louise? But having said this, what else could he say? He did not want to take a wife. He had some vague ideas that he had not yet worked into reality, even in his thinking. He was not at all sure that he wished to continue much longer here at the hospital. What it was he wanted to do he did not know and if he took a wife, he would be compelled to stay here, particularly if it were a young modern woman such as Louise. Yet he recognized the danger of staying near her, and of allowing his eyes to see her every day. Yet what was he to do? James would certainly demand the truth from him, and he would be ashamed to tell him that this younger sister stirred up his blood at the same time that he knew he did not want to marry her. This was coarse and he did not wish to reveal such coarseness in himself. He had always prided himself on being a better man than Su, for example, or Kang, or any of the exquisites in the hospital, and now he was feeling just as they did over a pretty girl.

When he left her thus abruptly, Louise had looked after him thoughtfully. She had waited daily for a letter from Philip or even from Estelle. To Estelle she had poured out her hatred of everything in this medieval city and all her longing for New York. To Philip she had written six heartbroken pages. Neither had answered. When the days began to slip into weeks something hard appeared in her heart. She had refused to go to school and on the pretext of keeping house she had stayed at home, idling her days away. There was nothing to do. Little Dog and his mother under the supervision of Young Wang kept everything smoothly running. The house was comfortable in its fashion, while the weather was still warm. She slept a great deal, and she borrowed books from the English library at the hospital and read novels. There was a motion-picture theater and she went there sometimes, although always with Little Dog's mother as chaperone. Chen had spoken to James about that.

Now, leaning back in the wicker chaise longue in which she spent so many hours, she toyed with the idea of making Chen love her. Then she frowned restlessly. What was the use of it? He would only want to marry her, and she did not want him. She was so cold to him for a few days that he felt relieved.

In the hospital as at home Mary was almost completely happy. That she was not altogether so was because of her sincere anger whenever one of the doctors failed to be as careful of the children under her care as she thought he should be. Dr. Kang especially she heartily hated and she quarreled with him often. He evaded her laughingly, secretly angered that she was not a nurse whom he could simply dismiss.

"Can I help it that I prefer adults to children?" he demanded one day.

"But a *child!*" she breathed at him hotly, her eyes filled with fury.

"I am a hardhearted wretch," he agreed. "I am all that is hateful. But I do not like children."

She retorted by never calling on him, and by insisting on James as the surgeon. It was her habit to dismiss from her thought and her life all whom she disliked.

One Saturday morning, as she was preparing to go home for the midday meal, she stopped at the hospital post office to fetch the mail, and there she found her mother's letter. She took it out with warm pleasure. It was thick and it would be full of news, and they could read it aloud at the table together. She did not open it, therefore, thinking that to do so would be selfish. She tucked it into the bib of her apron, and later, at their noontime dinner, when their first hunger was over, she drew the letter out.

Saturday was always a pleasant day, for they did not hurry back to the hospital and Peter had a holiday from the college. This afternoon they had planned to walk to the chrysanthemum market. James had been a little late, and she waited for him to finish his first bowl of rice. Then she said, "Here is a letter from Ma."

"Good!" James exclaimed. "I was secretly beginning to

worry, for Pa has not written at all, although he promised he would."

Chen rose. "I will go away," he said politely.

James pressed him down, his hand upon Chen's shoulder. "Sit down, sit down," he said. "Now you are our brother."

"There is no telling what is in Ma's letters," Peter said with mischief.

"I will go," Chen said, starting to get up again.

"Stay," James insisted, putting out his hand again.

Louise had taken no part in this. She continued to eat, her large discontented eyes downcast.

So Mary began to read. Every now and then she paused and turned the letter this way and that, for their mother's writing was entirely individual and she went by sound rather than by the correct way of shaping a character. Upon this Peter gave some advice. "You make a mistake to examine Ma's writing," he said. "Take a deep breath as though you were about to run a race, and then go as fast as you can, by sense only, and not by sight."

They laughed and Mary, in fun, did what Peter had told her to do. Thus she rushed straight into the part of Mrs. Liang's letter where she told of the possibility of a concubine and her determination to leave the house in such case. There Mary stopped. They looked at one another aghast. Even Louise was startled and put down her chopsticks.

"I told you I should not be here," Chen said.

"Why not?" demanded Mary. "If Pa has been so foolish—"

"I do not believe it," James said severely, but in his heart he was dismayed to find that he was not sure that his father could not be foolish.

Peter turned to Louise. "You know Pa better than any of us," he said. "Can you think of anyone who seemed—special to him?"

Louise looked thoughtful. It was painful to remember all the gaiety of those days in New York in comparison with the dullness of her present life, but she forced herself to do so. "It is hard to think of anyone," she said at last. "You know how women are about Pa. They gather in a circle so close to him—to hear what he says."

"Louise!" Mary cried. "That is not Pa's fault."

Peter grinned. "Pa never pushes them away," he remarked.

"Pa never puts his hand out to touch anybody," Mary retorted.

Louise continued to look thoughtful. "I do think that Pa used to talk more to Violet Sung than to any of the others," she said.

Peter groaned loudly. "Oh—that female!"

"Hush!" James said. "Who is Violet Sung?"

Louise cast a sidelong look at her brother. "She is a friend of Lili's," she said.

James compelled his face not to change. He had only once spoken to Mary of Lili. There had been but a few words. "Is —Lili married yet?" So he had asked Mary.

"No, she is not," Mary had replied. "And please do not ask me about her. I never saw her except that once after you left."

Since Lili had not written him one letter, it seemed folly to speak more of her. Yet he had wanted to talk about her, perhaps to heal his own heart. "I know that she and I could never marry," he had said. "We would make each other very unhappy."

"I am glad you see that," Mary had said. Her round pretty face had looked so severe that he had said no more.

Now that he heard her name on Louise's lips, however, it occurred to him that Louise was the one to whom he should have spoken. But this was not the time or the place. He put on his most elderly brother look and he said quietly, "In any case I feel sure that Pa will do no such thing. Give me the letter, Mary. I will finish it in private, and then I will write to him for us all. Of course if we are wrong about Pa, it is quite true that Ma must come to live with us."

"Then I will go and take care of Pa," Louise said eagerly. "I am sure Violet will not be a good housekeeper. She is very beautiful, in that French sort of way—she has always lived in Paris. And you know how Pa is—he's very intellectual, but at the same time he's used to the way Ma looks after him, and Violet would never put a hot-water bottle in his bed or see that his ties are cleaned and his shoes brushed." Her face was eager and her eyes shone and they all pitied her, for they knew that it was not to their father that she wished to return.

"Louise," James said, "I wish to speak with you alone." He rose and went into the other room, and Louise, pouting, followed him.

The others left behind ate what they wished for the remainder of the meal. Mary's appetite was gone, and Chen, feeling sorry for her, had not the heart to seem hungry. With his chopsticks he picked a bit of meat here and a strip of vegetable there. When she put down her chopsticks he put down his and taking the tea bowl he went out into the court and rinsed his mouth thoroughly and spat behind the pine tree. Only Peter ate another full bowl of rice, and to him Mary talked in subdued angry tones.

"If I thought Pa really were so wicked, I would declare myself not his daughter," she said. Every day in the newspapers in Peking daughters and sons declared themselves free of their parents, because, they said, these parents were too old-fashioned and did not have the interest of the nation at heart.

"Pa is very deep," Peter said. "He is full of Confucianism and all that rotten old stuff. You should hear the fellows here at college talk about Confucius. Why, Confucius was a reactionary, and he kept the old traditions alive that have made the nation weak and the people slaves."

"Don't be silly," Mary said impatiently. "You know the people here are not slaves. Everyone does as he wishes. In the hospital we have signs everywhere that there is to be no spitting but everybody spits just the same wherever he likes."

"That, too, is because of Confucianism," Peter declared, with his mouth full of steamed duck. "Hygiene and science are equally unknown here, because Confucius has held back our people."

"I don't see what this has to do with Pa!" Mary cried.

"It has everything to do with him," Peter said, filling his bowl with rice again. "Pa is a reactionary, too. That's why he doesn't dare come back to China. He is afraid someone will stab him in the back in a dark alley."

He said this terrifying thing so solemnly that Mary held her tongue for a half minute. Seeing the impression he had made, Peter went on. "I have already learned a lot at the college. I never knew before how much the fellows here hate Pa. Everybody knows him and everybody hates him. They say he is an old-fashioned intellectual, that he wants to be considered a scholar of the old school, and those old scholars are in league with the warlords, the landlords, and the government to oppress the people."

"Peter!" Mary cried. "Take care how you speak."

"I'm only saying what I hear," Peter said doggedly. "It is not pleasant to be Pa's son, I can tell you. I have to say openly that I don't agree with him."

"You ought to be ashamed of yourself," Mary said warmly. "Your own father!"

"Yours too," Peter said. "It was only a minute ago that you were talking about being independent of him."

Thus caught, Mary lost her temper. "Oh, shut up!" she said in English, and feeling the tears come to her eyes she rose and went into the court to be alone.

Chen, however, was still there. He had sat down on the bench under the great pine to pick his teeth and to consider how he could be useful. When he saw Mary he hid the tooth-pick in his hand and rose politely. With her he was always formal.

"Do not get up," Mary said. "I am only passing through the court."

"Please," Chen said, "sit down for a moment. I have been thinking about the letter. My conclusion is that your mother has made some mistake. If your father were really considering such a step he could not take it in America, where a concubine is not a recognized person. Whatever he did must be secret there. Since he is so famous, it would be difficult to keep anything secret. Moreover, I have discovered that intellectuals seldom carry on a genuine love affair. They do not have the physical strength for it. Take the doctors in our hospital—they talk a great deal about love and women when we are alone together. Actually I do not know of one who does more than talk. For them love is entirely theoretical. Your father is no longer young. He is the less likely then to undertake a love affair in practical terms. Please write to your mother and tell her that she is probably mistaken."

Mary had listened to this somewhat long speech without removing her eyes from Chen's face. Never before had she looked at him so steadily. As he stood there under the pine tree with the sunlight falling through the branches she saw as if for the first time that he had a broad honest face, a square big mouth, a large strong nose, and fine eyes. The look in his eyes was good, friendly, and true. She spoke with involuntary thanks. "Chen, you are very kind to say this to me. I think you are right. I think it is Ma who is old-fashioned and suspects Pa. I shall tell her so."

Chen smiled somewhat timidly. "Do you think with all this trouble that we must give up our walk to the chrysanthemum market?" he asked.

She had forgotten it, but now when he spoke of chrysanthemums it seemed to her that this visit to the famous market where she could choose pots of her favorite flowers and bring them home would comfort her more than anything. "I don't see why we should not go," she exclaimed. "I will go and find James."

"Wait," Chen exclaimed. "Listen!"

They stood and listened. They could hear the murmur of James's voice, and then Louise's, in earnest conversation.

"They are still in the stream of talk," Chen said. "Let us give them a little longer."

"Where is Peter?" Mary asked.

Chen smiled and pointed his forefinger toward the open door. Peter, filled with rice and duck, had thrown himself down on the wicker couch that stood against the wall and was sound asleep lying on his back, his hands folded under his head.

"Come and rest under the pine tree," Chen said to Mary. "The air is cool and fragrant. You need not talk. Let us just sit in quietness."

In the other room, a small room which they had made into a study and library, James was listening to Louise, asking a question now and then, guiding her to talk, but saying little himself. This sister of his with whom he had lived in one house for nearly all the seventeen years of her life, he now realized had been a stranger to him. He knew how she looked, and he could even remember how she had looked as a baby and a little girl. In those years she had been for the family a toy and a plaything. Mary had been serious and impetuous, always a person, but Louise had seemed to have no life except as she drew it from others. She had always sat on somebody's lap until only a year or two ago, when suddenly she had stopped of her own accord, and yet none of them had noticed it. Imperceptibly she had ceased to be a little girl and had become a young woman, and they had not noticed this, either. She had done well enough in school, but it had not mattered that she did no better. None of them expected or indeed wanted Louise to be bookish or brilliant. She had seemed al-

ways gracefully unselfish, because she was the one who brought
Pa's slippers, or filled his pipe; she was the one to fetch a book
somebody wanted or to bring in the dishes from the kitchen
and take them out again. No one noticed that she never did
any real work, even to make her own bed. Behind the façade
of prettiness and graceful unselfishness she had grown into
someone quite different, a small hard separate woman, James
now perceived as he let her reveal herself. How had they let
her grow up without heeding what she was?

"I hate it here," Louise was saying. "You may think these
crumbling old palaces are wonderful, Jim, but they repel me.
I don't like living in a country where everything is falling to
pieces and all that is worth talking about is the past."

"But, Louise, you are wrong. Something wonderful and new
is taking place here."

"What is it?" she asked doubtfully.

"I don't know," he said honestly. "But I feel it. We have
finished with one age and we are about to begin another. I
stay here because of the future, not the past. I know Pa is
always dwelling on the past, but I do not."

"It happens that I don't like anything here!" she said pas-
sionately. "I don't like the young men. I don't like the people
on the street. The children are filthy. Jim, I wish I hadn't
been born a Chinese. I wish I could stop being a Chinese. Oh,
Jim!"

Here she broke down into tears and he let her cry.

"All this," he said after a moment, "is because you have
let yourself fall in love with an American. At your age love
shapes the universe."

She continued to sob, and he went on gently. "I know, too,
what it is to love someone. I think I loved Lili with all my
heart. Even now, when I know we shall never marry, when
I think of her, or someone speaks her name, the world trem-
bles. But it does not crash about me. I know that there is a
life that must be lived happily without Lili. Just now I feel
as though for me it would always be lived alone. But I know
this is only feeling. I shall marry and have children. I want to
marry here and have my children here. And I shall never let
them leave our country. They must stay here until there is no
possible danger in their going away, because however far they
go, they will always come back, and wherever they are they

will dream of coming back and whatever they do it will be for our people. And they must marry here, too, and their children must be born here. So much I have decided."

Louise stopped crying and looked at him half angrily. "You are very old-fashioned, Jim."

"There is something here that I want," he said. "I don't know what it is, but I shall find it. And I shall find it not with this—" he tapped his brain cap—"I shall find it by my blind roots pushing down and down."

She was not stupid and she listened to him. "You are a man," she complained, "and you can do what you like."

"Now it is you who are old-fashioned," he said heartily. "A woman can do what she likes too, nowadays, even in China. You must change what you want most. Instead of grieving for Philip, who does not want you, you must keep saying that you do not want him. And after a while it will be true. Then you will be free to find what you really want."

She did not answer and he could not tell how much she believed. He gazed somewhat wistfully and with great tenderness at her lovely and still childlike face, and it crossed his mind with a sort of wondering shyness, that of all of them, only this child knew what the mystery of the flesh was. And yet she did not really know, for she had not crossed the valley and slowly climbed the hill of life to the forts of happiness. Instead, like a child she had rushed up that hill and had beaten at the gates and clamored until they opened. She did not know anything about love and its true consummation. He felt a great pity for her, because what she had done could never be undone, and whenever the true consummation came, if ever it did, it would be spoiled.

"We really came here to talk about Pa," Louise said suddenly.

"And now I do not feel that I want to talk about him," James said.

"I don't think Violet Sung would have him," Louise said. "After all, Pa is old. He looks handsome enough, especially in the evening, and of course he has a wonderful speaking voice —so deep and gentle. Women like it. But any woman would soon know he has no passion in him. And Violet isn't intellectual—not really. I mean—" she broke off.

A great revulsion fell upon James at the ease with which

this young creature spoke these words. "I daresay you are right," he said, getting to his feet.

"Ma is so simple," Louise said ruthlessly.

"And very good," James said gently.

9

Dr. Liang received his son's letter on a cool night in autumn. He had just come home with Mrs. Liang from a very enjoyable occasion. Mr. and Mrs. Li had announced the formal engagement of their daughter Lili to Charles Ting, the son of Timothy Ting who, it was expected, would be China's next ambassador to the Court of St. James. It was said that the most important ambassadorship was in Washington but the most pleasant was in London, for English life, next to Chinese, was the most civilized in the world. The wedding was to be soon, for the young couple were to go with Mr. and Mrs. Ting to England.

It had been a distinguished party. The great wealth of the Li family was joined to the high position of the Ting family, and the Waldorf-Astoria had done its best. The ballroom had been decorated with Chinese works of art belonging to both families, and two close friends of the families, both great art dealers, had lent their best pieces. Invitations were at a premium, and special guards had been hired and stationed at the doors to keep out gate crashers. The food was superb, the best of Chinese and American, and champagne and the finest teas were served. Mr. and Mrs. Li and Mr. and Mrs. Ting had stood in a row of four and with them the young couple. All the men wore formal Western garments and the Chinese women were in beautiful and sumptuous Chinese satins. The Western women were striking in décolleté but the Chinese women were equally so in their shortsleeved high-necked robes. Lili was the most beautiful girl in the room. She was ivory pale, and her black hair was cut to her shoulders and curled loosely under. Across her forehead it was cut in a straight bang, and she wore jade earrings and bracelets on her pale cream-colored arms. She was as slender as a willow, and the apricot shade of her robe melted into the warm pallor of her flesh. Her lips were flame red, and her long black eyes were dreaming. Charlie Ting stood only a little taller than she, and he kept looking at her until people began to notice it and tease him.

Dr. Liang had reached the party with carefully timed lateness and immediately he was surrounded by people. Mrs. Liang drifted away with her usual quiet and found herself a comfortable chair and sat down. She disliked evening parties, and this one was hateful to her because Lili had refused to marry James who, as everybody knew, was worth fifty of Charlie Ting who was only a playboy. She sighed and ruminated mournfully on the importance of money. Liang made enough money but they spent it as fast as he made it. She had often suggested that they should move into a smaller apartment, but he always refused, saying that the house must be worthy of its master. She was sure he had not sent any money to the children and tonight—no, perhaps tomorrow morning after he had got up—she would surely ask him.

She gazed at the crowd of people around him and wondered jealously which of the women was the one he imagined when he talked about concubines. He had said no more since that day when she had written to the children and she began to regret the desperate letter. He would be angry if he knew about it. Still—

Her eyes were now caught by the figure of a beautiful Chinese woman who had something foreign about her. Perhaps it was only that she looked too Chinese, more Chinese than a real one could look. She wore a tight perfectly fitting robe of pale violet, and pearls at her throat and in her ears. Her high-heeled slippers and handbag were gold. She sauntered near Dr. Liang and stood somewhat aloof and alone. But he saw her. How well Mrs. Liang knew him! She saw him move almost imperceptibly toward the beautiful lonely figure, and in a moment or two they had clasped hands. It was nothing but an ordinary handclasp, but Mrs. Liang instantly felt that this was the woman who had made him think of concubines. She leaned toward another stout middle-aged Chinese lady who sat silent a few feet away.

"Who is the woman in the velvet robe?" she asked.

The Chinese lady looked toward Dr. Liang. "That is Miss Violet Sung," she replied.

"I never saw her before," Mrs. Liang said.

"She is from Paris," the lady said. "But nobody knows who her family is. She seems to be here without parents."

"She is probably older than she looks," Mrs. Liang said.

"She is said to be very clever," the lady replied. "She writes verse. It is also said that she is the mistress of that Englishman."

With her little finger the lady pointed toward a tall gravelooking foreigner who was smoking his pipe and smiling at a small earnest-looking American woman whose gown was slipping from her shoulders.

Mrs. Liang looked at them vaguely. "How do these Western women keep their dresses from falling off their breasts?" she inquired.

"I do not know," the lady replied. "I have often wondered, but I do not know one of them well enough to ask such a question."

"Standing above her like that," Mrs. Liang went on, "that Englishman must be able to observe her bosom."

"Doubtless," the lady agreed.

They fell into silence and Mrs. Liang's eyes returned to her husband and Miss Violet Sung. She felt better now that she knew Miss Sung was already attached to a man, but still she disliked her. Also she knew her own old man. He would play about a woman with renewed zeal when he knew she was attached to another man, and that she was a man's mistress lent her added sweetness.

"Exactly like a moth and a candle," Mrs. Liang thought.

She decided that the time had come for her to be active and so she rose and walked rather stiffly to where Dr. Liang stood talking to Miss Violet Sung. They were a handsome pair, and others had fallen back to let them talk alone.

"Eh, Liang!" Mrs. Liang said loudly in Chinese. "I begin to grow hungry."

She came near and he looked at her. His face, so lighted with happiness a moment before, grew cold. "Ah, yes, yes," he said.

Mrs. Liang stared at Violet Sung, then she put out her plump hand. "How do you do, Miss Violet Sung," she said in English. "I have heard your name. I am Mrs. Liang, and this is my husband."

Violet Sung's slim hand touched hers. "Oh, how do you do, Mrs. Liang—we were just going to get something to eat."

"Come with us," Mrs. Liang said, "there is food enough for everybody."

"Thank you," Violet Sung said. She had a sweet deep voice. "But please excuse me—"

She smiled and slipped away, and they saw her join the Englishman and go toward the dining room. Mrs. Liang stood solidly beside Dr. Liang. "She is mistress to that Englishman," she said.

"Please don't speak so loudly," Dr. Liang replied, with too much politeness. He led her to the dining room, however, and they ate in silence, each determined to show independence and displeasure.

As the evening proceeded, Mrs. Liang found two old friends whom she had known in China and the three ladies sat in a quiet corner and told each other of their difficulties with white servants and the thieveries of American grocery clerks with shortweight scales. In China everyone took his own scales to market. There was also the problem of squeeze.

"At home," Mrs. Liang said plaintively, "I expected a ten-per-cent squeeze by my head cook. Here, although I must do my own cooking if I want food fit for my husband to eat, I am squeezed at all places. If I ask the elevator man to buy something for me, I find he has charged me half again what it costs. Even my female servant Neh-lee takes something from the laundry and the tailor."

"White people are all dishonest," Mrs. Meng said in a loud voice. She was the wife of an attaché at the Embassy and with her husband had come from Washington for the occasion.

"If the government at home would only kill all the Communists and bring peace, how quickly we would all go home!" Mrs. Chang sighed. She was a small sweet-looking woman who had been one of the famous Wu sisters of Soochow, about whom Hsiang Lin, the poet, had written three of his most popular pieces. Now, as the wife of a rich retired banker, she had almost forgotten her girlhood and Hsiang Lin was dead.

All of the ladies had children and the rest of the evening was happily spent talking about them. Mrs. Liang confided that her eldest son James was the most brilliant student ever to have graduated from his medical college here in New York, that now he was in Peking where he was to be the head of the hospital next year, and that once he had thought himself in love with Lili Li. This had been only a momentary feeling, however, for he soon saw that while Lili was very pretty, she was also spoiled and selfish, and not at all the wife for a man who would one day be famous.

"It is difficult, indeed, to be the wife of a famous man." Mrs. Liang sighed. "For example, my husband—what he will eat and what he won't eat, the sort of undershirts he will wear and he won't wear, the color of his ties, the texture of his socks, the hours when he cannot be disturbed and the hours when he must be amused, what is too hot, what is too cold; one day the bed is too soft, another day it is too hard—all these tortures cannot be imagined. And I assure you everything is the wife's fault. Look at him!"

The two listening ladies looked at Dr. Liang who was now talking with the Englishman. Violet Sung was not near either of them. She was dancing with a young Frenchman and so beautifully that people were standing about to watch.

"He looks all spirit and good nature," Mrs. Liang continued, seeing only her husband. "But tomorrow—eh! I tell you, I dread tomorrow."

"I don't think you can expect the return of Hong Kong," the Englishman was saying to Dr. Liang. "In fact, Britain needs Hong Kong rather more than before. Now that India is to be free, we must contain her, you know. And besides there's Burma free, too, also to be contained. And one doesn't know just what will happen in the East Indies—or, for that matter, in Indo-China. We're rather more responsible than before the war for the peace of the East, especially with Russia kicking Burma free, too, also to be contained. And one doesn't know about in Manchuria. And there are your own Communists, my dear sir—what are you going to do about them?"

Dr. Liang smiled gracefully. "I'm a mere man of letters," he said softly. "I don't occupy my mind with such things."

"Ah, yes, well," Ranald Grahame said, "somebody has to, you know." His eyes wandered about the room and fell on Violet dancing with that chap Pierre du Bois. He watched them in silence so suddenly grave that Dr. Liang with his delicate intuition felt alarmed. He would not like that English look directed against him! Thus thinking, he said that he must be going home, and then he drifted across the room and found Mrs. Liang.

"I'm feeling a little tired," he said. "Shall we go home?"

She rose at once, bade her two friends a warm good-by with many promises of early meetings and invitations to meals, and Dr. Liang bowed twice and they went home, stopping only to thank Mr. and Mrs. Li who were sitting side by side on a settee near the door. Lili was now dancing with the Englishman, and Mrs. Li, disapproving, could only nod her head to her guests.

"Does it not cast some reflection on Lili to dance with this Englishman who owns Violet Sung?" she asked Mr. Li after the Liangs had gone.

"Well, well," Mr. Li said, "I see Charlie is about to take her away. He will take care of her now—we can rest." Even as he spoke Charlie Ting cut in on his lovely fiancée and Ranald Grahame was left alone on the floor. He looked half angry for a moment and then he went to the bar. Violet was still dancing with the Frenchman.

Dr. and Mrs. Liang rode home in total silence and Mrs. Liang leaned her head in a corner of the taxi and dozed. When they got home they found two bills and a letter on the hall table and the letter was from James.

"It is from the children," Mrs. Liang cried with pleasure. "Come, let us read it at once."

"I would like a cup of hot tea," Dr. Liang said. "While you make it I will just cast my eyes over the letter."

She looked wistful, but being anxious to keep him in good humor, she went obediently to the kitchen, lit a match, and shut her eyes while she applied it to the gas range, jumped when there was a loud report, and then set the kettle on to boil. She longed to go back and hear at least part of the letter but she waited until the kettle had boiled and she had infused the tea. Then with teapot and two bowls she went to the study.

What she saw caused her to set the teapot down hastily on the table. "Liang, what is wrong?" she cried.

He was tearing the letter into small pieces. "So," he said, between set teeth, "you think I am about to take a concubine!"

She turned pale and sat down. "I did think so," she faltered, "and I told the children I could not stay here if you did."

"And whom would I take as a concubine?" he demanded.

"I don't know," she said. She was terrified at the look on his face and the children were not here to protect her. She faltered on. "One day you came and asked me what I thought about concubines—"

"Fool!" he said bitterly. "I was only writing an essay about women."

She looked at him confounded. "Was that all?"

"That was all."

She turned and tried to pour a bowl of tea, but her hand shook and she gave it up. "You will have to pour your own tea," she said, beginning to sob.

She made for the door blindly, her handkerchief at her eyes, but he stopped her. "Why did you think I would take a concubine?" he asked. "Have I ever been unfaithful to you?"

She shook her head, her eyes still hidden behind her handkerchief. "Not altogether," she murmured.

"What do you mean not altogether?" he demanded. "Either I am or am not unfaithful!"

She was very tired. She disliked large parties and she still felt that the Li family had slighted James and through him the Liang family. She was tired of Dr. Liang's rather windy fame, and she longed for the solid substance of money and American bank accounts. It seemed to her that the Li family had everything. She was so tired that she felt reckless and inclined to tell the truth, even though the children were not here to protect her. So she opened the gates of her being and the truth flowed out. She took away the handkerchief and faced Dr. Liang.

"What is this faithful and unfaithful? It is all in the eyes and the mind. Yes, I am your wife, and that is how I know when you are being unfaithful. Do you think I do not know the look in your eyes and on your mouth when you are being faithful with me? And when I see the same look, when you look at Violet Sung and—and any other such woman—do I not know what you are being? And perhaps when you are being faithful with me, you are in your heart thinking about Violet Sung, so that even when you are being faithful with me you are also being unfaithful with her. You are not a man with a single kind of mind in you. You are like this—" Mrs. Liang's fingers described in the air contradictory and secret convolutions, unfathomable in their contortions—"winding this way and that way and this way. I know you!"

Upon this she burst into loud sobs, put her handkerchief to her eyes again, and rushed out the door. Tomorrow morning, she told herself, she would empty the wastebasket herself in the kitchen and collect the scraps and piece together the children's letter.

Dr. Liang heard her stump upstairs and go into the bedroom and lock the door fast. He sat quite still for a moment. Then he got up and poured himself tea and drank it slowly. When this was done he took out his Confucian classics and began to read them. The book fell open of itself at the pages upon which Confucius, more than two thousand years ago, had recited his hatreds. Smug people Confucius hated, rumor mongers he hated, spies he hated, and wily persons who pretended to be honest gentlemen. He hated cockleburrs that mix themselves with corn, and dishonest men who mingle with the honest, and he hated glib talkers. He hated also the music of Cheng, because like modern jazz it confused classical music. He hated the color purple because it put to confusion the good color of red, and he hated prigs because they confused themselves with virtuous people. Then Confucius ended the list of his hatreds with these words: "Women and uneducated people are the most difficult to deal with. When I am familiar with them they become impudent, and when I ignore them, they resent it."

Dr. Liang read these words thoughtfully, smiled, drank a little more tea, and prepared himself to sleep all night upon the couch here in his study.

He took off his coat and shirt and trousers and wrapped himself in a warm old quilted robe which he kept in the closet. He took off his socks and shoes and drew on a pair of knitted bedsocks. A steamer rug lay folded on the couch and this he put over him. A velvet-covered cushion made a good pillow. But when he had laid himself down and had put out the light he found he could not sleep. He felt lonely. That was the worst of going to an evening party. One was deceived by the noise, the glitter, the appearance of friends. The home seemed cold and empty.

Perhaps he had been hasty about sending the children away. Or perhaps, indeed, he and their mother should now think about returning to China. A pleasant home in Peking with a garden, his children there, James a distinguished surgeon, the home a center for scholars and beautiful women, his grandchildren running about the rooms, he and the mother growing old, honored and respected as only in China are the old honored and respected. Perhaps he might even be the presi-

dent of a university, since he did not want to go into politics.
All this flitted through his wakeful mind. He was on the brink
of going upstairs to find his wife to tell her impulsively that
at last he was about to yield to her wishes and go to China.
He hesitated, however. He did not like to seem afraid of her
and it was his habit never to allow himself to appear reconciled in less than twenty-four hours. Before that time had
passed she was sure to make some small sign of repentance
and then he could forgive her generously. He put out his
hand therefore to turn on the radio, since he could not sleep,
and at the same moment the last news commentator was finishing his summary of the world's news for the day.

"In Peiping the day was marked by stormy protest from the
students. Five thousand university students went on strike
against the arrest of twenty-five of their fellows who had been
in jail here since yesterday for—"

He winced and turned off the radio. He could live only in
safety—that is, in peace. He had better stay where he was. A
scholar must have peace. Resolutely he closed his eyes and in
a slow murmuring voice began to recite the Book of Songs,
written hundreds of centuries ago. It was better than a bro-
mide and in less than a quarter of an hour he was fast asleep.

In the big parlor of the Li apartment Lili was listening to
Charlie Ting talk. He had a fluent tongue which spoke an
idiomatic American dialect much better than he spoke his own
native Shanghai. He sat on the divan beside Lili, his arm
thrown behind her. Her mother sat silent and dozing in a
distant corner. At the exact moment when her head fell upon
her breast he would kiss Lili. He talked on, his eyes upon the
dozing figure.

"I wish we were going to Washington instead of London.
But everybody says London is fun. I wish the food weren't so
scarce there, but Violet says the black market in Paris is
wonderful and of course we can have things sent over. As for
that, you and I aren't diplomats and we can slip over to
Paris. What say we get a little apartment there and spend a
lot of time in it? Officially of course, we'll be with the old
people, like nice dutiful children, but actually we'll be on our
own. That'll give them face and give us what we want."

Mrs. Li's head fell upon her breast and Charlie pressed his
lips to Lili's soft red mouth. She yielded with entire abandon,

throwing back her head and closing her eyes exactly as she had seen movie stars do. She always watched the screen kiss closely in order to learn the American way. Charlie's head swam a little. He also learned from the movies. It was really the only place to learn modern ways of making love, or perhaps it had better be said, ways of making modern love. There was nothing in China to teach him. He had seen a few motion pictures made in Shanghai and they seldom showed even a kiss. Chinese lovers still only talked, or at most touched hands. He had once read an English translation of an old Chinese book which had been recommended to him as spicy, and it had seemed dull indeed, full of references to flowers and dew, clouds and valleys and wooded mountain-tops, which he had not understood, and where the little feet of women were supposed to be something wonderful.

"Sure you've never loved anybody but me?" he inquired jealously of Lili.

She looked at him with large thoughtful eyes and kept silent. She spoke very little, and he was not always sure she understood his English. She did not speak very well herself— cute, of course, the way she talked, but certainly not good American.

"Tell me, darling," he urged.

"Only once I thought I maybe love a little," she confessed.

He felt a punch in his chest, where his heart beat against his ribs. "You never told me that," he said solemnly. "Who was he?"

"Never mind now," she said softly and laid her head against his shoulder.

"But I do mind," he insisted. "I can't be happy till you've spilled the whole thing."

"S-pilled?" she inquired in two syllables.

"Told me," he translated.

She smiled. "Is nothing at all, truly. When I first came here, I didn't have experience." She spoke the long word syllable by syllable. "At that time James Liang fell into love of me— I didn't understand. I only saw how it is in the movies and I was excited. I let him love only a little."

"Where is he now?" Charlie demanded.

"Oh, very far away in Peking!"

"What is he doing there?"

"He is doctor in a big hospital."

"Does he write to you?" Charlie asked.

"Oh, no!" Lili replied in a soft scream, "only once he wrote a long letter asking me to come there. But I don't answer."

"That's all?"

"All," she sighed.

There was silence for a moment. "Did he kiss you?" Charlie asked in a tight voice.

"Sometimes he did."

Charlie drew his arm away and sat apart from her. She stole a long look at him. Enough jealousy was good but too much was dangerous.

"I didn't like it," she said sweetly. "When he kiss me, I feel it is not nice. And I do not want to live in China any more now when it is so nice here and I think it will be nice in Paris and maybe London, too."

She leaned toward him and pressed the fragrant palm of her hand against his cheek. "Now I am sorry I s-pill," she whispered, "but I think I must because I must s-pill everything for you."

He resisted her for a brief moment and then he turned to her and kissed her again, long and hard. In the corner Mrs. Li began to snore slightly.

Still later did Ranald Grahame sit up talking to Violet. They did not so much share one apartment as live in connecting ones. He had, of course, to seem to live alone, and so for that matter did she. He was not the sort of man who wanted domesticity, and certainly she was not the woman to provide it. He had never married and he never intended to marry. He had explained to Violet so there would be no misunderstanding. He believed in being as honest with women as he was with men.

This honesty compelled him now to demand an explanation of her behavior. He had left the party early because he would not allow himself to make a spectacle before others. After his dance with Lili had been interrupted he had taken a whisky and soda at the bar and then he had gone to pay his respects to Mr. and Mrs. Li. They had looked at him rather vacantly as though they did not remember who he was and this had not made him feel better. He knew Chinese well enough to believe they were only pretending when they seemed not to know one. They knew everything, actually. They were much more difficult to deal with than the mercurial people of India, who were always bursting with talk and feelings, so that you knew what they were about and could circumvent them easily. Chinese contained their feelings so thoroughly that any more containment was self-immolation.

For this reason he did not believe for one moment that Violet did not know what she had done. He had waited two hours for her in a state of cold rage mounting to absolute frigidity by the time she came in, beautiful in her pallor.

He was waiting in her sitting room, and she lifted her eyes in surprise at him. "You still here, Ranald!" she said in her lovely modulated voice. She threw off the short sable coat. "Shall I make you a drink?"

He had risen meticulously when she came in and now he sat down again. "No thanks—I shan't stay but a moment. You must be tired."

She sat down gracefully weary and pushed back her hair. "I am, rather. Pierre wanted to show me a new nightclub—a French one. A lot of his friends were there. It was fun—or would have been if I had not been already tired. That was a stupid big party, wasn't it? But curiously distinguished, too— frightfully Chinese, I thought. It looked as though everybody were there, but when one examined the crowd, there was really not one person who was wrong, you know." She had the trick of speaking English in various ways, to an American as an American, to an Englishman as an English woman. She spoke five other languages as easily, one of them Russian.

But she was not a spy, nor anything indeed except what she seemed to be, a rootless beautiful woman, floating on any surface, and without depths of her own into which to retire. Frequently she did not like her life, but she did not know how to make another. Her father had been an old-fashioned Chinese, whose origins even she did not know, and she had never known her French mother. She might have become a famous model for artists, but to her they seemed dingy men, and she had continued to live strictly as a nun in her father's great dark Paris house, which was filled with Chinese furniture and rugs and paintings. What he did not want he sold and what he liked he kept. Such goods reached him in secret ways from China, and imperial treasures passed through his hands or stayed in his house.

Among ivory statues of Kwanyin Violet had grown up to look like one herself, consciously modeling herself upon the goddess. When her father died, leaving no will and no other family, she had continued in the house, except when she traveled with her servants, a married French couple who made her home wherever she was, hiring transient help in whatever country they were. Until she met the Englishman, she had had only one lover, an impetuous, jealous White Russian who had made her wretched and yet who had made it impossible for her to live alone. She had fled from him, and then she had really fallen in love with Ranald in her quiet peculiar way. She liked his subdued heat and his tenacious strength, and she liked his complete self-control. He was restful and he gave her a sense of security. She hoped that she need never have another lover, and that they could keep their relationship steadfast until they grew beyond the need of such things. By that time she hoped she could find something she really enjoyed doing.

This steadfastness she wanted above all else, and she had felt it threatened tonight by the passionate and handsome young Pierre du Bois, whom she had met for the first time. He had immediately told her that he was nobody, only a third secretary to somebody, but he thought she was the most beautiful human being he had ever seen. She had missed something of the Russian in the quiet Englishman and his quiet rather selfish way of making love.

"I quite realize that you and I have no claim on one another," Ranald was saying, "and I make no claim now." He was very straight and tall and his pale firm face was distinguished looking. "Nevertheless, I cannot have it said that you allow yourself to be exhibited by a Frenchman or any other man. I demand of my mistress the same good taste I might demand of my wife."

She leaned forward when he said this and she looked at him earnestly. Her face was molded in soft curves and flat bones, and her body was slender at the waist and more full-breasted than it would have been had her blood been purely Chinese. She smiled somewhat wistfully.

"You needn't say that to me, Ranald. All my Chinese common sense tells me I shall never find as good a man as you. There are times when you seem a little dull to me, you know, and then Pierre or somebody like him is fun—just for an hour or so. But if you don't like it, I can easily do without fun. I'd much rather be able to count on you and have you count on me."

He acknowledged to himself at once that her honesty was equal to his. "Thank you, my dear," he said with some heartiness and entire sincerity. "So long as we understand one another! All the same, I'd advise not dancing too long with one man—or too often. Or sitting too long, for that matter. You went to the extreme with Dr. Liang the last time. I didn't say anything, for I felt you couldn't be interested in him—a wishy-washy sort of man, I thought."

"Distinguished," she murmured in her Chinese way. "With us a man does not have to be brutal or strong. Delicacy is also appreciated. Subtlety is admired."

He was not without his own subtleties. "You are more French than Chinese under that smooth golden skin of yours," he reminded her.

She laughed. "That is exactly what is the matter with me," she agreed.

He allowed himself a smile. He was really very fond of her. She knew how to be comfortable as well as passionate. The combination was irresistible.

10

THE WHOLE THING BEGAN AT the chrysanthemum market on that bright autumn day when James had written the letter which had so disturbed his parents. With some delay they had proceeded with their afternoon's jaunt. Indeed they were the more impatient to get out of the house and into a change of scene, because they felt helpless. James had written the letter at once and had read it aloud to them, even Chen being there at the demand of everybody except Louise, who had kept silent, and they had waked Peter to listen. The letter was approved. James had made it short but clear.

He had written to his father: "We cannot be sure that Ma has understood you rightly. We think she has not, for we cannot believe that you would take a concubine now when it is illegal by Chinese modern law to do so and would certainly bring disgrace on the family and shame us before all Western peoples, who know your name. Our faith is in you and we hope you will set Ma right on this matter. We are only concerned because she seems unhappy. If, on the other hand, it is we who are wrong, then please let Ma come to us at once, and we will look after her. You can say you have divorced her, and then there will be no public disgrace, at least, since many people in America are divorced.

"We are well and Mary likes her work and Peter to his own surprise enjoys the university—"

Peter had interrupted James to deny this. "I don't enjoy it," he said. "But I see there is some sort of a job to be done here. In America the students only have a good time and they do not trouble themselves about other people. But here where the people cannot speak for themselves we have to speak for them. Yesterday, for example, a bunch of us saw a policeman beating a ricksha puller over the head with his club. We stopped and asked him what the man had done, and it seemed he had

170

only let the wheel of his ricksha run by accident over the policeman's foot. There was no law broken. We made the officer let the miserable fellow go."

"But that was enjoyable," Mary said warmly.

"No, it wasn't," Peter retorted. "Actually we were more angry at the ricksha coolie than at the policeman. He should have stood up for himself instead of cringing. He hadn't done anything wrong. We followed him and when he tried to thank us we gave him a couple of whacks over the head ourselves for being such a coward."

"Peter!" Mary cried. "How wicked of you!"

"It wasn't," he insisted. "I get into a rage with our stupid common people, letting themselves be run by anybody with a club or a gun. Why don't they fight back?"

"Because they have no clubs and guns," James said quietly. He folded the letter and put it into the stamped envelope, sealed and addressed it. "Come, let us go now to the market and see the chrysanthemums. Mary, you must not spend too much money."

"What do you call too much?" Mary demanded. "Today a hundred dollars in our paper bills is worth something under ten American cents."

"I mean you must not pay more than half what the vendors ask," James replied.

"We'd better get there before they double their prices to get ahead of inflation," Chen said, laughing still more loudly than the others.

Money had become a joke and yet an inflated paper had to be given for purchases, and so with their pockets stuffed with rolls of bills they had gone to the flower market. Young Wang followed behind them to bring back the flowers. Imperceptibly they had lost their American ways enough so that they yielded to Young Wang's determination not to allow the members of his master's household to be seen in public places carrying any load, however pleasant.

They all agreed afterward that there was something peculiar about the day. The air was so still and clear as to seem almost solid. People were magnified by it, faces were sculptured, eyes made bright. Especially beautiful were the faces of old people, for every line seemed drawn with meaning. Since there was not a flutter of wind, the garments the people wore fell in quiet folds, the colors even of faded blues and red were sure and rich, and human flesh looked brown and warm. Smiles and white teeth, the sounds of voices and musical instruments, all were enhanced by the silent magnetic atmosphere.

When James led his brother and sisters and Chen to the great square which was the market place, the scene struck him with all the force of a magnificent stage. An old palace stood in the background, its heavy roof of blue porcelain tiles lifted against the clear sky. Maple trees had been planted on either side of it centuries ago, and these were gold and red with autumn. Since there was no wind the leaves did not scatter, but now and again in the ripeness of the season a leaf loosed its hold upon the parent branch and fell slowly to the ground. In the leaves little children played. They were drunk with happiness, although they were the children of the poor and they wore ragged clothes. Some of the boys had laid aside their shirts and their smooth brown bodies glistened with sweat.

The whole center of the immense court was filled with the chrysanthemums which vendors had brought to be sold. They stood in pots, hundreds together, and each owner with his wife or son watched over his own. Between the pots the people walked, exclaiming and praising until they saw one bloom irresistibly beautiful when reluctantly they felt themselves compelled to buy. Rich and poor were here together, for all alike revered these flowers, imperial in their size and hues. There were even a few foreigners and among them an occasional American soldier, on leave, perhaps, and out to see the sights. Yet here, as everywhere, the poor far outnumbered the rich. They were unable to buy any flowers, they could only stand and admire wistfully, and yet seemingly without envy, the purchases of the rich. Even when a flower by some ill chance was broken off, these poor did not dare to pick it up. They watched while the woman servant of some rich lady took up the flower and thrust it into her hair. It was the same quality in these poor that had made Peter so angry at the ricksha puller, and that James himself had seen in the wards of the hospital, where they received gratefully everything that was done for them, and if one of them died, there was no thought of revenge for his death.

Mary was at his side, and her seeing eyes perceived this difference between the people. "Look at the poor ones," she said to James. "They think it is enough to gaze at the flowers."

"I wish I were rich enough to buy a pot for everybody," James said.

They had separated by chance. Chen and Peter were strolling along one side of the square and Louise was wandering at a little distance alone. Young Wang stood waiting and meanwhile watching a juggler who performed for those who might weary of the flowers.

Mary stopped beside a small group of common-looking men with their wives and children who were staring with wide eyes at the purchase being made by an old lady in satin robes and her two daughters-in-law. A steward called out the pots as the ladies pointed their delicate fingers toward the ones they wanted. The vendors sprang forward to set aside these choices. There was not so much longing in these watching eyes of the poor as a pure and dreamy pleasure that there should be in the world beings who were able to indulge themselves in the possession of beauty. A child touched a flower and his father reproved him in a low voice. "Eh, do not touch, little heart. One flower would take a seven days' wage."

"I can't bear it," Mary said suddenly. James looked down at her and saw tears flooding into her eyes and shining like crystals in the clear sunshine.

"You can't change what has been going on so long, Mary," he told her, and yet understanding all she felt. He too knew very often this catch of the heart, this sense of shame, before the poor here in his own land. Yet what could any of them do? It was all too old. One could not change eternity.

They walked away beyond the square, apart from the others. The square was set in the park belonging to the palace, and huge old trees stood in it here and there. "I am not satisfied, Jim," Mary said. "I want to go farther into the country. We're still on the surface here."

He knew what she meant but he did not answer her quickly. She had their father's fluency of words and he did not. In his own way he had been thinking and feeling deep under the surface of his daily life. Peking was now a pleasant backwater, a charming ancient pool. But it was not in the stream of life. One could live here and even do some good work and yet never reach the roots and the source.

"I'd like to go back to our ancestral village," Mary said. "I want to know what kind of people we really are. Behind Pa and Ma who are we?"

She did not ask him the question. She put it to herself and he knew this and did not reply. She went on, "Let's ask for a week away and let's go to our village. Then I think I shall know what I want. Maybe it is what you will want, too. As we are now, we are almost as far from our people as we would have been had we stayed in New York."

He was not prepared to agree altogether to this distance, but he felt that with her usual directness Mary had chosen the next step. It would be good for them to go to the village of their origins and see it for themselves. Whether they liked it did not matter. His natural caution kept him from making up his mind too quickly. "I think it a good idea," he told Mary. "Let's keep it in our heads for a few days and see if it holds. And now we must go to Louise. Do you see that she is talking to an American soldier?"

So indeed it was. Louise, wandering alone, had attracted the eyes of a fair-haired young man in foreign uniform. He had drawn gradually nearer to her, and though she had been aware of it, she had made no sign. Yet so subtle was the perception of their youth, and of sex, that he became confident that she would not repel him, and he had come to her side as she paused to admire a pale lavender flower, huge in its size, with petals curled loosely inward.

"Do you like this one best?" he had asked boldly.

She answered in English. "It's nice."

He moved to her side. "I'm in luck—you speak English! But somehow I knew you did."

"How did you know?" she asked, looking at him from under her eyelashes.

"There is something American about you," he declared, and knew that he had pleased her.

After that it was easy to talk. They exchanged names and ages, and she told him that her real home was in New York, and found that he, too, had come from New York. Here in Peking this was a miracle for them both, and they had just discovered it when James and Mary, Peter and Chen converged on them from different directions. Louise introduced the uniformed boy. "This is Alec Wetherston, and he comes from New York, not terribly far from where Pa and Ma live."

"West of the park," Alec said, smiling frankly and showing fine white teeth.

They bowed, Mary somewhat coldly, and then she said in

Chinese, "Now we must buy what we want and go home, Louise. It is nearly sunset and the best flowers will be gone."

Somehow or other their backs were all turned toward the American. But he was not to be discouraged. His face took on an indignant and set look and he said loudly to Louise, "Where do you live, Miss Liang? I'm coming to see you if I may."

She gave him the name of the hutung and the number of the house, and he tipped his hat. "I'll be there one of these days real soon," he said, and giving a full stare at Mary and Chen and James, and a grin to Peter, he went away.

"Louise!" Mary cried, "how can you?"

Louise shrugged. "I didn't do anything," she declared. But all of them saw that the look in her eyes had changed in this short time. The despondency was gone and instead there was a look of life and even of triumph. Chen turned away.

"Come," James said, "let us buy this white one, this yellow one, and this fine red one."

"I will choose also this red and gold," Mary said. She was too indignant to speak again to Louise. Young Wang came forward and argued the price with the vendor, then they gave him handfuls of paper bills and set out for home. Louise, Peter, and Chen went ahead, and Mary and James walked behind. Still farther behind came Young Wang seated in a wheelbarrow he had hired to take himself and the pots home.

They walked along resisting the pleadings of ricksha men to ride. Evening was settling upon the city in sunset colors caught in a mist of dust. Along the street near them a blind violinist walked, playing as he went. He was a tall fellow, stalwart and strong, and his whole heart sang through the two vibrating strings under his bow. The melody was joyful and loud.

"See that man," James said. "I wonder if he can be cured." He stepped a little nearer and then back again and shook his head. "No hope," he told Mary. "The eyeballs are quite gone."

The musician had passed without hearing him, walking in great powerful strides. People gave way before him, fearing him because he was blind, and had, therefore, so they thought, a special power of magic intuition.

"I cannot bear so much that cannot be helped," Mary said.

"You are getting too tense," James answered. "I think that idea of yours is a good one. We need to go back to the place from which we sprang or we'll not be able to live the life we have chosen."

Neither felt like talking more deeply. Thoughts were going very deep indeed, and speech must wait.

When they got back to the old house, from which now all weasels had fled, Young Wang set out the chrysanthemum pots and Mary ran about changing them. Young Wang watched an arrangement take form from under hands which he considered only haphazard.

"According to the rules, young mistress," he said in a lofty voice, "everything should be set in pairs and if there are two on this side the door there must be two on the other side or life has no balance."

"Thank you for telling me but I have my own ideas," Mary said without meaning to be unkind.

Young Wang said no more, but he went away to the kitchen where, without any wish to do so, he kicked Little Dog on his left ankle as he stood stirring the rice cauldron for supper, and shouted to Little Dog's patient mother, who was behind the stove feeding in knots of fuel grass, that yesterday the soup had tasted of kerosene oil, and the person who tended the lamps must not wipe her hands on the dish towel.

Mary, when the chrysanthemums were arranged to her liking, went to find Louise. She was in her own room, experimenting with a new way of combing her hair. Mary sat down, and seeing her sister's face only from the mirror, she said, "James and I have decided that we ought to pay a visit to our ancestral village."

"Why?" Louise asked. She had separated the front half of her hair into a long curling bang over her forehead.

"You look like one of those poodles that American ladies lead about on strings," Mary said. "We want to see the village so as to understand ourselves better."

"I don't need to see it for any such reason," Louise declared. "It has taken me long enough to learn to endure this place and if I see more it will be too much."

"You cannot stay here alone," Mary declared.

"Peter will stay with me," Louise said. "Peter won't want to go."

So it proved. After the evening meal they sat about the table in a pleasant mood of satisfied hunger and good exercise and Mary announced again that she and James were going to visit the village. Peter said that he would not be able to leave the university for so much as a day. He spoke so promptly that Mary knew that Louise had already prepared him.

"What is going on at the university?" James asked. He was pleased that Peter had not said any more about going back to America, even though the time would come when of course he must go for his training as an engineer.

"We have been studying our own ancient history," Peter said earnestly. He seemed to have grown taller since he came and his looks had changed. He had a student haircut and his hair, clipped close at the sides, stood upright on top. Moreover, he had stopped wearing his American clothes, except for special occasions, and he wore instead a blue cotton Sun Yat-sen uniform. James and Mary had both welcomed the change, partly because there was no hope of buying new Western clothes, and partly because it proved that Peter was changing in secret hidden ways. Just what his inner change was they did not know, but certainly he was far more serious than he had ever been in New York.

"Well, what has ancient history to do with you?" James inquired.

He himself felt years older than when he first came a few months ago. It was not only the work at the hospital and the continual presence of the desperately ill. There was something in the air of this city, so old, so stolidly beautiful, that sobered everybody. Yet this soberness was not sadness. He was actually enjoying life more than he ever had. There was time enough here to enjoy the changes of the sky, the goodness of food, the quiet of night, the frolic of kittens—for the two old cats sent by their landlord to fight the weasels had instead devoted themselves to the birth and rearing of large families. So must even the poor here, he thought, savor their days and their hours.

"Scholars in our history have always undertaken the reform of the government," Peter said in a firm voice.

James was mildly alarmed. "I hope you will undertake nothing so dangerous!" he exclaimed. "Pa put you in my charge and I would fail in my responsibility if I let you get into trouble. You might even lose your life if you go too far."

Peter looked with disgust at this cautious older brother. "How do you propose to help our country?" he asked in a lofty voice.

"I don't know," James said honestly. "But I think it would be of no help if I were killed before I could do anything at all."

Mary listened, torn between her two brothers. She admired Peter's fire and forthrightness, and yet she held James in love and respect.

"Peter, you would learn more about the people if you came to the village with us," she now said.

"The people!" Peter exclaimed impatiently. "You and Jim are always talking about the people. It is their fault that the country is so rotten. Had they had even a little energy, a little less concern only for their daily bowls of rice, things could never have come to this pass. I tell you, reform must be from the top."

There was no agreement in this argument and the end of it was that some weeks later, before the cold weather set in, James and Mary having received a leave of twelve days, set out for their ancestral village, Anming. Chen, after much indecision, stayed with Peter and Louise, but Young Wang was fearful for his master's welfare, and with many curses and threats to Little Dog and his mother, he went with James. The baggage he had prepared for the journey was formidable. Insisting that no one could sleep on the beds in the village inns, he had three rolls of bedding, a small portable earthenware cookstove, poker and tongs and tea kettle, earthenware pots and dishes, chopsticks, several pounds of tea, two loads of charcoal, mosquito nets, and foreign flea powder. The journey was by muleback and Mary wore Chinese trousers and jacket and James, too, put aside his Western garments.

The approach to an ancestral village is one of the spirit. Mrs. Liang had told her children a great deal, in her desultory way, about the village and the Liangs who lived in it. Thither she had been taken as a young bride, less than twenty years old. Her own home had been in a suburb outside Peking, although her family had come three generations before she was born from a small town in the province of Hupeh, whose people are noted for their fiery tempers and virile frames. More revolutions have sprung up in Hupeh than in any other part of China, and revolutionary leaders are born there any day in the year. They lead revolutions with equal zeal for large reasons or for none at all, and they eat red pepper with every meal. From this province an obscure ancestor of Mrs.

Liang's had become a traveling peddler of cotton cloth, had married a poor girl, and had settled with her in a cheap mud house outside the city wall. With what was left of his pack he had set up a minute shop which had prospered through the generations to something like modest wealth. There Mrs. Liang had grown up into a girl, so buxom that her father had decided to betroth her early.

How is a son betrothed to a daughter? The Liang family went to Peking often at the festival seasons, especially at New Year, when the theatricals are best, and there the girl's father, who had come to the city to buy goods, met the boy's father at a feast with mutual friends. The father, anxious to settle his daughter and hearing of a boy unbetrothed, approached the mutual friend, who approached the other father and thus the parents arranged the lives of their children.

For Mrs. Liang's family the marriage was an advance, and so fine a one that when Dr. Liang, then a rebellious student, had refused marriage and demanded that his wife know how to read and write, Mrs. Liang went unwillingly and yet of her own accord to a girls' school.

"Ah, that was torture," she told her own children in a solemn voice. "I who knew already how to do all that a wife should do was compelled to sit in a room with small children and learn letters! Only for your father I did it."

To her children she could not, of course, tell the agonies of marrying a proud, discontented, even scornful young man. So she told them about the Liang village and the gentry into which she had married.

"The Liang village, your ancestral home," she had often said, "does not lie on low ground where it can be flooded. True, there are no high mountains such as those to the north of Peking. But the ground swells and the village stands upon the swell. It is not a large village but neither is it a small one. A mud wall, strengthened with crushed brick, stands around the village. The gates are of wood, studded with brass nails. They are closed at night. Inside the gates the main street runs across, and there are many alleyways. Our house, your ancestral home, lies to the north, so that the rooms and the courts face south. There are sixteen rooms, four to each court. When I went there the old parents were still living. Ah, my mother-in-law, your grandmother, was very severe! I cried every night.

Whenever your grandfather coughed or sneezed, I was blamed."

Dr. Liang, hearing the tale often, always smiled at this point. "Yes, Liang," his wife would insist with solemnity, "it is true. You do not know how much I suffered." She turned again to the children. "When your pa's feet were cold I had to rub them warm with my hands. When he did not eat I had to find special dishes. I tell you, to be the wife of a learned man is not easy. Your father's father was, on the other hand, a large easygoing person who, while he never spoke to me, was kind to everybody. When he came into the room I must go out, but he always said to somebody else, 'Tell her not to hurry herself.' I wept when he died, I can tell you, because that left me alone with my mother-in-law. When she died, there was only Uncle Tao left. He is still there. Eh, that Uncle Tao!"

Mrs. Liang always began to laugh when she said this name.

"What about Uncle Tao?" the children had demanded.

At this point Dr. Liang always stopped her. "I forbid you to talk about Uncle Tao," he said.

When she heard this she covered her face with her hands and laughed behind them until Dr. Liang began to grow angry. Then she took her hands away and tried not to laugh but her face was very red. "I cannot tell you about Uncle Tao," she told them. "Your pa would be angry with me. But some day you must go to your ancestral home, and then you will see Uncle Tao."

"But suppose he dies first?" they had clamored.

"Uncle Tao will not die," Mrs. Liang had said. "He will live for one hundred years at least." And she would say no more.

When James and Mary and Young Wang approached the ancestral village there it was before them, exactly as their mother had told them. It sat upon a swell of the land, and the mud wall surrounded it. The north gate was before them, and inside the gate would be their ancestral house. They were tired, for they had been riding muleback all day and the roads were rough. But in spite of weariness Mary began to laugh quietly.

"What is it?" James asked. They had spent a happy day together, talking of nothing much and enjoying the soaking sunshine. Mary, feeling free and comfortable with James, had sung songs and laughed often, and yawning had all but fallen asleep in her saddle in the afternoon warmth. To hear her now begin suddenly to laugh was only part of the pleasant day. She turned her laughing face to him, for she was riding ahead of him on the narrow earthen path that ran beside the stone road.

"Uncle Tao!" she cried. "Do you remember?"

"The one Pa would never let Ma tell us about," he answered.

"Now we'll see for ourselves!"

"Unless he's dead——" Jim suggested.

"He won't be dead," she declared. "Ma said he'd live a hundred years."

She struck her mule smartly with the braided rawhide whip and he quickened his pace for a few steps and then plodded again.

"Oh, go on!" she said impatiently to the mule. "I've wanted all my life to see Uncle Tao!"

Uncle Tao at this moment was sitting on the inner side of the spirit wall, impatient for his supper. The house was in a turmoil, for his third daughter-in-law who was in charge of the kitchen had mistaken his pronunciation of chicken noodles for lichen noodles. She was somewhat stupid at best and terrified of Uncle Tao, and while lichen is easily prepared, a chicken has first to be caught and then killed and plucked and properly stewed. The sun was over the wall before the mistake was discovered and then Uncle Tao declared that he would wait until midnight before eating lichen noodles. He sat down firmly in the large speckled bamboo chair which some ancestor had once brought from Hangchow, and there he waited, smoking his yard-long pipe with ferocity. Meanwhile the lichen noodles were hastily fed to the children and the three daughters-in-law devoted themselves to the chicken, which was hiding in the cabbages.

They were further frightened to discover when the fowl was dead that by some mischance they had killed their best laying hen. The one due to be eaten was a yellow hen who laid eggs only occasionally, storing up her energy in fat. But this good hen laid at least three eggs a week and had for several years hatched and cared for flocks of chicks, whereas the yellow hen could never be kept on the nest long enough to hatch anything.

"At least let us not tell Uncle Tao," the first daughter-in-law said.

"He will find out," the second daughter-in-law replied dolefully. "As soon as he sets his five teeth into this fowl's flesh he will know what we have done."

They united in turning upon the third daughter-in-law, who, with her face quite pale, was busily getting the cauldrons hot. "How you could be so stupid!" said the eldest.

"Why did you not look at the fowl before you wrung its neck?" said the second.

Thus they cried at the poor soul, who could only tremble. "I caught her under the cabbages," she faltered, "and I wrung her neck before she could escape again."

Uncle Tao's loud voice bellowed from behind the spirit wall. "I want to eat!"

"Hurry," the eldest daughter-in-law commanded. "We can lay the blame afterward."

As one woman they proceeded to chop the favorite into small bits, that the flesh might be cooked the quicker. In one cauldron the bits were browned in oil with onion, ginger, soy sauce and a little water added, and all covered tightly under the heavy wooden lid. In the other cauldron the water simmered waiting for the noodles.

"I want to eat!" Uncle Tao bellowed again.

"Coming, Uncle Tao!" the eldest daughter-in-law cried.

Everybody called him Uncle Tao, although properly speaking his own family should not have done so, and in no other village was such a thing to be found. It had begun when he had returned to the village to live, the first of the family to do so in this generation. Dr. Liang's father had left the ancestral home to study in Peking and he never went back except to pay a visit of duty to his parents and to bury them when they died. He had been given a good post in the Imperial Court in the days before the revolution, and was thought even to have had some influence upon the young Emperor, who lived so pitifully immured by the old Empress, his mother. When the young Emperor died, the Empress exiled Dr. Liang's father because he was one of those who had urged the Emperor to reform the nation. He had been exiled to Mongolia, but he had gone only as far as his ancestral village. There, by an extravagant use of gifts to the chief eunuch, he was allowed to live and even to visit Peking occasionally and no one told the old Empress that he was not in Mongolia. Before the exile Dr. Liang himself had visited the ancestral village only at the time of his grandparents' funeral when he had been a boy of fourteen or fifteen. It was during the exile that his father had betrothed him, and there the wedding had taken place some three years later after she had learned to read and write.

When after the Empress died the family returned to Peking, old Mr. Liang as the eldest son and the guardian of the family estates had left Uncle Tao in charge. Uncle Tao was the younger brother, younger only by one half hour, for the two were twins, and all that remained alive of the once large Liang family of the previous generation. There were numerous cousins and remote relatives, who when they were without jobs and were hungry returned to the village to live, but of the Liang family direct there were only these two. They were very different. Dr. Liang's father was dignified and a scholar. Uncle Tao had no dignity at all. As a boy he had driven his parents to despair with his mischief and his waywardness, and one day when his kind mother swallowed opium because she feared that her younger son would die under a headsman's ax, her husband had firmly sent the boy away to a distant city, where a third cousin kept a medicine shop. The mother did not die, and the boy came home ten years later to his parents' funeral. By then he was a handsome red-cheeked man with a loud laugh.

Mr. Liang rather liked his younger twin brother then. He himself had been the dutiful elder, the soul of rectitude and good behavior, and the tenants on the land cheated him continually. It was too easy to cheat Mr. Liang, who believed any who told him that the rains and the excessive sunshine, the heat and the surprising cold of the season had ruined the crops.

Uncle Tao soon saw what was going on. One day after the parents were safely under the earth he said to Mr. Liang, "Elder brother, I can see that if you continue to care for our family estates we shall all be out in the fields one day with the oxen and the tenants will be sitting here in our places. You had better put me in charge. I understand all about cheating."

Mr. Liang was only too happy to agree to this. He began the series of bribes which could make it safe for him to return permanently to Peking, and fourteen months after his son's wedding, some years after the funeral of the Empress, and

after the revolution, the family went to Peking, leaving Uncle
Tao in charge. During these fourteen months Mrs. Liang had
got to know Uncle Tao so well that she laughed every time
she thought of him, while Dr. Liang grew more and more
ashamed of him.

Behind the spirit wall Uncle Tao now rolled his head round
and round and shut his eyes tight, preparing to shout yet
another time that he wanted to eat. Before he could get up his
wind, however, a tenant sauntered in from the street. He had
been at the wineshop when two strangers and a servant stopped
to ask the way to the Liang house. He had purposely mis-
directed them in order to leave himself time to come and warn
Uncle Tao that he was to have visitors.

Uncle Tao opened his eyes. "Who are they?" he asked in
his rumbling husky voice.

"They look like foreigners," the tenant replied. "A man and
a woman. The woman has her hair cut short. Perhaps they are
only students of some sort. They have no red hair, purple eyes
or chalk skin, but they look like city people."

Uncle Tao hated city people. "Tell them I am dead," he
said, shutting his eyes. In a family of country gentry known
for its courtesy and breeding Uncle Tao showed these qualities
only when he was in good mood.

It was too late to obey him. At this very moment Young
Wang appeared around the spirit wall. Uncle Tao opened his
eyes and stared at the dapper young fellow in a strange uniform. Young Wang smiled and for a moment only stood,
looking pleasant. Then he coughed to show that he was
ready to introduce himself.

"What man are you?" Uncle Tao demanded.

"I am my master's head servant," Young Wang began
glibly. "He sends me to say that he and his sister wish to pay
their respects. They are son and daughter of the Liang family,
children of the Honorable One's elder brother's son."

Uncle Tao heard this with stupefaction. So long had it been
since he had even thought of these relatives whom he had
long considered as dead in some foreign land, that now his fat
underjaw hung down. "Where are they?" he demanded.

"At the gate, Honored One," Young Wang said. He could
scarcely keep back laughter. This old gentleman, for it could
be seen that Uncle Tao was still a gentleman, was of a sort he
knew very well. Every village had someone more or less like

him. True, he had never seen any country gentry so huge, so fat, so dirty as Uncle Tao, so like the Buddha in a forgotten temple, except that now he frowned instead of smiled. His great belly creased his soiled gray silk robe and his bare feet were thrust into old black velvet shoes. Upon the vast yellow face were a few sparse white whiskers, and the head, while almost entirely bald, had a handful of hairs at the back which were actually braided into a tiny queue secured with a dingy black cord. This queue should have been cut off more than thirty years ago when the revolution came, and that Uncle Tao had kept it was a sign of obstinacy, for he hated all governments alike. Indeed long after the revolution had come and the Empress was dust he still persisted in declaring that she was alive and in ignoring the new rulers.

"At the gate!" Uncle Tao exclaimed. "How inconvenient!"

"May they come in, Honored One?" Young Wang asked.

"I have not yet eaten," Uncle Tao replied.

Young Wang began to grow angry and turning his back abruptly he went back to the gate.

"Old One," the tenant said apologetically, "it is none of my business and I ought to die, but after all they are the children of your elder brother's son who after all is the first in the next generation after you."

Uncle Tao lifted himself up by his hands on the arms of the bamboo chair and made as if he were about to heave himself at the tenant who fled at once around the spirit wall and out of the gate. There the miserable man saw the guests who stared at him in surprise. He smiled in a sickly fashion, and jerked his thumb over his shoulder. "The old man is getting his anger up," he said, hurrying away.

"I thought that old relative looked as though he had temper," Young Wang said.

A hearty red flew into Mary's sunburned cheeks. "Why should anybody be angry with us?" she demanded of James. "I'm going straight in. We belong here, too."

"Wait," James said. "Perhaps we had better go to the inn."

"I won't," Mary replied. "The inn is sure to be dirty." So saying she walked briskly up the two cracked marble steps of the gate, went under the portal and around the spirit wall where she came full upon Uncle Tao. She knew at once that it was he. No one else could have looked at the same time so absurd and so formidable. Their eyes met. Uncle Tao frowned and drew down his full lips.

"Uncle Tao!" Mary said.

Uncle Tao did not reply. He continued to stare at her.

"My elder brother and I have returned to our ancestral home," Mary said. "We are Liangs, and our father is Liang Wen Hua."

"Little Bookfool, I always called him," Uncle Tao said suddenly.

Mary laughed, and small wrinkles crossed the severe expanse of Uncle Tao's flat face. "Go away," he said. "I never talk to women."

As he so spoke James appeared at Mary's side. He bowed slightly. "Uncle Tao, you must forgive us," he said in his best Mandarin. "We have rudely come here. Yet we think of ourselves as your children also, and of this as our home. If it is not convenient for us to stay here for a few days, please tell us."

Uncle Tao wagged his head. "Where have you come from?" he asked.

"From Peking today, but some months ago we came from outside the seas, from America."

"I heard some twenty years ago that the Bookfool had gone there," Uncle Tao said with some show of interest. His thick lids lifted slightly and he began to breathe through his mouth. "How does he earn his rice?"

"He teaches school," Mary said.

"Do they pay him well?" Uncle Tao demanded.

"Well enough," she replied.

At this moment Uncle Tao remembered again that he was hungry. "I have not eaten," he announced.

"Neither have we," Mary said.

"We can eat at the inn," James said quickly. He was a little ashamed that Mary talked so much. Old-fashioned gentlemen did not like to hear women speak.

Before Uncle Tao could answer, his eldest daughter-in-law came briskly to the door. "The fowl is ready, Old Father," she called. Then she stared.

Uncle Tao heaved himself out of his chair. When he stood up it could be seen that he was a very tall man, in spite of his weight. He pointed a long and dirty thumbnail at the two guests. "These are my brother's grandchildren," he told his daughter-in-law. "It is very inconvenient that they have arrived without telling me. Now we have only the thin yellow hen to eat."

The daughter-in-law felt that this was the moment to confess the grievous mistake that had been made. Uncle Tao would perhaps restrain himself before strangers. She began smoothly, "Old Father, the gods have guided us. Doubtless they saw these two coming hither. We chased the thin yellow hen under the cabbages and the youngest one among us reached her hands under and caught and twisted her neck off before she could escape us. When she brought out the fowl, it was not the thin yellow hen but the fat red one. We longed to die when we saw this, but now I see the meaning of it. The gods know better than we humans can know. There is enough chicken flesh with the noodles and some eggs we found in the hen to make a meal for these two also."

Uncle Tao heard this and he glowered for a moment but he did not speak. He lumbered toward the door, rolling his thick lips as he thought of food. There he paused and turned to his daughter-in-law. "I suppose you have filled those rooms of my brother's with your children and that we have not an empty bed in the house."

"There is no truth in what you say," the daughter-in-law retorted. "I can brush the children away like flies." She turned to Mary. "Come in, do! In a few minutes I shall have two rooms empty for you."

"We have brought our own bedding," Mary said gratefully. She liked this honest round-faced country kinswoman.

"Ours is clean," this kinswoman replied, somewhat hurt. "We have no lice in this house."

"That I know," Mary said.

"Do not be offended," James said. "We are only glad to be under the roof of our ancestors."

"Then come and wash yourselves and eat," the woman said and she led them into the house, and Young Wang, who had been standing waiting at the spirit wall, went and led in the mules from the other side of the wall where he had tethered them to a date tree, and tethered them instead in the court to a thick and old pomegranate tree laden with hard red fruit. There he unloaded the bedding and bags and he, too, came in.

In the night rain fell. Mary heard the quiet drip from the tiled eaves above her bed and she woke. The bed was harder than any she had ever slept upon, being only a bottom of boards set upon benches. Nevertheless she felt rested. A thick cotton mattress was under her body and a clean cotton quilt was folded over her. The kinswomen had refused to allow the other bedding to be opened. "We have plenty of everything," they had insisted. "Is this not your home? Our ancestors would rise against us if we let you sleep under other bedding as though here were only an inn."

The night was so cool that there were no mosquitoes and Mary had not let down the heavy flaxen bed curtains. She lay in the darkness listening to the rain, breathing in a faint mustiness in the room, the smell of old wood and plastered walls and generations of her family. The house was none too clean—that she had seen during the evening—and her kinswomen, alas, were not often bathed. They had gathered in her room to watch her prepare for bed, cheerful, curious, friendly, and she had not the heart to send them away. They had exclaimed at the whiteness of her undergarments and at the cleanness of her skin.

"We country people," the eldest had proclaimed, "cannot have time to wash ourselves. In the summer it is true we pour water over our bodies every day. But now with storing the harvest and getting ready for winter we cannot wash every day. In winter of course it is too cold to bathe."

Why had she not resented their curiosity? It was sweet and childlike. They had admired her much, remarking tenderly upon the natural narrowness of her feet which had never been bound, upon the smallness of her waist, the beauty of her breasts. There was nothing coarse in their eyes, and there was no envy in them.

"Are you betrothed?" they had asked and when she said she was not they felt it a pity and that her parents had neglected their duty. She had tried to explain that she did not want to be betrothed but here they could not understand her. "Ah, but you must be betrothed," one had exclaimed and the others nodded. She had not argued with them. She could not, indeed. They belonged to another world.

And Uncle Tao! She laughed silently in the dark when she thought of him. He had ruled over the evening. What was that song she had learned in kindergarten long ago in New York?

"Old King Cole was a merry old soul and a merry old soul was he!" That was Uncle Tao. Fretful until he was full of food, when he had cleaned the bones of the fat hen and had supped up the final fragments of noodles, had eaten the last of the side dishes and the sweets, he became genial. Around him the family relaxed into ease and the children who had stayed far from him came near and leaned on his enormous knees and laughed at the size of his belly, reposing like a pillow in his lap.

He rumbled with husky laughter and laughing made him cough until he was purple, and while the children ran for the spittoon, his sons rubbed his back. He recovered to emit loud belches and to wipe the tears from his eyes, and everybody relaxed again.

It was James who had persuaded him to talk of the past. "Tell us about our grandfather and the old times, Uncle Tao," James said.

They had sat far into the night listening, and children went to sleep in their mothers' arms while Uncle Tao talked. Mary had listened with strange warm feelings. The crude old room with its plastered walls and cobwebby rafters, the open-faced kind of country people, these were real and they were her own. She curled herself down into the huge bed. "I like it here," she murmured. "I like it better than anywhere in the world."

On the other side of the wooden partition James too was awake. It had not taken him long to see that his kinspeople were ridden with trachoma. The eyes even of the children were red. No wonder when they used the same gray towel, the same tin basin! If he were not mistaken, the middle son had tuberculosis. And these were the gentry!

Uncle Tao, James saw, would not like any change. Nevertheless change, James decided, was what he would bring to his ancestral village. He got up out of bed and lit the candles on the table. They stood in brass holders wrought in the shape of the character for long life. He would bring long life to them with health. His heart grew soft when he thought of them, even Uncle Tao. "They're good," he thought. "They're really good people."

The next morning began with a quarrel between James and Mary. When they came out of their rooms and met in the big central room of the house there was only the eldest daughter-in-law there.

"The outside persons," she said, meaning the men, "have gone to see to the planting of the winter wheat. They asked me to excuse them to you, and to say they would be home before noon and they beg you to eat and be comfortable. Uncle Tao does not get up early. One of the children is by his door listening and when Uncle Tao begins to rumble the little one will come and tell us. It is like this every morning."

"Please do not trouble yourselves about us, good aunt," James said.

"It is no trouble," she replied. "What will you eat? Our food is poor."

"Anything," Mary said, "I'm hungry." Then she said impulsively, "Don't treat us as guests. Let us come to the kitchen with you and fetch our own food."

The kinswoman laughed and did not refuse and so they followed her through the courtyard to the kitchen. The morning was clear and bright, and alas, the sunshine showed all too plainly that the kinswomen were not careful housewives. Mary looked at James with meaning, and James said in a low voice and in English, "Never mind, most germs die with heat."

There was plenty of heat. The kinswoman opened the wooden lid of the great cauldrons, and steam poured from fragrant millet. The iron ladle was so hot it could not be touched without a cloth, and Mary, when she saw the dark rag offered to her, used her handkerchief instead. Cold salted duck eggs still in the shell were clean enough and salted fish was safe, and so they heaped their bowls and went outdoors in the sun to eat. The house was quiet, for the other kinswomen and the older children had gone to the fields and to the ponds to wash clothes, and only the smallest children played about in the dust.

"Let us go to the fields, too," Mary said to James.

When they had eaten and washed their bowls they found their kinswoman again, who now was weaving cloth in a back room. They heard the clack-clack of the loom and going there they saw her seated high in the loom, hands and feet both at work in the midst of a mighty dust.

"We are going out on the land," Mary called to her, and she nodded and took up her work again.

Now it was that the quarrel began. So near were brother and

sister that their minds came together often as one, and Mary did not doubt that James felt as she did this morning. She turned her glowing face to him as they walked along the village street. "Jim, let's come here to live!"

Along the street children stopped to stare at them and women ran to the doorways. It was not a small village and there were crossing narrow alleyways running back to the four-square walls. In all there were perhaps a hundred houses. The center of the main street was cobbled with blocks of marble smoothed by generations of Liang feet and the houses were made of home-dried brick and the roofs were of black unglazed tiles. Here and there was a poorer house of earthen walls under wheat thatch. The children were cheerful and dirty.

James looked at them and saw adenoids and tonsils, reddened eyes and bad diet. "What would we live on, Mary?" he inquired. She came to his own conclusions too quickly and though in the night he had made this same decision, it was an irritation to have her announce it first. He would not agree with her at once, without heed to the necessary difficulties.

"We belong to the Liang family, don't we?" she retorted. "I suppose we can have our food and our rooms as well as Uncle Tao and the others can."

"We could not do only with food and shelter," he said prudently. "I would want to set up a hospital and you I suppose would want to do something about these children. That takes money."

"It wouldn't take much," she said, reluctant to grant that he was right. "I could run the school in an empty room and the people could pay for books and things. It wouldn't cost anything to get these children clean, at least."

James did not answer for a moment. They had reached the south gate in the village wall, and passing through it they were in the country. All but the biggest of the children had now gone back and with a trail of not more than a dozen or so, they struck off into the paths that led between the fields. As far as the eye could reach the level land stretched brown and shorn under the brilliant blue sky. The harvests had been cut and only cabbages and onions showed green. The blue of farmers' garb showed pure and clear, and a flock of white geese, strolling across a newly cut field to pick up lost grain, lent an accent of snow.

"Oh, but it's beautiful," Mary sighed. They were speaking in English as they always did now when they were alone. In New York instinctively they had spoken Chinese when they were alone.

"Why don't you say something, Jim?" she demanded.

She looked at him and saw as she never had before how handsome a man he was. He had put on old clothes this morning, an old pair of brown trousers and a faded red sweater. He looked foreign and young, and yet his profile, strong and smooth, belonged to the landscape.

"I am thinking," he replied. "I know very well that we have to do something about this, Mary. I felt it coming over me in the night, as you did too, I suppose. It's a strange thing. We exiles coming home seem to take two directions. Some of us, like Su and Peng and Kang and those fellows and their wives and girls and all that, want to ignore and escape. Then there are those like us. We are stunned, because nothing is like what we thought it was, yet we can't separate ourselves."

"Do you suppose Pa knew it was really like this?" she asked.

"Like what?"

"Well—to put the worst of it—dirty," she said frankly. "Dirty and the children filthy and the people ignorant."

"I imagine Pa has forgotten all that except in his secret heart," James replied. "There are dirty people everywhere—plenty of them in New York."

"Jim, you know what I mean! You know as well as I do that you didn't expect so many poor, so many dirty, so many ignorant people as we've found. We've lived well enough, but we haven't lived among them."

"I don't think Pa thought any of this was his business. What makes you think it is ours?"

"Because it *is* ours," Mary insisted.

"I am not so sure," James replied.

Here the quarrel began. While Mary argued, James resisted, until at last in a passion she stood her ground and refused to let him walk another step.

"But why are you so angry with me?" he protested.

"Because you know, and I know that you know, that you are not saying what you really think," Mary said loudly. A flock of crows that had settled in the field by the road looked up startled and with a great flutter they whirled away.

"You've even scared the crows," James said, laughing.

"Jim!" she cried, stamping her foot in the dust. "Answer me!" But James did not answer, and throwing him a flashing look Mary walked ahead.

Now they reached a wall temple to an earth god, a tiny dwelling scarcely taller than Mary was herself. Within, looking through the opening, they saw the little god and his wife. Upon the low surrounding wall Mary sat down and James sat beside her. Behind this temple were grave mounds.

"Our ancestors, I suppose," James said. "They put them anywhere in the fields, apparently."

Mary looked at them only for a second and returned to her quarrel. "Jim, if you don't come to live in the village, I shall come alone."

He looked grave at this. "My dear, I am sure you would," he said. "But I am not saying I won't come. I am only asking how—and perhaps when—and with what. Merely to come here to live among ignorant people might make us ignorant, too. We have to think how we can make our lives here. We don't want just to bury ourselves—with our ancestors."

His gravity, his gentleness, subdued her. She sat still for a long moment, curbing her eager thoughts. He was right. There was a world of difference between themselves and these kinfolk, centuries of difference, space and time crowded together into a single generation.

James went on. "I want to talk with Uncle Tao, first of all. We would have to get his help, you know. If he were against us, we could do nothing. He'd have to understand."

"Do you think he understands anything except his food and his sleep?" Mary demanded.

"Underneath that mountain of flesh I think he understands a great deal," James said.

The quarrel had faded away like a mist but she could not quite let it go. "As long as I know you are thinking about it," she said, "as long as I know you really want to come back to our people and not just drift along with those Sus and Pengs and Kangs and people like that—"

"I don't want to drift," James said.

"As long as you are thoroughly discontented with everything, as I am," Mary went on with a hint of laughter.

"I am quite discontented," James replied.

Mary laughed. "Then let's enjoy ourselves." She got up and

peered into the tiny temple. "Poor little gods," she murmured. "They look terrified!"

When they got back at noon Uncle Tao was awake and walking slowly up and down the courtyard, digesting his late breakfast. The harvesting being over, the three meals of working days had been cut to the winter schedule of two, and there was as yet no preparation for the next meal. On the table in the main room were a plate of persimmons and a square sweetmeat dish divided into compartments which held watermelon seeds, pumpkin seeds, and some stale sweets.

"Eh, eh," Uncle Tao said negligently when James and Mary came in.

"How are you, Uncle Tao?" James asked.

"Busy, busy," Uncle Tao said, putting his fat hands to his stomach. "Where have you been?"

"Out in the fields," James replied. "But we saw none of our kinsmen."

"They went to a distant part of our land," Uncle Tao said carelessly. "I sent them there to measure seed wheat. These old men of the earth will cheat the landlord every time if they can."

"How do you decide the rent?" James asked.

"We take half," Uncle Tao said. Now that he saw there was to be some real conversation, he sat down in his bamboo chair which no one else used. "Half the seed we furnish, half the harvest we get. The land is ours, the oxen are theirs. They have the easy work, we have the hard."

"How is that, Uncle Tao? You look easy enough sitting here."

"Ah, you don't know the truth of our life here," Uncle Tao said with vigor. Now that he was awake his huge body was responsive to his mood. His large head stood round and bald upon his wide shoulders, and his brown neck rose thick from his unbuttoned collar. He never bothered with buttons. His gray robe was held about him by a wide soft girdle of old silk and from the long sleeves his big hands moved in unison with his talk, gesturing with peculiar grace. These hands were smooth, though dirty, and the knuckles were dimpled.

"All you young people," he said in a loud voice, as though addressing millions. "You do not understand. You think the old men of earth are all good and honest. Nothing is less true.

I tell you these sons of hares who rent our Liang land, they are thieves. They sell the seed wheat and then complain of a poor harvest. They harvest early and sell our part of the harvest. I and my three sons, we trudge everywhere watching and weighing and measuring. Now when the seed is given we must see that it is sown. When it comes up we must judge the harvest month by month. At harvest we must be everywhere at once, lest the grain be cut before we can know how heavy it is. Pity the landlord, pity the landlord!"

Young Wang had come in during this talk, and not daring to break in, he had stood waiting. When Uncle Tao said this his face grew red and the veins on his smooth temples stood out. James saw this and understood it very well. Young Wang belonged to the men of earth. He turned aside to hear him. "What do you want?" he asked.

Young Wang began without noticing Uncle Tao. "Master, I see you are very well off here. How long do you stay?"

"Seven or eight days, if Uncle Tao will allow us," James said.

"Stay, stay," Uncle Tao said indulgently.

"Then it is long enough for me to go and visit my old parents," Young Wang said. "I ought to have gone long ago, for I left them in the city after the floods. The water will be gone now and they will be back in their houses, if these have not melted into the water. If so, they will be making new ones. They have a very evil landlord who will not help them, and I must go back to see that he does not compel them to sell the very oxen who must plow the land if all are not to starve."

James knew well enough that Young Wang said this for Uncle Tao, and he said at once, "Do go, and we will plan to leave here on the eighth morning from now."

"I go then," Young Wang said, and without more ado he went.

Uncle Tao had shut his eyes during this interruption and seemed to be asleep. Now he opened them and took up where he left off. "Had it not been for me," he announced, "the Liang family would have no place on the earth today. Your grandfather, my older brother, was nothing but a scholar. He understood no more than a child about life. Full of good talk he was, and anybody could cheat him by agreeing with him. I suppose your father is the same way."

"Perhaps," James said.

"How does he make his real living over there?" Uncle Tao inquired with lively interest. "School teaching cannot fill the stomach. I send him so much of the rent each year, but I suppose it is also not enough."

"You send him rent?" Mary exclaimed.

"His share," Uncle Tao said, without looking at her. He never looked at any female creature in the daylight. "Before New Year each year I divide everything in exact proportion, to each his share according to his place in the family. Thus your father gets what my elder son gets in the same generation."

"Pa never told us that!" Mary exclaimed.

"Eh," Uncle Tao said. "Now why not?"

"I suppose he didn't think of it," James said reasonably. "What he earns at teaching is a good deal more."

"Is it?" Uncle Tao exclaimed, his eyes lively. "Does he teach the foreigners how to read and write?"

"They know already," Mary said.

"Not our language," Uncle Tao replied.

Mary seized upon this change of subject. "Uncle Tao!" she said, firmly.

Uncle Tao looked at the ground. "What now?" he asked.

"Do you believe in reading and writing?"

"I can read and write," he replied.

"But for other people," Mary insisted.

"Not for women," Uncle Tao said firmly. "When a woman gets her belly full of characters there is no room for a child."

"For men, then," Mary said, swallowing her pride for the moment.

"It depends upon what men," Uncle Tao said. "For men like me and my sons, certainly we all read and write. Not too much, you understand, but enough."

James looked at Mary with warning in his eyes. "Proceed slowly," these eyes advised her. "Leave it to me," they said. She rose. "I will go and see if I can help in the kitchen."

Uncle Tao looked slightly in the direction of her voice. "Very good," he said, "very right, entirely proper."

He waited until she was gone and then he looked at James. "You must get this sister married quickly," he said in a solemn voice. "To allow a female to run hither and thither is tempting the devils. Come, come, what have you done?"

"She wants to teach school," James said boldly.

"Now you see," Uncle Tao said triumphantly. "I told you —no reading and writing for women. None of my daughters-in-law can read. I insisted on that. Your father, I remember, would have your mother read. Well, I suppose she runs about everywhere. Never at home, eh? How many children?"

"Four of us."

"Do you teach school, too?" Uncle Tao asked.

"No, I am a doctor."

"A doctor!" Uncle Tao exclaimed. "A cutting doctor or a medicine doctor?"

"Cutting," James said, "although sometimes I treat first."

"Cutting!" Uncle Tao said darkly. "I don't believe in it. I have never seen anyone who was cut who lived."

"Have you ever seen anyone at all who was cut?" James asked, smiling a little.

"No," Uncle Tao said flatly. "I don't believe in it."

He yawned, fell silent for a moment, and then began to rub his belly slowly round and round with his right hand.

"What is it?" James asked.

"Nothing, nothing," Uncle Tao said. But without opening his eyes he added somewhat anxiously, "There are times when I could think I was a woman about to have a child. Being a man, it is impossible."

He continued to sit with his eyes closed while he rubbed his belly and James waited.

"Eh, isn't it?" Uncle Tao said suddenly opening his eyes.

"I think it is impossible," James said, trying not to laugh.

"Then what is here?"

Without further warning he pulled at his girdle, and jerked open his robe. His enormous belly sat revealed. "Feel this," he told James.

James bent over him and pressed the huge soft mass.

"Do you feel something like the head of a child?" Uncle Tao asked anxiously.

"Yes, but it is not that," James said gently.

"What is it?"

"A lump and it should not be there."

"Crabs," Uncle Tao said dismally. "I ate too many crabs one year, and soon afterward this began."

"It is not crabs."

"Then what is it?"

"I do not know. I should have to look at it through a special glass."

"You can see through me?"

"Only partly."

"And then what?"

"I should probably have to cut," James said very gently.

Uncle Tao wrapped himself up again. "I don't believe in cutting," he said. "Let us talk of something else. The men of earth, for example."

But James was not listening. Everything seemed to fall quite clearly into place. The future, which had been confused this morning when he talked to Mary, came near, and he saw it step by step before him. Uncle Tao, with a tumor in his belly, would lead the way and without knowing it.

Young Wang came back after seven days and in unwonted silence he packed the bags and retied the bedding which had never been used and brushed the mule which he had ridden south to his own village and reclaimed the other two which had been at the inn stables while he was away. The next morning he appeared soon after dawn, for the return to the city, and James and Mary were ready for him. Everybody in the house had got up to see them off and to cry out invitations for their return. Even Uncle Tao with heroic effort hauled himself out of bed, and tousled and bleary he staggered to the door to nod his head and murmur vaguely, "Eh, eh, meet again—meet again!"

As soon as the two had gone he fell upon his bed to slumber. Sleep was the one way in which he could escape the horrible fear which now sat in his heart every waking hour. The young man who was his grandnephew had said he must be cut! He thought of this for one instant before he fell asleep and the withers melted in his enormous mass. Then he spoke stoutly to himself. "Whatever is in me is mine, and no one can take it away from me unless I allow it." Upon this momentary comfort he was carried down into sleep again.

Dawn was breaking over the village as they left it. The sky was illuminated with many small golden clouds, for the sun had not yet come over the horizon. The street looked fresh in the new light, and the smoke curling from kitchen roofs was purple. Children's voices were cheeping behind doors, like waking chicks, and only the white geese were up and about their business. They came home at night, as decent as good men, and took shelter under the walls, but at dawn they bestirred themselves and walked in dignity and silence to the fields, in contrast to the noisy quacking ducks who went anyhow and kept no ranks. Between geese and ducks there is no communication.

The village gate was already ajar and James had to bend his head, he sat so tall upon his mule. Outside the wall the land lay with that pristine glitter of dew which is gone as soon as the sun rises full. The fields were richly brown, for in these days they had been plowed for winter wheat, and the willow trees were golden about the villages which dotted the plain.

"Look at these villages," James said, "we can reach fifty of them within a day's journey."

"We will begin with our own," Mary said.

They had talked very little in the last days they had spent in their ancestral house. Both were fermenting with ideas, and until these were clear they kept themselves separate. Mary had joined in the life of the kinswomen. She had worked with them and sat with them, answering their constant questions about herself, her clothes, her parents, her education, about America and all the strange folk there and their strange ways. Wherever they had got it, the women had heard something of the outer seas and the farther lands, but their information was woven upon dream and myth and imagination. Thus they thought that in the outer lands children were born with white hair which grew dark with age, and they thought that men and women did not mate and produce children in human ways— that is their own ways—but in some unaccountable mystic fashion. The food in the outer lands horrified them, for they had heard that it was raw meat and cow's milk which disgusted them. They had heard that the people were covered with hair from head to foot and that their skin was of all colors and that their eyes were blue and purple and yellow like the eyes of wild beasts. With the passion of one born to teach Mary told them what she thought was the truth and in her turn she asked them questions. She learned that the elder daughter-in-law alone dared to speak to Uncle Tao, and then only since the death of Uncle Tao's wife, a mild gentle small woman whom everybody had loved and who had disobeyed Uncle Tao in everything without rousing his anger.

"Ah, Uncle Tao's wife, our mother!" the middle daughter-in-law sighed. "How good she was! She was even famous as a mother-in-law. Some women fear the mothers of their husbands, but we did not fear her. She thought of us as her own flesh and blood and she would tell us not to work too hard, and so we worked the harder."

The eldest daughter-in-law laughed aloud. "She was too wise for any man! Whenever Uncle Tao scolded any of us she would resign from her position as his wife. 'Tao!' so she called him. 'Eh Tao, I am no use to you. I see that I cannot manage your house. I beg of you to get yourself a good strong concubine and I will retire and let her control everything.' So she said."

"Did he never do it?" Mary asked. She found undying interest in these small affairs of which the kinswomen told her.

"He?" the daughters-in-law cried in chorus. They fell into fits of laughter.

It was a merry household, and the fear of Uncle Tao's anger only added liveliness to the day. He was a god under his own roof, and his wrath, while it cast them into terror, made them proud also, for they believed there was no other like it in the world. Even his sons boasted of their father's rage and fatness, of his bellow and his roars of laughter. They loved him well, while they cherished their fear of him and he gave direction to their lives.

All this Mary saw, but she herself could not like Uncle Tao. "For example, Uncle Tao," she now said to James as their mules jogged along the narrow footpaths to the main highway to the city. "What is he but a mass of ignorance and dirt? I shall not be thwarted by him. He despises women but I despise him. I shall go my own way and do what I plan to do."

"What do you plan to do?" James asked, smiling at his downright sister. She made a picture anything but formidable. Her short hair was blowing in the sharp autumn wind and her cheeks were red and her eyes bright and dark. Her profile, against the horizon of earth and sky, was young and exquisite and she held her small body lightly straight upon the shambling bony mule.

"Whatever you do, Jim," she said briskly, "I am going back to the village to live."

"On what?"

"On Pa's rents," she said calmly.

James was mightily amused at this but he kept his face grave. "How do you think you will get the rents out of Uncle Tao?" he asked.

"I shall tell Pa to write to him that I am to have them. If Uncle Tao doesn't listen to Pa, I will make him miserable until he listens to me. After all, I belong to the family and I have a right under that roof."

"Until you are married," James reminded her.

"I shan't marry."

"You are declaring eternal war against Uncle Tao," James said.

"Yes!"

They pulled their mules aside for a few moments, for they now met a long line of farmers carrying their grain to the city. It was heaped into baskets made of bamboo, and carried at either end of a limber wooden pole. Although the air was cold, the men were already sweating and they had thrown open their cotton jackets, showing brown bodies rippling with muscles.

"We are a handsome race," James said as he watched the men.

"We are wonderful," Mary agreed. They exchanged a long look of pleasure in themselves and then they went on again.

"You know," James said thoughtfully, "Uncle Tao is also wonderful in his way."

"He likes you because you are a man," Mary retorted.

"Well, he is a man, too, and perhaps in the bottom of their hearts men do like men best," James said. A glint of mischief showed itself in his eyes. "So do women like men best, Mary, and here is the root of the quarrel between men and women."

She rejected this lapse into theory. "Uncle Tao is more of a mountain than a man," she said heartlessly. "What you found in that lump of meat I cannot imagine. I never heard him say anything worth hearing."

"He did not talk when you were around," James replied.

She refused to be moved. "Jim, please don't pretend you really like Uncle Tao. You know that he will be your chief obstacle and enemy when you go there to live."

"Who said I was going there to live?" James demanded.

"I know you are. You may say even to yourself that you haven't decided. But you have. I can feel it in you."

James yielded gracefully. "You are right, Mary, though I

don't know how you know. I am going back there to live out my life. I don't know how or when. I scarcely know why. But I am."

All Mary's good humor returned. "And how do you think you will make your living?" she asked with loving sisterly malice.

"I don't know. I haven't gotten that far yet. But I have an idea that somehow Uncle Tao will help me."

Mary shouted with laughter. "Oh Jim, oh Jim!" she cried. "Jim the Silent Dreamer!"

It was night when they drew near to the house in the city. The hutung was quiet, for rain had begun to fall, the cold rain of autumn, and children were inside their homes. At the gate they had got off their mules stiffly, first shouting for Little Dog to come and fetch the baggage, and Young Wang led the beasts away to the owner. Little Dog came running and then Peter and Louise and lastly Chen came out to meet them. Chen had been somewhat distressed when he was left in the house with Louise, having only Peter to be a third, but they had laughed at him for being old-fashioned. Nevertheless he had been very scrupulous and so busy at the hospital that he had not been alone with Louise while James and Mary were away. A strange thing had shown itself at the hospital and he was disturbed by it and he was glad to see James home again. But he said nothing of it now.

"Eh, you two," he said amiably, his spiky hair standing on end about his big honest face, "you've come back safely from your ancestors, have you?"

"You both smell of garlic," Louise declared.

Peter stood grinning, his hands in his pockets. "I thought maybe you wouldn't come back," he suggested.

"We'd have to come back for a bath if nothing else," James said gaily.

They walked together into the house. A rich smell of cooking hung about the rooms. Little Dog's mother ran out, her face black with soot. "Oh, Heaven, let it be that you have not eaten yet!" she cried. "I have the meal ready."

"We have not eaten," Mary replied. "But wait, good mother, until we have washed ourselves."

"Little Dog shall run to the hot water shop quickly and buy hot water," the woman promised.

So it was that in a very few minutes the hot water was brought in great steaming buckets and poured into the glazed pottery tub in the washroom. This was for James, and Little Dog's mother fetched a wooden tub and put it in Mary's room for her, so that the meal need not be held back too long.

How good was the hot water, and what a blessing the soap! "When I get to the village," Mary mused in the midst of this comfort, "I shall make a bath house first of all for the women."

In his pottery tub James sat cross-legged like a smooth young Buddha. "A bath house for the men," he thought. "That will be the first thing for the village."

They came to the table with monstrous appetites, eager to tell everything, and to hear all. "First to hear," James said, "and then to tell."

But it seemed there was not much to hear. Louise was very silent. Questioned, she said that she had read some books Chen had brought her from the hospital library, and she had gone to a party the new Mrs. Su had given, where there was dancing—the first time she had danced since she left home, as she persisted in calling New York. Neither James nor Mary corrected her. Home for them was now becoming the brown walls of the village rising out of the brown plain. They could not imagine Louise there.

"I want to talk to you alone about the college," Peter said abruptly to Jim. "There's stuff going on there that I don't like."

Chen made a brief report of the hospital. "The healthy season is coming in, and we have had no more cholera. We've had the usual number of childbirths already half ruined by stupid old midwives, and Peng is threatening to resign because foreign auditors want to examine the books he kept during the war." He hesitated and then went on, "Later, Jim, when you have time, I want to tell you something."

"Why have each of you secrets?" Mary demanded.

"I have no secret," Louise said quickly. She glanced at Chen who did not look at her or speak, and Peter paid no attention. His appetite was always excellent. He had his bowl to his mouth, and he was ladling in a combination of rice, gravy, cabbage, and duck livers which he had arranged in the exact proportions he considered perfection.

And James, sensitive to some entanglement here which could not now be unraveled, began to speak of the village.

"I don't know how to explain to you Uncle Tao—" He began to laugh and everybody laughed with him as he went on.

Sitting around the table lit by candles they all listened to him and Mary did not interrupt. When this tall brother of hers set himself to a task, he did it supremely well. Chen was deeply moved. He opened his hands upward upon the table. "All that you say is as known to me as the palms of these two hands," he said when James had finished. "Yet I never understood before that it had anything to do with me."

"We can do all that I have said," James went on, "but we must move in ways that seem slow at first. The people must be with us."

"Slow!" Peter cried. "So slow that we'll all be dead before we see the change."

Only Louise was not moved. Her face was set in its lines of prettiness. "It all sounds horrible," she said and wiped her hand daintily on the napkin, which to the astonishment of Little Dog's mother she insisted on having fresh at every meal.

Alone that night for a few minutes after the others had gone to their rooms, Chen said to Jim, "Do you remember the child that was born while you were away in Shanghai, whose mother died, to my shame, because she was my patient?"

"The one I gave into Mary's charge?" Jim asked.

Chen nodded. "Rose came to me a few days ago and asked me to come and see him. It is a boy, you know."

Jim nodded.

"That child," Chen said with peculiar emphasis, "is not all Chinese."

"No!" James cried. "But you said the mother—"

"The mother was certainly Chinese. She was a young girl— not a student, not a girl of good family, but one of these young moderns—you know them, Jim. She had left her family. I supposed she was a prostitute but she was quite clean and the child is healthy. Well, that's not too strange. But—" Chen pressed his lips together.

"Go on," Jim said. "How can there be anything you fear to tell me?"

Chen said, hesitating very much and turning red. "Here it is, then. After the dance, late that night, Louise went to see this child."

"But why?" James exclaimed.

"I don't know why," Chen said. "She came alone and she asked the nurse in charge to show her the child. She used your name to get in."

11

THE WINTER WAS DRAWING ON in New York and for Dr. Liang the best part of the year was at hand. Now that he had got used to a quiet house he was beginning to like it. Moreover, the presence of the children in China gave him protection. When some of his enemies, and he was always pained by their number, mentioned their surprise that he continued to stay abroad when his country so obviously needed all well-educated citizens, he could smile rather sadly and say, "I am supporting four young citizens now in China. Somebody unfortunately has to pay the bills, and with inflation what it is, this is done more easily with American money than Chinese."

The fact that he had not yet sent them any money was beginning to weigh on his conscience. Neither he nor Mrs. Liang had ever mentioned the concubine quarrel again, but she had asked him several times whether and when he was going to send the children money.

"Even though James and Mary have jobs, I am sure it is not enough," she said one day with the stubbornness natural to her. "Besides, we are the parents and we should support the younger ones at least enough to pay for their rice."

"Certainly you are right," he replied with unusual politeness to her. "As soon as the lecture season begins, I intend to double my engagements and send them a generous amount."

"Meantime?" she asked.

"Well, well," he said impatiently.

The end of this was that Mrs. Liang began another private savings account. One she already had. She had begun it aimlessly, merely for her own comfort in case she should decide someday that she could not bear America any more and that even respect for a husband was not everything in a woman's life. The money was not deposited in a bank. Instead she had put it thriftily out to loan in Chinatown, and Billy Pan managed it for her, as a favor to the famous Dr. Liang, who knew nothing about it. Each month the capital increased with pleasant regularity. Mrs. Liang was sometimes a little angry because the interest rate was low, but Mr. Pan declared that he could not break the American law, which could be invoked if those who borrowed felt themselves ill used.

"It seems strange that I cannot lend my own money on my own terms," Mrs. Liang said.

"Well, you can't except in China," Billy Pan said flatly. He did not propose to break American law, however absurd. America was still greater than the Chinese Dr. Liang.

"It is another way of stealing," Mrs. Liang exclaimed. But she did not withdraw her accumulating capital.

The second savings account she merely put into a box which she kept behind the towels and sheets in a closet. She thought of it as the children's money, though she had no idea how to get it to them. Had Lili married James it would have been easy to ask Mr. Li to exchange the American dollars for Chinese ones in Shanghai, but the Liangs now saw very little of the Li family, who, it was said, were about to join Lili in England. Yet the important thing was to have the money in hand. Mrs. Liang got it by charging Dr. Liang more for everything she bought. This, she told him, was the high cost of living, and if he looked at American papers, he could see for himself that prices were rising every day. She herself followed the price lists closely and made a new rise whenever they did, at the same time continuing to inquire of Dr. Liang when he was going to send the children some money.

Thus, Mary's letter could not have reached them at a better time. It was written to them both. After some thought Mary had decided not to try to explain any of her feelings about the village or even about Uncle Tao. She would merely say that she and James thought they ought to do something for the ancestral village, where the people were very poor and Uncle Tao himself was sick and James said he needed an operation. "We think of going there to live and to see what we can do for them," she wrote. "It made me sad to see the children growing up with no chance to go to school and no one even telling them to wipe their noses. Really, Pa and Ma, you should have told us what things here are like, instead of letting us think that our country is one beautiful cloud of Confucianism. But maybe you have been away so long that you have forgotten."

Her father was displeased with this. "I don't see what Confucianism has to do with wiping children's noses," he said.

"That is not what she is really talking about," Mrs. Liang said. "So Uncle Tao needs to be cut! Eh, I hope James won't do it. It is much better to let Uncle Tao die naturally. Sooner or later it must happen. Why prevent fate?"

"When you talk like that I wonder whether you have learned anything in all these years you have had the advantages of America," Dr. Liang said angrily.

"Please excuse me," she replied, having learned submission in small matters.

Dr. Liang read on. "Now you will wonder what we can live on," Mary wrote. "We have thought that all out. Food and room we can have under the ancestral roof. But I need money if I am to have a school, and James will need some too."

Here Dr. Liang paused and looked severely at his wife. "Why should she need money for a school when the government sets up schools everywhere free?"

"You know they would not put a school in that dead little village of your ancestors," Mrs. Liang exclaimed. "Please go on."

Dr. Liang hesitated, decided not to answer and read on, "Uncle Tao says he sends you some money every year for land rent. Pa, I want this money. Put into American money it will mean very little to you. It is so little that you have never even mentioned it to us. But in the village it will be enough for me. And there is something good in using that money for the ancestral village. It comes from our land. I feel it is right to keep it here."

At this point Dr. Liang became really annoyed. "I cannot understand why Uncle Tao said anything about that money," he said. "It is no one's business but mine."

Mrs. Liang's surprise was great indeed. "But Liang, you have never told even me you had this money!"

"It is too little to think about," he declared.

"So you kept it for some use of your own," she said with evil suggestion. She knew to a penny what he earned and while he signed all the checks she studied the checkbook and could foresee the balance at the end of every month. She had never seen any notice of the deposit of rent funds from China.

"I buy a few books," he said gently.

"If that is all, then certainly you can give our children so little a sum," she retorted. "I will write and tell them that you will do so and they can show the letter to Uncle Tao."

"Uncle Tao will scarcely accept your letter," Dr. Liang reminded her.

She immediately went into tears, and this destroyed his peace. "You know I cannot do the work which supports you, let me say, as well as myself, if you cry and make the house miserable," he told her.

"Let me go home!" she sobbed.

The scene proceeded according to old pattern, and the end of it was that Dr. Liang sat down and wrote a letter to James, which he was to show to Uncle Tao, asking that the rent funds be given to his son. "I have been stirred by my daughter's letter," Dr. Liang wrote. "She tells me that the village needs repairs and so on. I make my contribution thus to our ancestral family. Let the land keep its own."

Mrs. Liang did not wholly approve this way of putting it. "I hope Uncle Tao does not think that you mean for him to keep the money," she said, taking the letter.

But Dr. Liang would not change what he had written. It sounded too well.

Nevertheless the whole transaction made him melancholy. He went into his study and shut the door and sat down in a deep leather chair and held his head in his hands. He felt harried and confused. His privacy was invaded. He was vaguely ashamed that his children had seen the village as he was sure it must be now. All these years since his childhood had passed doubtless without any repairs being made. Centuries had passed over the village and each had left its mark. No one had made improvements. As young men in the Liang family grew up they had simply gone away if they did not like the village and its ways, even as he himself had gone away. The ones who had stayed were the ones like Uncle Tao, who, although they belonged to the gentry, were very little above the coarse peasants. Those peasants! How he despised them in his heart! Stubborn, strong, fearing no one, there was none to control them. His own parents had been afraid of them. He remembered his mother pleading with his father to allow the peasants lower rents and larger sharing of the harvest, lest in their anger they come against the Liang house and destroy it. Such things did happen in other ancestral villages. Were the landlords firm in maintaining their just dues, the peasants could and did willfully come against them with hoes and mallets and clubs and axes and while they seldom killed anyone, they would break valuable furniture and slash silken bedding and rip satin curtains and hack and hew walls and beams. Once this had happened even in the Liang family and he could still remember that when he was a little boy his own paternal grandmother had paused on the way home from the funeral of an old cousin, and she had pointed with two delicate fingers to a deep ditch beside the Liang burying ground.

"There I hid once, when your father was a child," she had told him.

"Why did you hide, Grandmother?" he had asked.

"The men of the earth rose against us," she had said.

"Why?" he had asked, and even as she spoke a dart of fear ran through his bosom.

She replied coldly, "Your grandfather wanted to raise the rents. We had many sons and their weddings came close together and we could scarcely pay for everything that had to be done. Of course men of earth understand nothing of such needs."

He had asked no more questions. Even as a child he knew what had happened. He had heard whispers of it in the courts. He had seen anxious looks on women's faces. The peasants were the ogres of his childhood. They were necessary because they tended the fields and reaped the harvests. Without them there was no food. They had to be ruled and yet they had to be placated and cajoled because they were men without reason. He grew up afraid of them and hating them.

Yet even now he remembered certain moments. In the spring, when the young wheat was green, the figures in blue that moved across the landscape were beautiful in the distance. When he came near he saw good brown faces. In the spring the peasants were always happy and they laughed and were kind. They were kind even to him, the landlord's son, and he remembered a big brown fellow kneeling on the earth so that his eyes could be on a level with the child's and he had smiled and brought out of his pocket a piece of steamed bread and offered it to him. His nurse had drawn him back crying that he had already eaten. But the child that had been he was willful and shouted that he wanted the bread. So the big brown man had given it to him and had continued to kneel there smiling at him as he ate.

"Is it good to eat?" the man had asked the little boy in the satin robe.

"It is good," the boy had replied.

"It is my bread that I eat when the sun is yonder," the man said pointing to the zenith.

Then the man had pointed to the earth. "Sun above and earth beneath, both together make man's bread."

He had said this gravely, as though he meant something special, but the child did not know that.

Dr. Liang pondered that saying now, as he sat in his quiet study, his head in his hands. He still did not know what the peasant meant. People, he reflected, must live at these different levels. Some must work with the hands, some with the mind. The peasants should not be lifted from their places as workers with the hands, or the higher ones would starve. He himself would, if he lived in China, be quite helpless without the peasants. Even here, he supposed, there were the workers with hands, men on American farms who had to do the crude work of producing food. Such persons must not be taught falsely that they could or should do other work.

At this moment he began to distrust his daughter Mary. James was safe enough in his profession. It was all very well to see that peasants had sound health and strong bodies for their work. But Mary spoke of schools. Surely there was no reason for a peasant to know how to read and write. This would give him the means of rising out of his class. What would happen if the whole world were scholars? Who then would provide the food? Besides, the peasant mind was a crude one. It had not passed through the centuries of refinement which he, Liang Wen Hua, for example, had in his own ancestry. He frowned and determined to write a letter to Mary. He began to regret his generosity in the matter of the rents and he got up impetuously and went to find his wife.

She was gone. The house was silent except for the maid Nellie, banging something in the kitchen. He never spoke to Nellie if he could help it. Doubtless the letter was mailed. He stood for a moment, irresolute, wondering whether it would be worth writing a second letter which he would post privately. But of course Mrs. Liang would hear of it, and now that there were only the two of them in the house, his peace was peculiarly dependent upon her.

The telephone rang, and soon the maid Nellie came into the room. "It's the Woman's Art Club," she said. "They want to know if you can come to a luncheon tomorrow. The speaker is sick and they need you bad."

"I am quite busy," he murmured in the distant tone he reserved for her. "Stay—I will speak to them myself."

He went to the telephone and listened to an arrogant woman's voice explaining the crisis. American women all had arrogant voices.

"I wouldn't think of giving up my own work to fill in for another speaker, Mrs. Page," he said gently.

Her arrogance changed hastily to persuasiveness.

"Well," he conceded, "only because I am profoundly interested in art and the American public has so little knowledge—"

He paused for her gratitude, and then said with mild firmness, "My fee is one hundred dollars."

He heard a gasp at the other end of the telephone and then a quick recovery. "But of course, Dr. Liang!"

He regretted that he had not said two hundred. They were in a pinch. He subdued the thought as unworthy of him.

Mrs. Liang had posted the letter at once, and then she had taken a taxicab to Chinatown. The expense was severe, but she had never been successful in finding her way underground and she was ashamed to be seen riding a bus as though she were not the wife of Dr. Liang. In the subway she would not meet anybody she knew, but she had never been able to understand what train to get on, or once on where she should get off. Several times she had tried to get to Chinatown by subway, lured by the cheapness of such travel, but after an hour or so underground she had been compelled to come up and take a taxicab. The last time she had come up near a suburb called Queens, and the cab fare had run into dollars. Besides, who was the Queen? She supposed it must be Mrs. Roosevelt.

"Does Mrs. Franklin Delano Roosevelt live this side?" she had asked the cab driver from sheer curiosity.

"Lady, you're nuts," he had replied pleasantly. This also she did not understand. There were many things said by Americans which could not be understood and she had learned by experience that questions did not make them any plainer. So she merely accepted this reply.

Today she wanted to go to Chinatown to shop for various groceries which could not be bought elsewhere. Since she had plenty of time, this being one of Neh-lee's days, she would also inquire into the state of her savings account and perhaps visit a little while with Billy Pan's wife whom she had learned to know. True they did not understand one another entirely, since Mrs. Pan was Cantonese. Still, it would be pleasant just to sit a while with a Chinese woman of whom she need not be afraid. With Liang's friends she was easily ashamed. They were, she feared, secretly surprised that the great Dr. Liang's wife was not young and beautiful. But with Mrs. Pan she was the superior one—the wife of the great Dr. Liang.

The taxicab, she thought as she sat squarely in the middle of the seat, was after all the American ricksha. In Peking she had her own private ricksha, and how pleasant that had been! She had paid Old Yin, the puller, seven dollars a month and he had eaten the kitchen scraps and had slept in the gatehouse. Yet whenever she had wanted to go anywhere in the city he had been ready to take her there, thinking himself lucky to have his food and bed sure every day. While she spent long hours talking over everything with her many friends and playing mah-jongg, Old Yin had slept in the footrest of the ricksha, his head against the seat. Thinking of him she smiled. Where was he now? So genial, so faithful, so polite, so much better than the taxi driver!

She looked out of the window anxiously, convinced as always that the driver was taking her many extra miles. However often she came to Chinatown she was never quite sure of the way. She leaned back and closed her eyes. In any car she easily felt seasick. When they had crossed the ocean she had been sick every day. There was another anxiety. When they went back to China, if Liang was ever willing to go, who would hold her head? On shipboard one of the children had always stayed with her. Liang could not bear to see anyone sick and he always left the room. She smiled, remembering something. One day the sea had been evil and even Liang had got sick. How nice that was! He had lain in the lower bunk groaning and insisting that some lobster he had eaten was not fresh. But of course he was only seasick.

Ah well, Liang was her husband and she would never have another. Even had she been young and beautiful she would not have run from man to man as women did nowadays. But she was neither young nor beautiful and she was grateful for Liang. It was honorable to be his wife, and if he had a peevish temper at home, he might have been worse. He had never beaten her, and she had learned, after all these years, how to torture him.

The driver woke her. "Where are you going in Chinatown?" he asked gruffly.

"Corner Mott and Pell," she said instantly.

He growled and whirled about a few streets and then stopped with a jar. She tried to get out and could not. "Up, up, up!" the driver said angrily.

"Up?" she said blankly, looking at the glass in the ceiling. "I came in the door."

"Handle!" the driver shouted. "Push it up!"

Mrs. Liang suddenly hated him. "You do it," she said and waited. She counted out the change carefully. cutting his tip in half for his being rude. She held the money in her hand while he moaned and opened the door. Safely on the sidewalk she gave him the money and turned instantly into the grocery store, catching a glimpse of his glowering face before he drove off. She sighed.

"What you want?" an American voice demanded. She saw a Chinese boy behind the counter, a new clerk.

"Eh, you," she said. "You don't talk like Chinese."

"I'm American," he retorted. "What you want, lady? Got some nice green cabbages today—also fresh ginger roots."

"Two pound cabbage, one-quarter pound ginger," she ordered.

So it was, she reflected. This Chinese boy an American! Why, Louise was an American at that rate. She was the mother of an American! That was the way these foreign nations did. They took even your children. It was a good thing Louise was in China. When she had finished shopping, and had stopped in to see Mrs. Pan, she would go home and write a private letter to Mary. "Let your sister be friend with some nice Chinese boy," so she would coax Mary. She ordered shredded chicken and small dried shrimps and a brown jar of soy sauce. She bought pickled mustard leaves and salted turnips and fresh bean curd and salted fish. Then she waited while it was all tied together.

"What your name?" she asked the boy.

"Louie Pak," he replied.

"You go to school?" she asked with her endless human curiosity.

"Yeah—just finished high school."

"Now you go back to China?"

"Naw," he replied with scorn. "Whadda I wanta go there for? I'm gonna go into drugstore work."

She felt scarcely less alien to this boy than she would have were he blue-eyed and yellow-haired. There was something outrageous about him and she felt vaguely indignant. "All boys must go back to China," she said firmly. "China needs educated boys."

He tied the string in a double knot. "Yeah? Well, they hafta get along without me," he retorted.

She took her bundle and walked away, feeling his bold eyes upon her, critical doubtless of her stout figure and Chinese dress. When she reached Mrs. Pan's house she went in full of protest about such boys. Mrs. Pan was ironing children's clothes in her small compact kitchen. She was the mother of many children and her ironing was never done. But when she saw Mrs. Liang she put the iron away and hurried into the clean little parlor.

"Eh, Mrs. Liang," she called in a loud cordial voice. "Come in; I was just wishing to stop my ironing."

Mrs. Liang sat down. "Mrs. Pan, I don't know how you feel, but I think we must do something to make our boys want to go back to China."

"Mrs. Liang, drink some tea, please, and have a small cake. You are so lucky your children are still patriotic. This is because you and Dr. Liang are so good. Our children are too bad. I tell Billy every day he is no good father. The children all want to be American. Of course they have no chance here. Look at Sonia, wants to be stenographer! We try to teach them better but what can we do?"

Mrs. Liang, remembering that Sonia had once been in her mind as a possible wife for James, asked with melancholy curiosity, "How is Sonia?"

"Oh, Sonia is such a smart girl," Mrs. Pan answered in a lively voice. "Her boss is selling electric stove and refrigerator and Sonia gets me one special price as consequence."

Mrs. Pan with seeming carelessness flung open a door to reveal a tiny kitchen and an enormous cabinet, glistening like a mountain of snow.

"How good!" Mrs. Liang exclaimed, her voice sharp with regret for the daughter-in-law now impossible to attain.

The ladies were well launched on their morning.

Just before noon Mrs. Pan said, "Please eat with us today, Mrs. Liang. It is a long way to your house, and now it is nearly twelve o'clock."

Mrs. Liang gave a start of surprise. "Can this be? But my husband is getting hungry."

Mrs. Pan laughed robustly. "You are too good to him, Mrs. Liang. Learn like American ladies not to be so troublesome! Ring the telephone to him and say you will stay here to eat with us. My Mr. Pan never comes home noontime. I say, 'Billy, go somewhere. I can't cook three times every day.' For Sonia I say, 'You eat drugstore, please!' So, Mrs. Liang, just a little common food for you and me together. Tell Dr. Liang I want you to help in hospital drive here for Chinatown and this is true."

Mrs. Liang could not resist. Encouraged by the rosy-cheeked Mrs. Pan she called Dr. Liang and said somewhat timidly, "Liang, I am here with Mrs. Pan. We are busy. We are planning hospital drive."

Dr. Liang did not answer for a moment. Then he said rather coldly, "In that case Nellie can get me something. But please do not promise any money from me."

"Oh, no," she agreed. But he had already hung up the receiver.

"Is he mad?" Mrs. Pan inquired.

"Not at all," Mrs Liang said proudly.

"Good," Mrs. Pan exclaimed, "you see he is rather nice."

She bustled into the kitchen and scrambled eggs foo-young and chopped green cabbage to braise in peanut oil, and boiled water for noodles. In less than half an hour the two ladies settled themselves to a simple but substantial meal. When they had eaten heartily and had drunk several bowls of tea, Mrs. Pan was telling Mrs. Liang what she did when an American Chinese young woman tempted Mr. Pan from the path of virtue, and Mrs. Liang yielded to the temptation to confide in Mrs. Pan and told her that only her own firmness had kept Dr. Liang from taking Violet Sung as a concubine. Furthermore a young American had fallen in love with Louise and that was why Mary had taken her to China, and Peter had gone along to care for them both.

Mrs. Pan listened avidly and then she said, "But why did James go to China?"

Mrs. Liang leaned closer. "Lili Li," she whispered. "It was Lili Li who—well, we told him she was not good for him. Rich girls are too lazy. James is very hard worker. So he went to China now."

"How I wish you live in Chinatown," Mrs. Pan said warmly.

"I wish, also," Mrs. Liang said with equal warmth. She confided still further. "In that case I wished your Sonia for my daughter-in-law."

Mrs. Pan was overwhelmed. "Oh, Mrs. Liang," she exclaimed. "So much happiness for us! But Sonia would not go to China, perhaps."

"If she had married my son James, maybe he would also be here."

Both ladies forgot China and mourned silently for a moment over what was now never to be.

Mrs. Pan recovered first. "Anyhow," she said with renewed cheer, "maybe sometime you live here as neighbor."

"How nice!" Mrs. Liang replied. "But I think not. Liang likes to be lonely."

It was midafternoon before Mrs. Liang went home. She entered the quiet apartment. It was quite empty. "Neh-lee!" she called, but there was no answer. The maid had finished her work and gone. Dr. Liang was nowhere to be seen. She could do nothing except try to settle herself. But the day had been exciting for her and she went into the kitchen and feeling restless she decided to clean out the icebox.

In a remote corner of a small French restaurant Dr. Liang was talking with Violet Sung. Some vague feeling of revenge had prompted him to call her when his wife telephoned. Violet Sung was at home, feeling, she said, at loose ends.

"So am I," Dr. Liang had said. "Will you lunch with me?"

She hesitated a moment. Then she said delicately, "Are you sure you want me?"

"Quite sure," he said.

So they had met in the restaurant she suggested, a place where she often went when she was alone, because Ranald did not like French food. They were quite reconciled, the mutual bond between them stronger than ever. But she knew now that there were arid stretches in Ranald's mind. He was profoundly intelligent and spiritually undeveloped. Physically he was far more passionate than she, and he often wearied her. Yet after the first few acknowledgements of weariness she had learned to pretend, for he grew angry with her did she seem less desirous than he. English women were like that, he declared, but he had not expected frigidity in a combination of France and China. At this she had smiled and said nothing and after that pretense was easy. Her mind at all times was free of her body, and within the privacy of her skull her thoughts roamed the universe. Ranald, acute rather than intuitive, did not perceive her absence from her body.

With Dr. Liang she felt an intimacy that had nothing to do with the flesh. She was deeply attracted to the handsome tall Chinese gentleman, whose black hair was silvery at the temples. Physically he pleased her without rousing desire. His pale skin, clear-cut lips, and long intelligent eyes, his beautiful hands and slender graceful figure, were pleasantly symbolic of his cultivated mind. The coarse red and white skin of Western men, their hairiness and thickness, their high noses and protruding bones, were privately disgusting to her. Yet she had always been shy of Chinese men. Her father's strictness and rectitude had moved her and yet had made her afraid of him. She could not imagine a Chinese lover. The approach was different to any she knew. Chinese men, when they noticed women at all, gave them a grave courtesy which implied the conviction of equality.

When Dr. Liang had telephoned her today it had been almost telepathy. She had been sitting alone in her room in one of her long fits of musing which were trancelike, and she had been thinking of him, not romantically, but with a divining imagination, as she thought of many persons, men and women, who interested her. Had she been more active physically, she might have put down some of these musings on paper and made stories out of them, but she never moved if she could help it, except to dance. She could sit motionless for hours when she was alone, merely thinking about one person and another, remembering, probing, hearing again the sound of a voice, seeing the trick of a gesture. Thus was her inner solitude peopled. Upon such a reverie the telephone had broken and when she lifted the receiver she had heard Dr. Liang's voice.

Now seated opposite him in the restaurant which at this late hour was almost empty she felt a deep sense of peace. She had little wish to talk at any time and she floated upon the restfulness of the moment.

Dr. Liang looked at her with appreciation. She had slipped her brown mink cape from her shoulders and the deep violet wool of her simply fashioned gown and small hat melted into the richness of her dark hair and eyes and her creamy skin. He had never seen so beautiful a creature.

"When I am with you I always feel like speaking only truth," he said. "So I will tell you that you are entirely beautiful today."

"Only today?" she asked half smiling.

"Always, but today with an aura."

"Let's speak Chinese, shall we?" she said. "I can't very well, but I long to be able to—perfectly, I mean, with one word slipping into another, and yet each quite clear."

"Then we will speak Chinese," he replied. "I also prefer our own tongue. It has been spoken so long by human beings that it is shaped to human need. Had your father one of those hand pieces of jade or amber?"

"He held always a piece of onyx," she said, smiling. Her Chinese was pure and good, but her vocabulary was not large and she longed to know all the words she needed.

"And it became shaped to his own hand," Dr. Liang went on. "It was polished by his flesh until it shone in the light of a candle, did it not? It lay in his palm and he felt never empty handed."

"He did find comfort in it," she agreed. "When I was a child I never knew why. I said to him, 'Baba, why not hold my kitten or some flowers? Why always the same thing?' And he said, 'I like it because it is always the same.' "

"Yes," Dr. Liang replied. He murmured a few words to the waiter without asking Violet what she wished to eat, and she liked this. She avoided making up her own mind even about food. It was easier to eat what was chosen for her, and she had confidence in his choice. When a delicate broth appeared, a sift of crisp croutons upon the clear surface, she drank it well content, and in silence, and after it she enjoyed the small fresh fish, browned in butter. It was a change from the beefsteak and mashed potatoes which Ranald ate every day.

French pastries were almost Chinese, and Dr. Liang made a long and careful scrutiny of the tray before they chose. She liked his Chinese carefulness about food, that every mouthful might be savored.

They talked very little during the meal and this was Chinese, too. When tea came on, and he was very firm in his directions that the tea leaves should be brewed without the cloth bags, they looked at one another across the table and Dr. Liang felt the impulse, rare indeed, to speak from his heart.

"My wife is jealous of you," he said with his hint of a smile. "That, for you, doubtless, is no new thing in wives."

"I like your wife," she replied. "She gives me a feeling that is good."

"What is it?" he asked.

"It is like firm hard earth under the feet."

"You see what she is," he said. "That is why I am always faithful to her. I do not pretend to be better than I am. My thoughts like to play sometimes—I own it. Ours was an old-fashioned marriage, made by our parents. Yet I insisted that she learn to read and write, and we met once before the wedding day."

"What a moment!" she murmured in French.

"Yes, was it not?" he replied in the same language. Then he went on in Chinese. "I looked at her—short, even then a little fat, rosy-cheeked, and frightened of me."

"So she is now," Violet said, in Chinese again.

"I did not love her," Dr. Liang said, "but I knew that she would be a good wife."

"A good wife," Violet repeated. "It is what such a man as you must have."

Their eyes met and she laughed with a soft delight in him. "How Chinese are you!" she exclaimed.

Something naughty gleamed in the demure lines of Dr. Liang's smooth face. "At the same time," he went on, "there are other sides to my nature. A man's mind, if he be intelligent, seeks also female companionship. Yang and Yin are not made of flesh alone. Mind and spirit are in the circle too. That is why I telephoned you today."

He had never been so daring before. He had made clear to her that he had no wish for a passionate relationship. Nevertheless he had said boldly that he wanted a female mind to complement his, a female spirit to fulfill his. Whatever she was to the Englishman, he had implied, had no more to do with him than Mrs. Liang had to do with her. They could ignore such persons.

She understood and was pleased. Now these long musings of hers need not be entirely silent or lonely.

Dr. Liang leaned toward her slightly. "I should like to penetrate your mind with my own," he said. "I should like to pierce the mysteries of your soul."

12

Mary knew that her father's letter had been mailed by her mother, for she had written a postscript. "While your father agrees to let you have his share of the Liang rents do not think it came out of him easily," she wrote. "I stood at his side and I took the letter at once and I hastened from this foreign pagoda house in which we still live to put it in the box. I will not give it to the man in the up-and-down because doubtless he will steal the stamp. For myself I am glad you and your brother will have this money."

Mary's pleasure in being thus one step nearer to the village was tempered, however, by two events which were not so much events as something still going on. Louise was excited and Mary recognized certain signs within a few days after the return from the village. Her sister's eyes were bright, her cheeks pink, her voice high, and she was easily angry as she had been in the Vermont summer. This could mean only one thing. Louise was falling in love again. It was as plain as though she were about to succumb to an illness, and Mary went to James the first evening that he was free to be at home. She had learned that it was useless to approach him in the hospital. There his mind was too busy to give her heed unless she brought the message of some new illness among the children she taught in the hospital school. Meanwhile she watched Louise who, it seemed, went nowhere and received no visitors.

"What have you done all day, Louise?" she asked each evening when she came home.

The answer was always idle. Louise had made a new dress, or she had washed her hair, or she had read a book or she had slept half the day away. Several times Mary, perceiving her sister's excitement, wondered if she had had a secret visitor. She was sorely tempted to inquire of Young Wang, but antipathy forbade it. Young Wang still disliked a mistress in the house he served and often he pretended not to hear what Mary told him. When she complained to James of this he only laughed. Of Little Dog no one could inquire for he would lie as the moment demanded. Little Dog's mother also was too frightened of everybody and everything to be worth talking with. Therefore was Mary constrained to wait until such a day as James came home with the cheerful look on his face which meant that he expected no one in his care to die at least before morning.

On that evening after they had eaten and Louise had gone early to bed and Peter had gone to a meeting of students at the college, Mary found herself alone with James and Chen. She pondered whether she should speak in Chen's presence, since she imagined him half in love with Louise secretly. When he left them for a moment, therefore, she took her chance and said quickly in English, "Jim, I am sure Louise is in love with somebody again."

James lifted his eyebrows. "This time with whom?" he inquired. Yet strangely he did not seem surprised.

"Who knows? Unless it is with Chen?"

James shook his head. "Not with Chen."

At this moment Chen came back, and James went on easily. "Chen, Mary thinks that Louise is in love with someone."

Chen looked thoughtful at once, as though he knew more than he wished to tell. "I can see that Chen agrees with you," James said, turning to Mary.

It was an evening too cold to sit in the court, and they were gathered in the main living room of the house. Young Wang had bid Little Dog light a brazier of charcoal, and this was heat enough for the early season although in the corners of the room the air lurked chill enough to make them talk of going to the thieves' market to find a big American stove.

The oil lamp burned on the table and gave a soft yellow light to the walls. Mary had cut a stalk of Indian bamboo with its scarlet berries, and this stood upon the table in an old brown jar. The room looked cheerful and warm.

To Chen this was exceedingly precious. "I do not like to see any change in this house," he said sadly, "but we must all perceive now that Louise is not here with her heart."

"Yet I never see her with anyone," Mary said.

"Young Wang has already told me that she leaves the house

every afternoon," James said quietly. "He says she meets an American."

"An American!" Mary echoed, stupefied at Louise and her deception. Then she was hurt. "Why didn't you tell me?" she demanded of James.

"Because you are such an impetuous little thing," he replied, looking at her with eyes both fond and humorous, "because you are like a brimming cup, always ready to spill over, or a small firecracker, ready to explode—"

He dodged Mary's open palm, and Chen put out his hand and pretended to give James a mighty slap. They laughed and settled down again, and Mary's face took on its look of lively concern.

"But why does Louise hide it from us?"

"I suppose she thinks that since Pa sent her here to get away from Americans, we would prevent her," James said. He was smoking his old American pipe and suddenly he looked weary.

"We must stop her!" Mary exclaimed.

This James did not answer. He continued to smoke, his eyes very dark.

Now Chen began to talk gravely. "Several things begin to be plain to me," he said. "That boy child at the hospital— Mary, have you looked at him lately?"

"He is quite well," Mary said with surprise. "The nurses care for him and not I, as you know, but every day I pass his crib and he is sleeping or eating or lying awake. He cries in such a loud voice."

"Louise went to see that child," Chen said cautiously.

James took the pipe from his mouth. "There is no reason why you should shield Mary now," he told Chen. "We had better tell her everything." They were still speaking in English, lest a servant overhear them.

But it was no servant who overheard. Louise, always sensitive to Mary's watchfulness, had seen her sister's eyes follow her thoughtfully as she left the room that night. She had thrown her good night gaily at the three who sat on after Peter had gone, and when she said she was sleepy Mary had not answered. Mary had only looked at her with large quiet eyes, too full of thought. Therefore Louise knew she would not be able to sleep. In a few minutes she had stolen with noiseless feet along the corridors and had hidden herself behind the curtains which divided one room from another. Now she heard what was being said, and filled with horror, she fled back to her room. There she put on a coat and outdoor shoes and still silent she slipped through the dark court, passed the latticed door of the living room, now closed against the sharp night air, and thus she went on through the gate. In the alley she was frightened but she went on to the street where she waved to a passing ricksha. Seated in it, she directed the puller to the house of Dr. and Mrs. Su.

Mrs. Su was her only friend. At her house she met Alec every day. Dr. Su knew nothing of it, but Mrs. Su welcomed the excitement of the romance. All Mrs. Su's best friends knew about the rendezvous, and most of them had told their husbands. Therefore in the hospital nearly everyone knew that Dr. James Liang's younger sister was meeting an American, who had returned to Peking after his discharge as a soldier, because he had been in love with a Chinese girl, a nobody, who had died in the hospital after giving birth to a boy who was now a hospital foundling. Louise thought her secret safe with Mrs. Su, and no one had told James or Mary, and no one told Dr. Su because everybody liked the new little Mrs. Su and nobody liked him. The Chinese gossiped prudently. Where it did not matter all was told and discussed, but beyond prudence no one went.

The danger tonight, Louise reminded herself as the ricksha carried her through the darkness, was that Dr. Su was at home. It was only good fortune that could prevent this. Alas, such fortune was not hers. When she had paid the ricksha man and had entered the brightly lit foreign-style house that stood beside the street, she heard Dr. Su's voice. It was Mrs. Su, however, who came out to meet her when the servant announced her.

"My brother and sister know!" Louise whispered.

At this moment Dr. Su came to the door. "Miss Liang!" he called with the bantering smile that was his approach to all young and pretty women. "Have you run away from home?"

Louise tried to laugh. "I am really only on my way somewhere else," she said. "I just stopped to see if Mrs. Su would come with me."

"Where?" Dr. Su asked with ready curiosity.

"Some foreign friends," Louise said, frightened that everything she said was too near the truth.

"Don't go, don't go," Dr. Su exclaimed. "Stay here with us."

"Then I must telephone," Louise said, seizing upon the chance.

Mrs. Su was immediately helpful. "Su," she said to her husband, "please return to our other guests. I will take Louise to the study."

Dr. Su turned away and Mrs. Su led Louise into the small study where the telephone stood on the desk and she closed the door.

"Now," she whispered, "what will you do? Your brother will be angry with my husband if he finds that I have let you meet Alec here. You know I like to help you, Louise, but I must think of my relations with my husband. Su has a very bad temper."

"You mean Alec mustn't come here tonight?" Louise faltered.

"He must not come any more if your brother knows," Mrs. Su said. Her small pretty face was pale. "You know, Louise, what you do may be all right in America but here it is serious. And I am my husband's fourth wife. He is not too patient with me. Such a fine man as Su with a good job can get plenty of women to marry him."

Louise felt her heart grow hard toward Mrs. Su and all Chinese women, but she asked, "May I telephone?"

"Certainly that," Mrs. Su said quickly.

"Then please—may I be alone?"

Mrs. Su hesitated. "I ought better to stay here," she said, "but then I like to say I didn't know anything about it. I will stand outside the door."

So saying she went out and closed the door and Louise called the hotel where Alec Wetherston was living. His voice answered, a pleasant tenor at whose sound her lips quivered.

"Alec, it's me—Louise."

"Why, darling!" His voice took on depth. "Where are you?"

"At the Su house. Alec, my brother and sister know about us."

There was silence for a long moment and she said anxiously, "Alec, do you hear me?"

"Yes, I was just thinking fast, darling." His voice was somewhat breathless. "What will they do?"

"I don't know but I've got to see you."

"Shall I come over there?"

"Mrs. Su is afraid."

"But what'll we do, darling? I suppose you couldn't come here to the hotel?"

"People would recognize me—you know how they are."

"I could meet you at the hotel door and we could walk."

"All right—in fifteen minutes."

She hung up the receiver and went out into the hall. Mrs. Su was still standing there, watching the door of the living room. A burst of laughter pealed out.

"I am going home," Louise said. "Just tell Dr. Su I had to go on, after all."

The two young women tiptoed down the hall; Mrs. Su opened the door, and Louise went out. She was beginning to be frightened because for the first time in her life she was acting quite alone. In New York there had always been Estelle to praise her for her independence and here, until now, there had been Mrs. Su. Now she had no one. Estelle was far away and Mrs. Su was a coward, like all Chinese—cowards when it came to real courage. How she hated being Chinese herself! She must go back to America. If she married an American she could be an American, almost. At least her children would be American and she, their mother—it was her only escape.

The dusty wind blew down the wide street. It was several minutes before she could find a ricksha in the dim light. With nightfall and cold the Chinese went inside their houses and put up the boards. All the open gaiety of the city in summer was gone. She felt still more frightened when a wild-looking old man pulling a dirty ricksha offered it to her, but seeing no other she got in. He ran slowly as though he were too weary to walk, and when he let the shafts down at the hotel gate, his face glistened with sweat and his cotton jacket was streaked with damp. She ought to pity him she told herself, but he only repelled her and she gave him as little money as she dared. He was too exhausted to protest beyond a moan and a grimace at the money outspread on his grimy palm. She paid no heed to him and walked quickly up to the door. Then her heart was released. She had been afraid that Alec would not be there but he was waiting for her, his coat collar turned up and his hat pulled down.

"Hello," he said in a guarded voice. "You were a long time coming. I began to freeze."

He put his arm into hers and they walked down the street. "Tell me everything," he said.

Who could have foretold what now happened? Before she could reply six or seven students coming along the half-lit street saw a Chinese girl walking with an American. They surrounded the pair swiftly and a flashlight in the hands of one thrown upon the girl revealed Louise's pretty face. "You American man!" a student shouted. "Leave our girls alone!"

Then incredibly the students began to hustle them. Alec felt himself pushed against a wall. He put Louise behind him to shield her, but the yelling students were trying to pull her out from behind him.

"We'll have to cut and run," he said to her over his shoulder.

Where could they go in this whole city?

"We'll have to go home," Louise said.

"When I start, you keep up with me," Alec commanded. "Come now—get ready—get set—let's go!"

By the suddenness of their dash, by the swiftness of their pace, they took the students by surprise and got a head start. Both Alec and Louise were strong and long-winded. Good food and care had gone into the making of their young bodies, and the students were underfed and weak. The chase was uneven and one by one the students halted and gave up. When the two reached the hutung no one followed.

"You'd better leave me here," Louise said.

But Alec Wetherston had been thinking hard while his legs ran. He was deeply attracted to this pretty Chinese girl. Perhaps he was really in love with her—not as he had been in love with his little Lanmei who had died when the baby was born. The baby worried him terribly. He had come back to China when he knew there was going to be a baby and he had made up his mind to marry Lanmei as soon as she got out of the hospital. When he reached here she was dead. He had gone to the two rooms she had shared with another girl, who had told him the story. Lanmei's room had already been taken by a man whom the girl had accepted as her lover. Alec had listened and gone away again, not knowing what to do. "Better leave the baby in the hospital," the girl had advised. But his heart clung to the child, although he had never seen it, hesitating to own it as his. What could he do with a baby? He had told no one at home about Lanmei. At last he had told Louise everything, even about the baby, and she had gone to see it.

"The kid is cute," Louise had reported. "He has big eyes

and he smiles when you look at him." The father in him wanted to see his child.

Now he took Louise by the shoulders and pinned her against the wall. "Look here," he said. "I'm not going to leave you, darling. I'm coming in to see that big brother of yours and tell him I want to marry you."

Louise looked up at him wistfully. She would never love anyone as well as she had loved Philip. She had told Alec about Philip, too. They had exchanged the stories of their sorrows. He even knew that Philip did not want her, and it was sweet of him not to mind. But before she could speak they heard footsteps in the hutung. In the darkness they stood quite still, waiting. Again a flashlight was thrown upon them and in the beam they saw Peter.

"Peter!" Louise gasped.

Without a word Peter jumped on Alec and tore him away. "You devil!" he cried.

Alec leaped at him. In a second the two young men were rolling on the ground locked together and Peter struggling up seized Alec by the hair and beat his head against the cobbles. Louise shrieked and fell upon Peter.

"Jim, Jim!" she screamed for help.

Down the hutung doors opened. Their landlord's servant came running out. "These foreigners are fighting," he shouted, and he hastened into the rented house and beat on the closed door of the living room. "Your brother and sister are killing a foreigner!" he yelled.

So it happened that the next instant James and Chen and behind them Mary carrying the lighted lamp saw three disheveled young people rising from the ground. Louise was crying.

"You leave my sister alone!" Peter was bellowing, and Alec leaped on him again.

It was James who separated them, James who commanded Louise to get into the house and who led the young men into the house behind her. He locked the gate firmly upon the gaping crowd and they stared a while at the closed gate and went home telling each other that a house haunted by weasels could give no happiness even to foreigners.

Into the living room James led his captives and Young Wang came out of his room and Little Dog and his mother followed.

"Get us some food," James commanded them, "and fetch

hot tea. Then we will talk quietly." He turned to Peter. "What were you doing?"

Peter, his eyes still blazing at Alec, replied, "I had just passed a crowd of the fellows who said they had run after an American going with one of our girls. They can't stand that now, after all the things Americans have done here. I didn't dream the girl was my own sister."

"And you?" James said still more quietly to Alec.

"I was coming here to ask your permission to marry Louise," Alec said bluntly.

"Who are you?" James asked with the same fearful quietness.

"Alec Wetherston, formerly of the U.S. Army," Alec said in a firm voice. "Louise and I met the day she came to the chrysanthemum market. You won't remember me."

"I do," Mary said. She saw that she was still holding the lamp and she set it down on the table.

Alec looked at her. "Yes—well, I know you, too. I wanted Louise to tell you about us, but she seems to be afraid of you all, for some reason."

"Because they don't want me to marry an American," Louise put in, beginning to cry again.

"Mary, take Louise away," James said.

Louise allowed herself to be led as far as the door. There she paused, the tears wet on her cheeks. "I tell you I will marry Alec," she declared.

Mary pulled her away, and James went on quietly. "Mr. Wetherston, sit down, please. I have no objection to my sister's marrying the man she wants to marry, but he must be a good man."

They were all sitting down now except Peter, who stood with his hands in his pockets, his hair on end. Chen had sat down. His face was very pale and he had said nothing.

"I guess nobody is perfect—not these days," Alec said frankly. He was beginning to feel better. Louise's brother looked like a regular fellow.

"Please tell me everything," James said sternly.

Alec looked startled. "How do you mean—everything?"

Chen spoke. "The little boy in the hospital—"

Alec leaned his arm on the table. "I guess you know," he said simply. "I guess it's nothing different from lots of other fellows during the war. Only I came back—I guess that was my mistake."

"Listen to him!" Peter said contemptuously.

"Be quiet, Peter," James said. He leaned forward and looked at the American. He liked this tall angular young man. His brown hair was mingled with the street dust and his face was grimy. But it was an honest face and for an American the features were delicate and quite good. It might be true that Louise would never marry a Chinese. Perhaps the first human perceptions stamped by life upon a newborn child were the ones which finally seemed most real. He and Mary had been born in China but Louise and Peter were American born. Some American nurse in a hospital in New York had lifted her from the bed of birth and had cared for her in the first weeks, and at home Nellie had taken her place. The first instincts of the child's flesh had entwined themselves with blue eyes and blond hair and white skin. Louise could not change these instincts now.

"You really want to marry my sister?" James said to Alec.

Alec lifted his head. "I've been thinking it all out," he said. "I want to marry her and go home. We'll take the baby with us. She's told me all about herself and she knows all about me. Lanmei was the first girl I was ever in love with and I'll be happier with Louise than I would with any regular American girl. Besides, the baby will be easier to explain. And people aren't as old-fashioned as they used to be. You can't marry a Negro, but most people don't mind a Chinese."

Peter burst at this. His clenched hands flew from his pockets. "Don't mind a Chinese!" he bellowed. "But we mind Americans, let me tell you! We've had about enough of Americans, I tell you! At the school tonight we framed up a protest to the government—about the way Americans are interfering in China. Gosh, when I tell them my sister is marrying one of them!" His anger ended in a wail.

James turned on him with forbidding eyes, but Peter gave him look for look. Then he yielded and rushed from the room.

Alec tried to smile. "You can't blame them, I guess," he said. "But what they don't see is that fellows like us can't help what any government does. We're helpless, too. I want to get the hell out of here myself."

James had been thinking hard and swiftly. Now he spoke with sudden clarity. "I think it is what you ought to do. Tomorrow you can come and tell me about your family and your situation. If I am satisfied I will tell Louise that so far as I am concerned, she may marry you."

Alec lifted his head. "I want to thank you, sir," he stammered. "I wish I knew how to thank you."

Chen said, "Jim, what about your parents?"

"I stand in my father's place," James replied. "He has put my sisters and my brother in my care."

Alec was on his feet. "I'll come around tomorrow—here?"

"To my office in the hospital, please," James said. "Then we will see the child together. Louise is very young for the care of so small an infant. But I suppose she can learn."

They stood while Alec shook their hands and while he went to the door, smiled back, and went away. Then James turned to Chen. "Tell me I have done right," he pleaded.

They sat down opposite each other at the table. "I think you have done right," Chen admitted. "Yet how do I know?"

There was a footfall at the door and Mary came in.

"Done what right?" she asked. She sat down at the third side of the table between them.

"I have told him he can marry Louise," James said simply.

She sat for a long moment. Then she got up and said, "I'll go and tell her. She keeps crying."

But she paused a moment and looked at Chen. "I thought you were going to be in love with Louise," she said bluntly.

Chen opened his eyes wide. "I? In love?" He gave a great shout of laughter, and she left him still laughing.

The wedding took place quietly. Alec and Louise wanted no guests. They were both American citizens and they went to the American Consulate one afternoon with James and Mary as witnesses and there, before an acquiescent though unwilling consul, the marriage was performed. Peter would not go and Chen had refused, saying that only two witnesses were needed and he would stay with the baby. The baby was at the hotel waiting for them in Chen's care when the wedding party came back.

"I am a good amah," Chen declared. "A better amah than a doctor."

He had the baby in his arms, and the baby, dressed in new yellow rompers that Mary had made for him, was holding Chen's thumb tightly and staring into his rugged face. The few days before the wedding had been busy with new clothes not for the bride but for the baby, everything made American. Louise and Alec had devoted themselves to the study of formulas and schedules, and Mary had lined a Chinese basket with cotton padding and blue silk for a traveling cradle. Another basket with a lid carried bottles and sterilizer and all that a child would need for a long journey.

That night the bride and groom with the little boy took the train southward to Shanghai. It was a strange wedding party, and yet a happy one. James and Mary and Chen saw them off and stood until the train disappeared into the night, shades drawn against possible bandits and only the great engine headlight flaring.

Gazing after the moving train, James buttoned his coat about him tightly. "Now I must cable Pa," he said.

Mary clung to his arm as they turned to go home again and Chen fell in beside her. "I know we have done right," she said with her old sweet stubbornness. "It doesn't matter what Pa says."

"Louise would never have been happy here," Chen said. They began to trudge together in common step down the half-empty street. The night was cold and there would be frost. People walking by gathered their robes together and hurried on.

"It takes a certain kind of person to live in China now," Chen mused.

"What kind of person?" Mary asked.

"Someone who can see true meanings; someone who does not only want the world better but also believes it can be made better, and gets angry because it is not done; someone who is not willing to hide himself in one of the few good places left in the world—someone who is tough!"

They were passing an ironmonger's shop and the ironmonger being behind with his work had not yet put up the boards. Upon his anvil he beat a piece of twisted iron that he was making into a knife which a student had ordered that day. The flaming metal threw out sparks and lit up his black face in a grimace of effort. His white teeth gleamed. This same light fell on the three and Chen looked down into Mary's upturned face as they passed.

"Somebody tough," he repeated half teasingly, "somebody like you—and me—and Jim." Mary laughed and she took her other hand out of her pocket and put it in Chen's arm, and they marched along, in step.

Peter stayed in his own room during the wedding. Young Wang had been amazed and horrified and when the others had gone he went to Peter's door. He liked this younger son of the family and longed to come to good terms with him. He imagined them almost friends, rather than master and servant. Sometimes, brushing Peter's large shoes after a rain and cleaning cakes of Peking mud from under the soles, he imagined himself talking thus and even saying Peter's name. "Pe-tah, hear me! I am older than you, although born in a low family. Your family are gentry, mine are small farmers only. Nevertheless in these new times who is high and who is low? Let us be friends. I tell you, students are no good. In the old days we common folks looked up to scholars and students. They were the governors. I tell you," here Young Wang brushed the shoes with fury, "now we know that it is we common folk who must resist scholars and warlords and rich men and magistrates. These four are the enemies of the people."

Was Peter a Communist? That was what Young Wang continually wished to find out. He himself was not, since the government cut off all Communist heads or else shot them dead. But he listened sometimes in the corners of the teashops and winehouses. At his village when he had gone to rescue his family from the island to which they clung he had heard a young man and woman who came together and helped them move and stayed while they put up fresh earthen houses on their fields, and they had kept saying, "Where are your landlords? Where are your wonderful students? Where is your government? Does no one come to help you? Only we help you, we the Communists."

The villagers had been much troubled by their help, well knowing that in this world no one does anything for nothing, and they had been casting about in their minds as to why this young pair with such bold faces had come to their aid. When they found they were Communists they fell into awful terror, for no one in these regions could be Communist and live, seeing that the government sent armies every day against Communists. Worse even than their own government, for they were used to their own, were the Americans, who now demanded, the villagers were told, that every Communist be killed. So Young Wang and his family had joined with the villagers in driving these two young Communists away with hoes and rakes and bamboo poles. The two had gone off singing one of their songs and they shouted back at the villagers.

"We offered you peace, but now you reject us and we will come back with swords and guns!"

Young Wang had been as frightened as the rest. Nevertheless, this stuck in his mind as truth—no one did anything for men like him and their families. They struggled along as best they could, starving in famine, dying with sickness, their children were dirty and unlearned, and all this was in spite of their continual labor. Who indeed had helped them build anew their houses after the flood?

That Peter was angry at something Young Wang well knew. He had heard the young man argue with his calm older brother and with Chen. "You with your tolerance and your patience," Peter had said bitterly to those two. "The only way to wake our people up is to use violence on them."

"You mean kill them?" Chen had inquired politely. "Alas, people do not wake from the dead!"

"I mean kill everyone who will not change," Peter had declared.

"Oh, Peter, don't be silly," Mary had exclaimed.

James had listened in his usual thoughtful manner. Then he said, "When men start killing other men, a craving for death enters their heart, and to kill becomes the solution for every difficulty, however small."

"There is something of Pa's Confucius in you," Mary exclaimed.

"Perhaps there is," he had replied.

Now Young Wang walked softly to Peter's room and looked into the window. The young man sat by his desk writing furiously. Even as Young Wang looked at him he put down his pen and sat frowning and troubled. Young Wang went to the door and coughed.

"Go away," Peter said, recognizing the cough. "I am busy."

Young Wang opened the door enough to put in his head. "Will you not even go to the train to see them off?" he asked in a mild voice.

"Get out," Peter replied.

Young Wang weighed the tone of his voice. The words were harsh like an American's, but the voice was not too much so.

He came in looking meek and stood with his back to the door. "I said get out, didn't I?" Peter cried, looking up with high impatience.

"I will get out," Young Wang promised. "But first I tell you what I heard today. Something is being planned at the marble bridge."

Peter shot him a sharp look. "Where did you hear that?"

"A chestnut vendor told me."

Peter had taken up his pen but now he threw it down again. "Go on," he commanded, "tell me what you heard."

"He passed by at midnight a few nights ago," Young Wang said in a low voice. "He had been to a theater to sell his chestnuts. That is why he was so late. He passed by and he saw some people under the bridge. Of course he thought they were beggars sheltering there. Then one of them cried out with pain. One of the others had let a spade or a hoe fall on his foot. And this cry was no beggar's cry, the vendor said. It was the voice and the curse of a student."

Young Wang paused.

"Well, what of that?" Peter asked.

"The vendor went back the next night and the next," Young Wang went on, "and he goes every night. He is being paid now by the secret police." Young Wang looked down at Peter's shoes. "I brush your shoes every day," he said suddenly. "Yesterday they were clean. But tonight there was yellow clay on them. I know there is yellow clay under the bridge. Our soil elsewhere is sandy and dusty. But under the bridge there is clay. Doubtless when our ancestors sank the great stones into the bowels of the river, they brought yellow clay here from the south to hold hard the foundation."

Peter leaped from his chair and rushed at Young Wang. But Young Wang slipped through the door like a tomcat.

Nevertheless Peter locked the door after him and went to the desk and taking the sheets of paper upon which he had been writing, he tore them across again and again and he emptied the bottle of ink upon them and threw them into the wastebasket. Then he began most restlessly to pace the floor.

13

DR. LIANG WAS VERY ANGRY. James's letter had come by air-mail and had thus reached him some two weeks before Louise could be expected. He who had proclaimed so often before audiences in classroom and lecture hall the wisdom of the doctrine of fate could scarcely persuade himself of the in-evitability of what had already happened to his family and therefore to him. It now seemed to him that it would have been better to have had Louise marry Philip Morgan, whose father was in Wall Street and therefore rich. Who knew what this new fellow was, this Alec Wetherston? James had put the address of the family in his letter. It was an address of a somewhat middle-class sort. Dr. Liang had a flair for a good address, and he knew that this one was only partly good. It was not distinguished and very wealthy people would not be in that part of the city. He decided to ignore the Wetherston parents, refusing to recognize publicly his own secret fear that they might not be pleased with a Chinese daughter-in-law.

To his wife, however, he spoke with complete frankness, and in the height of his irritation at fate, he bullied her a good deal in small ways. "It would be very pleasant now, wouldn't it, if this soldier's family did not like to be connected with us?" he demanded of Mrs. Liang.

"On the other hand they might like us," she suggested rea-sonably. "For example, can we not ask why this Alec does not object to a Chinese wife? He has received no teaching against our people. Doubtless his parents also have no strong objec-tion."

The reasonableness of this incensed Dr. Liang. He tasted his coffee and set the cup down again. "How strange that after twenty years you still cannot tell good coffee from bad," he remarked.

"Neh-lee!" she called, but he put up his hand.

"She drinks anything herself," he said. "Therefore she has no taste. It is you, my wife, who should be able to know the difference, even by the aroma, between good and bad coffee."

"But I don't like coffee, Liang," she objected.

"That has nothing to do with it," he retorted.

She sighed. She must prepare to bear upon her own shoulders the brunt of her husband's displeasure. She brooded in silence, her eyes downcast, while he finished his scrambled eggs, broiled kidneys, and the bad coffee, munching as she did so on a piece of toast.

This munching next annoyed Dr. Liang. He looked at her and compared her large somewhat flabby face with Violet Sung's exquisite one. "What a noise you are making with that toast!" he exclaimed. "It sounds like a mill crushing grain."

She stopped and looked at him across the table. Her mouth was full of the half-chewed toast and she did not know what to do.

"Swallow it," he said violently.

She drank some tea, held her handkerchief before her face, and swallowed. The bit of toast she had been holding in her hand ready for the next bite she put down. She sat neither eating nor speaking until he had finished his breakfast and rising with dignity had gone to his study and closed the door. Then she finished the toast, took another piece, and spread it with strawberry jam. Butter she could not abide for it tasted of cows and milk. The teapot was empty and she called cautiously, "Neh-lee!"

Nellie came in wiping her hands on her apron. "Want more tea?" she asked kindly. She and the madam got on all right.

Mrs. Liang nodded. "What you think, Neh-lee?" she asked in a half whisper.

"What?" Nellie asked, with the teapot in her hand.

"Louise is marrying," Mrs. Liang whispered, "American fellow and a baby!"

"Louise got a baby?" Nellie exclaimed in the undertone they used when Dr. Liang was in the house.

"He got baby," Mrs. Liang explained. "Before time another Chinese wife." It was the one thing that James, after some thought, had decided not to make clear. The baby's mother, he had written, was the former wife of the American. Why, he asked himself, should the child assume a stigma when it reached America? In China people did not blame a child for the failures of its parents.

"Whaddya know," Nellie said. "Will they live here? It'll be kinda nice to have Louise home at that. Though a baby—still, there's the diaper service."

"His father and mother live also in New York," Mrs. Liang told her. "So maybe they live that side. But I am so glad to have some child again." She touched the corner of her napkin to her eyes.

"The mister is kinda tough on you, ain't he!" Nellie said with sympathy. "Well, cheer up now, madam. I'll fetch the hot tea."

She went away and Mrs. Liang sat alone and thinking, the lines of her face growing kind and soft. She would go down to Chinatown and find Mrs. Pan and tell her everything. It was so nice to have a woman friend again.

Behind his closed study door Dr. Liang sat moodily staring out of the window. Nothing in his philosophy, so closely derived from Confucius, prepared him for what had now happened. He did not know what to do. Louise had suddenly become no longer important to him. She was not a favorite child now that she had chosen to defy him and marry an American. Neither was the man important. Dr. Liang could, for his own part, live as though neither of them existed. He would not disown his daughter or dignify her by any such notice. The young couple could come here and pay their respects to him and he would greet them carelessly, as though nothing they did mattered to him. Children were disappointing. One produced them and cared for them and taught them and paid huge sums in school fees and then they did what they liked. It was America that spoiled them. In China—the old China—children remained subject to their parents as long as the elders lived. For this they were recompensed by becoming elders in their turn. Thus society was sound and the generations proceeded in order. That China, he knew, was gone. It was already passing when he himself was young, and had insisted that he would not have an illiterate girl for his wife. But he believed that the old wise ways would return. A nation that did not organize its generations in proper relationships was doomed to disintegration.

All this philosophy did not help him at the moment. The important thing, he discovered after he had sorted his thoughts, was what the Wetherston family was like. Were they entirely mediocre? How could he approach them? Should he approach them or should he wait for them to approach him? He could answer none of these questions, and his wife, he knew, would not even understand why he asked them. It would be her nature to rush over at once to see the new family and get on a footing of immediate and absurd friendliness which might involve him later in all sorts of obligations unsuitable to his position. If the Wetherstons proved to be poor and crude, for example, they might even seize at the chance to be connected with a famous man, though a Chinese.

In his indecision he took up the receiver of the telephone and dialed the number of Violet Sung's apartment. They had never mentioned Ranald but Violet had said, "It is quite safe to telephone me in the morning, but please not at night."

So he waited for a moment and then heard her voice, still rather drowsy. "Yes?"

"Violet?" he said very softly, for Mrs. Liang had an acute ear.

"Oh, yes," she replied, recognizing him.

"Please forgive me for calling you so early. I have had bad news. I need you."

"Tell me," she said with the warmth in her voice which was so charming to him.

"My youngest daughter has unexpectedly married an American. The letter came this morning. His family, unfortunately, is here in New York."

"How strange," she murmured.

"Yes, so I feel it," he agreed. "Now I must have your advice. What shall I do?"

She hesitated a moment, then she repeated his question. "What shall you do? But what can you do if they are already married?"

"Yes, that I know," he said a trifle impatiently, "but how shall I behave with the family? How can I know what they are and how they will feel? Doubtless by now they know what their son has done and perhaps they will be expecting me to— or ought I wait for them?"

"Where do they live?" Violet asked.

He gave the mediocre address and she considered it thoughtfully and so long that he asked rather piteously, "Can you suggest anything?"

"I will go to see them," she said at last. "I will call upon them, saying that I am a friend of your family."

He was relieved and deeply grateful, for he had not thought of such a thing. Yet it was in excellent Chinese tradition—a go-between, so to speak, someone who would break the blow of compulsory acquaintance.

"Who but you—" he murmured, breaking his sentence there. "Who but you would be so kind, so beautiful, so understanding—" any of these things could be said. But he preferred not to be explicit.

She laughed a soft wistful laugh. "I am really not much use in the world," she said. "I'd like to be of use to you."

"Of such use," he said gravely, "that I cannot live without you."

He put the receiver down upon that.

14

THE HOUSE FELT EMPTY after Louise had left it. While she was there each separate member of the family had felt her discontented presence and each had tried to please her in some small way, to make her smile at least for the moment. Now there was no more need for such effort. When the four came home at their various times, they could go their own ways, give greeting or not, and they had no duty to a lonely little sister.

Yet they missed her. Because of her very loneliness Louise had compelled them all, James and Mary, Peter and Chen, to come out of themselves and to enter into her being. And there were times when she was not sulky, times when she played with the kittens and laughed, times when she found a fledgling bird, or a new flower growing in the ancient court. She was so pretty, her little face so pleasant to see when she was happy, that they remembered her tenderly now that she was gone. Only Peter seemed careless, and when the others spoke of her he put his mind elsewhere and sat silent.

That Louise was gone made only one of the reasons for restlessness through the winter that now came upon the city. The old landlord, who had during those months kept prudently to his promise not to ask for the rent in advance, forgot himself in his need and became troublesome to them. The manservant had come to Young Wang and had put to him the matter of money.

"My old lord and mistress are very poor," he told Young Wang. "It would be a good deed if your master were to forget the signed paper and give him the month's rent in advance."

At first Young Wang refused but the man came back again with a present in his hand of two pieces of jade which he gave to Young Wang, saying, "My mistress gives these to you as a present that you may sell. Only plead with your master for a month's rent."

The jade was a worthless pair of ornaments such as in old times were once sewn on the sides of a woman's crownless cap. They were thin as paper. When the man was gone Young Wang took them to James. He opened his hand and there were the jade bits on his palm. "These things were given me by the landlord as a bribe to ask you to advance the rent," he told James. "I could not give them back because it would cause offense. Here they are."

"What can I do with them?" James replied. "Give them away or sell them. As for the request, I will think of it."

So he saved Young Wang, who when the man came back again was able to say, "My master considers it."

When Chen came home, and it was a cold bitter dry night at the end of the year, James told him what the landlord asked, and Chen grew angry. "We had better move away," he said. "Once these old opium lovers swallow down their shame and begin to beg we shall have no peace."

But James was more tender, and he decided that he would go to see the old pair and persuade them if possible to go into the hospital to be cured. So a few days after that when he had an hour he came house earlier than usual and he knocked at the landlord's gate and was admitted by the manservant who was all smiles at the sight of him.

"Is your master at home?" James asked.

"My master is always at home," the man replied smartly. "Where has he to go?"

James did not answer this impudence and he followed the man into the middle room of the house. It was a dreary room. Everything of worth was gone from it, and a few cheap benches and a broken bamboo table were all that remained. The manservant left him there and after a long while he came back, bringing his master. The old landlord tottered into the room, the manservant supporting him from behind, his hands under his arms like crutches. He was a pitiable figure. His padded winter robes were torn and the cotton was hanging out in a dozen places. On his feet he wore farmer's shoes of woven reeds, the woolly tassels twisted inside for warmth. On his head was a felt cap, once black but now rusty brown, and it had a hole at the side whence a tuft of gray hair came out. So wasted was the old man, so yellow, so withered, that he was all but dead. He tried to give greeting to James and was in such distress that he could not speak.

"I had to wake him," the manservant declared. "He was deep in dream."

"Eh—eh—" the old landlord stammered.

James leaned toward him. "Sir, you look very ill," he said gently.

These words and the kind tone in which they were spoken reached the old man's dimmed mind.

"I am very ill," he moaned.

"Then you ought to go to the hospital," James said in the same gentle voice. "Let me entreat you. Come with me. I will see that you are put into a warm room and a good bed. We will give you food and we will help your illness. We can cure you so that you will crave no more for the thing that makes you ill."

The old man slowly came to his senses while James was thus speaking. He fastened his dead black eyes on James's face and listened.

"It is cold here," James went on. "You have not even a brazier of coals."

"He sleeps on the k'ang," the manservant broke in. "When we have any food to cook, the smoke from the stove creeps under the k'ang and warms him."

"But only for a little while—unless you use charcoal," James remonstrated.

"Who can pay for charcoal?" the man said rudely.

The old man sighed. "I have no money."

"If you were well," James said, "you could perhaps earn some money. Were you not once a scholar? A scholar can write letters for other people. You could even teach children again. Or I might be able to find a desk in the hospital office for you where you could copy records."

The old man listened to this and he thought a while. Then he shook his head. "I have nothing to live for," he said at last. "My sons are gone. There are no grandsons here. Why should I work?"

"You see what he is," the manservant put in.

James spoke again and yet again, but each time the old landlord said again that he had nothing for which to live and why should he come out of his sleep? "I sleep and I return to that place from which I came before I was conceived in my mother's womb," the old man said. "There I am at peace."

Beyond this James could not go. It was the end of persuasion. When he saw that all was useless, he put his hand in his pocket and brought out a bundle of money. The servant stretched out his hands at once to receive it, but James would not see this hand. He took the landlord's hands and into those thin yellow shells he put the money. "This is a month's rent," he said. "Try to keep it for food and a little charcoal."

He knew even as he said the words that the hope was idle. At the gate he looked back and the manservant had taken the money from the old man and was helping him out of the room again.

He told the story that night when they were together at the evening meal and Chen rebuked him for what he had done. "You have made it impossible for us to stay here," he said. "Now every few days this manservant will be after us."

"I think James did right," Mary declared. "Only I think he should have insisted that the old man come to the hospital."

"When the Japs were here opium was cheap," Peter said.

"And how do you know that?" Chen asked.

"Fellows at the college use the stuff too," Peter said. "Not the crude opium, of course, but heroin pills. It makes me sick to see them. They can't get it now. One fellow is always after me." He closed his lips firmly as though he could not tell more.

James, listening to all this, now decided to speak what was in his mind. He looked around at them all. They had put on padded Chinese garments. Only thus could the intense cold of the house be borne. Here in the middle room which they all shared, there was the foreign stove which they had found at the thieves' market, not the large stove they had hoped to have but a little one which blazed red when coal was put into it, and turned cold soon after. Yet it was far better than nothing. This room was the only place which held any heat except the kitchen, and there the grass and reed fuel gave but a quick warmth that passed as soon as the flames died down. Padded cotton garments on their bodies and padded cotton shoes on their feet kept them from frostbite. They looked no whit different from the people on the streets.

"The time has come, I think, for us to move to the village," James said. "I know we thought of spring. But we cannot be colder there than here. And the cost of food and fuel will soon be beyond us. We cannot be worse off there."

Money was indeed becoming worthless. There was no true money. What the people used were baskets full of paper printed in America with Chinese letters and figures, signifying gold and silver that did not exist. All that James and Mary and Chen could earn barely paid for their food and rent and fuel, besides wages to the ones who cared for them. There was nothing left for clothing or pleasure. And soon, as the paper stuff grew more abundant and the figures were printed higher, even this would not be enough.

"Why should we wait for spring?" Mary exclaimed. "There is food in the village, and there is plenty of room. I want to go now."

James turned to Peter. "What do you say, brother?" he asked. He dreaded the answer, for what would Peter do in the village? There would be no students there and he would be lonely and unhappy. He would refuse to go. To his surprise Peter said no such thing. He lifted his head which so often he held down as though he were thinking of something secret and far from them all. "I am ready to go," he said. "I shall be glad to get away from here, at least."

Chen slapped his two hands on the table. "It is all folly," he declared, "but I will follow you three fools." They laughed and the thing was decided.

Yet so large a move could not be done in a day. First Uncle Tao must be written to, and this James did, telling him of his father's permission to receive the rents. Then the hospital must be told of their decision to leave. Never did James know that he had so many friends among the doctors and the nurses. Dr. Kang gathered together all the other doctors and they gave a small feast, not for farewell, Dr. Kang declared, but for advice. It was given in Dr. Su's house and Mrs. Su herself supervised the dishes. Since only men were present Mary was invited to come and help Mrs. Su, and these two young women busied themselves in the kitchen and ate in Dr. Su's study, while the doctors kept to themselves in the dining room. In the kitchen Mrs. Su apologized for everything before Mary, although secretly she was proud of her small clean foreign-style house. "Before the Japanese came," she said, stirring long strands of flour noodles into a pot of chicken broth, "I would not have thought it possible to keep a house without five servants at least. Now I am lucky to have this one Lao Po."

Lao Po was an old woman who kept perfectly silent and did nothing but wash the dishes which Mrs. Su dirtied and sweep the floor upon which were dropped flour and bits of grease and bone. She understood only a country dialect, for she did not come from the city.

Mrs. Su spoke to Mary in English. "Now of course money is nothing. I pay Lao Po food and room and bedding and some clothes beside her cash. She is not clean, but what can I do? Su will not look at her because he says she is so unclean. I say, 'Su, it is true Lao Po is dirty, but find me someone clean.' He cannot for no poor people can be clean. Let us tell the truth about ourselves. Our poor people are very dirty. After all, we are not Americans here today. We need not be ashamed before each other."

"Everything is nice," Mary said politely. Indeed the little house with curtains at its windows and wicker chairs with cushions in the living room seemed a palace of comfort to her.

Mrs. Su moved her chopsticks to a pot of pork bits simmering with chestnuts. "Louise is really very lucky," she said next. She did not know whether Mary knew that Louise had met the American here, and she could not be easy until she found out. "Of course it is better to marry a Chinese—we all agree to that. But Alec is a good American—not roughly chewing gum and swearing words all the time. He is nice family, I am sure. And I think Louise can never be happy here. She is really quite American herself."

Mary, slicing big white winter pears for a dessert before the meal, did not answer this.

Mrs. Su felt that by her silence she assuredly knew. Therefore she plunged into a half confession. She laughed first to show that she thought it nothing. Then she said, "You know Louise begged me so hard to come here and see Alec sometimes—of course always I was here with them. I felt very unhappy. I should have come and told you first. But I did not know how to say it to Louise. And they are so modern—we are all modern, of course. But I must ask you to excuse me if I did wrong."

Mary looked up with her large too truthful eyes. "I didn't know anything about it," she said. "Louise didn't tell me."

Mrs. Su regretted her queasy conscience and she made haste to talk about something else. "It does not matter now, with such happy ending," she said quickly. "Of course I knew Alec would be good husband and not just fooling. Now tell me, do you really leave our city?"

"We want to go to our ancestral home," Mary said. She began piling the thin slices neatly in a pyramid on a flowered dish.

"I am sorry," Mrs. Su said. She covered the pork and uncovered a skillet of shrimp and bamboo shoots. "And I think you will be sorry, too. For people like us, well educated, village is very hard. I never was in some village. That is, not for sleeping. Sometimes in spring and summer we go outside the city for picnic and of course we stop at village to rest. Even then it is too dirty for us. Su will not eat food there. The people are very wild and dirty and all the children are sick with something."

Mary did not reply to this. "Shall I take the pears in now?" she asked.

"Yes, please," Mrs. Su said briskly. "Just ask them to eat with watermelon seed and small things and in few minutes dinner is there." She began to spoon the shrimps into a bowl and Lao Po, seeing that the moment had arrived, brought bowls for other food.

"Lao Po!" Mrs. Su said loudly in Chinese. "I told you, put on a clean coat and wash your face and brush your hair!"

The old woman put down the bowls on the table and went away. By the time Mrs. Su had the bowls full of food, Lao Po came back looking quite clean. "Lao Po, you take the bowls, and put them on the table. I will put the rice in the bowls. Then you can serve us all."

Mrs. Su was a busy little figure in all the pride of her kitchen. Over her neat Chinese dress of rose-red silk she wore a white apron and her plump and creamy arms were bare.

Mary came back from the dining room. The men had greeted her pleasantly but with reserve. There was much gossip in the hospital that Mary was more willful than James and not so easy in temper, and that she, rather than he, guided the family destiny. It was for this reason that Dr. Su had invited only men to the feast.

"Shall I take in these dishes, too?" she asked Mrs. Su.

"No, Lao Po will do everything now," Mrs Su said, taking

off her apron. "I don't mind to cook, but I don't like to appear servant."

She led the way to the study and they sat down. Mrs. Su enjoyed a friend with whom to talk. Mary was not so pliable a friend as Louise had been, but she was a woman and a listener. "Sit down, please," Mrs. Su said. "Have some tea. Then our stomachs will be ready for the food. Lao Po will bring us the dishes when the men finish."

So sipping the fragrant tea, Mary sat and listened. Long ago she knew that women like Mrs. Su were of a kind to which she did not belong.

"Now, really," Mrs. Su began. Her round little face was not so pretty as it had been in the days before her marriage. It was less delicate and her eyes were no longer shy. "What shall we talk?" she asked in a bright voice.

"You talk," Mary said, smiling, "and I will listen."

Mrs. Su smoothed down her short skirt. "Shall I tell you how I marry Su?" Her voice was at once demure and cozy.

"If you like."

"It all begins like this," Mrs. Su said. "I was teaching English in Kunlun girls' school. Naturally I don't have to teach since my father is head of the bank, but still I cannot do nothing. One day my father say to me, 'Someone say Dr. Su, very famous and rich doctor, is going to divorce. Of course he cannot live always divorcing. He must have wife and how would you like to be that one?' At first I didn't like. I told him, 'Baba, suppose he has divorcing habit how I feel if then some day he also divorcing me?' But Baba say, 'No! All his other wives have been too stupid. They think only he is husband, they don't think also I am wife. Now you are not so stupid. When you marry, you think of him first.' So I say all right. Then my father asking Su's friend Dr. Kang to suggest Su I am rather nice. Of course my father gives something. Then at a party Dr. Kang introduces me and I look rather nice, I must say. Su is very handsome. There are two sons, but they are nice and they don't live here."

The cheerful little voice chirped along like a cricket at the door.

In the dining room, crowded with the doctors, James and Chen were listening to a steady chorus of disapproval and dissuasion. The food was excellent. Mrs. Su was a good cook, and Lao Po faithfully watched for an empty bowl.

"You will waste yourselves in a village," Dr. Su declared loudly. His last marriage was turning out well and he was beginning to put on weight. His handsome oval face was no longer thin and intellectual looking. He had a prosperous air, he smiled often and his voice carried the dominating note of the well-satisfied man. He heaped shrimp upon James's bowl as he went on talking. "Now, you know, Liang, the Generalissimo was very wise when in the recent war with Japan he decreed that our educated men were to stay in the colleges and not to go to the front. The youths from the villages were made into soldiers. We have too few educated men. We should conserve ourselves. We must live long. We must breed children."

"Eh, Liang!" Dr. Peng called jovially across the table. "You are not even married yet!"

"Liu Chen is not married, either," Kang retorted. "Two bachelors! We must penalize them! They must get drunk!"

"Of course they do not live in continence," Peng said with some malice. "Look at Liang—see, he is blushing! Eh—eh—everybody look at Liang!"

Dr. Su as host took pity. "Now, now, Peng—because you make love to every pretty nurse does not mean that all men are like you. Come, Liang—come, Liu Chen—you two fellows —tell us what you think you can do in this village!"

James had been all but silent until now. He was heartily enjoying his food. The cost of good food made this dinner a pleasure. He had not tasted pork and shrimp and sharks' fins for a long time. Where did Su get so much money?

"Perhaps I am only going to the village to learn." His voice was cool and quiet.

A shout of laughter answered this. "Learn what?" Su demanded. "How to eat sheets of pot bread and raw garlic?"

"How to kill lice?" Peng screamed.

"Now, now," Dr. Kang said, spreading his fine pale hands, "we are getting too coarse. I respect Liang and Liu Chen. They wish to serve the people, I am sure. Serve the people— ah, yes—it is very fine!" His voice, his manner, carried sarcasm, mild but tinged with apology. Liu Chen was saying nothing at all. "Liu Chen, why do you not speak?" he asked smiling affably at Chen.

Chen lifted his bushy eyebrows. "Me? Why should I talk when I can eat such good food? I am not so foolish." He held out his bowl to Lao Po. "More rice, old mother," he commanded. "I've only eaten four bowls."

They laughed again and James smiled. "Liu Chen is going to the country to eat," Peng declared.

But after they had eaten and had drunk their wine in tiny pewter bowls these doctors became serious with the two young men. "Now seriously," Dr. Su said, "in a sense what you are doing is to betray us all. You go to the country, you say to learn, in order that you may be more useful. But think in what light this puts the rest of us! You say, in effect, you are doing the right thing and we are doing the wrong."

"No," James replied. "We are only doing what we wish to do—not what is right, not what is wrong."

Liu Chen clapped his hands. "Truth—truth—" he declared.

Yet this truth continued to make them all uncomfortable with each other. Why did anybody wish to go to live in a village? Those who did not wish to go could not understand, and those who did wish to go could not explain. When the feast ended, the separation was already made. James and Chen had cut themselves off from the others and none would oppose their going.

Uncle Tao had not written an answer to the letter James sent him, but it was not expected that he would. Doubtless years had passed since he had put brush to paper. The preparations went forward therefore. Young Wang sold the furniture at the thieves' market and rejoiced when it brought many times the money it had cost. This was not all pure gain, since money was not worth nearly as much, but there was some gain. The stove was a cause for argument. Mary wished to sell it, so that they might live exactly as their kinfolk did, but Chen was prudent.

"You will find the village is just as cold as the city," he declared. "It is necessary that there be one place where we can get warm."

"We can sit on the k'ang," Mary said.

"You will not always want to sit on the k'ang among your cousins and all their children," he retorted.

"We cannot get coal in the village," Mary declared.

Chen had to yield. "You will not be content until you have us plowing," he said in mock complaint.

Little Dog and his mother made a great lamentation, since they were not to go. Where would they find so pleasant a place in which to live and to sleep and to eat? But Chen said sternly that the fewer the mouths that were brought to the village the more welcome James and Mary and Peter would be to their kinfolk. He himself was enough, and Young Wang was one more. Plenty of servants would be in the village, and so Little Dog was paid well and his mother was given a new padded coat. Nor were they turned out of the house at once. They could stay as long as the landlord allowed and it might be that a new tenant would need them.

As for the landlord, they did not go to bid him farewell. Chen's prudence was against this. A small parting gift was made of some cakes and at the last moment James kept back an easy chair for the old gentleman, so that he might sit in the sun and sleep.

Thus on a fine cold sunny morning in February they rose early and ate their last meal in the city house and bidding farewell to the weeping Little Dog and his mother, they mounted their hired mules and the muleteers yelled and brandished their whips and they began the long day's ride southwest to the ancestral village. The wind had died down in the night and the clouds of fine sandy dust which hung over the city for a week had settled. The air, made clean by the sandstorm, was as pure and dry as desert air, and the sun shone as though through glass. The landscape sparkled with light and distance was shortened and the rim of the earth seemed near. Under a gray sky this same land could look gray and dispirited, the people gray mites upon its surface, the villages scarcely to be seen. But on this day the houses were clear and the people no less clear in blue and gray flecks of red. The very brown of their skins was rich and lively.

Thus as the sun rose higher the spirits of the riders rose, too. They were young; they had set forth on the adventure; they had cut themselves clean from all that had been before. None had been content with life, and what was to come must have some good in it. Only Young Wang was gloomy. He who had lived all his childhood in a village under a landlord could not think with pleasure of Uncle Tao. Nevertheless, even he allowed himself to be cheered as the day wore on, remembering that those whom he served were kinfolk to Uncle Tao, and that they would protect him in time of need.

Only Peter was less cheerful than the others. He looked doubtful when they stopped at an inn for their noon meal. It was an inn like any other, the floor of beaten earth, the tables unpainted wooden boards set on legs. The innkeeper's wife was snaggle-toothed and unkempt, as all decent country women are lest it be thought they make themselves beautiful for men, and her hair was unbrushed for many days and the sandstorms had left it brown and dusty. Yet she was cheerful and when she asked them in a loud voice what they would eat, her breath came out hearty with garlic.

"What have you?" James asked.

"Bread and garlic," she replied.

"What else?" Chen asked.

"We have millet and cabbage."

"Nothing else?" Chen insisted.

"Bread and garlic," she said again.

They laughed and she laughed and James told her to bring all she had. Nevertheless, she brought a little more, for these, she saw, were no common guests. When the meal was served she put before them homemade noodles in boiling water and dipping out the noodles she sprinkled them with sesame oil and a little vinegar and soy sauce and on top of this she put chopped green onion sprouts.

"No meat?" Peter said with some discontent.

"Come, you American," Chen replied, "you will see little meat from now on."

"The food is hot and good," James said.

They ate themselves full, Young Wang sitting at some distance from them. James had motioned to him to sit with them but Young Wang, feeling what was fit, would not do this. While he ate the woman sat near him on a bench and talked. Thus he learned that this village feared greatly the coming of the Communists who were now only a short distance away.

"What are Communists?" Young Wang asked, to see what she would say.

"Who knows?" the woman retorted. "I have never seen one alive. But some were caught a month ago near here and beheaded by the soldiers of the government and I went to see them. Well, they looked just like all dead men, except they were young."

"Why do you fear them?" Young Wang asked.

"They take away the land," the woman replied.

"And they are all young men," Young Wang said slyly, "and I suppose you fear them for that, too."

The woman laughed very much at this and looked sidewise at Young Wang, and made such answer as this, "You and your mother! Eh, you son of a hare—" all of which was designed to reprove him and at the same time to signify that she took pleasure in his wit.

Later in the day, while Young Wang rode beside Peter, he told Peter what the woman had said, and Peter looked so thoughtful that Young Wang was curious, and he grew bold. "What do you think of the Communists, young master?" he asked.

"How do I know what they are?" Peter replied. "Some say they are good and some say they are bad, but I have seen none of them."

"If some are good and some are bad then they are like all other men," Young Wang said, and they rode on without more talk.

Ahead of them the other three rode together, side by side when the road allowed, and falling into single file when it went narrow. Mary was always between James and Chen, and both talked to her but Chen talked the more. James was deep in thought. He saw every line and accent upon the landscape, but it was not of the landscape that he thought. His mind was already in the village. He must begin small. For a month or so he would seem to do nothing. Then he would heal a sick child, and then a few more and then he would be willing to treat others, and then he would find a room for a clinic and this room could become two and three until in a simple way it was a small hospital. When the time came he would write to Rose and Marie and Kitty and among the three perhaps one would be willing to come as a nurse to aid him.

In the same small quiet way must Mary begin her school. Nothing must be done with noise or fanfare. They were only Liangs coming home to their kinfolk. Chen was their friend. Chen would advise and keep the accounts. He would begin from the first to ask a little money for medicine. He had brought with him a small dispensary, loaded in boxes upon the backs of two mules, and Mary had brought some schoolbooks.

It was good that they were not farther from the city, for Young Wang could always ride back for new supplies. But they had enough for some months.

James repeated to himself like a song, like a ritual, like the rhythm of his heartbeat, that he must go slowly every day and win his way. The dream was a hospital, not a great foreign building standing stories high above the surrounding countryside under a great curving temple roof. He saw his hospital low, a spreading shelter for the sick, the walls of earth and the roof of common tiles, so that when the sick came in it would not frighten them. They would see only a house like their own homes, bigger, for the family of the sick was large, but under their feet would be the beaten earth, and above their heads the rafters would be beneath the tiles. This hospital would be the center but out from it everywhere would reach living hands of healing. He would teach as well as heal. Under his teaching men and women would go out everywhere to find the sick, to treat them for simple illness, and to bring back to the hospital those who were too gravely ill. And they would not only heal the sick. They would teach the young mothers who were the creators of life, and the children who loved life enough to cling to it, and the young men who took pride in their families.

So he wove his dreams that day as he rode through the countryside until he saw them reaching into every village through which they passed, and every blind man and sickly child he saw healed and strong again. What had seemed impossible in the city and in the great hospital now became plain and possible to him.

"It is well enough for you two," Chen was grumbling to Mary, "you and Jim know what you will do. But I am here for nothing. This is all folly, I tell you. I am the son of a villager and I know that village people cannot be changed unless you catch them young and drag them away. They like their faces dirty and they do not want to bathe themselves. Dirt is their garment."

"We will change all that," Mary said briskly.

"Ah," Chen said sagely, "do not think that you will do all the changing! They will also change you."

So the day passed. They rode steadily except for stopping for the noon meal and again at sunset. The several mules went more slowly than the two had come on their first visit, and it was well onto midnight before they came near to the ancestral village. The night was as clear as the day had been and the great yellow stars hung in the sky and quivered in the cold night air. In the darkness the villages sank back into the earth. Gates were barred and they could no longer pass through the streets. They were compelled to find paths around village walls, and only the baying of watchdogs, wakened by the sound of horses' hooves, disturbed the silence of those who slept early and deep.

They, too, were full of sleep and their bones ached from the rough riding. Peter rode with hanging head and a slack bridle and Mary, though wakeful, was made solemn by the vastness of the land spreading in darkness about her. She was not given to meditation or imagination, being one of those creatures easily busy in many things, but even upon her did the spell of the land fall.

Chen buttoned his coat closely about him and wondered at himself. He was no dreamer of dreams, having all his life seen life hard and clear and cruel. He had not come to save anyone from death or even sickness. Often did he wish that he could live as callously as Su or Peng or Kang and their kind, and he cursed himself that he could not. It was their fault, he told himself. Had they been larger men, less selfish and trivial in their minds, he would have accepted them. But they repelled him with their smallness, even while he admired their skill. He loved no villager or poor man and yet he tended any man or woman or child with care and with respect for life. Thus unwillingly was he the bondsman of his own soul.

It was soon after midnight when they saw ahead of them the low walls of the ancestral village. The square of these walls, the squat tower over the gate, were not different from those of any other village they had passed, but some homing instinct led James to know the village was his own. The gate was locked and Young Wang beat upon it with a loose brick he found and he raised such a clatter that every dog inside the walls snarled and bayed his belly out. This woke the watchman who slid back a small panel and looked out with terror shining on his face in the light of the paper lantern he held. Who but bandits and Communists would come to a village at midnight?

"We are of the Liang family!" James called to him. "Do you remember us? Look at my face!"

The watchman stared and saw him. "Eh, you bring too many with you," he objected.

"My sister, who came before, my younger brother, my friend and our serving man. The rest are muleteers," James replied.

"The inn cannot hold all these muleteers," the man objected.

Young Wang came forward at this moment. "Elder brother, the muleteers will not sleep here if there is no room," he said with courtesy. All this time he had been counting money inside his bosom and now his hand came out clenched about a roll of bills and he went close to the gate and somehow the money met the watchman's hand through the small open panel and after a moment the gate swung open. Dogs were waiting inside and they sprang at the mules, but the mules, long used to them, plodded on, only breathing hard and kicking at the leaping dogs if they came too near.

Thus they went in single file down the street and so came to the gate of the ancestral house. This gate, too, was closed but the middle son of Uncle Tao had been waked by the dogs and he had risen and stood near the gate. His heart beat fast, for why should horsemen pass through the village now? When he heard a knock upon his own gate that heart stopped for a second. Did not the Communists always come to the house of the landlord first? He slid back a little panel and looked out.

"It is I, Cousin Brother," James said.

The gate was thrown wide then, and the cousin stood holding his robes about him as he had thrown them on when he rose from his bed.

"Come in," he said, "welcome, even at this hour. We knew you were coming one day or another, and we have been expecting you any day. Come in, come in—"

It was a pleasant welcome and they all came in while the cousin ran to wake the women. They rose, with such men cousins as waked themselves, and millet soup was heated and water was boiled for tea, while Young Wang paid the muleteers with much loud argument and anger over the wine money which was to be given above the price agreed upon.

At last all was settled, and the loads were in the house and the mules gone. In the middle room all gathered to eat and drink before they slept again, each feeling somewhat shy because of the new life ahead. Kinfolk they were, and yet they were strangers, too, now that they were to live together under the same roof. Uncle Tao had not waked and none had called him. Let that be for tomorrow.

Yet the kinswomen were kind and they pressed the new-comers to eat and drink and the kinsmen were courteous and asked how the journey had been. They looked often at the boxes which James had brought and one asked if they contained money. "Only medicines," James said. "You know I am a doctor."

To this none answered and he felt them afraid and bewildered by a new thing under the roof.

Peter said not a word. He ate a little and drank some tea and from under his dark eyebrows he looked at these kinfolk of his. He felt not one drop of blood in him that was like the blood in them. Yet they were all Liangs. His father, thousands of miles away, in a world as different from this as though it were upon another star, was still a Liang, with these. Mind knew, but could not comprehend, and heart rebelled. Peter only longed to sleep.

Chen was cheerful. There was nothing here too strange to him. This village was like his own, and these frowzy women and slovenly men were like those who lived in his own father's household. He made small talk, and asked questions in courtesy and they laughed once or twice at what he said and their eyes were lively. This he did with intent. They must like him, because in days to come he must stand often between them and Mary, and even perhaps Jim. He pitied these two with all his heart for he loved them well. Peter? Peter would not stay here, that he believed. But Jim and Mary were bound by their own wills.

"Now we must sleep," Chen said at last. "You, Elder Brothers, are too good. Please go back to your beds."

So saying all rose and the kinsmen took the newcomers to their rooms, and the kinswomen led Mary to her room where she had slept before. Young Wang lay down upon three chairs in the middle room and wrapped his quilt about him.

All tiptoed as they passed Uncle Tao's room until they heard his great rumbling cough and then they paused and looked at one another.

"Can it be he has been awake this whole time?" the eldest kinswoman whispered.

For answer there came a second great rumbling cough from Uncle Tao. They waited listening, but he did not speak and neither did he come out. After a long few minutes of such waiting they crept on, each to his own bed.

Uncle Tao lay listening to their footsteps creeping away. He knew very well what had happened. The first dog had wakened him. But he did not get up. He lay slowly making up his mind and only mischief made him cough when he heard them pass his door. Let them know that he was awake and would not get up!

15

A PLEASANT HOME, Violet Sung told herself, a pleasant woman, this mother of Alec Wetherston, and Louise was lucky. Violet sat in a comfortable chair in a large living room full of too many things and now and then she looked through the wide window in the central garden of the huge apartment house.

"Dr. and Mrs. Liang will be pleased when I tell them how you feel," she said in her sweet deep voice. With her instinctive gift she appeared a gentle somewhat simple-hearted young woman before this gentle and very simple-hearted older woman. "You can understand that they have been a little troubled at such a quick marriage. Not everyone would be so generous as you have been. We Chinese pay great heed to the mother-in-law. Therefore it was natural that I should offer, on behalf of my friends, to come and see you first."

Mrs. Wetherston looked troubled. "I do hope," she said with pathetic emphasis, "that nobody will think of me as a mother-in-law!"

Violet smiled. "To us a mother-in-law is a revered figure. A son honors his mother, and the son's wife must both honor and obey."

"Oh, I don't want to be obeyed!" Mrs. Wetherston exclaimed. She was a small plump white-haired woman whose face was no whit different from that of any plump white-haired woman whom one might pass on the street. She was dressed in a gray wool frock, tight across her ample hips and bosom, and her feet, crossed upon a worn hassock of red velvet, were encased in black kid pumps, too tight across the instep. But she had grown accustomed to such restrictions and there was something pleasant and good about her. She was a woman sheltered and loved for so long that she did not know her own privilege. The mother of five children, of whom Alec was the youngest, she had already eight grandchildren. But the big apartment was empty now. Sons and daughters had scattered.

Mrs. Wetherston saw Violet's roaming gaze. "I know this apartment ought to be redecorated," she said apologetically. "But I just can't bear to have it done. The children grew up here and I want to keep it like this. That spot on the arm of your chair—Rob, that's my oldest, spilled his ice cream there when he was having his tenth birthday party. Of course it's been cleaned but I can remember him so well when he was ten. And the piano stool is a sight, but they would kick it when they were practicing—Lilian plays beautifully, but the others got tired of it except Ken, who sings tenor. Not professionally, of course! I'm sentimental, Miss—"

"Violet Sung—"

"Oh, yes, of course. Chinese names are so—but I can call her Louise right away so it doesn't matter if I can't remember—"

"Liang," Violet said gently.

"Oh yes, of course—though we will want to have them all over to dinner."

"You really don't mind having a Chinese daughter-in-law?" Violet asked. She gathered up gloves and bag and handkerchief, preparing to go.

Mrs. Wetherston struggled with truth. "I've always said that I would love the people my children married and I intend to love Louise," she said valiantly. She paused and her good, wrinkled face blushed a dull pink. "What really grieves me is that my boy didn't tell me about the other one—the first wife—who died—you know—the baby's mother. I can't understand—" Her lips trembled, and Violet who comprehended all men, hastened to comfort this mother who could never believe that her sons were only men.

"A first love is sometimes very deep," she said quietly.

Mrs. Wetherston's eyes filled. "There was even a child."

Violet felt danger about her. The innocence of American women was frightening and she must not disturb it. Mrs. Wetherston was the mother of five children and yet she was a virgin. She wondered what Mr. Wetherston could be. His business, she had learned, was prosperous and sound. He was the head of an old legal firm. Her mind toyed for a moment with the idea of Mr. Wetherston. Perhaps American husbands enjoyed keeping their wives virginal. It gave men more liberty. Then she shrank from all responsibility for Mrs. Wetherston's innocence.

"I am sure your son will tell you everything when he comes," she said, pressing Mrs. Wetherston's plump hand. "Meanwhile it is perhaps well that Louise is Chinese. She will look like the baby's mother and if I were in your place, dear Mrs. Wetherston, I should just forget that she is not."

Mrs. Wetherston was comforted. When Violet Sung first came in she had been afraid of her because she was beautiful and well dressed but now she saw that she was only a dear and charming girl, in spite of being Chinese. "I hope Louise will be like you," she said, clinging to Violet's soft ringed hand.

"She is much better than I am," Violet said, smiling. "Much younger, much prettier—"

"But you are so understanding," Mrs. Wetherston said. "You really aren't like a Chinese!"

These words, said so innocently, fell into Violet's heart like a dart thrown by a child. They made a little wound which she quickly concealed. "Good-by, dear Mrs. Wetherston," she said. "I will tell my friends how kind you are."

In the street again she took a passing cab and went directly to Dr. Liang's apartment. During the family distress Mrs. Liang had subdued her jealousy and now it was she who met Violet at the door.

"Come in, come in," she said warmly in English. "Tell us all about something."

She pattered into the living room ahead of Violet and as she passed the closed door of the study she raised her voice. "Eh, Liang! Violet Sung got here."

There was no answering voice. Dr. Liang heard her and was displeased at the rude summons. He did not therefore move for some five minutes. Had anyone opened the door he would have been sitting at his desk, a brush held upright between his thumb and two fingers as he wrote Chinese letters. But no one opened the door and after the five minutes he got up and walked with slow dignity into the living room.

"Forgive me," he said to Violet. "I was just finishing a stop-short."

He had taught her the necessary qualities of the four-line poem thus named, and she smiled at him. "You must let me read it," she said.

He made a deprecating gesture. "It is far from perfect yet," he replied. "I have worked on it for four days, but I am not satisfied."

"Now, Liang," his wife broke in, "don't talk some poetry. Sit down. Miss Sung wants to tell us how is Wetherstons."

In her eagerness she was to Dr. Liang's perceptions more than usually vulgar. To quiet her therefore he sat down and prepared to listen. Violet, glancing at his sensitive and handsome face, imagined that she saw suffering there. Certainly his pallor was deeper than usual. She proceeded very gently.

"You are fortunate. The home is a good one. It is not too rich, but there is some money. The mother-in-law is kind, and she wishes to do well but she does not know anything. Everything will depend upon Louise. The mother believes that her sons are all good and even great men, and Louise must learn the wisdom of agreeing with her mother-in-law."

Mrs. Liang cried out at this. "Our Louise? She cannot agree with anybody. What do you say, Liang?"

"Please go on, Miss Sung," he said.

Violet went on. "The mother-in-law, wanting to be kind and correct, is determined that she does not mind her daughter-in-law being Chinese. But in her heart she minds because it is something strange. It makes her different from other women she knows. Also she is not sure how Louise will fit into the home. I told her Louise was very American—is indeed by birth a citizen—and this comforts her somewhat but not wholly. And she is wounded that her son told her nothing of his first love affair or that a child was born."

Dr. Liang had been making up his mind rapidly as Violet talked. The Wetherston family was not distinguished. The Liang family was better. It was therefore an honor for the Wetherstons to be connected with him. He would maintain this position.

Violet Sung went on. "She hopes to invite you to dinner."

Mrs. Liang brightened. "I like to go and see," she exclaimed.

Dr. Liang rose. "Thank you very much, Miss Sung," he said formally. "You have done us a great service. Let us be glad that the family is respectable. I suppose we should not hope for more. The man might have been someone from the slums. It is useless to pretend, however, that I am pleased. I shall not feel the same toward my daughter Louise."

"Please wait," Violet said. "It may all turn out very well. I believe that blood and body differences do not matter if minds and hearts are the same."

Mrs. Liang agreed to this with enthusiasm. "Miss Sung, you say true. I also! Of course, it is much better to marry Chinese if possible. If not possible, then American is not too bad. Liang, I am not agreeing. I am happy seeing my daughter, and I am feeling nice to her husband. As for baby, it is boy, and that is some better than girl. I say everything is not too bad."

Dr. Liang ignored this. He spoke only to Violet. "I suppose," he said with a slight smile, "that it is only natural for me to maintain certain superiorities. Will you forgive me if I go back now to my studies?"

He bowed and walked out of the room, conscious that Violet was looking at him thoughtfully.

16

IN THE ANCESTRAL VILLAGE the four sat talking. James, Chen, and Peter had three rooms leading one into the other and facing south upon a small barren court. James kept for his own the central and slightly larger room which, having no windows, had a wide door that was now open to the winter sun. Here they were gathered. There was no other heat than the sunshine, and they were all clothed in padded Chinese garments and Mary sat with her feet on a small brass footstove within which were coals imbedded in ash. All of them wore half gloves which Mary had knit from gray camel's-hair yarn.

They had been here for nearly a month and under James's command had done nothing, apparently, except receive all who wished to come and see them. Yet within the house they had been quietly busy, except for Peter who read and studied much alone. The monotony of the country food had persuaded Mary to bid Young Wang to buy an earthen portable stove shaped like a jar with a small iron grate at the top. He put it in a sheltered corner of the barren court, and buying small pond fish and white cabbage and soy bean vermicelli with an occasional scrawny chicken, he set before them private and pleasant dishes. Other members of the family did the same in their part of the rambling earthen house and it was not taken amiss.

No one had expected Young Wang to remain in the village since he so enjoyed city life, but he had surprised all of them by falling in love with the daughter of the village innkeeper. Chen had first suspected it in the careless service and generally absent-minded behavior which Young Wang began to show soon after their arrival. Upon inquiry Young Wang confessed that he felt it was time for him to start a family for himself, and that it would be convenient if he settled here. He reminded himself and James that he had always dreamed of returning to the sea to be a ship's cook, but now that he had seen the innkeeper's daughter, he preferred to be a land cook. The inn was a good business, he further explained, and it was his luck that the innkeeper's two sons had died, one as a child and the other last year of smallpox, leaving the daughter the only offspring. This meant that her husband would be accepted in place of a son, and he could step into the business as heir.

"I suppose you care nothing about the girl herself," Chen had said teasingly.

Young Wang had grinned. "I have seen her once or twice," he admitted. "She is not too ugly."

Anybody could see the innkeeper's daughter any day as she served at the tables and Chen had laughed loudly. "You need a marriage broker," he told Young Wang. "Allow me to offer myself. I will ask no fee except a good meal cooked by your own hands and served by your wife after the wedding."

Young Wang was much pleased, and Chen had gone to the innkeeper and had made so handsome a picture of Young Wang that both parents had soon agreed to accept him.

"Shall we not also ask the young woman if she will consider him as a husband?" Chen had suggested daringly.

"No," the innkeeper said with decision. "It is none of her business. The inn is mine."

Nevertheless Chen took care one day before the betrothal papers were written to eat a meal at the inn and to ask for wine, which the girl always served. The hour was early and he sat alone at a table. When she poured the wine from the long slender spout of the pewter winepot, he leaned toward her and without looking at her he said these words in a low voice. "If there is any reason why you do not wish to proceed with the papers which bind you to Young Wang, remove the lid of the winepot as a sign."

He did this in order to spare the feelings of a young girl. But she was no shy and modest creature. All her life had been spent in the inn and she saw new men every day. Therefore she answered smartly though not loudly, "A woman has to marry some man or other, and if he has his two eyes and his two arms and two legs, he is as good as any."

Thus did she say that her heart was pleased with Young Wang, and so the wedding was set for the first lucky day after the opening of spring. Chen felt proud at this first achievement in the village and word went around that he had been a go-between and people praised him for his good common ways. He himself foresaw that his function in the years to come, if these two young Liangs persisted in staying here as they now swore themselves to do, would be to stand as bridge between the old and the new. With all the good intent in the world, James was too cautious and Mary too quick. James could not easily understand these country people in the very excess of his sensitive wish to do so, and Mary did not wait on understanding. If a child's face was dirty she wiped it clean without perceiving that the jealous mother was wounded thereby.

Yet Mary was more fortunate than James. She paid little heed to the elders but she had witchery over children. She was full of stories and songs and games, and following James's command she did not try to teach anything for a full month. The two dozen and more Liang children allowed her to wash them and to tend their scratches and cuts and soon they followed her everywhere, so that she had not one moment to herself.

Her danger was that she was impatient with Uncle Tao. She refused to respect him. She told him boldly that he would feel better if he washed himself all over with hot water and soap even though it was winter, and while he was washing she would put a powder into his clothes that would kill the lice.

Uncle Tao listened to her with astonishment. He was not quite angry for his real anger he never wasted on women. But he pursed his lips and rolled his eyes around and refused to wash himself. "I have never washed in the winter," he declared. His sleeves were wide and he withdrew his arms from them the better to scratch remote parts of his body. "As for lice, they are a sign of good health."

"They are a proof of dirt," Mary said severely.

Uncle Tao rolled his head round and round on his short neck to signify rage. "You know nothing about lice! I tell you, they will not stay on a sickly person or on any person about to die. I am healthy and I have many lice."

Mary walked away, her cheeks flaming and her head high. When Chen begged her to remember that this was China and not America, that it was country and not city, Mary flouted him. She said, "Uncle Tao is just a fat dirty old man."

Had she been a boy she might have suffered. But it was accepted in this household as in all others that women were like children and must be allowed a license which a man as a superior being could not have. Therefore although no other woman dared to quarrel with Uncle Tao, it became a matter for family respect that Mary was not afraid of him and that he, although he roared at her, did not demand that she be beaten.

Peter remained unknown and aloof. It was plain to all that something secret weighed upon the boy's mind. James, probing him, could not find what it was, for Peter would not tell him anything.

"I think you should go back to America, Peter," James said one day.

"I don't want to go," Peter replied.

"Then what do you want to do?" James asked with something as near impatience as he allowed himself.

Peter had shrugged his shoulders. "Leave me alone," he said.

So this day, too, he sat in silence while the others talked together. The first small sign of the northern spring had shown itself. Young Wang had found in the village market some lily bulbs and he had brought them home and had shown Mary how by keeping the water tepid about their roots they could be forced, though the room was cold. Now the flowers hung in rich golden-hearted clusters and their fragrance filled the room. In the court, too, a small bare lamay bush had begun to show buds of waxen yellow even before there was a leaf, and the brown buds on the plum tree were beginning to swell.

"I must begin to do something," Mary declared. As usual when they were together they spoke in English and as usual James reproved them.

"Please," he said, "there is nothing we need hide, and if they hear us speaking a foreign language it makes them think us foreign."

"You are overcareful," Chen said lazily. He sat in the sun and the warmth was creeping into his heart. "They know we speak English."

"I shall begin by teaching a few of our own Liang children how to read," Mary said. "Then others will join us. And I shan't ask Uncle Tao."

"I think I shall not begin on our own family," James said thoughtfully. "And I will ask Uncle Tao."

Chen laughed. "We will see how far each of you goes," he said.

Peter had been listening and now he suddenly broke forth as though he could not contain what was in his thought. "You are all foolish—as if it matters what you do in one little village to a handful of people among so many millions!"

His angry young voice stilled them in the midst of their pleasure in the coming spring and in each other.

"What do you suggest?" Mary asked. She put the bitter question in English for Peter had cried out in that tongue.

"It's all rotten," Peter cried. "Nothing will be any use except a clean sweep from top to bottom." He got up and walked about the room and sat down again but this time out of the sunshine and beside the table.

"Go on," James said, "tell us what you think. None of us know."

"I don't know what to think," Peter said. "I have been trying to find out. The dirt—the disease—the stupidity!' He stared at them all in a sort of rage. "I shall never forgive Pa as long as I live—letting us believe that everything was wonderful, hiding it all under a Confucian mist! No wonder he doesn't come back!"

"I suppose you wish you hadn't come back," Mary flung at him.

But Peter would not accept this. "I don't wish that. I am glad I came back. If this is the way things are in my country I'd rather know it."

"Still you wish they weren't," Mary argued.

"Of course I wish they weren't!" Peter reared his head like a young stallion and glared at them. "I wish the president of my college weren't a pussy-footing old fool! I wish he didn't love tea parties and flattering sycophantic professors—and women! I wish we had a decent government! I wish we needn't be afraid of secret police sneaking everywhere like rats in sewers! I wish I didn't have to see my college mates jailed—tortured—killed! I wish we even had the guts to rebel—and stand together—which we haven't—because we're all rotten through and through—" His voice broke, tears rushed to his eyes, and he turned away his head.

James had listened, his eyes steadily on his young brother's flushed face. Now he spoke. "We all wish that some things were different. It is like coming home from college and discovering that your parents can't read and write. But they are still your parents. We have to take our people as they are and change them as we can."

"They won't change," Peter muttered.

"I suppose we have to prove to them that change would be better," James said reasonably.

"How can you prove anything to a lot of village dolts?" Peter demanded.

"What else can you do?" Mary demanded in return.

Peter gave her a strange dark look. "There are other ways," he said.

They gazed at him with blank looks and he rose to his feet impetuously. "Oh, I don't belong here and we all know it. The sooner I go back to the city the better it will be for us all. I can board at the college."

He went into his own room and shut the door. They were silent for a moment after this. Chen looked very grave. He sat on the high wooden threshold of the door, his hands clasped about his knees, and he gazed out into the barren court surrounded by the low earthen wall. "The innocents!" he murmured. "We must pity them. But they are terrible in their innocence—and dangerous."

"What do you mean?" Mary asked.

"Peter is American," Chen said. "He has been brought up innocent. He believes that anything can be done and done quickly. You do it by force, either of money or arms. What can the innocent understand of the long slow years, the thousands of years? What can they know of the incorruptible people?"

"Are the people incorruptible?" Mary asked. Her voice was troubled and wondering and not at all like Mary's voice, usually brisk and firm.

"There are corruptible men but no corruptible people," Chen said.

"You give me hope," James said.

They talked long together that day without Peter. They planned how they would begin, in what small ways, with what few people. They would begin at once, tomorrow, Mary gathering the children together, James setting up his small clinic. They would let the people of the ancestral village lead them, and as they themselves were led, they would lead again.

"And Peter?" Mary asked.

"Peter must decide for himself," James said.

Young Wang was much troubled. He had been told to go with Peter to the city and see him settled in his room at the college and then come back again. This he would do. But should he first tell his master about the marble bridge? So long as Peter was safe in the village he had felt no need to tell. Yet were Peter to be alone in the city should there not be warning to the elder brother?

He took his chance to talk with Peter himself as they wound along the country roads northward. "Now, young master," he argued, "I am older than you, though a serving man only, and I beg you to have nothing to do with such students as do not read their books and who instead spend their time complaining against the government. All governments are devouring beasts, and they feed upon the people. Avoid officials, I pray you. This we are taught even when we are children. And especially now, avoid our present officials, who are beside themselves with greed, since money is worthless. They will destroy all who complain. The nearer a government is to its end, the more cruel and hungry it becomes. Was it not so in the days of the old empire?"

Peter did not answer this and Young Wang, stealing a look at his sullen face, went on. "I have not told your elder brother anything about the marble bridge, and I will not if you will promise me only to read your books and not mix yourself with those who read no books."

"I do not need to promise anything to you," Peter said rudely. "Let me tell you this—I do not care what you say to my brother."

Young Wang did not say any more after this. He became again only the good silent servant and he went with Peter to the college and there they found no room empty. But after some search Peter found a friend, a youth from the province of Hupeh, whose name was Chang Shan, and this friend said, "There is space in my room for another bed, and you are welcome to the space if you can find the bed."

So Young Wang ran to the thieves' market and found a bed and put it up in the narrow room and he spread quilts and he bought some fruits and sweets and did all he could for his young master. When there was nothing more to do, he waited until he could find the Hupeh youth alone for a few minutes and then he said, "This young master of mine is wholly ignorant, coming from America, and he does not understand anything here. I beg you to shield him and watch over him and warn him and do not let him fall into evil hands. He walks with his head high and he does not see where his feet are going."

The Hupeh youth smiled at this and said, "Yes, yes," and Young Wang gave him a parcel of food he had bought as a gift and then having indeed done all he could, he returned to the village. There he made no report to James beyond saying that he had seen Peter safely to the college and had bought him a bed and that he was among friends. Young Wang was a prudent man and he was loath to make trouble in the family he served. It might be that Peter would heed his warning. At least he would wait and see. Meanwhile the affairs of his own marriage began to press him. His father-in-law was a canny man who did not wish to yield up his authority in the inn too easily. The first necessity therefore, Young Wang decided, was to marry the daughter and get her with child and so establish himself secure in this family.

Young Wang's wedding day dawned clear and calm, a good day in the midst of days of wind and sandstorm and this he took to be a favorable omen. The wedding was a common one without extra show, but Young Wang in his thriftiness considered it money soundly spent to pay for a meal at the inn for everybody. The gentry ate apart from the others, and the Liang family were put in the inner rooms. Uncle Tao let his hunger loose and he ate and drank mightily, and all admired his capacity.

Chen, delicately perceiving what was his proper place, did not sit down long with the Liangs and yet he did not sit anywhere else. He wandered about among the guests making jokes and teasing the bride, who ran here and there with the feast dishes as though it were any wedding except her own. James sat near to Uncle Tao but at the outer edge of the tables, and from here he looked at the villagers and country folk. They were hearty people and good, ignorant of letters and yet wise in the ways of human life. They were not innocents. They did not expect much and they were happy with what they had. Yet they would gladly be more happy if it were possible. They liked Uncle Tao and they despised him, too. They bore with such gentry; they did not wish them dead, but they watched their own scales when they measured seed rice and harvested grain. No, they were not innocents. They granted to every man his own right to the life he liked best, or the life that he had been given by Heaven.

From this wedding feast James returned to his own room late that night and he sat thinking and alone for a long time. He was not here, he perceived, only to do what good he could. Perhaps he was not here to do good at all. He was here to release some force of life now hidden in his people. To heal their bodies was to release force, to teach them to read and to write was to release yet more of such force. What was this force? It was good sense and strong wisdom, and it was an inheritance. It was also his inheritance. While he gave his people the tools of health and letters, he gave himself the means of learning what their wisdom was, and when he knew them he could enter into his inheritance, from which he had been cut off. Thus would he find his own roots.

In this humility he began his new life.

Spring delayed that year, and week after week the cold winter nights covered the city. On one such night the sky clouded soon after sunset and snow began to fall. Many poets of ancient times had written poems about snow falling upon the roofs of the palaces, but Peter could not read these poems and he did not even know of their existence. And the peaceful times in which they had been written were gone. It was one thing to look out from a snug and comfortable house set in a prosperous nation and see the snowflakes drifting upon imperial roofs. Today the palaces were empty and poet and emperor alike were dust. The city was desolate, the people without good rulers and the enemy only newly driven away. The past was no more, and the future could not be seen.

Peter, pressing his face against the small dirty windowpane of his friend's room, saw the lamplight reflected only upon large wet snowflakes that tomorrow would make the day's work harder, the classrooms more chill and damp, the streets slippery. Here inside this heatless room the temperature was already freezing. Like most students, his friend Chang Shan had contrived a small stove upon which to boil hot water to drink, or at best for making a little tea. The stove was only an oil can bought from someone who had followed the American army and had salvaged all tin cans. But Chang Shan, being inventive, had lined the tin with clay and had made a frame of heavy wire to support a small copper kettle. The hot water, poured into cheap pottery bowls, kept their hands from being too chilblained for writing, and the same hot water in their stomachs gave them momentary warmth within.

Peter looked at Chang Shan. He was a tall very thin young man of twenty-two. Anyone could see that he had tuberculosis, as most of the students had. His head was large and the bones of his skull protruded. A big slightly arched nose, full pale lips and solid white teeth were nothing uncommon in his looks, but these, combined as they were with fiery eyes, gave his head nobility. Everybody secretly admired Chang Shan, but few dared to be his friends. In these times when life depended upon many things besides food, friends could be more dangerous than enemies. Peter and Chang Shan were friends.

"You will not believe me when I tell you that the place where my father lives is warmed in every corner by pipes carrying hot water," Peter said.

"It is a pity you do not return to your father," Chang Shan said. He was reading a badly printed book and he did not look up.

"I do not know why I cannot return," Peter replied. They spoke in Chinese because Chang did not speak English. Peter had learned to speak the Peking Mandarin, partly that he might talk with Chang Shan. Yet he had never taken Chang Shan to the city house. James and Mary, he had felt, would not like this friend. Chang Shan was an absolutist. When anything was not good, he believed in its total destruction. Thus he believed now in the destruction of the old family system, of the president of the university, of all capitalists, of the Chinese written language, of inflation, of the high cost of living, of the gold standard, of Confucianism, the classics, and the government. It was only a matter of time until Chang Shan would be caught by the secret police and killed. He knew it and for this reason he did not allow himself to fall in love with a girl who loved him. He refused even to see her and the only way she could comfort herself was to come to the room when he was away and leave small packages of food. Chang Shan tried not to eat these but sometimes his hunger compelled him to do so. The girl, Fengying, was a plain ugly female student, and she waylaid Peter as often as she could to ask if Chang Shan had eaten the food and to beg Peter to persuade him to do so. She did not hide her adoration. She declared to Peter, "Chang Shan will be a great revolutionary leader. It is our duty to keep him alive." In her heart she hoped Peter did not consume her gifts, but she did not say so, fearing he might be angry and so refuse to answer her questions about Chang Shan.

"Yes, yes—" Peter had agreed. She was so ugly, her bulging eyes so pathetic behind her steel-rimmed spectacles, that he escaped from her as soon as he could.

"I do not know why I do not return to my father," Peter said now to Chang Shan. He, too, was trying to study but he had found it impossible to read the assignment for the next day. It mattered little enough whether he read it or not. The professor would doubtless not come to his class through the snow. His shoes, like those of his students, were only of cotton cloth, and the snow would soon wet them and he had not another pair. He had long ago sold his leather shoes for money to buy rice and so could buy no more leather shoes.

"You are weakening again," Chang Shan said scornfully. "You have been wet-nursed on Confucianism. You are, I suppose, the superior man."

"You are very unjust," Peter said bitterly.

"I am not unjust, then, to myself," Chang Shan said gravely. All this time he had not lifted his eyes from the book. Now suddenly he looked at the window. When he saw the reflection of the light upon the falling snowflakes, he got up quickly and went out.

Peter did not ask where he went. Chang Shan might have gone out for any reason. Since there were no indoor toilets, he might merely have stepped outside in the street to relieve himself. Or he might have decided that this was a good night to go to the marble bridge.

He came back in a few minutes. "The night is dark and even the police will not be out in the snow," he announced. "I am going to the bridge."

Chang Shan never asked anyone to go with him to the bridge. He merely told a few other students that he was going. Then he went off alone. Usually before he reached the bridge two or three others would follow him. At the bridge they would work in silence, digging into the yellow clay, making a hole big enough for dynamite. Did they have the pure dynamite that Americans used it would not have taken them so long. But they had only the poor stuff left by the Japanese in a warehouse—lucky at that, for the students had found it first. The bridge was huge. Built centuries ago of marble with granite foundations, it was as strong as the day it had been finished. The only signs of time were the hollows worn by the feet of generations upon its surface. Since these were even now only an inch or so deep, the bridge could exist for thousands of years longer. But the students were planning to blow it up for the very reason that it was so old and huge and because its size and permanence made them angry. It signified the glory of an age that was gone, and it was a bridge not only over the water beneath it, but also from the present into the past. The past was what the students wanted to forget because they could not share its glory, and dead glory did them no good now. It was the present which they wanted to build, and they craved hope for the future. Yet the people, those who lived in villages and upon the land, remained on the other side of the bridge, separated from the students in the university. These people still lived in the past, they were content with themselves, they trusted the land, which is eternal. Therefore the students wanted to destroy the bridge in protest.

In protest against what? They said, against the government. But actually it was in protest against their tuberculosis and their poverty and the miserable teaching they were given when they were hungry for true knowledge; in protest, too, against their wretched childhoods and against their own ambitions, never to be fulfilled, and most of all in protest against their broken pride and the hopelessness of their future. But the students did not know all this. They blamed only their rulers, who they insisted, had sold the country to Western imperialists.

Alone now in Chang Shan's room Peter determined that he would not follow his friend. Yet he felt so lonely that he was terrified. He knew that he could never return to his father. If he went home he would quarrel with his father. Sooner or later he would tell his father that he was a liar and had cheated his own children. His mother had become a fool in Peter's eyes. He did not want to see his parents again as long as he lived. Neither did he want to see his American friends. He could not tell them about China. There were no more dreams to be made, now that he knew the truth. Yet he was more impatient with James and Mary than with any of them. The paltriness of what they planned, the folly of finding satisfaction in it! There was something splendid in Chang Shan's determination to destroy. Chang Shan was not a Communist. He did not believe that the Communists were any better than others. They, too, Chang Shan said, should be destroyed. A clean country, the old gone, the selfish swept away by the storm—this was the only hope. "Even if I destroy myself in the storm," Chang Shan argued, "I leave cleanness behind me."

For sheer need to have something clear and definite Peter sat down at the table and began to write on a piece of paper. It was only a small piece for even paper was too dear to waste.

"Our country is foul," so he began to write in English. "We must make it clean. Our country is rotten. We must ruthlessly cut away what is rotten and burn it up. A prairie wind, a prairie fire, that is what I see. After the fire the ashes, the clean ashes. Who will light this fire? It can be lit by a single match held in a human hand."

He sat a long time in thought and he kept seeing the match struck against the substance, and then the flame blazing into a fire as wide as the world. Chang Shan was right. He rose, and catching up his padded coat from the bed as he went, he wrapped it about him and went out. He was better off than Chang Shan who had no padded coat.

Whether any other friend of Chang Shan had followed he never knew. For that night he walked through the snow with his head down that it might not creep down his collar and chill him with wet. Thus he came near the bridge by the path he knew so well. Snow is so silent that it hides even footsteps. Therefore Peter heard no one and he did not know that he was followed until he felt his shoulder seized. He looked up and saw a fierce wet face under a ragged felt hat.

"Are you going to the bridge?" a voice hissed in his ear.

How do the secret police dress themselves when they spy upon children playing under a bridge? They dress themselves as common men, in ragged hats and dirty robes. These robes are better than smart uniforms for there is room under the skirts for pistols and knives and ropes.

But what did Peter know of secret police dressed as common men? He nodded, and the next moment he felt a round cold piece of metal at his temple. But this was only for the fraction of a second. Then upon a roar of thunder he felt himself lifted from earth into heaven and he knew no more.

"Dear Mr. Liang," the president of the university wrote to James some weeks later. "For a number of days now your younger brother has not appeared in his classes. Neither has his roommate, Chang Shan. We do not know whether they have met with some unfortunate accident, or whether, as has been the case with a few others, these two have unwisely joined a brotherhood of some kind in the northwest. Unless you have further information, the name of your brother will be removed from the roll of the university."

Upon receiving this letter, James forbade Mary to be frightened. He went at once to Peking. But where could he search? He called upon the proud and dignified president, who, as a great scholar and a famous man, received him with courtesy but without interest.

"It is unfortunate that your brother was the friend of Chang Shan," the university president said in a loud clear voice. "I reproved Chang Shan many times for his daring behavior. A scholar, I told him, ought not to concern himself with outside affairs. Alas, Chang Shan never obeyed his elders."

There was no more help than this to be had from the scholar who sat wrapped in his quilted satin robe, nursing his soft hands and long fingernails, and James went to Chang Shan's room, which was pointed out to him by a shabby girl student, whose eyes were red, and there he found some of Peter's clothes. The padded coat was gone, he saw, and this made him wonder whether Peter had run away with Chang Shan. On the other hand, his toothbrush was there and his hairbrush and comb and such small things as are needed for daily life—that is, for Peter's daily life. But perhaps he had deliberately left them behind because to Chang Shan they would not seem necessary. Someone had already taken all the books, for books were precious.

But the shabby girl student who had been hanging about the door now drew a bit of paper from her pocket. "This was found," she whispered.

James saw Peter's handwriting and he took the paper and read it.

"Does it tell you anything?" the student asked. She could not read English.

"Nothing that I did not already know," James replied.

He put the paper in his pocket, and after a few more such fruitless days he went back to the village again with his miserable news.

There, with Chen and Mary listening, he told them what

he could and he showed them the paper. Young Wang, hearing that James was home again, came from the inn with a rack of steaming hot spinach dumplings. He set it down upon the table and listened, too, for a moment. Then very unwillingly he told them what the vendor had once said and of the yellow clay upon Peter's shoes. "I believe they were plotting to destroy the marble bridge," Young Wang said.

"But why?" Mary asked. "What good would it do?"

"Young men do not ask what good it will do," Young Wang said. "They only wish to make a big noise."

"But the bridge is not blown up," James reminded them. "I passed it as I came and went. It stands there exactly as ever it did."

Young Wang shrugged his shoulders. "Maybe they were caught before they could set the dynamite."

This was all guess and conjecture and no one could know.

"Peter will write to us," Mary insisted. "Wait—and we'll hear."

"Nevertheless, I should tell our parents," James said gravely.

So he sat down that same day and wrote down all that he knew, how discontented Peter had been and how unhappy and yet that he would not go back to his father and mother.

"I feel myself at fault," James wrote. "I blame myself. I should have compelled him to tell me what he was thinking about. As soon as we hear from him, I will go to him whereever he is."

But he did not tell them of the bit of paper upon which Peter had written the words of destruction. When the letter was gone James sat reading again and again these words, and slowly he began to believe that Peter was dead. But how and by whose hand?

These questions were never to be answered. For at this moment Peter's body was in an old well. The fall had not been hard, even had he known that he was falling, for Chang Shan had been thrown down before him, and his body lay upon others. Such old wells were deep. They had been dug in the palace gardens, long ago, so that the Empress might have ample water with which to water her peonies. Now they were foul with age and death and nobody drank their waters, and all the flowers were dead.

17

DR. LIANG RECEIVED THE LETTER and immediately he refused
to believe that Peter was dead. Who would kill the son
of Liang Wen Hua? Even the secret police, whose existence
he had never acknowledged, would not dare to do such a
thing. It was therefore probable that Peter had joined the
Communists. This being the case, he, Liang Wen Hua, as
a loyal citizen of China, would disown his younger son. His
first feeling upon putting down the letter was one of swift
anger. Peter knew how his father felt about Communists.
To run away from school, to leave no message, to join the
traitorous ones, was unfilial beyond measure. He would disown Peter publicly.

Upon the first impulse of his anger he went to find Mrs.
Liang. She was in the kitchen, since this was Nellie's day
off. A fine aroma met his nostrils as he opened the door.
Mrs. Liang was heating a combination of fresh ginger and
onion in lard and soy sauce, ready to brown a whole fish.
She looked happy when he came in and immediately burst
into speech.

"Liang, look! I made the fishman leave on the head. That
is good luck, for once."

He took a dark pleasure in spoiling her joy. "We have no
luck," he said bitterly. "Here is a letter from James. Peter is
gone."

Mrs. Liang felt her legs tremble. She sat down quickly on
the kitchen stool. "You mean—" she could not say the unlucky word "death."

"Who knows?" Dr. Liang shouted. Now that he took
thought he perceived that it was possible that they would
never see Peter again, dead or alive. In his heart of hearts
he was a soft and tender man, and tears came into his eyes.

When his wife saw these tears she was terrified. She remembered the first time she had ever seen him cry. It was after he had been told that he had failed an examination, many years ago. It was in the first year of their marriage and she had wept with him. In old times scholars not only wept but sometimes they hanged themselves or swallowed opium if they failed in an examination. She had watched Dr. Liang for some time after that and had not felt wholly safe until two years later he had taken the examination again and had passed successfully and so had removed the shame from himself.

Now seeing his tears she burst into loud wails. "He is dead!" she sobbed. "You are afraid to tell me!"

This dried his tears again with anger. "Why should I be afraid to tell you?" he retorted. "He is your son. No, he has simply run away."

To his surprise she turned on him with fury. "This is your fault! You sent him no money. He has nothing to spend. He took money from somewhere and now he is afraid. Sit down at once, Liang, and write to James and send him money to use to find Peter. I will not eat until you do this."

So it was. She finished the fish and prepared the meal and she would eat none of it. Dr. Liang ate alone until he could not endure it. Then he threw down his chopsticks and with much complaint he wrote the letter and enclosed a check which he made twice as large as he wished.

After this they both felt better, as though now it was certain that Peter would come back. They finished the fish together and Dr. Liang went to his study for his nap and Mrs. Liang went to mail the letter.

"I will just go to see Louise," she told him. "I will talk with her about Peter and see how he was when she was with him."

Dr. Liang, outstretched upon his couch and covered by a light silk quilt, listened to her footsteps and the closing of the front door. The rooms were very still. He tried not to think of Peter but he found himself remembering him. Of all the children Peter was the most American. He had gone to the excellent public school of the district and he had stood often at the head of his class. But he had not written one letter to his father after he went to China. They had not thought this strange, for it was natural that James as the eldest should make the report to his parents, and when

Mary wrote it was to her mother. Now, however, in the silence about him, and thinking of Peter's face, Dr. Liang wondered if there was something he did not know about his son. Strange that the face he saw was not Peter's at eighteen, but the face of twelve-year-old Peter, coming home from school, his books in a strap, a boy always gay and always hungry. The door would burst open and Peter would shout, "Ma, I'm hungry!"

He lay, listening to that boy's voice, and for some reason which he could not explain, the tears began to flow again. Why should he weep for Peter? Was it an omen? He got up from the couch and walked up and down the room, his hands clasped tightly together. Perhaps he ought not have let Peter go to China. Yes, he should have kept the boy here. He had allowed him to grow up with a sentimental notion of what China was like. He had even helped to make the notion— let him be honest, now while he was alone. But he had wanted the children to understand the glory of China, the honor, the dignity of an ancient race and country. He himself purposely dwelled upon these things. It was necessary to do this in order to have a perspective upon the disagreeable present. The present was always transient. It faded away. Only the past and the future were eternal. Therefore he had done well to teach his children of their people's greatness. It was what Confucius himself had taught. Confucius too had lived in troubled and divided times, and he had not allowed himself to be troubled or divided. Instead he had gathered together all the greatness of the ancients and he had put this greatness into a book which had lived through the ages.

Dr. Liang stood still, his head lifted. Here was inspiration. He would write such a book about the past that it would inspire the young of today. They would know their roots and they would feel fresh life come up into them. He should have done it long ago, but perhaps it was not yet too late.

He sat down at the desk and took up his brush and began to make the exquisite letters for which he was famous among Chinese scholars. Then he paused. Should he not dedicate the book to his own children? He would write it first of all for them. Over this he pondered, then he decided. If Peter came back before the book was finished, the dedication would be to James, Mary and Peter, citizens of China. If Peter never came back? Then he would simply dedicate it "To Peter, whom China has lost."

The tears stung again but he refused to allow them. He had immense work to do.

Mrs. Liang mailed the letter and then she took a taxi across town. The day was gray but it neither rained nor snowed and she rode through the park and stopped at the Wetherstons' apartment house and took the elevator to the twelfth floor. She liked Mrs. Wetherston very much and the two had become good friends. True, she thought the American lady was too fussy about the baby, but this was natural since it was her own grandchild, though by an unknown woman. The child was fine enough. He grew well; he was trying already to walk; he looked much like his father. A grandmother naturally would be proud of all these things. She herself, also naturally, was more interested in the child Louise herself would bear before the year was over. Mrs. Wetherston hoped this child would be a little girl, but Mrs. Liang said frankly that for herself she wished a boy. It was true that Alec was not her son, and this child could be only an outside grandchild, but she had grown fond of Alec, and with all her own sons away, it was nice to have a tall young man call her Mother, even though he was not Chinese. With much that she did not approve, it could be said for the Americans that here both mothers-in-law received attention, and not only the mother of the son, as in China.

Mrs. Wetherston opened the door and the two ladies greeted each other with affection. Mrs. Liang produced a small gardenia that she had bought on the street and Mrs. Wetherston thanked her for it as she pinned it on her dress.

"You always bring me something," she said with pleasant reproach. "It that a Chinese custom?"

"Only when we like," Mrs. Liang replied. She spoke in a loud voice in order to help Mrs. Wetherston to understand her English. "Suppose we don't like somebody better, we don't bring something else."

Mrs. Wetherston laughed. "Come in and sit down! I'll have some tea made."

"No, thank you," Mrs. Liang replied. She remembered Peter and the smile faded from her face. "I must talk to Louise, please, Mrs. Wetherston, because I have bad news of my younger son. He is gone away, maybe dead, but I don't think so."

Mrs. Wetherston's look was instantly concerned. "Oh, my dear—dead? But I can't believe it—you look so—" cheerful, she was about to say and stopped herself.

"Who knows? I want to ask Louise how was Peter when she saw him before," Mrs. Liang told her.

"Of course." Mrs. Wetherston tiptoed to a door and knocked. "Louise dear?" she called.

She had grown fond of the young girl that her son had brought home. Louise was lively and gay and yet docile. When Alec was not in the house she stayed alone in their rooms and seldom came out. But when she did join the family she was good-natured and talkative enough to give life to them again. "You mustn't be afraid of me, dear," she had told Louise after the first few days. "And I don't want to be obeyed."

"I am not afraid," Louise had said sweetly, "and I like to obey you." No one knew how grateful she was to be in this kind house, where everything was clean and comfortable and where she could take a hot bath whenever she wanted it. She liked to sit in her room and Alec's and look around it and think, "This is really my home, I belong here. I am really American."

Now she heard Alec's mother's voice, even in her sleep. She slept a great deal so that when Alec came home she could stay awake as long as he liked. Curled under the down quilt she had slept and now she rose from it, her eyes dewy and her lips folded sweetly in content.

"I am here," she called softly and opened the door and saw her own mother. "Why, Ma!" she exclaimed.

"I shall leave you two alone," Mrs. Wetherston said and went away.

Louise drew her mother into her room. "Ma, what is the matter? You've been crying."

Mrs. Liang began to cry again without let. She put her handkerchief to her eyes. "Peter—" she sobbed.

Louise looked stricken. "Is he dead?" she whispered.

Mrs. Liang let the handkerchief drop. "Why do you say that?" she asked sharply.

"Oh, I don't know. Yes, I do know. Ma, he was in trouble over there."

"Why?"

"He hated everything over there too much."

"Then why didn't he tell us and come back here?" Mrs. Liang asked. She went on without waiting for an answer. "That's what you did. Yes, I know, Louise. You never told me you didn't like it in China, but you didn't, I know. And so you were glad to marry an American."

"But I love Alec," Louise retorted.

"Yes, now," Mrs. Liang said stubbornly. "At first I think you only loved him for this nice house and for New York and hot water and electricity and clean streets and so on. I know how you are, Louise. You are too American. I told your father too many times."

Mother and daughter were preparing for one of their hearty old quarrels when Mrs. Liang suddenly remembered Peter again and her anger cooled. "I am glad you are come just the same," she said quickly, "and I wish Peter would come, too. After all, you are not used to China. So strange there, isn't it? Now I am homesick all the time for China. My own children don't like it. Oh, Peter, why don't you come away from it, then?" she moaned softly.

Louise accepted her mother's offer of peace. "Ma, if you want the truth from me—Peter hated it but he wanted to stay, too. He was afraid of Pa."

"Afraid?" Mrs. Liang cried. "Why, when I am always there?"

"He blamed Pa," Louise said. "Once when we talked together he told me Pa told lies about everything and if he ever saw Pa again he would have to tell him so and he didn't want to see Pa any more."

"Peter must be crazy," Mrs. Liang exclaimed.

"No, he wasn't. He was angry and he was sore and he was ashamed and it was all mixed up in him. He wanted to be proud of his country, and he had thought there were things to be proud of, and so he began worrying when he couldn't find them." Louise looked thoughtfully at herself in a long mirror opposite the chair where she sat. "Maybe I would have been that way if I had been a boy instead of a girl."

Mrs. Liang rebelled at this. "You can't talk that, Louise. Many women in our country do very much."

"I guess I'm American," Louise said. "Women here are taken care of."

Mrs. Liang was not a little shocked. "You are too selfish. What about poor Peter?"

Louise looked away from the mirror. "I just don't know what to say, Ma." Her mother spoke as usual in Chinese mixed with English, but she herself spoke always in English, and the conversation had gone along in the two tongues. "I have a queer feeling that anything could have happened. I mean—" she broke off and then went on again with a catch in her voice. After all, Peter was her brother, and they had played together much when they were children. "Well, a lot of things could happen," she said unwillingly. "Students disappear, you know, if they do anything except their books. And Peter belonged to some clubs and things. He never brought his friends home—I don't know why."

Mrs. Liang's heart froze. She had heard stories whispered even at parties and dinners. Newcomers said—

"You think maybe Peter is—" Again she could not say the word.

"I just don't know, Ma," Louise repeated. She saw her mother's face melt into weeping and she began to weep, too.

It was nearly dusk when Mrs. Liang opened the door to her own handsome apartment again. She had not stayed all this time with Louise. When she left her daughter her eyes were swollen and she felt she wanted to be alone instead of coming into the house. When she climbed out of the taxi she had gone to the river and had sat down on a bench there. The bridge loomed above her, high and silver. At first it had seemed to catch and hold the light, and the sunset had stained it pink. Then its own lamps began to spring out, and in the deepening darkness it became an arch of light from shore to shore. She sat there a long time remembering how when the children were little she had brought them here to play. Peter had always loved the bridge. He would look up from his toys to gaze at it. The first word he had said, after her name, had been that word. He had lifted his tiny hand and pointing he had said, "Bridge!" How proud she had been!

She cried again, softly, her face toward the river, where no one could see. Yet who cared if an elderly Chinese woman cried? Somehow she was coming to believe that Peter was dead. So many young men died in China, she knew. But she had thought that Liang's name would protect her children. Liang! Why had he sent the children away? He had not wanted Louise to marry an American and so he had sent them all away. Now Louise had married an American, and he pretended that he believed in such marriages. Liang was always pretending. He pretended that Confucius was so big. Confucius was only a man, probably a man like Liang, but his wife could not read or write and so she died unknown. Men were all alike.

She stopped crying and now she felt cold, although the day had been warm. She got up and walked slowly homeward. She would not tell Mrs. Pan or anyone about Peter. She would wait and wait. If James could find out nothing she would ask Liang to let her go home. She would find Peter herself. A mother could always find her own child.

She opened the door and was frightened by the utter silence. Where was Liang? "Liang!" she called. Then she saw the line of light under the door of his study and she ran to open it. He was sitting there with his brush upright in his hand, a happy smile upon his face, writing. He neither saw nor heard her. She shut the door without noise and went into the kitchen and began to cook his supper.

18

THE MONEY THAT HIS FATHER SENT James used to begin the search for his brother. How does a brother make such a search? James learned soon that the ways were devious. Young Wang went with him everywhere. Leaving his bride and the inn, both of which were now equally dear to him, he followed James, and yet led him. There were no lawful ways to seek justice for what had been done without law. But Young Wang, shrewd and accustomed to getting what he wanted and using money freely since there was hunger everywhere, heard from one hungry mouth or another, and so he was led to the palace gardens, not because of one dead lad or two, but because the old wells there had been used long ago for such things as death. Did not the concubines of emperors drown themselves in the imperial wells?

Why tell of how James and this faithful manservant crept about in the dark human caverns in a great and ancient city? These caverns were human sewers, not of the filth of bodies but of the filth of souls. Men who starve for food, who starve for opium, who gamble away wives and children, men who will kill rather than work—among these James came and went in silence, and Young Wang was always there and hidden under his coat was the big butcher knife which he had brought from the inn.

James lived during these days with Su and his young wife. They were kind to him, but they were afraid of him, and so he went out of the house before dawn and entered it after dark. James was the brother of Peter who had been killed, and it was dangerous to be a friend of James, even though he was the son of Liang Wen Hua.

There came a day at the end of sixty-three days when a vendor told of a gateman who told of a beggar who told of a band of beggars who paid him to allow them to sleep in the shelter of the empty pavilion in the imperial gardens. Among these beggars one was found who told of a night when he had heard voices muttering and whispering about an ancient well. Money—money! James spent all that his father had sent, but American money was true money and it changed for a fortune and this fortune James offered the beggar in exchange for his brother's body.

He and Young Wang with him went to the imperial gardens on a dark night, and they waited until the moon was gone. The gate swung open and there was no gateman to see what went on, and the two of them went in and sat down under a vast old pine tree and waited half the night through. His thoughts were strange, and scarcely thoughts so much as unspoken feelings, perceptions, fears, and resolutions. From the vast gardens, miles within the high four-square walls of past empire, there came dying scents, no longer perfumes, from old trees and long grasses, from fungus upon wet bark and mosses creeping between stone and tile no longer trod by human feet. The silence was profound and yet there were sudden small gusts of wind and somewhere small bells upon a roof tinkled in a ghostly tremor. He felt life about him, dead and no longer human, and yet clinging to these haunts. Strange and horrible it was to think that Peter's young rebellion had been quenched here, where all the evils of history had culminated and died! There was something so solemn about this possibility of his brother's death that James could not weep. He sat crouched upon the deep bed of pine needles and leaning upon a mighty root of the pine tree that canopied above him he waited, resisting with his own inner forces the forces of the dead past that encircled him here. He was young and he was alive, and he would not allow himself to be overwhelmed. A stubbornness for life and his own life began to steady his heart and cool his mind. Peter had chosen the swift way, the gamble of violence against violence, and he had lost. He, James, the elder, would take the slow plodding path and live, he hoped, to see his goal clear, if not to reach it.

Calmness came to him as the hours passed, and in all this time Young Wang had not spoken. Had the beggars betrayed them, after all? Young Wang had prudently held back half the money lest there be no body brought, and he promised that cash would be given after its delivery.

In the small cold hours of the night, when the owls hoot in the trees, he whispered harshly, "They are coming!" James rose and stood waiting and behind him he heard Young Wang take a stealthy step. They saw the glimmer of a paper lantern through a marble colonnade and the light fell dimly upon a cluster of human feet, staggering under a load. A half moment, and the beggars brought three water-soaked bodies and laid them under the ancient pine. It was too dark to see, but James heard the footsteps and he heard the beggars' voices. "Take care—they are already rotting—"

Then he rose and took from his pocket the small flashlight he had brought with him from America, and this light he lit upon each dead lad, and Young Wang peered over his shoulder. The first he did not know, nor did Young Wang. The second one James did not know, but Young Wang cried softly, "It is the one in whose room he slept!" The third they both knew, for it was Peter.

Thus was certainty made sure. Now they moved quickly to do what they had earlier decided must be done. No one in the whole city would have dared to bury these bodies. Under the ancient pine the earth was soft and rich, and Young Wang had brought a spade hidden under his long Chinese coat. He began to dig swiftly and the earth came easily away. Soon he had made a bed, narrow but wide enough for three and deep enough for safety, and the bottom lay upon the stout old roots of the tree.

When it was ready the beggars helped to lift the lads, and James stooped to hold his brother's head. They laid Peter in the middle and upon his right his friend and upon his left the unknown. Then Young Wang covered them, and when the earth was smooth he spread over them the deep pine needles which had fallen here year after year since the Old Empress herself died and was buried.

Young Wang paid the beggars and they crept away into the night. But James stood motionless under the tree and beside the new-made grave. All in him was feeling and not only that Peter was dead. For the first time he felt how small he himself was, how solitary, and how vast was the people which surrounded him, and how miserable. Had not Peter died, James could never have known of creatures who never saw light or comfort or safety. They swarmed beneath the surface of life, breeding and counterbreeding, and life pressed down upon them and held them under. In his own fashion Peter had known people more quickly than any of them and in passionate tragic fashion he had tried to help them. Yes, James told himself, in his young foolish way Peter had died to save their people.

Young Wang touched his arm. "Come," he whispered. "This is not safe."

And taking James's hand with simple tenderness he led him away.

Long before dawn they were on their road again to the ancestral village. James could not quickly enough be quit of the city. Upon the surface of his mind as he rode along he thought of such things as what to tell his parents and what to tell Uncle Tao. To his parents he would simply say that he had found Peter dead and had given him burial. He might say that Peter had doubtless mixed himself with rebel students of some sort. To Uncle Tao he would only say that Peter would not come back again. It was hard to tell so half a truth but James weighed the matter well, and he knew that Uncle Tao would take fright if he knew the whole truth. Only to Mary and to Chen would he tell exactly what he had found. Beneath such surface thought he dwelled hour after hour upon the meaning of Peter's death and how it had come about and why. It would take his lifetime to answer all he asked himself this day.

So at nightfall he rode into the village, very weary and silent, and he bade Young Wang return to his wife and his inn and never to tell even his wife what had taken place in the night.

Young Wang was somewhat offended at this and he pursed his mouth and said, "Master, I am not the sort of man who tells his wife everything! I am trustworthy and you ought to know it by now."

"So I do," James said to comfort him, and the two parted.

James went first to his own room. He hoped to find Chen there, but the rooms were empty. He washed himself and then he went to find Mary, but she too was not to be found. Next must he then go to Uncle Tao to announce himself returned, as younger should do to elder, and Uncle Tao he found sitting in the main room doing nothing. He was waiting for his pipe to be filled, for he had declared the tobacco damp and the grandchild who served him for the day had gone to find a dry handful by the kitchen stove.

"Eh, you are back again," Uncle Tao rumbled, when he saw James come in. "Did you find that young mischief?"

"Yes, I did," James said and he tried to smile. "He will not come back, Uncle Tao. I arranged everything in the city."

"If he likes the city I do not want him here," Uncle Tao said. The grandson came running in now with the tobacco and Uncle Tao took it in his hand, felt it and smelled it. He forgot Peter in this task. When he found himself pleased he commanded that his pipe be filled. Then he was ready to speak again.

"Eh—eh—" so he began.

James leaned forward to listen. "Yes, Uncle Tao."

"What do you want to do here, eh?" Uncle Tao went on smoking between every word.

"What would you like me to do, Uncle Tao?" James asked. By now he knew that Uncle Tao must seem to give direction everywhere.

"Anything—anything," Uncle Tao said. He was feeling amiable tonight, having eaten well. "That is," he said after a long draw of smoke, "you are not to meddle with the land. Your grandfather meddled with it and we were all but in the hands of the tenants before I took it back. You young ones who have been to school, you cannot understand the land."

"There is only one thing I can do which will be useful to you," James said with proper caution. "I see that many of our tenants look sickly. Surely they cannot do a day's work. If you will allow me, I will try to discover what their sickness is and heal it."

Uncle Tao's small eyes half closed. "No cutting!" he said sternly.

"Not without your permission," James agreed.

"Well, well," Uncle Tao replied. "How will you begin?"

"With your permission I could take one of the empty rooms and keep it as a medicine room. I have a few medicines which I brought with me when I came, and when I need more I can get them through the city hospital. To that room the sick ones can come."

Uncle Tao turned this over and over in his mind. "What if you kill someone?" he asked after some minutes. This thought filled him with horror. "No, no," he said in alarm, "it is better to let them die naturally."

"I will kill no one," James said.

Uncle Tao wagged his head. "You would be blamed if one dies, and then I as your eldest relative would have to pay for it."

"Consider," James reminded him. "When a tenant declares himself sick and cannot work, then I will see if he is truly ill or only pretending. Moreover, there are the children. It is a pity for children to waste away. And the women who die in childbirth—"

"You cannot concern yourself with women," Uncle Tao said firmly.

"A doctor concerns himself with all human life," James replied.

Thus coaxing and persuading he led Uncle Tao to the place where he agreed that James might use a certain room which had a door of its own to the street. This door had been barred for generations and it had been made long ago secretly by a wicked Liang son who went out at night against his father's command.

James was weary indeed by the time Uncle Tao had reached his permission, but when he rose to go Uncle Tao stayed him again. "As to your sister—" so he began and James sat down once more.

"Your sister is—one of those new ones," Uncle Tao said solemnly. He laid aside his pipe, now grown cold. "She makes a disturbance in our village. Already I see my daughters-in-law are growing forward. The youngest one spoke to me the other day. Such a thing has not happened before. I speak to command her, but I expect no reply."

James could not but smile at this. "What shall I do with my sister?" he asked.

"She should be married," Uncle Tao said in the same solemn voice. "Women who are not married go about cackling like hens who lay no eggs."

James did not reply to this. It would make a disturbance indeed if Uncle Tao stepped in to arrange a marriage for Mary! Yet Uncle Tao now prepared to do so. "In this village," he said, "there is a very decent fellow who does not belong to the Liang blood. His father came here as a peddler and then settled himself as a tailor. I gave him permission. The son is a tailor also. I will speak to the father."

James made haste to avert this catastrophe. "Uncle Tao, let me talk with my sister," he begged. "If I fail I will come and tell you."

"Well, well," Uncle Tao granted him. "But let it not be too long. Women are a family burden until they are married."

So James went away at last and now he found Chen in his room, the one next to his. He was changing his garments from his old working uniform to the Chinese robe which he wore when he was at ease.

"Where were you?" James asked. "I have been home this hour and more. You and Mary—I could find neither of you."

"I was helping her clean the schoolroom," Chen said with an air of lightness.

"Is there already a schoolroom?" James asked.

"Mary has taken one," Chen replied. "I told her it would be better to ask Uncle Tao first, but no, she said she would go and tell Uncle Tao when it was done. The young mothers are all on her side. They are helping her. They want their children to learn to read, and some even talk of learning themselves. The youngest daughter-in-law is quite determined." All this he said in the same light voice, half carelessly, as he usually spoke.

"I want to tell you and Mary about Peter," James said. "I will go and find her. We can meet in my room."

All through that evening they sat together and they talked about Peter and why it was that he could not be happy. They well knew. The weight of their country, vast and old, lay heavy upon them all, and they were of such conscience that they could not escape.

"What Peter could not see," James said at last, "was that destruction does not heal. For what can be destroyed except people? Yet the people are the treasure of the nation."

"And our people are good," Chen said.

"I tell you ours are the best people in the world. Ignorant and dirty and fighting disease with nothing except their natural health—" James broke off here and shook his head.

"Peter was too young for this life," Chen said.

"Perhaps too spoiled," Mary said in a low voice.

The two men did not argue this and they sat a while not speaking and watching the guttering candles on the table.

"When I have children," Mary said at last and as though she had been thinking of it for a long time before she spoke, "I will not let them go to America. They must grow up here, where our life is. They must learn to do with what we have and if they want more they must make it with their own hands. They must not dream of what others have made."

So she spoke of her own marriage and it came into James's mind to tell her what Uncle Tao had said. But he did not. The time was not fitting. They were speaking of solemn things, and what Uncle Tao had said was only cause for laughter.

The next day, after sleep so deep that he was ashamed of it, James began the clearing of the room Uncle Tao had given him. Plenty of help he had, for the place was full of children eager to see any new thing. These children he put to work so pleasantly that they thought it all a game, and thus were carried out old baskets of rubbish and broken furniture and rags and papers and all such stuff as gets itself together somehow in an old house where there are too many people. The room was large, having earlier been two rooms, and the floor was of beaten earth and the walls of brick. James bought lime from the village store and he mixed it with water and brushed the walls and sprinkled the floor. The children stood amazed to see him do everything himself, for they were not used to their elders so bestirring themselves. None had seen Uncle Tao so much as fetch his own pipe. When after this James bought boards and nails and put them into shelves they were even somewhat ashamed of him. Who had ever heard of a man who knew books turning carpenter? By now all the ancestral Liangs wondered at these new Liangs and their friend Chen who had dropped upon them from the skies. Behind their backs be sure there was much talk about them, but which of the three knew it? They went zealously about their business, full of faith that the ancestral village could become a place where all were clean and healthy and learned.

It was a healing thing they did, and the first to be healed were themselves. The spring came and went and summer spread over the land. Uncle Tao slept like a vast half-naked Buddha under the date tree, and at night the whole family moved their beds into the courts and slept there and the village street was lined with such beds. It was a gay season, for children ran about together and women gossiped and men sat late drinking hot water and tea and fanning themselves so that when they burst into sweat they were cooled. Day after day James rose early and let the sick come to him before the sun rose too hot. The fame of his healing spread over the countryside and people came to him from a long distance away and Chen helped him always, so that they worked together as closely as two hands.

Even so they could not tend all who came, and in the midst of summer James wrote letters to the three good nurses at the city hospital, Rose, Marie, and Kitty, and invited them to come and help. Of the three he hoped one might come. Yet he made his letter stern, for he did not want them deceived. "I can pay you a tenth of what you are getting now," he wrote. "But you will have food and shelter. How then will you be paid? As I myself am paid, by healing those who have nowhere else to turn for healing."

Out of the three two came, Rose and Kitty, for Marie had married herself to a young doctor, and he would not let her leave home and he would not come with her.

At the city hospital it was still considered folly indeed that James and Chen had buried themselves in a village and long tongues wagged and said, "They like to be lords over the poor. Who can believe that they live like the villagers?"

"We will tell you what we see," Kitty promised.

"Why should they live like villagers if it is their wish to make the villagers themselves better?" Rose asked. The Liang house opened to these two also, and they lived together in one room next to Mary.

It must not be supposed that all things went well. Rose was a cheerful careless girl and she was happy enough. But Kitty was a third, and as the months passed she was sometimes peevish because she thought that Mary and Rose were a close two and did not take her into their friendship deeply enough, and then Chen saw with some alarm that she showed signs of leaning upon him for friendship. He went sheepishly to James one night and said that Kitty should be sent back to the city.

"The country is a hard test, Jim," he said. "Only those who are full of their own richness can bear it. Kitty is too thin of soul. She will make you trouble sooner or later."

"I will keep her busy," James said. He tended as he spoke the growth of a culture from some unknown disease which had come to him that day. He had never seen it before. It settled in the legs of men and women and children and they swelled monstrously from the hips down, while above the hips they withered. Whether it was contagious, whether it caused death, these things he was trying to discover.

So Chen was obliged to speak out. "This Kitty is looking toward me, Jim," he said with a wry face. "A woman who does not marry and cannot find her happiness in work—well, a man must be careful of such a woman."

"Why do you not marry her?" James suggested. "Then I would not lose a helper."

He heard Chen choke and he looked up to see his friend fiery red. "No, I thank you," Chen said.

But James would do nothing quickly and so for a while he saw to it only that Kitty had much work to do. As for the redness of Chen's face, he took it as a sign of his friend's habitual delicacy where women were concerned.

At this time of his life it must be said that James was not acute to such matters. He was delving too deeply into the lives of many to dwell upon the life of any one. Thus he had begun to see that many of the illnesses which he had to heal were the fruit of other evil things. The food which the people ate was not good enough, and when he tried to teach mothers that measles could be a deadly disease here where it was new, and that one child could give it to another, they were too unlearned to understand such things, and never could they believe that cucumbers were dangerous if they were first soaked in pond water and that while it was good to boil the water they drank, it was useless if they rinsed their mouths with water that was not boiled. A cut, however slight, could not be rubbed with mud, he told them, and above all the cord that tied a child to its mother must not be cut with her kitchen scissors. The curse of this whole region was the "ten-day seizure," as the people called it, of newborn infants, and the cause of it was in the use of rusty iron scissors.

"What shall we use then?" women asked him.

Then Rose told how in her village far to the west they had learnéd to use the inside leaf of a reed, and the nearer to the heart it was the more likely was the child to live. This seemed magic to the mothers, but James tried to make them see that it was still only what he had said, for the heart leaf of a reed was cleaner of invisible soil than was a pair of iron scissors used to cut anything else as well as the child's cord. Still the truth was beyond their understanding and none could believe that what could not be seen could be a cause of death.

Uncle Tao himself declared all this was nonsense, and what Uncle Tao said had great force upon others. This was strange enough for it was not long before James saw that Uncle Tao was not well loved here in the Liang village nor by the people on the surrounding Liang lands. But he was admired and people told one another what he had said, and his half-bitter, half-joking words were carried from mouth to mouth. Yet he had a grasping hand and it could tighten secretly, and the people feared him because he was always on the side of the rulers, and their rulers from long habit the people hated. When the emperors were ended the people had rejoiced but now they were beginning to say that the emperors were better than their present rulers. There had been only one emperor, they said, and under him one viceroy in every province and under the viceroy one magistrate in every county, and though these all took their tribute, there was a limit to it. Now little rulers popped out everywhere and who knew where they came from? Each collected tax, and if a farmer refused to pay the tax a band of soldiers appeared with foreign guns. One soldier with one gun is too many anywhere.

Uncle Tao was always friendly with the tax gatherers. He himself paid no taxes, for he declared that all he had belonged to the people and from the people must the tax be gathered. So saying he fed tax gatherer and soldier and what could the people do?

All this the country women poured into Mary's ears when she went out to visit among them, for she was one who listened to any tale, and after she had heard these things she took them to James and Chen, and demanded that something be done with Uncle Tao. They talked long and argued much, shut up in their private rooms so that no ears could hear and no mouth run to tell Uncle Tao. For these three too had their lesser enemies, in spite of every effort they made to keep all friendly. Thus the eldest daughter-in-law was jealous of Mary because the younger women followed her and learned to read, instead of spending all their time in washing and sewing, and the eldest one said she had no time for reading and would not learn. This daughter-in-law went to Uncle Tao and complained that Mary made trouble in the house and that all was better before these new Liangs came. She talked with her husband too and turned him against the new Liangs and their friend Chen. And when autumn came it was known that Uncle Tao did not like so much learning in the village and Mary found her schoolroom half empty.

The village was split in two by the time the midautumn festival came, and some were with the new Liangs and some were against, and those who were against were all for Uncle Tao and the old ways. As if this were not trouble enough Rose said one day to James that Kitty was with those who were against them, and therefore she should be sent back to the city. James sent for Kitty then and in the midst of the evening's work when bandages must be wrapped and tools boiled in the tin tank Chen had made to set upon a charcoal fire, he told her gently enough what he had heard. At this, such a stream of venom came spitting out of Kitty's mouth as he had not imagined could be in a woman's heart.

"You and your sister and that Liu Chen!" she cried. "You are too good for me—and for everybody. Why are you here? Is it likely that you are here for nothing? Who does anything for nothing and can it be that you are here only because this is your ancestral village? Are you so old-fashioned as that? Nobody believes it. You are here because you are secretly Communists—I know it! Your lives are in my hand. One word to that old fat uncle of yours and one word to the county police and you will be gone!"

For a moment James could not speak, so aghast was he at this wickedness and so ashamed of his own stupidity in not seeing early that Kitty was not the good young woman he had thought she was in the city hospital. He looked at her thin face and unhappy eyes, and it came to him that she was not evil but weak. When all went well with her, she could be good, but the soil in her heart was shallow, and goodness was a plant that must have deep roots with which to live. So he spoke very gently. "Why did you come to our village?" he asked. "No one made you come. I told you the life here was bitter." He saw that she was brimming with some secret, but he did not want to hear it. Instead he took half of his scanty store of money which had come in as his share from the autumn harvests and he said, "You must leave at once. Pack your box and roll up your bedding. I will hire a cart to take you back to the city. If you go today, I will not send a bad report of you to the hospital. You can return to your old work and forget that you ever were here."

She pouted for a while and struggled with her wish to speak out her whole mind, but prudence was in her too and she obeyed. When she was gone Rose had the courage to tell the truth, which was that Kitty had come because of Liu Chen, whom she had loved for a long time. At this Mary grew indignant in her turn, and she said, "Such women cannot understand that marriage is not everything and that work comes first," and she could not understand why Rose laughed so much when she said this and at last Rose had to give over lest she make her friend angry.

Yet for James all this was still only upon the surface of the day's life. He was beginning to understand that sickness and health, that ignorance and learning, poverty and comfort, war and peace, sorrow and joy were all fruits of human confusion or of human wisdom. Here in this one small village set in a spreading countryside was the whole world. What was true here was true anywhere. Something was wrong here and nobody knew why. The Liang family had plenty of food and yet there were others, even outside the gate who starved. James, himself a Liang, had learning enough to raise him high, and yet there were those here, even his kinfolk, who could not read their own surname if they saw it written down. These differences remained in spite of all he could do. James could eat plain food and wear cotton clothes and walk barefoot in his shoes and yet the deep difference remained. And what could he do, he asked himself?

Upon such thoughts James fed and he grew moody and downcast and wondered at his own discontent. He began to think of himself as a man apart, one destined for some great thing, and yet he could not discover how he was to do anything great in the midst of such ignorance and stubbornness as the people had. Ignorance and stubbornness went together in them. Yet some were grateful for what he did, and when he saved a child for a mother, he was warmed for a moment by her joy. But then he asked himself, what was one child saved among these millions? He thought constantly, without telling anyone of his discontent with himself. He said in his heart, "I am cut off from the very people whom I want to help." This was true. While he could speak very kindly to the people who came to be healed or whom he met on village street or country road, he felt no link of flesh or spirit with them. He grew more solitary as the months passed, and this frightened him. Must he say that Su and Peng and Kang and their kind were right? Could there be no bond between himself and his own people?

In this state of mind he looked with new eyes at Mary and Chen. For a long time he had not talked with them except of the day's needs as they rose. Mary had moved her school outside the Liang house when she found the trouble it made, and once outside these walls, others in the village dared to come to it, and her room was full again. People who could not read or write themselves believed that there was some great good fortune in learning and mothers sent their little sons to Mary, hoping that with learning these lads need not be only common farmers and muleteers and carriers. These poor mothers dreamed their dreams, too. "Why can not I be content as Chen is content?" James asked himself. Both Chen and Mary had found a way to root themselves here and he had not. James watched Mary and he could discover in her lively looks not one hint of discontent. And Chen too was happy. Asking no profound questions of himself, he did the day's work well, and he it was who taught the village ironmonger to make a knife so keen of edge that it could lance a boil or cut a surface ulcer. His homemade sterilizer he declared better than ever and he used it daily.

Not one man or woman had yet allowed the cutting away of any inner part, and James and Chen had both to see some waste away and die rather than be cut. Uncle Tao was everywhere loud in his words against cutting and the people knew that he would not let James cut away the thing that grew larger month by month in his own belly. The stout old man still contended with this inner growth and he ate much and slept much and no longer walked far from his room, and by dint of such eating and sleeping he was still strong. Yet some day, as James and Chen both knew, he would be weaker. When that day came they must be ready for it.

The autumn drew on gloriously, and the moon swelled to harvest size. The frost came down and then went away again and autumn warmth returned and one day after another passed in golden silence. The people were quiet and happy for a while, for with the harvests all could eat. The bandits, always lurking over the horizon, were not yet hungry with winter and the people could take a little ease. The war withdrew farther north once more and this fear eased, too, though only for a space. The end of autumn before winter strikes is the best time of any year, and this year it was more than good, for the harvests had been heavy. Yet James alone was not content. All that he did was too small, and he had with him day and night a constant loneliness.

And then one day in midwinter he discovered the cause of his own discontent. The one room where they worked had grown into two and now they were building a third for a bath house. There was no warm place in this whole village for people to wash themselves. In the city can be found bath houses, but not in a village. Much skin disease came from filth, and while in the summer a man can stand behind his house and pour a bucket of water over himself and scrub his body with the rough dried shred of a field gourd, in winter no man longs so heartily to be clean that he will do such a thing. The bath house therefore became a dream of Chen's own and he had hired two men to come with their mallets and pound down earth into walls. He devised an earthen stove in one corner and a pipe to carry hot water from a cauldron to a great round wooden tub and a drain to carry the soiled water away into a ditch in the village street. The fame of this miracle went everywhere, and whole families came from miles around to see it for themselves.

Chen took much pride in the bath house, and he explained to all who came how easily it had been made, how cheaply, and how any man who had a little energy to spare could make his family such a bath house. When women saw in what comfort their menfolk came home after a hot bath in winter, they went to Mary and asked why one should not be made for them and Mary carried the demand to James and Chen. Chen laughed at her as he always did, and he said with mock ruefulness to James, "You see how these new women are, always wanting everything men have!" and Mary, who never understood quickly enough that he made a joke, flew to women's defense and Chen pretended to be frightened and he said, "Well—well, who said I would not do it?"

So a bath house was made for the women, too, and they were thrifty and brought their children to bathe with them and thus bathing became the fashion, and the village was proud and felt itself as good as any city. Even so there were those who complained and the eldest daughter-in-law grumbled and said, "All this bathing is nothing but a wasteful habit. Look at me! Now that I bathe myself, I itch all over in twenty days or so unless I bathe again. Yet before we had this bath house I went all winter and did not itch."

Uncle Tao would not bathe at all at first for fear of getting cold, and then for fear of seeming to yield to Mary. Then when he saw how rosy the children were after a bath and how well his sons ate and how sweetly they slept when they were cleaned, he mustered up courage and one day before the new moon year he declared himself ready for a bath, too.

Neither James nor Chen had urged him, but be sure that they rejoiced at this sign of change in Uncle Tao. Chen himself saw that the room was warm and the water hot and that some sheets of cotton were ready to dry Uncle Tao's vast body. All others were held off while Uncle Tao was bathed. He had decided that the bath should take place at high noon on a sunny day when there was no wind, and he waited some ten days or so before he found a day good enough. Then he was anxious about what he should eat, and James advised him to eat nothing until after the bath.

Uncle Tao agreed to this but he said, "As soon as I am in my clothes again I must eat well, for much strength will be drained out of me with the bath," and he ordered all his favorite dishes to be ready for him.

On the chosen day when the sun was high over the roofs, Uncle Tao allowed himself to be led into the bath house, and two menservants helped him to undress while his sons stood by, and Chen saw to the pouring of the water and James helped Uncle Tao get into the tub. Lucky it was that they had made that tub as large as a wooden vat, for when Uncle Tao lowered himself into it, the two men holding his arms and James holding his waist, the water spurted up around him like a fountain. At first Uncle Tao was fearful that he had done a foolish thing, but while James and Chen scrubbed him well with soap they had made from raw lye and the fat of an ox that had died, Uncle Tao began to feel better and he grew cheerful.

"To bathe is a good thing," he declared proudly, looking about at them all from the tub. "Of course it cannot be done quickly and carelessly. Nor should it be done too often. The day must be a lucky one, the water must be hot, and I must not sit too long in this tub. Add some hot to it."

When he was clean they poured two or three buckets of fresh hot water over him from the head down and he sat like a great baby gasping under the flow, his eyes shut and his mouth open and licking in the water. Then slowly he rose again, all helping him, and James wrapped him immediately with the cotton sheets and he was dried and the clean clothes he had ordered prepared were put on him. At last he was ready to eat and he ate with great pleasure and good nature, and then he slept, and when he woke he was so comfortable in all the mountain of his being that he commanded his whole household to be bathed at once, from his eldest son down to the smallest grandchild. This caused much trouble, but Chen was well pleased. "Behold me!" he cried to James, and pointed at himself with his thumb to his breast, "I have made a successful revolution!"

How could Chen be so happy with such small things? This James asked himself. This Chen was no small-minded man, neither did he dream small dreams. Sometimes when the two friends talked into the night Chen ceased for a while to make his jokes and then James saw him for what he was, a sober-minded, large-thinking man, who was making plans far beyond the daily tasks.

"You keep me in heart," he said on one such evening to Chen. "When I grow weak and think that perhaps Su and Peng and Kang are right, and that these villagers are beyond our strength to help, when I fear that the centuries are stronger than we are, then I think of you."

Chen heard this thoughtfully, rubbing the crown of his head slowly with his right hand in the way he had. "Of course the people on the land are stronger than we are," he said. "They are the strength of our nation and they cannot be easily changed.

"Yet why do we think we must change them? All we need do is to prove a thing is good and they will change themselves. Remember the bath house!"

These few words opened a door in James's mind. He sat thinking about them and in silence. A small earthen pot of charcoal stood between him and Chen, and he warmed his hands over it. His one care was his hands, that they stay supple so that the skin would not break. He needed these hands for

healing and he wanted them whole, so that when he put oint-
ment on the scald head of a child or washed out some old
ulcer on a farmer's leg, or cleansed the sores of a leper, the
poison would not spoil his hands.

Upon his thought Chen broke. "Jim, I have something to
say and I cannot say it."

James looked up surprised. "You and I have always spoken
to one another easily, Chen."

"Yes, but this is about something else."

Chen's face was suddenly fiery red and James remembered
that red. "You do not regret sending Kitty away?" he asked,
half in play.

Chen gave a snort. "That Kitty! No—no—but what made
you think of a girl, Jim?"

"Your red face."

Chen began rubbing his crown again. "Ha—yes—well—"
So he stammered.

"Come—come!" James said.

Chen swallowed, clenched his hands together on his lap and
plunged in. "I want to marry Mary," he said abruptly.

"Eh?" James said stupidly.

"You hear me," Chen said. Even his eyes looked red.

"But you are always laughing at her," James said still
stupidly. "And she never knows what you are laughing at. And
you quarrel how often!"

"Married people always quarrel," Chen said.

"Ah, but Chen, you two do not act like people in love!"

"And have you been in love?" Chen asked.

How seldom James thought of Lili, how resolutely he had
put her away, and yet now her soft charming face, her childlike voice, came creeping back into his memory. He remembered his love for her, and how while it lived that love had
wrapped him about in a dream. Mary and Chen did not walk
in dreams. She was busy and brisk and she commanded Chen
to do this and that and Chen laughed at her and sometimes he
made a great show of obedience and sometimes he only
laughed and did nothing, and when she flew at him he pretended terror. It was not at all what had been between him
and Lili.

"I have been in love," James said gravely.

"Did she die?"

"She married someone else."

"What a fool she!" Chen exclaimed cheerfully. "Well, better luck for me, Jim—and for you too, someday."

"I shall not soon marry," James said.

"I shall," Chen retorted. "But the question is—how can I tell Mary?"

He sat with his legs spread wide, his hands on his knees, his hair standing upright, and his square face so rueful that James burst into laughter himself. "You tell her everything else. Why can you not tell her this?"

But Chen was grave. "No, no. This is different. It is serious. A man cannot just go and speak to a woman so."

"Why not? You are not a villager in love, are you?"

Chen continued to look grave. "It is delicate. The old way is not good—for us, that is. Yet I do not like the American way for us, either. I saw it in the movies. It was too disgusting to me—also insulting to Mary."

It was so amazing to see Chen, who was always ready for anything, thus confounded by love, and by love for Mary, whom he saw every day and whom he teased as easily as he breathed, that James was speechless for a few minutes, half amused, half impressed. In this silence Chen continued to talk. "Besides, how do I know she thinks of me as I wish her to do? It may be that she will need a little education—you know, someone to say to her for instance, 'Eh, Mary, this Chen, who is such a rough joking fellow—at heart he is different. He is rather good. He is very faithful'—some such thing, Jim."

"Shall I say this to her for you?" James asked.

"Will you, good brother?" Chen said, very red again in the face. "That is what I want to ask."

"Why not? I will say that and much more."

"You like me well enough?" Chen asked with a little new anxiety. "Your father, for example—would he object to me?"

"My father seems so far away that I had not even thought of him. As for me, you are already my brother, and I will gladly give you my sister to bring our two bloods into one."

Chen sat back and he wiped his face with his sleeve and blew out a great sigh of relief. "Now then, I feel better," he said in a loud voice. "Of course—I must not be too happy yet. She may not like me for a husband."

"To this I cannot honestly reply," James said. "I have never seen her thinking of any man or even of a husband."

They considered Mary, and Chen asked excitedly, "Jim, eh—why not ask her now?"

"But she will be going to bed."

Chen got up and looked through the court. "The light is still behind her window," he said. "Eh—how can I sleep now until I know?"

"But how will you sleep if she does not want you?" James asked in reply.

This could not be answered. The two young men looked at one another. Chen was suddenly pale. He set his pleasant lips grimly. "I must know," he muttered.

James lingered one moment more. "Then I will ask her," he said, and he went to do it.

Mary was brushing her short straight black hair when she heard the knock on her door. She had taken off her outer garments and she had put on a bathrobe of red wool that she had brought with her from America. She opened the door and saw her brother.

"What's the matter?" she asked.

"I want a few minutes with you, Mary."

"Come in," she said. "But what is it that can't wait until tomorrow?"

They were speaking in English, and somehow in this language he found it difficult to say what must be said, and he dropped back into Chinese. "I come for a strange thing."

"What is it?" she asked still in English.

"I am a go-between, a marriage broker, and I bring an offer."

"Don't be silly!" she exclaimed.

"Is it silly? Perhaps it is," James replied. "For I told him to come to you himself, and he cannot. He is shy of you when it comes to love."

Did Mary know of what he was talking? He thought she did. Her eyes were wide and dark and her cheeks were pink and her lips parted. He waited for her to speak and she did not. She sat on the edge of her bed and he sat on the stool by her table and they continued to look at one another.

"Chen loves you, Mary," he said simply and he spoke these words in English.

"Oh," Mary said and it was a sigh, very soft, like a child's.

"Is that all?" he asked.

"But—but how does he know?" she demanded.

"He seems to know," James said tenderly.

She sat gazing at him, her cheeks pinker.

"And do you say nothing?" James asked.

"I am trying to find out how I feel," she said. "I think I feel—happy."

"Good! Take a little longer." So he encouraged her.

They waited and he saw her eyes drop to her small bare feet. "I didn't have time to put on my slippers. My feet are getting cold."

"Where are they? I'll find them for you."

"No, they're here, under the bed." She found the slippers for herself and put them on.

"You ought to be careful on these earthen floors," James said. He rose. "Well, shall I tell him that tomorrow you will speak to him yourself?"

She raised her long straight lashes. "Yes," she whispered. She turned and picked up her brush again and stood watching for an instant the dark straightness of her hair.

"I want you to be happy, Mary," he said at last.

"I am always happy," she said with a look of sweet firmness which he knew so well, and he left her to go back to Chen.

He found that friend of his prowling restlessly around the room.

"How long you were!" Chen exclaimed.

"I wasn't," James retorted. "She hadn't thought of it—"

"Hadn't thought of me?" Chen moaned.

"Let us say—of marriage."

Chen sat down as though his legs were suddenly weak. "But all women must marry," he remonstrated.

"Not nowadays. Chen, you are too old-fashioned."

"Then I suppose she doesn't—"

"She wants to talk with you tomorrow herself."

"You mean she didn't—"

"She did not refuse you," James replied slowly and clearly. "She is thinking. I dare say she will think all night. But knowing her, by tomorrow doubtless Mary will know what she wants."

Chen groaned. "I shan't sleep all night."

"Then you will be foolish and tomorrow you will not look your best."

Chen was alarmed. "True—I had better go to bed now." He turned in haste and made off to his own room.

James lay awake long enough that night himself. This then was why Chen had been so well content here in the village. His love was here. A man could live and work if he had his love. His mind stole back to Lili—foolishly, he told himself, for she was married now and perhaps even the mother of a child. But he had known her for a little while as she was, and this fragment of memory was all that he had. There had been American girls in love with him, he knew well enough, but he had never loved them. When he had felt them grow warm toward him he had grown cold and had withdrawn into his work. Their flesh was alien to his. And yet was he to live solitary all his life? No, heart and body cried. Yet how could he find here a woman to love? He belonged neither to old nor to new. He wanted a wife who would be a companion to him as well as the mother of his children. He wanted love as well as mating.

He could not find an easy place that night upon his bed and it was nearly dawn before he slept.

But Mary lay quietly in her bed. She lay on her back and she gazed up into the canopy above her. The moon shone outside and the room was not quite dark. The night was cold and still. It was midwinter. They had been here in the village a year. She had known Chen for more than a year. She had never thought of being in love, because being in love brought so much trouble. Louise was always in love, and Jim had been in love. She and Peter never fell in love, and Peter was dead.

What was being in love? She had always thought of Chen and Jim together, but now she remembered she always put Chen first—that is, she always said it so—"Chen and Jim."

Once Peter had reproached her. "Why do you say Chen's name before your brother's?" he had demanded.

She had stared back at him. "I don't know," she had said honestly.

She shut her eyes and thought of all the people she knew. Chen's face came first against the dark curtain of her eyelids. When she wanted the schoolroom made she had gone to Chen, not James. They had worked hard but it had seemed like play. Chen made her laugh. Sometimes he made her angry, but then it felt good to be angry with him. He did not mind. She could be as angry as she wanted with him and he did not mind. She felt comfortable with him. She could be herself with him. Was this being in love? "I will ask him tomorrow," she thought.

It was not easy for a man and a woman to be alone in the ancestral village. Tongues wagged quickly, and it was taken for granted that man and woman were interested only in their differing sex. It was necessary for a new Liang to work while she talked with a man. So Mary the next day in the afternoon cleaned James's room while she talked to Chen. Children came by and a servant or two and a new tenant farmer looking for Uncle Tao and two women who wanted to send their children to school and some of the cousins and daughters-in-law passed through the court. All they saw was Mary working hard to clean her brother's room and Chen reading a book on the threshold of his own room which opened upon the same court. When no one passed, Chen and Mary paused. They talked in English for safety.

"Is this being in love?" she asked, when she had told him how she felt.

"If you are content to be with me, it is enough to begin with," Chen said joyously. "I cannot expect a good girl like you, Mary, to behave like a wild Western woman."

"But you must promise to let me go on teaching."

"I promise," Chen said instantly. "More than that, I insist upon it."

"I might want to stop," Mary said suddenly.

"I shall forbid it!" Chen exclaimed. His eyes were twinkling. Then he laughed. "You shall do exactly what you want to do, now and forever," he said tenderly.

She stood looking at him doubtfully and so adorable was her face, the eyes so big and black, her mouth so full and red, that he felt distracted with happiness. He looked hastily about and saw no one in sight. Overcome with himself he stepped forward impetuously and took her in his arms, broom and all, and kissed her exactly as he had seen such things in American movies. He had never dreamed it possible, nor had she. Both were astounded at the success they both made of it. Chen stepped back. "Do you mind?" he asked humbly.

She stood transfixed, gazing at him and clutching her broom in both hands. She shook her head at his question and her eyes were entranced.

19

DR. LIANG FELT RELIEF at the news about Mary. There was pride in his relief, also, for until his daughters are married a father has an uneasy sense of duty not yet done. Unwed daughters still belong to the parents, and like fruit clinging too long to the tree, there is something unnatural about it. Surely, Dr. Liang had often told himself, it was very difficult to be a father in these post-Confucian days. In the old days, the golden days, the father chose a suitable husband for his daughter, the wedding took place, and the father could think of other matters. Nowadays, however, all the old harmonies being gone and discord having taken their place, fathers could only make objections. They could object if their daughters married unsuitable men, or they could object if their daughters did not marry at all. Dr. Liang had done both. He had never wholly reconciled himself to his American son-in-law and he professed to his wife not to understand how Louise could sleep with an American.

"I suppose a man is a man," Mrs. Liang had said briskly.

Dr. Liang had been offended at this. "You are too coarse," he replied. "I do not think that I, for example, can be confused with this one whom Louise has married. Consider his appearance! His bones are large. He is crudely educated. When I mention some subject of literature or philosophy he does not know what I am talking about."

"In bed even you do not talk about literature and philosophy," Mrs. Liang told him in her too literal fashion.

Dr. Liang had not replied to this. He had formulated in his mind several good paragraphs which he would use in his conversation with Violet Sung. Then he remembered that she, too, was in some unmentionable and strange fashion connected with the Englishman. He supposed that this was still going on.

It troubled him with a growing disgust. Violet never mentioned the name of Ranald Grahame and Dr. Liang never allowed himself to think of that part of her life with which he had nothing to do. Their relationship, which was now infinitely deeper than mere friendship, continued on a purely spiritual level.

This level had remained undisturbed until Louise came back to New York married to Alec Wetherston. Dr. Liang found the Wetherston family uncongenial and after one dinner party at which he had been extremely uncomfortable he had refused any further meeting. Alec was, he told Mrs. Liang, an empty young man. He would never understand what Louise saw in him. The child they had brought back from China he considered worthy of no notice from himself, and Louise's child, who had been born in July, was a girl and therefore still unworthy of notice. A girl of mixed blood was the child of misfortune. He could not imagine who would marry her.

He had remembered Violet Sung at that moment and that she too was of mixed blood. But the French, he believed, were the nearest of all Western peoples to the Chinese. Then, too, it was Violet's father who had been Chinese, and the Chinese male strength always dominated. His feelings, however, Dr. Liang kept to himself and his wife. He spoke to Louise when she came home and he was kind enough to smile at the plump little creature to whom she had given such mongrel birth. Fortunately the child had dark eyes and hair. Still, it was a Wetherston child, and he had very little part in it. The Wetherstons, he persisted in thinking, were not connections in which to take pride. Mr. Wetherston was undoubtedly honest but he was the ordinary commercial American, thickset, jovial, bald-headed, and given to back-slapping, which made Dr. Liang shiver, and in conversation he was dull and even stupid. Apparently he read no books. Mrs. Wetherston was the sort of woman found in any country, a female who is no more than a mother to children. After she had produced these children little was left in her except residue of flesh. That both the elder Wetherstons and indeed the whole Wetherston family seemed fond of Louise, that they heaped her with gifts and concern, seemed to him no more than just. They acknowledged thus the superiority of the Liang family and indeed of the Chinese.

When therefore Dr. Liang received a letter from James, another from Mary, and a third from his new son-in-law, he was openly glad that Mary had chosen so well. He examined the handwriting of Chen's letter. It was not too good. He held the letter up before his eyes and he said to Mrs. Liang, "This fellow is not a scholar. Nevertheless, there is a certain rude strength in his style. He does not merely copy delicate handwriting. He knows the roots of the letters and he writes correctly and with vigor. He has temper and power. I hope Mary will not quarrel with him immediately."

Mrs. Liang did not reply. She was absorbed in reading Mary's letter, which was written simply and plainly so that she might read it easily. "Dear beloved Ma," Mary had written. "Please forgive me for engaging myself without your or Pa's knowledge. James will tell you how it all happened. Chen is his best friend. I tell you he is a good man. He is ugly in the face but tall and broad and his mouth is square, which you know is a sign of brains and his ear lobes are long which Uncle Tao says is lucky. Chen laughs a great deal. He is kind to everybody. He is a doctor, but not so good as James, I think. His family lives in a village as ours does. Ma, I wish you could come here for our wedding but I suppose Pa will not let you. Dear Ma, there are many things I would like to ask you before I am a married woman."

At these words Mrs. Liang began to weep.

"What is the matter now?" Dr. Liang asked.

"Mary needs me," she said. She did not sob aloud but she allowed tears to stream down her cheeks.

"What for?" Dr. Liang asked.

"You would not understand if I told you."

Dr. Liang looked dignified at this. "I am not stupid," he remarked. "I have what is considered a good mentality."

She continued to weep. He looked at her from time to time with mounting impatience. "Well, well," he said at last and with severity, "I suppose you will be crying steadily now for these next few weeks. I had better get used to it."

She wiped her cheeks. "Liang," she said bravely, "let us go back to the ancestral village just for our daughter's wedding."

He looked horrified. "After all these years?" he exclaimed. "In these evil times?"

"I would like to go back," she said pleadingly. "There are things I should tell Mary before the wedding."

Dr. Liang looked displeased. "You mothers always think you know so much," he said. "The fact is that all that sort of thing comes naturally. Whatever you tell Mary, she will do what she knows already by instinct. Besides, what can you tell her?" He was moved with a faint curiosity.

"There are so many things," Mrs. Liang said vaguely, not looking at him.

"Whatever you tell her can only be out of your experience with me," he said with dignity. "This will not help her at all with such a young man as has written this letter." He touched Chen's letter lying on the table with his delicate forefinger.

"I want to go home," she said stubbornly.

The upshot of all this was that a week or two of steady dejection on the part of Mrs. Liang wore him down to such a low point of resistance that he agreed to let her have her way. He declared that he himself could not possibly leave his students at the college, but that if she felt no like sense of duty toward him and their home, she could go, to be back in a period of three months at the latest. He was deeply wounded at the signs of joy which she showed upon this permission, and he was only comforted when he had talked over the whole matter with Violet Sung.

They met now quite regularly two or three times a week, varying their meeting places, so that no gossip would rise about them. Each place was a small quiet restaurant in some part of the city. The routine was the same. They ordered a meal, or perhaps only tea, and they sat long, talking about their thoughts and never about their lives.

On the day when he had finally given his permission to his wife, however, Violet, with her delicate feeling instinct, perceived that he was unhappy. She herself was unhappy most of the time and this mood, so constant in herself, gave her a sensitivity almost abnormal toward all other human beings except Ranald Grahame. Toward him she had no sensitivity whatever. This puzzled her very much, for in hours she was with him more than she was with anyone else. But he remained strange to her. She met him each day, each night, almost as a stranger. She knew every line of his body, every look of his face as she knew her own physical being, but what was in his mind, what were his feelings and his emotions, she did not know. They were content together in a literal physical fashion, and sometimes, indeed, after hours of talk with Wen Hua, as she now called Dr. Liang, she went back to Ranald with a sort of relief that she need not talk or think or feel.

What, she often pondered, would have happened if these two men had been one? "I should have been utterly consumed," she told herself thoughtfully. As it was, between the two, she lived a life which though in some ways unnatural was nevertheless satisfying in its balance.

"Wen Hua, why are you sad?" she asked him gently today.

She was looking more beautiful even than usual. She wore a new frock of dull black silk and a black coat lined with scarlet, and a small scarlet hat. He saw this fresh beauty across the small table between them.

"It is nothing," he replied, trying to smile.

"Of course it is something. You cannot deceive me however you deceive others."

"Do I deceive others?"

"Nobody knows you except me."

He began therefore to talk. "I suppose I dread loneliness," he said very gently. "The mother of my children wishes to leave me for a while to return to our ancestral village. My elder daughter is to be married to a young Chinese doctor who is my son's friend. This is all good. I have no objection. I only wish I could go. But my work keeps me here. Yet I do not like to think of three months in my lonely house." He sighed. "Ah, I know I am a friendless man. I put my roots deep into only a few people. My children have left me. Now my wife, their mother, wants to leave me."

"She will come back," Violet reminded him.

"Of course—but still—"

He broke off. "It is a strange thing that one can live a lifetime with a woman without loving her, and yet—" he broke off again.

"In a way you do love her," Violet said generously. "Wen Hua, you are so complex. I understand you better than you understand yourself."

"Then explain me to myself," he murmured. It was delightful to lean toward this lovely woman and hear himself explained.

Her great eyes met his. "You are like the lotus. You need to plant your roots deep into the earth beneath the waters before you can flower and fruit. Your—the mother of your children has been your earth. She has given you a place for your roots." Her exquisite face turned the palest of pearl pink. "I ought to be grateful to her and I am. I honor her for what she is to you. For it is I who have enjoyed the flower and the fruit."

He was much touched by this sweetness and generosity. "You always teach me something good," he said. "I will be generous too. I will let her go. But be kind to me. While she is gone let us see each other often, very often—Violet!"

"Yes," she murmured, "yes."

Mrs. Liang closed her eyes and sat back in her seat. At the last minute she had decided to take the plane instead of the steamer. Just why this was so she did not know. She only felt it best. Liang had come back one evening quite himself and had said very kindly that she might go. She was surprised and disturbed.

"Liang, I think I better not go," she had exclaimed in English.

"Why not?" he had retorted. "I have myself all prepared and now you don't go!"

"I have been thinking—who will look after you?"

"Nellie will feed me, and I will work hard and expect your return," he had said too graciously.

She had stared at him, but he had returned her gaze unblinkingly. He looked placid and well and she was further alarmed.

"Then I must fly only," she said. "I fly there and fly back. Supposing I stay one month, I am satisfied."

"You will be seasick on the plane," he remonstrated. "Remember how in China you were sick even on the train—and for that matter, as a bride, I believe, in your sedan."

She refused the disagreeable memory of herself when, long ago, she had come out of the bridal chair, pale and shaken with seasickness. Chair bearers always tossed a bride cruelly, laughing when she was sick, for it was a sign of good luck and early pregnancy.

"Now I am older," she said. "If I am sick I will be sick and not mind too much."

So it was decided, and she made all preparations. She bought gifts for Mary of American stockings and underwear and a warm sweater and a sweater too for James and her new son-in-law. Had she been on a ship she would have taken boxes, and Dr. Liang was secretly thankful that on a plane she could take very little.

Yet it was not only in the matter of clothes that she made preparation. She went to see Louise and had loud exclamatory talk with Mrs. Wetherston in which she made known her joy at having another son-in-law. "So nice!" she had said briskly. "One American, one Chinese son-in-law! I am sure American is better, but anyway I take what my girls like. Alec is so nice. Thank you, Mrs. Wellyston, to be such a good mother with a good son. He is too good for Louise. She is such selfish girl, I know."

"Louise is a darling," Mrs. Wetherston said.

"Thank you too much, but I know," Mrs. Liang said. "She puts down things anywhere. 'Louise!' I say, 'now you have baby. You cannot to put down everywhere. It is too bad. Pick it up,' I say. But she is so spoiled. Please excuse me."

"I won't hear a word against our little girl," Mrs. Wetherston said warmly. She loved Mrs. Liang by now and she spent happy hours describing to her friends how interesting it all was since Alec had married a Chinese girl. "Of course, my dears, the family is exceptional," she always told them.

Dr. Liang she respected but disliked. After the one dinner the two families had taken together, Mr. Wetherston had refused to spend any more time with Dr. Liang. "We don't speak the same language," he had told Mrs. Wetherston.

"We ought to try to understand Chinese psychology, I think, dear," she had said gently.

This also Mr. Wetherston had refused to do. "I get enough psychology in my clients," he said firmly. "I don't want it in my relatives." He would have preferred that Alec had married a nice American girl and he made no bones about that. "Now, Dorothy," he had told Mrs. Wetherston, "I'm not going to say anything. For a Chinese Louise is a nice girl. But I'd rather Alec had married a nice American girl instead of bringing home a foreigner. Of course it can't be helped, and there was already little Alec. We didn't know about him. I guess I understand the circumstances—well, all I can say is, let's make Louise American as fast as possible, and forget the rest of them." Since he left home before nine in the morning and did not come back from his downtown office until after six in the evening, he was able to do this easily.

Mrs. Wetherston did not have the courage to tell him that she was beginning to enjoy her unique position as the mother-in-law of a pretty Chinese girl, especially one who was a daughter of the Liang family. Nobody had paid any attention to her before and now they did. Her bridge club, where she had always been inconspicuous except for a bad play, now made much of her and asked her many questions. Once even a reporter came for an interview, and the next day she was half proud, half embarrassed to see a picture of herself in an afternoon paper, set in the middle of a column of how it felt to be the mother of a son with a Chinese wife. She felt a hypocrite when Alec thanked her for being so good to Louise.

"Mom, you could have been so different," he said gratefully.

"But I enjoy her, dear," she protested. "And the baby is so good—and so pretty, Alec. And it was so sweet of Louise to name her Dorothy."

The marriage was turning out well. If Louise was growing more rather than less lazy, she was sweet tempered and content, for she had fallen easily in love with her husband. She had taken up her friendship with Estelle again and had laughed at her childish infatuation for Philip. Philip was married, too, but he had gone to California because his brilliant blond wife wanted to act in pictures, much to his father's disgust. Louise never went to the Morgan house, but Estelle, who was still single and working in radio, had at first come often to see Louise.

"Philip was only a boy," Louise had mused, smiling, and her long Chinese eyes were full of rich secrets which Estelle could not divine.

Then somehow the friendship began to dwindle. Louise, married to a handsome young American, nursing their pretty child, taking care of her lively little stepson, had become unendurable to Estelle. Since the war, girls married young. To be twenty-four and then twenty-five and still not married! It wasn't as if there weren't plenty of Chinese that Louise could have married. American men ought to marry American women. When Estelle stopped coming Louise did not miss her. She did not miss anybody.

"Louise," Mrs. Liang said when the door had closed behind her. "Now I want your listening."

Since Louise belonged to the Wetherston family, Mrs. Liang felt it her duty sometimes to speak in English to her.

Louise, changing the diapers of her adorable baby, did not look up. Little Alec was emptying the pin tray and she kept an eye on him. "Yes, Ma," she murmured.

"Now I am leaving your pa for nearly two months. Anyway six weeks," Mrs. Liang went on. "You must not just stay here and not see him. Every day or two days you must go to apartment and see what is Neh-lee cooking."

"All right, Ma," Louise said. She had no intention of such faithfulness, but she did not want to disturb her mother by truth. She lifted her baby tenderly in her arms, unbuttoned the front of her dress, and presented her full young breast to the child's obedient mouth. Sitting in a low chair thus she made a pleasant picture which moved Mrs. Liang's heart.

"Like I was with you," she murmured, her eyes swimming.

Louise smiled, unbelieving. Her mother could never have been pretty, even as a young mother. "Go on, Ma," she said.

Mrs. Liang hitched her chair nearer and began to speak in a low rapid voice in Chinese. "Eh, Louise, I tell you, your pa is a man, naturally. All men are the same. They like women too much."

Louise looked away. "Oh, Ma, when Pa is so old!"

Mrs. Liang looked indignant. "He is not too old. To you, yes, but to any woman over thirty, no! And I tell you—" She broke off and considered. Should she or should she not mention the name of Violet Sung? She could not control herself and she went on in English again. "You know Violet Sung? She is always—well, I don't say! But when I am away, your pa will be very weak."

"Oh, Ma," Louise murmured again.

"You don't need to keep saying so," Mrs. Liang said with irritation. "I will tell you later when you are not so young, and you will understand better. Now all I say is, sometimes see your pa, and listen to some friends, and hear if there is any talk. It is for Pa's sake. He is too famous and well known for talk."

Louise laughed. "All right, Ma. But you're funny."

Mrs. Liang laughed, too. She felt better. She had little time and she rose, remembered she had brought a pair of new rubber pants for the baby and fumbled for them in her bag. "Of course don't tell Alec. Your pa is not his family. Maybe I am suspicious but I know your pa too much. Now such pants like I got you haven't for the child. They button, like so, and when you wash, buttons out, and so—" Mrs. Liang demonstrated. "Good, isn't it not?" She laughed again heartily. "Well, now I go back to ancestral village, and I must get used to small watercloths holding to babies' bottoms and open pants to make some water on the ground. Never mind—in China it is not bad. Here, of course, it cannot. Carpets on the floor and so on. I think Americans are troubling themselves sometimes too much."

Louise laughed again. "Oh, Ma, you're really a scream, if you only knew it."

"Screaming? I am not screaming, Louise," Mrs. Liang protested.

"Oh, Ma," Louise repeated laughing helplessly.

From Louise Mrs. Liang had gone to Mrs. Pan. The two women had discussed thoroughly Mary's engagement until there remained nothing to tell. But Mrs. Liang after rending of the heart, had decided to ask Mrs. Pan also to let her know of any gossip. Whatever gossip there was would surely penetrate at once to Chinatown, where everything was known about everybody.

Mrs. Pan had been down on her knees scrubbing her floors when Mrs. Liang came and she was glad to see her. She had got up, wrung her cloth dry, and slapped her youngest child gently on its bare legs.

"You little thing—don't dirty floor," she said with mock severity. Then she had laughed. "Come in, Mrs. Liang. My children are terrible. Sit down, I have some tea already made. These little cakes mildew if we don't eat. My, my, so you really go on the plane! I couldn't dare. My stomach is too foolish."

The conversation ran on rapidly, most of the time in duet, until the tea was drunk, the cakes eaten, and Mrs. Liang came to the point for which Mrs. Pan had been waiting.

"Mrs. Pan," Mrs. Liang began, wiping her mouth on the edge of her sleeve.

Mrs. Pan looked solemn. "Yes, Mrs. Liang, please go on. Don't be afraid of me. I am very good friend to everybody and specially to you now."

Mrs. Liang cleared her throat. "You are old married woman too, Mrs. Pan," she said feelingly. "I don't have to say to you how are men anywhere. Liang is no worse than all. But I am going away six weeks now. I am only afraid—" She paused.

Mrs. Pan smiled at her tenderly. "I know. You are afraid of Violet Sung."

"How you know it?" Mrs. Liang exclaimed.

"Every woman is afraid of her. I am so glad my Billy Pan is just common old businessman from Canton. She cannot look at him, yet he looks at her when he sees her pictures in papers. I say to him, 'Billy, she don't know your name.' He say, 'Can't I just look?' I say, 'Sure you can look—for one minute. More I will scratch your face!'"

Mrs. Liang was frightened. "Have you heard some gossip?"

Mrs. Pan made haste to comfort her. "No—no—who can? But your Dr. Liang is handsome and famous and not common businessman from Canton. He is Peking man, very exceptional scholar, talks to American ladies and so on. I know!"

Mrs. Liang turned pale and Mrs. Pan went on quickly. "Now, don't you think, Mrs. Liang! And please be comfortable. I will listen all four corners and hear something. Anybody can tell me since they know I am your friend. Suppose I hear it, I will write you quick letter."

Mrs. Liang drew a deep breath. "Good! Then I am trusting your letter."

She rose, drew out a small stuffed doll from her bag for Mrs. Pan's youngest and then two cakes of fine soap for Mrs. Pan. "Thank you," she said.

"Thanking *you*," Mrs. Pan said gratefully.

Thus they had parted. But what Mrs. Pan had said was so disturbing that against her better judgment she had spoken even to Nellie on the last day.

"Eh, Neh-lee," she had said in a half whisper in the kitchen.

"What is it now?" Nellie asked, her hands in the dishpan.

"You take care good," Mrs. Liang said.

"I will that," Nellie promised.

"Neh-lee," Mrs. Liang began again, fumbling in her purse.

"Well?"

"I give you this, Neh-lee—please!"

"Thank you, I'm sure," Nellie said, taking quickly the ten-dollar bill held out to her. She was surprised and even frightened for Mrs. Liang had never before given her more than a quarter. Was she about to be fired?

"I tell you something," Mrs. Liang said urgently. "You don't please open door here to any ladies."

Nellie's gray eyes opened wide. "Well, I'm sure, madam—"

Mrs. Liang cut her off. "No, please, and specially to some

lady called Violet Sung. She cannot come here while I am gone."

"I'll never let her in," Nellie agreed.

Mrs. Liang patted Nellie's arm. "So I trust you!"

"But if the mister lets her in or if I'm not here?" Nellie asked.

"You look see every day," Mrs. Liang bade her. "Look see some lady's handkerchief, flower, or smelling—" Mrs. Liang went sniff-sniff, her nose in the air to illustrate.

"I get you," Nellie said succinctly. "I had trouble with my own old man—until he was hit by a truck."

So finally Mrs. Liang had been ready to go. Dr. Liang had taken her to the plane and had presented her with a gardenia. They held hands for a moment.

"Liang, please don't eat crabs while I am gone," she had begged. She felt no one else knew a really fresh crab as she did.

"No, no," he promised.

The next minute she was hurried into the plane and the door was shut. She had waved at the window and the parting was over. Now she felt the plane rise high into the air as it took off over New York City. A few minutes later it was humming above the Atlantic Ocean, its wings wide and its nose set toward the East. Her stomach soared, too, and she leaned back and closed her eyes.

20

IN THE VILLAGE James now began to wrestle with such loneliness as he had never imagined in his life. When he tried to find the cause for his melancholy, he found it hidden deep in himself. He examined himself secretly, his temperature, his blood pressure, and even took a sample of his own blood, searching for some new germ. The season had not yet arrived for mosquitoes and malaria, he had no fleas, and other insects, so far as he knew, had not crossed the border between the old-fashioned Liangs and the new. He was determined not to speak to Mary or Chen lest he spoil their happiness, and they were too constantly gay to notice that he was not.

He was introspective and yet able to be detached, even from himself. Thus he saw that he was not actually like Chen, who, he came to perceive more and more clearly, was really like Mary. These two were simple in their separate natures. They were both good; that is, they could not be satisfied with living entirely selfishly. They needed to feel that what they did, their daily work, was of some use to their people. Beyond this, both of them enjoyed simple food, plain clothes, and a house where they need not consider whether the furniture was damaged. Books were for amusement rather than instruction, unless these books taught them some better way of doing what they would do anyway. Mary read faithfully over and over again her few schoolbooks on teaching children, and she wrote letters to her former teachers in New York, asking for pictures and new teaching materials. Chen wrote no letters to America and he ridiculed Mary's pictures amiably, and he was not too careful as a doctor and everybody liked him. James would not allow himself to feel hurt when he saw that the people who came in even larger numbers to the clinic turned first to Chen. Chen's foolery and good spirits made them trust him first, even though James knew himself the better doctor.

Moreover, James was impatient because he had not yet had a chance to perform an operation. The people were frightened when he spoke of anything more than lancing a boil, and even a wen he could not remove, and Uncle Tao's stubbornness encouraged their fear. James had to restrain himself one day when a soldier came in with a gun wound in the arm, but when the man died with gangrene he could not but speak. "He would have lived, even though without an arm," he told the man's wailing mother. "Yet you would not let me save his life." The mother did not like him better for such truth and when she went home she told her neighbors how she had saved her son at least to live a little longer because she would not let the new doctor cut off his arm.

James was angry with the fearfulness of the people and their ignorance, but he would not let himself hate them for these things. He would not let himself even talk about them, and he kept inside himself his discontents and his impatience. But he felt more and more that he would make no true headway unless he found some sort of bridge which would carry him into that place, whatever and wherever it was, in which the people lived. His feet were upon the physical soil of his ancestors, but his mind was not, nor could it be, and his soul was not their soul, and they knew it.

Nor could he go back. He began to understand better now Su and Peng and their kind. They too had reached this place of knowing their difference. There they had stopped. They had accepted their isolation and this he was not willing to do. There must be some way of reaching his people. He was no longer content with the little clinic, enlarged by two rooms for patients who could not go home the same day. He would not be content even with a hospital. As the months went on he saw that nothing short of deep reforms would mend ignorance and ill health and bad government.

Yes, bad government! What had not been apparent to him when he first came was that Uncle Tao was in some way connected with the country police, who were in turn connected with the local magistrate and this connection put the people in the village at the mercy of the magistrate and of Uncle Tao. The magistrate came from elsewhere and having no blood ties in the village he oppressed the people very much. No one could get justice at his court and bribes must be given at the very gate, if one were to be heard at all. No matter what evil befell a villager, he considered it a greater one to go to court to get it righted. Taxes were high, except for Uncle Tao, and those who were poorest paid the most.

There were hours in the night when James, lying restless upon his bed, hated his very name. Because he was a Liang, he told himself, the people would never trust him. Yet how could he help what he was born? He promised himself fiercely that he would find a way, though he were a Liang, to break through to his own folk. Then sometimes even his determination failed and he remembered the beautiful clean hospital in New York where he might have become a great surgeon, and he thought of his father's fine home, and he thought of what might have been his own fortune had he stayed there and married Lili and what it would have been to have escaped the dust and filth and cold and heat of this village, and all the stupidities of his people. And yet he knew he could never have escaped. In spite of anything his heart was here. Somehow he would find a bridge to cross that short span, that fathomless abyss, between his eyes and the eyes of the man who would look at him in his clinic tomorrow morning.

In such mood James received from his father the cable saying that his mother was coming to China by air. The cable reached the city promptly enough but from there it had to be taken on foot by messenger to the village. This left James and Mary only the shortest possible time to meet their mother at the airport. As usual, Uncle Tao had first to be informed of the news.

The first difficulty, however, was that no one had yet told Uncle Tao even of the betrothal. As soon as it was known it would be impossible for Mary and Chen to meet face to face again without offending the proprieties in this ancestral village, and both Chen and Mary had been slow to give up the joy of seeing one another. Now all agreed the time had come. The mother was arriving for the wedding, which must take place soon, and James must therefore tell Uncle Tao everything immediately. He went to the elder one evening after the day's work was done.

Now James knew more surely with every passing day that at some time or other he must come face to face with Uncle Tao on very grievous matters having to do with the life of the people. It was no use, for example, to save from death a man who when he returned to his home would fall ill again from lack of proper food. Nor could James urge him to eat more and better food when taxes were so high that there was no money left with which to buy food. The people hid eggs as they might hide gold, for in these days of worthless money eggs were good tender even to the tax gatherer. Wheat was precious, too, and the tax gatherer or the local military lord took all except the seed wheat. The magistrate kept silent before these for he also must have his share. In the midst of soldier, magistrate, and idle scholar, none of whom produced food or clothing or shelter or tools for themselves, the man on the land who raised food and the artisan who made clothes and shelter and tools were slowly being squeezed out of life. Soldier, magistrate, and scholar clung together against peasant and artisan while they fought among themselves for the petty booty. James began to see that merely to heal the body was doubtful good. Often the man on the land came to him exhausted before he was old, with too little will to live. Something was wrong here in the ancestral village and James had determined one day soon to grapple with Uncle Tao, who allowed all to continue as it was.

But today was not the time, he knew, not only because he must think first of Mary and Chen and of his mother, but above all he had not found his own place here. He was not yet indispensable to his people. If he made trouble Uncle Tao would cast him out and the people would be silent. Before he tried to set up even one of the reforms of which he dreamed, he must have such strength in the ancestral village that Uncle Tao would not dare to cast him out. Ruthless as Uncle Tao seemed to be, yet even he in his secret heart feared the people in anger. For these people on the land and in small shops and crafts could be patient for a generation or two and then one day for some small cause their patience broke and they took up hoes and rakes and knives and mallets and went out to kill their oppressors. Men and women and children they killed. There were times when James felt the hour of the people's anger was near at hand again, especially as the bitter winter drew on and as the bandits began once more to come out of their nests in the distant hills to the northeast.

Yet today was still not the day to speak of such things. James went to find Uncle Tao, and he found him in his bed, where he always went as soon as he had eaten his last meal for the day. Three times each day Uncle Tao ate heartily, although in the winter when the work on the land ceased he allowed to others no more than two meals. He excused himself by saying that those like himself who must take care of others are valuable and should be kept alive.

When James came into the room the youngest son of Uncle Tao was hearing his last commands and all but going away for the night. The older grandsons took turns each night sleeping on a pallet bed in Uncle Tao's room, but tonight Uncle Tao bade the lad wait outside until he was called. Then he told James to shut the door and draw up a stool near the bed.

This unusual kindness from Uncle Tao made James wonder what was wrong here. In a moment he knew. When they were alone Uncle Tao put off the bedclothes, pulled up his night jacket, and pointed to his belly.

"Feel my knot," he told James.

James stood up and bending over the huge pallid mound of Uncle Tao's belly he delicately probed its depths.

"Is it bigger?" Uncle Tao asked anxiously.

"Much bigger," James said gravely.

"Am I thinner?" Uncle Tao asked next.

"You are thinner," James agreed.

Uncle Tao pulled down his jacket and covered himself with the thick cotton quilt. "The question now is this—am I to die or to be killed?"

"If you mean that you will be killed if you are cut, then you are wrong." He made his voice mild but excitement stirred in him. Uncle Tao was so afraid of death that he had refused the knife. Now even more afraid, was he about to ask for it? There was something piteous here. James went on still more gently. He said, "If you allow me to take this knot out soon instead of late, it is likely that you will live. Indeed, I will not do it at all unless I can do it within the next six months. It is only just to give me a reasonable chance to save your life."

Uncle Tao listened to this with unblinking black eyes. "Let us talk of something else," he said.

"I came to talk of something else," James replied. Excitement died. Uncle Tao was still more afraid of dying by the knife than of anything else. James hardened again toward the stupid old man. He sat down and seeing no reason for delay or bushbeating, he said, "You will remember that you told me my sister should be married. I am come to tell you that the betrothal is arranged."

As soon as he had said this he saw that he had made a mistake. Uncle Tao frowned. "How can this be so when I have known nothing of it?" he asked.

James knew that he must at once take a firm stand or Uncle Tao out of jealousy for his position might say that he did not want Chen even as a remote relative for the Liangs. "You know that my sister and I have been reared in America. It is not likely that we could grow up there exactly the same persons that we would have been had we stayed here in the ancestral village. In America the young choose their own mates. Then it would have been impossible for you or for me or even for my father to have compelled Mary to marry someone she did not like. She has chosen for her husband my friend Liu Chen. Nothing can be done about this."

Uncle Tao breathed hard and rolled his head. "Yet it is I who decide what persons are to live in our village! This Liu Chen—he is not a Liang and I can say easily enough that he must not stay."

Now James saw that for Mary's sake he must coax Uncle Tao. So he leaned toward him and he said warmly, "Any man who has power over others can work evil or good and so can you. We trust your goodness."

This set Uncle Tao back. His mouth hung open and he did not know how to reply. What could he say now that would not shame him? He wished that he might forget how he ought to act and act only as he felt, and in this dilemma he could not speak.

In the silence James went on. "I myself think that Mary has chosen well. Liu Chen likes you and he likes our village. Moreover, he is very useful to me in the clinic. Some day, with your permission, I shall make a hospital out of our clinic, and ours will be the first village in this whole region to have a hospital. This will bring honor to you and to the whole Liang family. People will come here from a long distance away and our inn will prosper and our few shops will grow into many and there will be markets for our men on the land."

All this James said in his smooth gentle voice and Uncle Tao could not speak against it. In some way of his own James had made Mary's marriage a part of good that might come about and so Uncle Tao still kept silent. James went on. "I have more news. My mother is coming very soon."

Here was something that Uncle Tao could oppose and he sat up. "Your mother should not come without your father," he exclaimed. "I suppose that man full of ink has forgotten his ancestors! He has breathed in foreign winds and drunk Western waters. What do I care? But they all depend on me still. What would they do without old Uncle Tao to keep the tenants in their places and to collect a little money for them and hold the house together?" He sank back again and closed his eyes.

"What indeed!" James agreed. "My mother has often said that."

Uncle Tao refused to be placated. "She had a loud voice as a girl. What has there been in these years in a foreign country that could improve her?"

James smiled and rose to his feet. "You will see," he said, and thanking Uncle Tao he went away. To Chen and Mary he only said that Uncle Tao did not oppose anything, and Mary and Chen were both cheered.

"You need not laugh," James told them. "Uncle Tao could if he liked put us all out of the village."

But they did not believe him. In these days nothing could make them afraid or sorrowful, and they laughed at everything.

"There are many other villages," Chen said.

Mrs. Liang looked about her in some anxiety. She had combed her hair but she had not tried to change her wrinkled garments. She was glad therefore when she saw James and Mary and not her new son-in-law. They saw her at the same moment and at once they were a knot of three, their arms about each other.

"Oh Ma, thank you for coming," Mary cried.

James took her bags and bundles and led the way to the cart which he had hired in the city. It was clean and he had folded a new quilt over the bottom. He helped his mother to get in.

"Ma, it has no springs," he reminded her.

"Eh, you need not tell me anything from now on," she said in a lively voice. She was feeling much better already. This was the air of home and she breathed it in deeply. "Such good smell!" she cried. "I am smelling hot sweet potatoes—"

So it was. A vendor had come near with his small stove and he was taking out roasted sweet potatoes and laying them on the tray he carried on the other end of his pole. Mrs. Liang fumbled for her purse.

"Let me, Ma," James said hastily and putting paper bills on the tray he counted four potatoes. Mrs. Liang shrieked. "James, you have made a mistake—so much money!"

"No, he hasn't, Ma," Mary said. "Money is worth nothing now, unless it is from America."

At this Mrs. Liang looked mysteriously cheerful. She fumbled inside her garments somewhere, gave a wrench or two at her waist, and brought out a small oilcloth package. Then she looked up and met the interested eyes of the mule carter and the vendor and she pursed her lips.

"We better get going," she said in a loud voice and in English. "I keep something to show you." She put the thin package into her bosom, made clicking noises to the carter and James jumped in after Mary and they were off. Mrs. Liang sat between them and she put her hand on the arm of each. The country road was cobbled and the cart bounced up and down, but she did not mind this. She continued in English. "What I have in this pack is something your pa also doesn't know. Why? Because I don't tell him. Your pa is good but too liking to keep his money for himself. So I take small squeeze for myself!" She laughed gaily and Mary and James smiled, looking at one another over her head.

"It's delicious to have Ma," Mary said.

"How will we ever let you go again, Ma?" James asked. Now that his mother was here he felt warmed and more confident. Nothing was strange to her. She would be able to help him in the ancestral village, with Uncle Tao, with the hospital, with everybody. He would tell her everything.

Mrs. Liang looked from one face to the other and continued in triumph. "When I come to you, children, I bring my money with me. Your pa thinking nothing and giving me only a little for myself and for you!"

The bumping cart was shaking laughter out of her in gasps.

"Oh Ma!" Mary said fondly. "I am so glad Chen is going to see you." She gave her mother's hand a squeeze, and then chanced to look at it. "Why, Ma, how dirty you are," she exclaimed.

Mrs. Liang was not embarrassed. "Never mind—it is not here like America," she said comfortably. "Now tell me, Mary, how is this Chen looking and all that?"

They were still talking in English because the carter sat on the edge of the vehicle, within a few inches of them. The mule took its own gait while the carter stared at them with bright and curious eyes. He was young and ragged and bold.

"James, you tell," Mary said with sudden shyness.

"Well, Mother," James said, "he is a little taller than I am, much bigger in the bones, a square head, a big nose—"

"Not too big!" Mary put in.

"Always making jokes, doesn't like the city, doesn't like to dress up, doesn't like scholars—"

"Sounds so nice," Mrs. Liang said. "Who is go-between?"

"I was, Ma," James said.

"And Uncle Tao?" Mrs. Liang asked shrewdly.

"Uncle Tao is willing."

"When is wedding?"

Mary looked shy again. "It depends on you, Ma, and when you have to go back to Pa."

"Six weeks only," Mrs. Liang said.

"Oh Ma!" Their voices rose in chorus. "We thought it would be six months at least," Mary cried.

Mrs. Liang looked grave. She glanced at the carter and lowered her voice and still speaking English she explained her anxieties. "Your pa is too valuable," she ended. "I cannot just to leave him loose. Violet Sung is like some hungry tiger outside door of apartment."

"Oh Ma," Mary murmured while James kept silence.

"Just like Louise," Mrs. Liang retorted. "Oh Ma—she says, oh Ma, you are screaming—such talking all the time! But I tell you I am older. Just now, Mary, you are engaging and you think men are too perfect."

"Only Chen," James said, smiling.

"Maybe just now Chen is too perfect," Mrs. Liang conceded. "But here is China and men have no such good chance as in America where ladies are waiting everywhere with open bust and leg. I tell you, men cannot continue perfect in such case. You mustn't think I am blaming your pa too much. No! I blame elsewhere—Violet Sung and whole America!"

"Tell us about Louise," James said, seeing his mother was growing agitated.

To tell all about Louise occupied many miles, and by the time they understood the happy state of their younger sister, it was time to stop for the afternoon meal. Mrs. Liang let her appetite have its way and she consumed several bowls of noodles, steamed vegetable dumplings, steamed meat roll, bean curd with chopped raw onion, and salt fish. Clearly she was happy. Both James and Mary were alarmed for her digestion but she was triumphant. "Many years my stomach is homesick also," she said. "Now I feel too good."

She slept for a while when they got in the cart again and it was twilight when they drew near to the inn where they were to spend the night. There when they were in their rooms, the door closed and barred after they had washed and had eaten a snack of bread in a thin sheet some twenty inches in diameter but rolled about garlic, they made ready for bed. Then Mrs. Liang delayed James as he was going into the next room. Alone with them she spoke Chinese.

"I had told myself I would not ask about your younger brother," she said sighing, "but I find him always in my thoughts. Tell me all you know, and then I will think of him in the night and be ready to put my sorrow aside tomorrow."

"Ma, you should sleep," Mary said.

But Mrs. Liang shook her head. "I know my old heart."

So James sat down on the edge of the hard board bed and he told his mother everything he knew. It was all too little, and because it was so little she wept bitterly. "At least we know where he is buried," she said at last. "When the times are good again, we will move him into the place where our ancestors have their graves and where he belongs because living or dead he is still a Liang."

She bade James leave her then, and when he was gone she said to Mary, "If you hear me weeping in the night, let me weep."

Mary promised, but she told herself that she would lie awake and listen for her mother's weeping. With all will to do so, nevertheless with health and youth and happiness and the long day's riding across the country in the cold clear air, she fell quickly asleep. When they woke in the morning her mother was her usual cheerful self, and when they had washed and eaten they climbed into the cart and set forth again.

Who could have known that the carter was an evil fellow? James had chosen him for his fresh face and his ready smile and for the agile way in which he leaped upon the cart. But like most men in evil times, he was made up of many parts. He earned a fair living by his mule cart but money was almost worthless, and he took goods too as tender. Thus he managed to feed himself and his young family and his old parents. Had the Liangs been ordinary traveling folk he would have dealt fairly with them, and had they been official folk he would have been fearful. But to him as he listened to the clack of some language he had never heard upon their tongues they were only foreigners.

Toward afternoon, having heard this clack for many hours, he leaned toward James and said, "What is this talk that you make?"

James smiled. "It is English," he said.

The carter stared at him. "Yet you have all the same color of hair and eyes that I have and your skin is like mine except that you are not under the sun and wind every day, and I can see you are always washing yourselves. What is your country?"

James was surprised. "We are Chinese, also, and the only reason we know a foreign language is because we have spent some years on the other side of the sea."

"What did you there?" the carter asked.

When James told him, he went on to ask many more questions, wanting to know how rich Americans were and what they ate and how they looked.

In the goodness of his heart James told him much, and the carter listened. Now Mrs. Liang did not like the way the carter began to look and so she broke in upon this talk in English.

"James, don't talk too much," she exclaimed. "I think this fellow is maybe bad."

"Why, Ma, how suspicious of you!" Mary cried.

"Maybe," Mrs. Liang conceded, "but he has something I don't like."

James smiled and ended the talk by saying he was sleepy, as indeed he was. Through the night before he had been wakeful after talking about Peter. But it was not only Peter. His mother had brought other memories with her, too, memories of his childhood and his boyhood in the comfortable American city. He thought of the great bridge by the river, and how he used to dream of what lay beyond it. Now he knew. There was no magic homeland. Here were poverty and oppression, and indifference to both. He began to sink again into the morass of despondence about himself and his life. Was he not throwing himself away, after all? Well, perhaps his mother would help him to answer that question. With some sort of return to childhood, which he fully recognized, he wondered if he should let her tell him, before she went back to his America, what he ought to do with his life.

Now the steady swing of the cart soothed him. They were traveling over dusty country roads now, and there were no stones. He fell asleep.

Out of deep sleep he was wakened by the sudden swerve of the cart off the road and by the shouts of men. Then he heard his mother's loud firm voice. He opened his eyes. The cart came to a standstill and he sat up. At the open end he saw a crowd of heads, rough and dark. An arm reached in and pulled him. He did not see his mother or Mary. He scrambled out of the cart, kicking aside the arm. Mary and his mother stood by the cart. Mary's face was fixed into angry calm but Mrs. Liang was talking loudly across her arms, folded on her bosom. Half a dozen young men in ragged garments stood pretending not to listen, yet hesitating as they stood. They looked half impudent, half sheepish. Clearly they had not counted on Mrs. Liang.

"Your mothers!" she said to them severely. "Where have you been taught morals? Have you no reason in your skulls? Can you behave like common robbers? Are we rich folk? No! We are not rich. I have no money on me at all that can be useful to you. Look at me—have I any jewels?"

She turned one ear and the other, and held out her hands. "That ring is my wedding ring and I have not taken it off in twenty years. Yes, you can cut off my finger but if you do, your head will be cut off."

The carter stood half turned away, pretending himself helpless. "You!" she shouted at him, "do not pretend anything!"

James broke across this torrent. "Ma, why didn't you wake me? You men! Who are you?"

"They are robbers and bandits, that is what they are!" Mrs.

Liang bawled. "They do not know we are Liangs! Wait until I tell Uncle Tao about them!"

At the name of Uncle Tao alarm spread over the face of the tallest and darkest young man. He turned to the carter and said in reproach, "How is it you did not tell us they are the Liang family?"

"How did I know?" the carter replied.

"You rice bucket!" the other retorted. "Now the old man will not want to pay us his yearly guarantee because we have attacked his relatives."

"You had better tell us that you have offended and for once we will let the matter pass," Mrs. Liang said in a hard voice. "If you get out of our way at once, I will not tell Uncle Tao, but if there is any delay—"

There was no delay. The tall rough young man spread out his arms as a barrier between his men and the travelers and with much dignity Mrs. Liang commanded Mary to take her seat in the cart and she herself climbed into it with James's help. Then James stepped in and the carter took up his whip sulkily.

"Wait," the young robber cried. "I have something to say."

Mrs. Liang looked at him with cold eyes. "Say it then, quickly," she commanded. "Can I waste all this time?"

The robber smiled, showing white teeth. "Lady, please know that we are not evil men. The times are very bad for poor folk like us. We belong to the earth and did we have good rulers and a kind Heaven we could work the land and find food for ourselves and our families. But the rulers are evil and Heaven looks the other way. Even so we rob only the rich."

Now this was the usual speech which robbers made when they had done their work, and so it had been from ancient times until now and Mrs. Liang was not deceived by it. "Did all do as you do," she said severely, "there would be nothing but robbers and then whom would you rob?"

The robber had no answer to this and he scratched his jaw and grinned and Mrs. Liang sat very straight and bade the carter go on. While they traveled the rest of that day she talked very much to the carter, until he became thoroughly frightened, and wanted to give them up as his passengers.

He stopped the mule and threw down his whip and turned to James as a man.

"Your honorable ancestor here has said so much good talk

that I dare not take you to your village. Please hire another carter." Only then did James intervene.

"Ma, let him alone," he said. "To change carts now would be to invite a fresh band of robbers."

So she subsided into muttering and then into silence and toward the end of the day they drove into the ancestral village.

Uncle Tao had not gone to bed. He had bade his sons help him put on his best clothes and his appetite for his night meal had been poor. Feeling that none of his children, who had lived all their lives in the village, could be of use to him in meeting a lady who had lived years in a foreign country, he had sent for Chen, who came with pleasure.

Chen knew far better than James the mass of iniquity, humor, and kindness that was Uncle Tao, for there was this difference between the two young men. James expected the best of all human beings and Chen expected nothing at all. Therefore he neither pitied Uncle Tao nor grew angry with him. He enjoyed the old man, good and evil alike, and laughed a great deal over what Uncle Tao said.

"I do not know how our honest Liang family got into all these foreign ways," Uncle Tao grumbled. "Until my generation we did not think of leaving our ancestral home and wandering around the four seas. My brother, the father of this bookworm Liang fellow, who now does not come home at all —well, my brother went to the northern capital but no further. In the city his children heard of foreign countries and nothing would do but this bookworm Liang must run over there, taking his wife and two small children, who have grown up as bad as foreigners, and then his wife gives birth to two more who are foreigners because they were born on foreign earth. All this has happened to us Liangs! Now they come back, these foreigners. The woman who is the mother of them—I remember her. She was a big mouth."

"On the other hand," Chen said, "I am grateful for everything, since it will give me a good wife."

"Old-fashioned wives are best," Uncle Tao grumbled. "When I frowned my wife trembled. When I shouted she wept. When I urged her she smiled. I did not praise her more than two or three times a year, for women and children cannot be praised. It makes them impudent. But this granddaughter of my brother whom you want to wed! Eh, I tell you, your life will not be too good. Begin strong, that is my advice to any man. Do not ask women anything. Do not tell them anything that is in your mind. I had a good wife, but I made her good."

Chen listened to all this, keeping back laughter. Uncle Tao looked magnificent, as he sat in the most honorable seat in the main room. He wore an ancient yellow brocaded satin gown which was frayed about the edges with age. It hung to his heels and though it was cut full, the sleeves covering his hands, yet it was tight across shoulders and belly. He wore new white cotton stockings which his elder daughter-in-law had made for him and a pair of large black shoes of quilted satin on thick padded soles.

Thus they were conversing of many things in the universe when a hubbub at the gate where the other members of the family waited in their best clothes told them that the expected ones had arrived. Chen got up quickly and left the room. He should not be the first to greet the newcomer, and he stepped into a side court.

Uncle Tao did not stand up when they came in. He sat like an old emperor in his big carved chair by the table, his long pipe in one hand. He stared hard at Mrs. Liang and nodded his head.

"Eh—eh," he mumbled, "so you have come back!"

Mrs. Liang stared back at him. "Uncle Tao, are you well?" she asked in a loud clear voice.

"At least I am not deaf," he said tartly. "Where is your outside person—where is Liang Wen Hua, my nephew?"

"He could not come, Uncle Tao. He teaches school, you know, and they would not let him come."

"What do they pay him?" Uncle Tao inquired.

She evaded this question. "He sent his obedience to you, Uncle Tao, and he bade me say that if there is anything you would like from the foreign country he will send it within his humble means."

"I have no foreign wishes," Uncle Tao replied with majesty. "Have you eaten?"

"Not yet, Uncle Tao," Mrs. Liang replied.

All the daughters-in-law clustered about. "Come and eat, come and eat," they clamored and she went with them.

Mary had not followed her mother. Instead she had gone to her room, pausing for a moment beside Chen who waited for her at the inner gate of the side court. They felt safe for this instant since everyone was with Mrs. Liang.

"Are you tired?" he asked in a low fond voice.

"Not too tired," she replied, looking at him from under her lashes. "You must go and see Ma."

"Now that she is come, I am frightened."

"Silly," she said softly. "She likes you already."

"Then you have said too much about me." .

Mary gave him a little push. "Go on."

"All by myself?"

"All by yourself," she decreed.

She waved her hand and went on, and he turned aside into his own room to take a last look at his hair and he stared at his face in a small old metal mirror that hung on the wall above his table. An ugly fellow, he told himself!

He shrugged his shoulders then and went to find Mrs. Liang. In a large side room, she was surrounded by relatives, men and women, who sat down to give her company while she ate, for the family had already eaten. James was with her and he rose when he saw Chen.

"Ah, here he is," he called. "Ma, this is Chen."

Mrs. Liang rose, her hands hanging at her side, and she looked at Chen. The first look was doubtful, her eyes grew warm, and next she smiled.

"So this is you," she said kindly. Then as though she were a foreigner she put out her hands and took his hand between both of them while the relatives stared. It was a good and warm clasp and Chen liked her then and there. If this was the woman that Mary would one day be, he was pleased.

"Eh, eh—" he said in Chinese. "You must sit down and eat your food while it is hot. I will sit down here."

Properly and modestly he sat down at some distance away and she sat down again and the relatives began their chatter. In the midst of the hubbub she stole glances at him sitting there and half the time their eyes met, with increased content.

James saw his mother take her place in this Liang household as though she had never been away. Despite the years she had been gone her roots were not disturbed. She was correct in all her relationships, and never once did her tongue slip into the wrong title for sisters-in-law, elder and younger, and for their husbands and their children. They liked her. What had been sharp in her as a young girl was gone. What had been sharp even in her life in her own home, James saw was gone. She had become mellow and mild.

"Ma likes it here," Mary said.

"It is her true home," Chen replied.

Yet Mrs. Liang did not sink back into old ways. She approved Mary's little school and she went about the village urging mothers to send their children to learn. In America, she told them, all people are compelled to go to school.

The villagers were aghast to hear of such tyranny. "Who then does the work?" they inquired. When she told them that learning to read did not spoil working men by turning them into scholars they could not believe her. They were used to their scholars who when they learned were too good for work.

One night she said a word of wisdom to Mary. "Now these ancestral people do not understand that a person can read and at the same time work. It is necessary that you continually show them it is possible."

She herself washed her own garments and helped in the kitchens and in all ways surprised the Liang women who expected her to act as a learned and idle woman. The fame of this went out over the Liang lands, and women began to come and see Mrs. Liang and then to tell her of their troubles and even, because she too was a woman, of how Uncle Tao oppressed their families. But Mrs. Liang was shrewd. She knew that oppression was like a sword in the hands of two who struggle for its possession.

"Right is not always with the poor," she answered James when he told her one day how much it troubled him that Uncle Tao had no thought for the people. "First you must ask why are people poor? Is it because they will not work or because they are thieves or because misfortune has overtaken them? Only when you know this can you know how they must be helped. With some the surest help is work or starvation."

"Uncle Tao is too hard," he said.

"He is hard," she agreed, "but do not you be soft."

To Mary she said, "Your brother James needs a good plain wife."

"He does," Mary agreed, "but where shall he find her?"

"I hope he is not looking at that little Rose nurse," Mrs. Liang said. She did not approve of any woman working at a man's side and she looked sidewise very often at Rose as she worked with James every day.

"James does not look at any woman since Lili married Charlie Ting," Mary said.

"James is stupid," Mrs. Liang exclaimed.

"Why not Rose, Ma?" Mary inquired.

Her mother raised her eyebrows, shrugged her plump shoulders, scratched her head with her gold hairpin, and cleaned her ears, all without answering. Then she said, "A bowl ought not to be too small for the hand that holds it," and would say no more.

Meanwhile the wedding day drew near. For the sake of decency before the relatives Chen and Mary kept apart, and did not meet at all until the day itself came. It was natural that Mrs. Liang should put her whole mind on this wedding, but James felt his mother's eyes often upon him. He knew her well. As soon as her mind was free she would have a plan concerning him.

On the night before the wedding he said to Mary, "As soon as you are married, Ma will be after me for something. I can feel it."

"She wants you to marry," Mary said.

He pretended to be terrified at this and begged Mary to prevent their mother. But in his heart he was amused, curious, and cautious.

The wedding day was a good one. The sun came up round and yellow, and there was neither cloud nor snow. Uncle Tao had been astonished when he heard that none of Chen's family was to come, but when he knew their circumstances, how they were held in Communist country, he could only pity them, and for once he did well. He ordered a good feast to last the whole of one day and all the village was invited to it, and such tenants as cared to walk the distance from the land. The wedding was an old-fashioned one.

"It is easier to have it so than to explain why I do not have it so," Mary had said.

So the marriage took place before the relatives, and Chen chose as proxy for his family a distant Liang cousin, and the papers were written, the wine drunk, the millet bowls exchanged, and so the ceremony was done. It was a bitter cold day, but the sun continued to shine and when men, women, and children were full of hot food it was good enough. There was no such thing as a honeymoon, for that was too foreign. Mary moved her boxes into Chen's room, and James gave up his room for their sitting room and he went into another room near his eldest cousin. The next day Mary went as usual to her school and Chen to the clinic and neither gave a sign of inner happiness. Yet James knew it was there. His very flesh was sensitive to their secret joy. He would not have lessened their joy by an iota, and yet suddenly it increased his own loneliness.

This he bore quietly and when Chen had given greeting that morning after the wedding night, James began to speak of the enlargement of the clinic into the hospital. This he had planned for early spring. At the same time he planned to set up classes for itinerant first-aid centers. There were two bright boys in the village who wanted to learn medicine from him, one a cousin of Young Wang's wife, for whom Young Wang had come to intercede, and the other the son of the village night watchman. When he perceived that Chen was answering "yes-yes" to all he proposed, and that his thoughts were not here, he stopped his talk, and it was at this moment that James felt his loneliness grow monstrous.

All through the day James and Chen worked side by side and Rose worked near them, tending the long line of the sick who now came from many parts of that region, some walking hundreds of miles, and the dying brought in litters or clinging to the back of some near relative. The old sorrow was that too often they came too late, having tried witchcraft and sorcerers first.

That day Chen watched Rose and he saw she was pretty and dextrous, and in his own new-found joy he considered within himself whether Rose might not be a good wife for his friend. In the middle of the morning's work when they had drawn aside to discuss the case of a child with a huge water-filled head, suddenly in the midst of their talk he said in English, "Jim, you too should marry."

James looked at him somewhat startled. "We were speaking of this sick child—"

"I am thinking of you," Chen said. "I tell you—"

"It is quite proper that the day after your own marriage you should think all men ought to marry," James said with a dry smile.

"Well, why not the little Rose?" Chen asked boldly.

"You!" James retorted. "No—Rose is well enough and we

ought to marry her off somewhere some day, I suppose, but not to me. Come, come—"

"Have you seen a better?" Chen urged.

"I have seen no woman that I want now for my wife," James said, too quietly.

They talked of the child again and decided to draw the water from its head, and so they did, warning the mother that she must come often, for this healing was not sure. But while he worked, Chen's mind was busy far inside itself. James had said he had seen no woman whom now he wished to marry. Then why not one whom he had not seen? If his heart was dead let it be waked by life itself, if not by love. A man should marry and have children, with or without love. Love was blessing but life was good enough.

In the middle of that night, being melted with love, he said to Mary, "Why should we not find a wife for Jim? He will not choose for himself—then let us choose."

"As if James would let us!"

The thought was too bold and Mary scoffed at it. Chen was pleased that even love could not change Mary. She teased him and opposed him as she always had and this made her yielding all the sweeter.

"No, I mean it," Chen insisted. "Jim is the very one to let us do it."

"He never would," said Mary.

The next day Chen waylaid Mrs. Liang as she came from the kitchens and drawing her aside into a quiet room away from the relatives he proposed to her that they should persuade Jim to return to ancestral ways and allow them to choose a wife for him.

Mrs. Liang was pleased indeed. "How is it I have not thought of this myself?" she exclaimed.

"Mary says he will not do it," Chen suggested.

Mrs. Liang considered this. "Had he not fallen once in love with that Lili Li, I know he would not. But he is a very single heart. When he was small he once had a dog and when it died he never took another. So when he had one friend it was enough—he never had many friends. This is his temper. We will plot together."

That evening Mrs. Liang went to Mary and Chen and together they planned what James should have for a wife. She must of course be schooled and she must not be too old-fashioned or perhaps too modern. Something between was well enough. For more important than schooling or fashion was the girl's own nature. She must be honest, she must be one who could love a man more than herself, a thing which not all women can do. She must be good at sewing and cooking, for James did not notice when his own garments needed mending, and when he worked he often forgot to eat. She need not be pretty, but since there was not love to begin with, neither should she be ugly. Certainly she must be clean, since James would have everything clean, and she must have a sweet breath and a soft voice.

With these matters decided, they laid their plot and let days pass perfecting it and inquiring where such a girl could be found. Chen offered to go to the city and Mary thought of writing to Dr. and Mrs. Su as the best among their new friends. Mrs. Liang even tried to bring to memory the young Chinese women she had seen in New York. She could remember no one except Sonia Pan, and she would be worse than any American, because while her body was Chinese, nothing else was. Besides, Sonia would certainly not live where she could not buy chewing gum, turn on the radio, or have a permanent wave in her hair. Uncle Tao, moreover, would not tolerate her, and she would be of no use to James.

At last Chen said sensibly that they had better lay the whole plan before James himself and with much timidity and laughter and arranging of who should speak first and how it should all be broached, they invited him to take a meal with them in a room at the inn, where Young Wang now being innkeeper and his father-in-law retired, they were sure of a good meal and of being alone in an inner room. They made the excuse of this being the first month day of Mary's marriage, and Mrs. Liang talked of having to go home in a few more weeks. She longed to stay on, to stay even another month. If James would get himself married—

Outside the little room the inn was full. Young Wang gave meals for barter of flour or wheat and for vegetables, fowl and eggs and for fish or a pig or cow's meat. Money was useless and the people did business without it.

Young Wang served them himself. He looked like an innkeeper now, his face was fatter than it had been and he ran with sweat as he hurried in and out of the inner room.

"Eh, do not be so busy," Mrs. Liang told him kindly, but

his zeal urged him on. Only when all the food was on the table and his young wife had poured out wine and tea, did he go away and leave the four alone.

Mrs. Liang had been chosen to begin and when they had eaten she said to James, "My son, as your mother, I beg you to let me see you married to a good wife before I leave you again. Then I will not worry. You are the eldest of all my children, and why should you live alone and my youngest be dead?" The tears came to her eyes.

Mary spoke next and she said, "We have been thinking of all our friends to find one whom you might like. Don't try to fall in love again, Jim. Just choose a nice girl and see what happens of its own accord."

"After all," Chen said in turn and before James could speak, "it is only this generation of our own which has so much as thought of choosing wives and husbands for themselves. Remember that it is the custom here still for parents to find husbands and wives for their children."

To their surprise James answered at once with a sensible gravity. "I have been thinking of such a thing myself, and I have told myself the very words which Chen has just used. Am I different from my ancestors? It may be that they understood better than we do the proper relationship between man and woman."

"Then who—" Mrs. Liang began joyfully.

James cut her off. "I will not choose for myself, Mother. You may choose for me. You gave me birth and you know me. Mary and Chen can give their advice."

All three were set back by their easy victory. "But have you no thought about the kind of girl you—you—" Chen ventured.

"Yes, I have thought," James said calmly. "I should like to have a good-tempered woman, one strong and healthy, and the daughter of a peasant—one of our own peasants."

The three listening were struck speechless. The daughter of a Liang peasant! This was something too strange even for them. This was going too far back!

James looked at the three solemn faces. "Why not? Goodness and health are all I want."

"But an ignorant woman, Jim?" Mary asked.

"You shall teach her," James replied smiling. He put down

his chopsticks. "Come, why are you all staring? I have only agreed to do what you have proposed."

"We did not ask you to go so far," Chen remonstrated.

"Find my bride," James said, half teasing them. "When you have found her, I will marry her. Now let us enjoy our feast."

Why not, he asked his own heart? There was no woman in the world whom he wanted for himself. To this his heart made no answer. It had become a machine to pump the blood through his body and keep him alive that he might do his work.

21

Mrs. Liang climbed into the great plane that was to carry her back to America. She walked to her seat, arranged her belongings, leaned her head back and closed her eyes. Only the fact that she had overstayed her six weeks by more than a month had compelled her again to fly across the sea. She had stayed until the very last moment with her three children. She now thought of Chen as entirely her own. Since Chen's parents were immured in Communist territory she thought of him as an orphan. She knew nothing about Communists or communism, but she had heard so much from Dr. Liang that she considered it only a matter of time until everybody in Communist territory would be dead. Since no letters came to Chen, nor did he write any letters, there was nothing to contradict this theory. Unless they were dead people wrote to their relatives. Since Chen had no letters, his parents must be dead. It was just as well, she thought privately, since the children could continue in the ancestral village under Uncle Tao's protection.

She reflected upon Uncle Tao. He was as intolerable as ever but circumstances had changed. That is, he was now old and he had a knot in his belly. Moreover, she also was older than she had been when she had rebelled against him as a girl. Aunt Tao had been alive then, and she had thought Aunt Tao weak and yielding too much to the quarrelsome and domineering man that Uncle Tao had been in those days. Now she realized that it was a rubbery yielding, and that actually Aunt Tao had been tough. But she only understood this from the years of her own marriage.

The most important thing about Uncle Tao nowadays, however, was none of these things. It was the simple fact that Uncle Tao had power. What this power was she did not know. But he had some sort of power over the magistrate, over the country police, even over tax gatherers. His hold over the tenants was of course absolute. She had warned James against defending these tenants too much.

"The men of earth are not what they were when I was young," she told James. "In those days what could they do? Sometimes they rose up, it is true, and killed the ones they hated. But when that man was dead another came down from the Emperor and when they saw it was no use to kill a man if another came at once to take his place, they endured again for a few generations. Now everything is different. They have heard too much. They even know that in America people can stop work and farmers can refuse to sell their food. It gives them ideas of what they can do also. And now too there are the accursed Communists to whom they can always go. We are pinched between these people and the Communists."

She had not at all liked the way that James had listened to this. He had not answered but he had smiled. Smiling silence is not a good sign in any man when he has been listening to a woman.

"Now, James," she had then said with real heat, "I don't oppose Uncle Tao so much. Everybody is still afraid of him. You better stay in his shadow. These are bad times."

To this James again had not answered and so she had talked to Mary and Chen. "You two," she had said to them privately and therefore in English only last night when they came in for a last talk. "Now you are married you have some common sense. I tell you, do not make Uncle Tao angry."

"I am not afraid of Uncle Tao," Mary said boldly.

Mrs. Liang looked at her with cold eyes.

"Everybody else is afraid. You better have some sense."

Chen had pacified her immediately. "Mother, I will not let Mary behave foolishly," he had promised. "Uncle Tao is a very big man here and certainly we need him, at least until we have established ourselves and the people see what we are doing for them."

"I hope he does not die first from that knot in his belly," Mrs. Liang had murmured. Then she had made a confession. "At first when I saw Uncle Tao is growing thinner and more yellow, I thought I better tell him let James cut him up. Then I tell myself, very good idea, but maybe James kills him, then who will protect my children here? Better I let him die slowly by himself."

Chen roared out great laughter but Mary was shocked. "Ma, how can you be so wicked?" she had demanded. "Poor old Uncle Tao! I swear I like him more now than I did before you said such a thing. I shall try myself to persuade him to let James help him."

Mrs. Liang sighed now, remembering this scene. Since she was married Mary had grown even more stubborn. If there was fault to be found with Chen it was that he did not deal firmly enough with his young wife. He laughed at her too much instead of scolding her. Mary had none of the softness which was so pleasant in Louise since she had married Alec. Mrs. Liang pondered on the strange contradictions in young people. One would have thought that Mary married to a Chinese husband would have become a docile Chinese wife. Instead, although she lived in the ancestral village, she behaved like an American, and without doubt she was planting rebellion in the hearts of many Chinese wives. But Louise, living in an American house, where women could be as willful as they liked, had grown sweet and obedient, as though she were in China. The world was very mixed nowadays!

The propellers had been whirling for some time, and now the engines were hammering and Mrs. Liang clutched her quivering stomach. She stopped thinking about her family in the ancestral village and her family in America and prepared to think only of herself.

Alone in his big apartment, except for Nellie rattling faintly in the distant kitchen, Dr. Liang was grateful for the added weeks before Mrs. Liang came back. Had she arrived on the appointed day she would have found him in the midst of his pain and distraction. He was still confused, still sore at heart, but pride and vanity were quelled, and he was able to be grateful that Violet Sung had made the decision. It was the wise decision for them both, although he had rebelled against it with his whole being. Indeed, after these weeks of utter solitude and quiet, he was somewhat astonished to look back on himself as he had been. He was still more astonished that he could have gone to London after Violet, as he had done. He leaned back in his deep red leather chair. Well, he had his memories—

After Mrs. Liang had gone, he had really lost his head. It was the only way he could describe it now. He had felt so free, so gay. The New York season had come on, and since he had no one to think of except himself he went everywhere. The most extraordinary thing was that he learned to dance. This would have been impossible had his wife been at home. Her astounded eyes would have accused him of unseemly behavior in his old age. But Violet had taught him and had praised him for his lightness. His one fault, which it seemed was a grave one, was that he had no sense of rhythm. When he was dancing with Violet, she supplied this for him, so that he had a feeling of dancing rather well. Since he was tall and he knew his own good looks, it was a pleasure to feel that people admired them together.

He supposed that they were together somewhat too much and therefore the Englishman was not to be blamed. Still, there had been nothing physical about it. There was no use denying, even now when everything was over, that there might have been. He had entered into a new phase, he told himself. He had been married so long and suddenly he had felt as though he were young and starting all over again. He refused Louise's invitations to come to dinner, and he had not invited her and Alec to dinner, simply because he did not want even to remember that he had children.

Yet he had felt no evil. On the contrary, never had he felt so exalted, so noble, so good as he had during those days when he and Violet saw one another every day. Yes, it was every day! He had not tried to write anything, although he had begun a new book, an anthology of Chinese love poetry. He taught his classes, of course, and he felt his teaching was inspired. Marriage, he then realized, had never inspired him.

After nearly three weeks of this well-nigh perfect happiness Violet told him one day over the telephone that she could not see him. She had said something about a headache and a cold. The next day she had called him again, and had said she was flying to London.

All the misery of that moment overwhelmed him again in memory. "But why?" he had kept insisting.

She had answered vaguely that she would write and that it would be better for them not to meet. She would tell him everything.

He had destroyed the letter, but first he had carried it with him to London, and when he had seen her for the last time, he had torn it in bits and dropped it from Westminster Bridge where they had met—wishing, but only almost, that he could throw himself after it. The letter had been unsatisfactory to him. She had not told him everything as she had said she would. She had simply said that Ranald Grahame had told her that unless she stopped seeing Dr. Liang, he would cut her off. She had thought about this carefully, she wrote him, and in view of all the lives involved, it seemed better to stay with Ranald. But she was his, always faithfully, Violet Sung. And there was no address below her name.

By the time he had this wretched letter in his hands she was already gone. He was beside himself and so badly did he conceal it that he caught Nellie's eyes on him hard that day and so he told her he was ill and locked himself in his room. She stopped at the door with the tray and he had to get up and get it, because she declared since they were alone in the house she had better not come into his bedroom. He was insulted at the evil suggestion in this intense virtue but he could do nothing about it, and it insured him privacy when his door was shut.

Twenty-four hours of solitude made the desire to see Violet, to talk with her and to demand her return to him, grow into a ravening hunger in his bosom. He did not care what anyone thought and he would divorce his wife, or at least command her to stay on forever in the ancestral village. He arranged his affairs and told Nellie that he had had a summons from London. This summons he provided for by cabling to old Mr. Li to ask if he might stay with them. The invitation came back at once and he left the cablegram on the dining-room table where Nellie would read it. He used the power of his famous name in the Chinese Embassy and got a priority seat and flew to London within the week.

Once there he had been compelled to submit to maddening delays. He could only say to Mr. and Mrs. Li that he had come on a holiday and he could not say that he wanted to know where Violet Sung was. London was far too huge a place to make it sensible to look for her. He could only pretend to enjoy everything that was done for him and meanwhile ask questions which he hoped sounded innocent. Mr. and Mrs. Li were living comfortably in a villa outside the city, and apparently had no idea of going back to China. If there was another world war, they said they might go to Rio de Janeiro. They were stout and unfashionable, and they were glad of a chance to have a famous visitor to show off and give parties for and provide return for some of the social debts they owed. At none of these parties did Dr. Liang see Violet Sung, and he was in a state of desperation which frightened him.

It was Lili who finally helped him. Lili had not changed at all to the eye. She had no child. She was slender and beautiful in the same pure calm fashion. Her voice was still high, sweet, and childlike, and what she said was still naïve and a little stupid. Beneath and behind all this, Lili was neither childlike nor stupid. She had added to the sophistication of Shanghai the sophistication of New York, London, and Paris. She was quite happy with Charlie Ting who was an interestingly degenerate young man and thought nothing was too bad for anybody to do, if it was fun. Indeed, the two words, good and evil, did not exist for him except for diplomatic use. With him Lili lived on several levels of life at once. On one of these levels she heard gossip about Dr. Liang and Violet Sung, and hearing it she had expressed surprise while she instantly and secretly believed all she heard. It explained Dr. Liang's presence in London and it explained what she saw was his restlessness. Out of indolent curiosity she found that it was true that Violet Sung was in London and that she had a very pretty, though small, flat looking out on a bombed area which was now a new park, and that she went nowhere. She also asked and got the address. Then she went to see Violet Sung.

All this Lili told Dr. Liang one Sunday morning in her sweet tinkling little voice. It came out very naturally. She was spending the week end with her parents and it was easy enough to find Dr. Liang alone after lunch in the garden, walking up and down the narrow flagged path of the small rose plot. She had sauntered out under her pink parasol, for she did not like the fad of being sunburned and kept her skin as pale as a white lotus.

After a few remarks made and exchanged she sat down on a Chinese porcelain garden seat and she said, "Dr. Liang, I saw your old friend yesterday."

He had looked at her startled and already half guessing.

"Violet Sung," she said thoughtfully and without a smile. "She is living now in London, do you know?"

"No, I did not," he had replied. "I have not heard from her for some time."

"Yes, now she is here," Lili went on. "I don't know if you like to have her address."

"It doesn't matter," he lied.

"I think she likes to see you," Lili persisted. By now she could speak English perfectly but she had discovered that it made her appear more exotic if she did not. "I think she seems somewhat like lonely. She doesn't talk much, and she looks too thin though quite beautiful."

He could not trust himself to answer this, for he had no intention of confiding in Lili or in anyone. He knew his own people. They could no more contain gossip than a leaky dish can contain water. They could keep a secret forever but gossip would be told to the next Chinese they met.

Lili opened a small satin bag attached to her diamond bracelet and she took out a bit of paper. "I write it down for you," she said.

He could not resist taking Violet's address but he did not look at it. He stuffed it into his pocket. "If I have time I will try to see her," he said, and hoped Lili could not hear the pounding of his heart.

He had been far too prudent to try to see Violet at once, for he had no intention of meeting the Englishman, whose very name he did not want to remember. He wrote her a letter and sent it by messenger and told the messenger to wait. Not trusting boys, he found an extraordinary old woman with only one arm whose lean rigid face looked reliable.

"Do not come back without an answer," he had commanded.

"Right you are, sir," she had replied.

Hours later she had come back. "It took a bit of 'angin' round," she told him. "The young lydy kep' tryin' to put me off like. Said come back tomorrow and all that. I said, me orders is, bring back the arnser. Here it is, sir."

He had paid what she asked and then had opened Violet's answer. It was brief enough to break his heart. "Now that we have parted," Violet said, "why should we meet again? It will only make it harder for us both."

That was all and it made him very angry. He sent a bold telegram, not caring this time whether the Englishman did see it.

"You owe me an explanation," he wrote. "I will meet you on the near end of Westminster Bridge tomorrow at six p. m."

Many people came and went on the bridge and at six it was winter's dusk. He was there at half past five, not daring to hope that she would come. She was quite capable of not coming. But she came. He saw her before she saw him. She wore a dark fur coat and a small fur hat trimmed with violets and fitting closely to her face.

She had come because she saw that he would never believe that she meant to cut herself off from him forever. She told him so in her lovely soft voice whose cadence he would hear as long as he lived. "Wen Hua, you shouldn't have made me come. It is really dangerous for me. I promised Ranald that I would never see you again alone."

"Yet you have come, and that means you wanted to come."

"You are wrong," she told him.

The evening had been strangely mild and still. Accustomed now to the violence of cold in New York it did not seem possible to Dr. Liang that it was a winter's night. The air was chill with river damp, but it was soft. Violet's cheeks under the lamplight were rose pink, like an English girl's.

"I did not want to come," she repeated. "I have made my decision, Wen Hua, and I shan't change."

"How can you decide against me?" he demanded.

They were leaning against the rail, their backs to the passing people, and looking down into the river she had mused for a moment.

"It isn't as if you and I could really love enough to give up everything," she said at last. "You only want to have me, too."

"That is not true," he had said instantly.

"Yes, Wen Hua, it is," she had replied. "And it is true for me, also. I am not better than you. More than that—"

She broke off and he waited. At last he said, "What is more than that?"

"I have thought so much," she said slowly. "I haven't much to do except think. People like you and me—we are not real people, you know, Wen Hua."

"We exist, don't we?" he asked with some indignation.

"Oh yes. We have these bodies—"

He waited again and this time he did not press her. He was afraid of what she was going to say—whatever it was.

She said, "We live on other people's roots. Wen Hua, what

makes you real is your wife. She is so real that were you and I to—of course she would not tolerate me. No real woman tolerates polygamy. Even in China, where we think we settled all human relationships centuries ago, the real women do not tolerate the concubine. They kill somebody—maybe the concubine—or they stop loving their husbands and then they stop being themselves and become cruel creatures."

"I was not thinking of putting away my wife," he said stiffly.

"No, but you see," she said, "Ranald is like your wife. I mean, he's real, too."

"He doesn't marry you," he said with purposeful cruelty.

"No," she agreed. "But I think I don't want him to. It doesn't mean enough to me."

He had grasped at this. "You don't love him?"

She shook her head and the little dark curls of her hair, given her by her French mother, danced against her cheek. "No, but I trust him. Some day we will part. Perhaps it will be I who make the parting. But when that day comes he will not leave me destitute. He will provide for me—"

"Money, I suppose you mean," he had said bitterly.

"Be reasonable," she had said. "I need a good deal of money and he has a lot of it."

"Suppose he marries?" He wanted to hurt her but she was not hurt.

"Even if he marries he will be grateful to me. He has a sense of obligation, you know, especially now that I have given you up."

She had used him to make the Englishman feel an obligation!

When he accused her of this she denied it. "It is not like that," she replied in her thoughtful musing way. "If you had been quite real, Wen Hua, I might have dared to—do anything. But for two people, both unreal, to leave the people they can trust—it would be very dangerous for us."

"Why do you not trust me?" he had demanded.

She had lifted her dark eyes to him then. "You know yourself," she replied.

He had not had the courage to press her. The truth from her lips might have destroyed him and he needed to believe in himself.

She had ended their talk by a soft touch on his hand. "Now

you must go away," she had told him. "You must go back to New York, to your home and to your wife. Please don't trouble about me. I shall be all right and really quite happy. I like London. I know many people and I don't lack friends. I am quite clear now in my mind. What has happened is what is better for us."

"What did the Englishman say?" he demanded.

She seemed surprised. "Do you really want to know? He is very honest and he just said to me that he had heard we were meeting almost every day and he would not forbid it—only I had to make the final choice. He said I could leave him or stay with him—he would not play second fiddle. If I stayed with him, he would look after me as long as I lived. There would be enough for me in his will, if he died in the next war, which he thinks will be quite soon. But if I chose to see you, ever, he would cut me off at once."

"Yet you have seen me," he had urged.

"Yes, I am going back now to tell him so," she had said. "It will be hard for a bit to make him understand that I did not want to see you, but that there was no other way. Then I shall promise never to see you again. I haven't quite made that promise yet. Tonight I'll make it—and keep it."

There was the soft touch again on his hand, and she turned and lost herself in the crowd. He had stayed on, staring down into the misty gently flowing river, and toying with the idea of throwing himself from the bridge. But a passing policeman looked at him once or twice and he grew self-conscious. He did not really want to die.

He had stayed on with Mr. and Mrs. Li for a few days more, accepting now an invitation from Charlie Ting's parents to visit them. To his surprise he found he quite enjoyed diplomatic life. It was gay and expensive, and money for everything was provided. He had a handsome Rolls-Royce at his disposal and a smart English chauffeur. He might, he thought, offer himself some day as a diplomat—an ambassador, perhaps. The idea gave him a new interest and while he considered it, he could stop thinking for a moment or so about Violet. Somewhere in the few days he found a chance to speak to Lili.

"By the by, I called upon Miss Violet Sung. She seems quite well and happy. I stayed only a few minutes because I was so busy that day."

The coolness of his voice astonished her but she only smiled. Then he told her that he was going home, that he was quite anxious to see his wife who had been to visit his two elder children in the ancestral village where they were enjoying the old home, and that Mary was married.

Lili gave a little scream, "Oh, can they enjoy such old-fashioned things? And what man is there to marry Mary?"

He had laughed with her. "They will grow tired of the village," he said. "I should not be surprised if they come back with their mother. My son-in-law, I hear, is a brilliant doctor of Peking—a friend of my son's, I believe. You remember James?"

Lili dimpled perfunctorily. "Of course, and Charlie thinks he is doing some wonders in China. I am sure it is true."

Dr. Liang did not believe that Charlie Ting had so spoken, but he inclined his head with the dignity usual to him when he received a compliment.

So he had come home again. In London he thought he had got over everything, but when he reached home he knew he had not. Mingled in his hurt love for a beautiful woman were her words: "You know yourself." He did not want to know himself. She had shaken him very badly indeed. The affair might have ended sublimely. It might have been a splendid rejection of a selfish love; it might have been a noble acceptance of the obligations life had already put upon them. But she had taken away both splendor and nobility. She had said merely the few words, "You know yourself." They included these few words more which she had not quite spoken, "and I know you."

He felt fretful in his loneliness and he began to long for Mrs. Liang to come home. He could be cross with her and she would not mind because he was her husband.

When he got her telegram saying that she would arrive at three o'clock the next day, unless there were storms, he immediately began to feel better. It was something like having been ill or away or out of his usual routine. Now soon his house would be what it had always been. He felt more kindly even toward Louise and he rang her up to invite her, with Alec, to dinner. It was the hour when she was putting her baby to bed and she was abstracted but good-natured.

"Sure we'll come, Pa," she said. "I think Alec would like it."

Before he knew what he was doing he was also inviting Mr.

and Mrs. Wetherston. "We may as well make it a real party," he told Louise. "If you think your parents-in-law would enjoy hearing the latest news from China, then bring them along."

Since her father had shown no interest in the existence of any of them ever since her mother went away, Louise was pleased. "I don't believe they have anything planned," she said. "I'm sure they'll want to come. It'll be nice. It'll be lovely to see Ma again."

"Indeed it will," he said with unusual warmth.

He was very much absorbed the rest of the evening in planning the dinner. After some thought he decided to order it sent in hot from a Chinese restaurant and he had a long talk over the telephone with the proprietor about special dishes and their preparation. When this was over he felt he should go to bed in order to be fresh for the next day. But he found it difficult to sleep. His mind, instead of being absorbed with memories of Violet Sung, returned to the earlier years of his life when Mrs. Liang had first come to his father's house. She had been a fresh-faced lively-looking girl with a full red mouth. His first disappointment had been that she was not pretty. But somehow or other she was living and strong in the house, simple creature though she was, and he had soon learned to depend on her. When there was something unpleasant to be done, such as asking a permission of Uncle Tao, it was always she who did it. She had many faults, and each one irritated him separately, but they did not combine to change her quality, which was that she never thought of herself. She was not interested in herself or in her own moods. She had very few moods and they were because of some external circumstance which could easily be changed. Usually she changed it herself and restored her own good humor, or she took a long nap or she bought herself a bag of chocolate drops which she enjoyed. She liked sweets, he now remembered, and he determined to buy her a large box of them tomorrow.

Mrs. Liang saw her husband waiting for her at the airport and she thought he looked tired. She blamed herself for having been away so long, and although she felt very tired herself after this dreadful journey, she braced herself to seem better than she was.

When he saw her she was smiling and cheerful as ever. She

looked younger than he remembered and her hair was becomingly loosened by the wind. When she saw him her face turned quite pink and this touched him. He took her hand openly. "Louise couldn't come," he told her, not knowing what to say at first. "She has the children and so on. But they are all coming to a welcome dinner."

"How nice!" she exclaimed. With him she began instinctively to speak in English. "You look a little bit of tired, Liang. Are you feeling quite well? Now I shall feed you something good."

"I am well enough," he replied with a touch of pathos. "Nellie has done her best. I gave her a little vacation, by the way, because I had an invitation to visit the Li family in London and I thought it would be a good way to pass the time until you came home. I got leave from the college." He wanted to tell her about London at once.

"I am glad you took some rest," she said briskly. She longed to get home and crawl into her own bed and put a hot-water bottle to her poor stomach. But if there was to be a welcome dinner she must not think of such things.

In the cab they sat hand in hand. He had put her suitcase on the floor so that she could use it as a footstool. He was surprised at his sense of comfort as he held her plump hand. He had not done such a thing in years.

"Eh, Liang," she said, smiling at him, "I think you do want me to come home again!"

He gave her his slight smile. "I was only afraid you would not want to leave the ancestral village and all its delights to come back to New York and your poor old scholar."

She began unexpectedly to chatter in Chinese. "Liang, nothing is changed! Can you believe that after all these years Uncle Tao is just the same, but more fat, except, poor old man, for the knot in his belly which must come out, James said, as soon as he is willing. And the street, Liang, even more dirty! Of course it is winter and so I did not see flies. But the children run everywhere as before, their faces dirty and their pants—well, you know. Mary teaches a school now and maybe things will be better in a few years. All the relatives are the same except some are dead." She counted off on her fingers the dead Liangs and what they had died of and when.

"Of course there are bandits everywhere now," she went

on, "but even they are somewhat afraid of Uncle Tao because he takes dinner with the magistrate and he is friends with the police and the tax men. In fact, Liang, Uncle Tao is quite useful and though he is troublesome, nobody dares any more to wish him dead. Later when government is better perhaps it will be all right for Uncle Tao to die. But just now——"

He laughed for the first time in days. "Nothing you say makes me want to go back there," he told her when they reached the apartment.

Now that she had been away and had returned she was surprised to find as she went from one room to the other that there was a strange feeling of home here, too. She could not have believed it possible, but so it was. The Wetherstons had sent flowers of welcome, and Louise called on the telephone almost immediately and Mrs. Liang listened avidly to details of baby's teeth and how much little Alec could say. Then she looked at the clock and screamed, "Louise, please! Only one hour or so and there is the dinner coming. Tell me something more, dahling, when you are here."

She hung up and then remembered Mrs. Pan and telephoned to her. It was just the time when Mrs. Pan was cooking supper and when she heard her friend's voice she cried out with joy.

Dr. Liang heard only his wife's end of the talk. "Yes, Mrs. Pan, I am here. . . . Oh fine, everything is fine. . . . Not so much as you think, Mary is fine—very nice man. James also is being married. . . . Yes, yes, I tell you everything. Tomorrow? Oh fine!"

"What's this about James being married?" Dr. Liang demanded. He had changed his coat for his old smoking jacket and had dragged out a pair of old slippers that he had not worn since she went away. He was smoking and reading and feeling almost entirely normal.

"I tell you later," she said. "It is surprise, but good. Now, Liang, you must dress yourself early. I and Neh-lee set the table. Supposing I am somewhat late you can be polite."

She was bustling about, but she found time to be alone in the kitchen with Nellie.

"How is everything went?" she inquired in a low voice.

"Good," Nellie replied. "For a while I thought something was funny, but I guess he was just restless. He went over to

London and come back like a lamb and hasn't hardly left the house since."

"Thank you, Neh-lee. Now better we use the second-good tablecloth on account Chinese dinner slops around fiercely."

Together they searched for the second-best tablecloth. Mrs. Liang had not seen a tablecloth since she left.

It was a very successful evening. Dr. Liang was at his best, dignified and quiet. He was courteous to Mr. and Mrs. Wetherston, a little distant perhaps with his son-in-law, and condescending and pleasant to his daughter. Mrs. Liang did most of the talking. Mr. Wetherston asked many questions of a practical nature, as he explained. These questions had to do with what she thought of Chiang Kai-shek, whether the graft was as bad as he had heard it was, how Communist the Chinese Communists really were, whether she thought the Chinese people would ever get together, and so forth. She answered everything briskly, declaring that Chiang Kai-shek was no better and no worse than any man in his position and with his history, that government graft was always bad wherever it was found but perhaps inevitable, that Communists were Communists, that Chinese people had been together on the same piece of land for four thousand or so years and probably would continue there. When Mrs. Wetherston ventured a question about the private life of Madame Chiang, Mrs. Liang laughed heartily behind one hand and said, "Madame Chiang is so special, isn't he?" Mrs. Liang was always weak on gender, and at this point Dr. Liang felt it necessary to explain. "In our language," he said, "we do not denote gender in the personal pronoun. Thus 'he' and 'she' are represented by a single third personal pronoun, namely, *ta*."

Mrs. Wetherston turned to her son with reproach. "Alec, you never told me that before."

"You never asked me, Mother," he replied, laughing lazily.

Alec, lounging his long frame on the divan, enjoyed the evening hugely. His marriage was turning out well. Chinese wives made a cult of marriage. He felt sorry for his friends who were coping with American girls in their houses. The Chinese had things right. Everything depended on relationships between people.

The many dishes which the Chinese restaurant chef served with a flourish provided conversation for two hours and more, and the last hour of the evening Mrs. Liang used in describing the fabulous ancestral village, its walls, its gates, the home of the Liangs with its courts and many rooms, the hospital which James was building, the school which Mary had already established, the relatives in all their beauty and cleverness and finally Uncle Tao, who presided over them all like a god.

"You make it sound wonderful, Ma," Louise said with some astonishment.

"In its way, it is also wonderful," Mrs. Liang declared.

She had not mentioned cold or filth or scald-headed children or beggars or rebellious tenants or quarreling relatives or Uncle Tao's tantrums or any of those things which Dr. Liang had feared she would. When he perceived she was creating a beautiful China before these foreigners, he felt for her a new and profound tenderness. This woman of his, this old wife, was doing it for him!

That night when she had made honest love to him in her downright wifely fashion, and after he had yielded pleasantly to her inclinations, they lay talking for a long time and she told him about her visit and each detail of each conversation with each relative. But most of all she talked about James and the girl she had found for his wife. The betrothal had been very quick—too quick maybe, she admitted. She had left the day after, which in itself was very bad, for she had not been able to divine anything from James's face. Of course he had said she was not to worry. Mary and Chen had promised privately to tell her everything.

"Liang," she now said earnestly, "I tell you, James is spoiled for common marriage. He loved that Lili too much, and yet it is a strange thing he does not love her now. She has killed the love power in him. If he did not marry a woman in an old-fashioned way, he would not marry at all. I saw that after a while. Now, Liang, you know a man cannot live without a wife. Any wife is better than no wife. But I did not take just any wife for our son. I went very carefully through our whole region and found a girl who is not blood kin to the Liangs. Her father came from Shantung when she was small but he never bound her feet because he had heard women do not any more, and he is a good man and he was glad to keep her feet free. They are farming people only, and their lands are beyond the Liang lands, and he owns his land. How he had money is this way: the Americans wanted some land to build a camp during the war and they bought his land and he moved far enough away from there so he would not see Americans and Communists and such strangers any more. I think our place is safe enough maybe, too."

"What sort of a girl is she?" Dr. Liang inquired.

"A big girl, maybe you would say," Mrs. Liang replied. "She is not fat, but very strong and she has a round face and big black eyes. She is old-fashioned, you know, Liang. She combs her hair as I did when I was a girl. She wears country clothes—no long robe. But she is quiet and she is very honest and she will think only of James, and their children will be very healthy. The family has five sons and she is the only girl, so maybe she will have plenty of grandsons for us."

He was so silent that she began to be fearful lest he did not approve.

She spoke in the darkness somewhat shyly. "Liang, I do not know how you think, but for my part I have been very satisfied in our old-fashioned marriage. I know that now our young people like to love by themselves, as for example, Louise and Alec. But Mary is somewhat more Chinese. Judging by everything, Liang, however, I don't think so much of love."

"Nor do I," he said, and then he added firmly, "very little indeed!"

She was so pleased that she could have cried, but she knew this would have been to show too much feeling. "Liang, you must go to sleep, please," she commanded him. "Tomorrow is your class day."

To him it was sweet to hear her voice thus bidding him what he wanted to do anyway and he obeyed.

Underneath all she had said Mrs. Liang felt the old bleeding wound that had been left in her by Peter's death. She did not speak of it because she wanted her return to her children's father to be without sadness. She had written to Dr. Liang the facts as she knew them, and she had not gone to see where Peter lay under the big pine in the imperial gardens. Later, when times were better, she wanted to go back and see that his young frame was brought back to the village and buried among the ancestors.

She heard Liang's deepened breathing and she knew he was asleep, and so, lying very still, she wept silently for the dead son. Then she lifted one hand carefully and turning her head she wiped her eyes on the edge of the pillowcase. What was past was gone, she told herself, and for the sake of the living she must think of the future.

She lay thinking instead of the village. Life was wonderful there, so warm and close, all the human beings so close and everybody knowing everybody else, good and bad. The days were crowded with life. It had been so good to be flat on the earth. When she got out of bed in the morning her feet were on the real earth, beaten solid by the feet of Liang ancestors. How intensely did she hate this living high up in the air, and knowing that above and underneath them were strangers!

Yet she knew well enough that Liang could never live in the ancestral village again. Without electricity or running water, he could not live. She understood that now. The fleas alone, jumping down out of the thatched roofs, would be too annoying for him. But nothing could clean the fleas out of the thatch of old ancestral roofs. Perhaps the next time she went back she could take some of this new stuff the Americans used for spraying flies. Of course she would go back again and again. She would not tell Liang so at once—maybe not for many months. But when James and Mary began to have children she must fly back to see them. Perhaps by that time the Americans would have better planes or at least medicines to hold down the stomach. She would go back and forth between the kinfolk, for she belonged to all of them.

She sighed as a truck rumbled by in the night; upon the river a steamer shrieked. In the ancestral village night was as quiet as heaven. A child's crying, a dog's barking—these were sounds of life and they did not wake the sleeping. Here the trucks, the ships—then it came to her suddenly that these were sounds of American life. Perhaps they did not waken Americans. They had not waked Liang. He had begun to snore delicately and at the familiar sound she too fell into old habit and dozed off into her own slumber.

22

THE ANCESTRAL VILLAGE seemed to settle back into the earth after Mrs. Liang left it. None had quite realized how her busy presence had drawn them into a new energy. Within her natural self she had means of communication with everyone. While she did no more than give greeting to the sons of Uncle Tao, elder and younger, yet they saw her good open face often and they heard her loud voice kindly advising and exhorting and talking. Her short heavy footstep was not the footstep of the younger women who had never bound their feet, and certainly it was not the stumping of the older women whose feet had been badly bound in childhood. Uncle Tao missed her when she was gone, for though she had not talked much with him she had devised small comforts for him. She had washed and turned his winter padded robes and she had made him a new bedquilt, light and warm.

But upon James she had left her greatest influence. He saw what he had never known before, that his mother was not at all a stupid woman. It was true that hers was a brain which could neither receive nor retain an abstract idea, that is, an idea which had nothing to do with the simple welfare of those she loved. Heaven, God, Government, Communism, War, Human Rights, Religion, all the large words which provided modern argument she tolerated as amusement only for men. While they argued and talked she was busy, hand and mind. She did not consider that people whom she did not know and to whom she was not related were her concern. Yet if any were brought within the orbit of her knowledge she busied herself at once with their needs, too. She saw men and women whole, both as they were and as they felt they were. James was surprised and even horrified that she had not insisted on Uncle Tao's operation, for example. He had talked with her about it and she could see for herself that Uncle Tao was gradually beginning to waste. Yet when James had urged her to persuade the old man, she had refused to do so. "Uncle Tao knows his own heart and body," she declared. "If I persuade him and he is not so happy afterward, I shall blame myself."

Because of her visit James understood his place in the ancestral village as he had not before. He and Mary and Chen belonged to the modern age in which they lived. The twentieth century was their atmosphere. But Uncle Tao belonged in the eighteenth century and he kept the village there with him. His mother, James saw, was the bridge between these centuries. Her interest in humanity was eternal, from the beginning of mankind and until the end. None could be too modern for her to approach with lively interest, and none too old for her to comprehend. That she was such a woman was unknown even to herself. She did not think of herself at all. She had no time for such thinking and no interest in it.

So James came to understand his mother in this ancestral village. He saw her in the strange unbalance of the world as it was, a world where new and old had to live together on their differing levels. She became significant to him. He told himself that she was the human creature most essential to men like himself, men who had sped far ahead of their native age.

Therefore when his mother had proposed to him one day that she find a wife for him, James had acquiesced with a sense almost of fatalism. He was unable to choose for himself. He might be misled again and again, and all his life could be spoiled by a wife who did not understand what he wanted to do. He did not need a woman to lead him farther away from their ancestral village. He needed and must have a woman who would root him here firmly by the force of her own life and understanding. When his mother told him, therefore, some six or seven days before she went, that she had found a young woman whom she thought suitable he had said, "I hope she is like you."

His mother had looked surprised. "Now how did you think of that?" she demanded. "The truth is she does make me think of myself as I was when I came here to marry your pa."

"Then sign the betrothal papers for me," he had said.

She had been troubled by his sudden willingness and had

probed him for a while. "You know, James," she had said earnestly, "if you marry such a girl as this Yumei, you cannot divorce her. She is not a new-fashioned girl. When she comes here to be your wife, it is for as long as she lives. You cannot put her away."

"I understand that, Ma," he had answered.

But she was still not satisfied until she had sent Mary and Chen to him, and from the wisdom of their good marriage they also besought him to think what he did.

"I think Ma has chosen too quickly," Mary said. "She wants everything settled before she goes back to Pa."

"Ma's instincts about her children are surprisingly sure," James replied. They were in his small living room, the door closed and barred, and they were speaking in English. "But there is so much you know that she will not know," Mary urged. "Now when Chen and I talk together, our minds are the same. We do not talk across a distance."

James smiled at this. "You and Chen both like to talk. But as you very well know I talk only a little. I can remember even when we were children, Chen, that this sister of mine complained against me because I did not talk much."

He did not want to explain everything to them, and indeed he could not. He knew only that his life was to be here in the ancestral village and in the country around it, and if from here the work he did could spread into other parts, then he would be satisfied. He could never live as his father did. Perhaps there was too much of his mother in him. He had to live from his roots up. Well, he had found his roots, and it was time to begin living.

When his mother saw that he was calm and sure, she went on with the betrothal. Of course Uncle Tao must be consulted, and there was no difficulty there. Uncle Tao was pleased except that he felt Mrs. Liang had gone ahead of herself in choosing the girl and that this should have been left to him. But when she told him about the Yang family and he heard that they owned their land and had some cash beside and that Yang Yumei could not read and write, he felt content. "Two like your daughter," he had declared, "would be too many for our village."

Mrs. Liang did not tell him that Mary was resolved to teach her new sister-in-law to read immediately after the wedding. With men like Uncle Tao it did not do to tell everything. A little truth at a time was as much as he could bear without losing his temper.

Before she went back to America, therefore, Mrs. Liang had seen to it that the betrothal papers were signed and sealed and the first gifts exchanged. Into the hands of the eldest daughter-in-law of Uncle Tao she put the final plans for the wedding and for the last gifts. Since the parents could not be present at the wedding Uncle Tao must stand in their place, and the wedding should be small. Dearly did she wish that she could stay and do it all herself, but she did not feel it right to hasten the wedding by so much. James should have a month at least in which to prepare his mind, and she dared not leave Liang alone for another month. His letters had been short and unsatisfactory and she had not heard from him for two weeks. Then she controlled her worry. "I cannot worry myself on two sides of the ocean at the same time," she confided to Mary.

"Oh, poor Ma," Mary had answered. "You mustn't worry about us, at least. I can't promise about Pa."

Mrs. Liang had bristled. "Your pa is fine," she had retorted, and was strengthened in her resolve to return quickly ↄ him.

She busied herself after that and arranged for James to have two more rooms for his share of the house and she bought some good furniture from the local carpenter, who was a Liang tenth cousin. Then she had wrenched herself away from the beloved village.

James had set the wedding day. During the holidays he knew he would have no new patients. He did not intend to take a honeymoon, for he knew that nothing would terrify his unknown wife more than that. Nevertheless he did not wish to have all the hours of the day and many hours of the night busy as they now were with the sick. His marriage, incredible as it would seem to Su and Peng and their kind, excited him with curiosity and wonder, and he wanted time to begin it well. It might be successful. Certainly he would love no one again as he had loved Lili. That fire had burned itself out even to the capacity for renewal. He did not want to love like that. It had been a destructive love.

Half amused at himself, he declared to Mary and Chen that there was sound wisdom in the ancestral way of choosing a wife for a man.

"Take Ma," he said one evening as they idled for an hou[r] before he went back to settle his patients for the night. "Surel[y] she knows me better than I know myself. She knows th[e] family traits. Who could choose better for me?"

They neither agreed nor disagreed with him. They smile[d] and listened, aware that this marriage was for him more tha[n] marriage. It was reunion with his own people.

Thus did James Liang wait for his wedding day. The ide[a] of this marriage pleased him more and more, and it please[d] Uncle Tao and the family, for it was like their own marriage[.] They drew close to James as they had never done, and h[e] felt this and was made happy by it. The tenants on the lan[d] and the villagers, who had so long thought him half foreig[n] now began to tease him and laugh at it and treat him as on[e] of themselves, and James liked this, too. He found himse[lf] laying aside his aloof ways, and he was more lively in h[is] talk and bearing than Mary had ever seen. She said nothi[ng] to him lest she damage this new nature, but to Chen she sa[id] with much wonder, "I believe Yumei is making a new ma[n] of Jim, even before they meet."

"He has chosen his way, and so he can stop thinking abo[ut] it," Chen said. He, too, did not speak to James of his n[ew] ways, although the two were together constantly.

Never had James worked so hard. He and Chen had a[l]ready begun work in the first three rooms of what was to b[e] their hospital. While masons and carpenters built added room[s] the sick lay on the floors and in tiers of beds against the wal[l] The courtyard swarmed with their families who came to sta[y] and see with their own eyes that no damage was done t[o] their helpless relatives. What patience did it take to try t[o] heal those who were near death! But James had put his dog[g]ed will to work at the level at which he found his people. H[e] would heal them in a house like their own, though clean an[d] filled with fresh air. The earthen floors were sprinkled with u[n]slacked lime and he caught sunshine in every corner that h[e] could. The hospital faced south, and the one-story room[s] stood in lines with open courts between, and the places wher[e] the sun could not reach were used for fuel and boxes. He ha[d] begun with three rooms, easily within the cost of the mone[y] his mother had given him of her savings. The people wou[ld] have to pay for each room as it was needed. He explaine[d] this and everyone paid a little and this little was put asid[e]

When he cured a local warlord or a petty official, he asked more and they gave more for the sake of pride. Su and Kang and Peng would have laughed, James knew, but this was his hospital and not theirs, and it was the only way he could build it.

Meanwhile his nights, when he was not called anywhere, were busy with teaching. He and Chen between them were training fifteen young men from neighboring villages as well as the ancestral one. These men when they had enough knowledge to know how little it was, so that they would not pretend to more power than they had, which is the danger of ignorance, would travel through the countryside to wash and disinfect sores and ulcers and bad eyes, to treat malaria and smallpox and to bring to the hospital such as they could not heal.

This was the simple but large plan which James and Chen had made for themselves. There was more than mere healing to be done. Every tool had to be contrived. They built their own operating table, with the Liang cousin's help. They put up a diet kitchen of earthen walls and plastered the ceiling to keep the dust of the thatch from the cauldrons, and Rose, the head nurse, took this under her charge. When Mary was troubled about her lest she be lonely, lest she should not marry and have her own life, Rose laughed as she laughed at everything. "There are already too many children," she declared, "why should I think that mine would be better than those already born?" There were many women like Rose in these times of change, women who did not want to submit to the old rules of marriage and yet who did not draw attention to themselves for any special beauty or ability. These are the good women of the world, and Rose was one of them.

His wedding day drew on, and out of deference to his unknown wife, whom now that he had decided upon the old way of marriage, he was determined to hold in respect, whether love grew between them or not, James gave up the hospital to Chen for three days. Since he could be a little idle, he took the time to see that his rooms were neat and his clothes clean and whole, in which Mary helped him. Young Wang came from the inn and they decided upon the wedding feast dishes, and then Young Wang stayed and shaved James's face for him and cut his hair, as he used to do when he was a serving man. He gave much good advice to his old master while he did so.

"I too married a local girl, as you know," he told James. "I has turned out well and we are expecting a child. But from the very first I let her see that I am the head and she is the hands. Women need to know their boundaries. They are lik fowls. If they see the whole world before them they ru everywhere squawking and laying no eggs. But if they see the wall, the fence, the yard, the closed gate, they settle down i peace upon their nests."

To this James listened with pretended gravity. Within him self he had already determined his course. He would be as h always was, neither yielding nor imposing, and from this van tage he would wait to discover the soul of the woman. H prayed only that she had a sweet temper.

The wedding day was one of those days which are commo in dry northern regions where the snow seldom falls. The sk was cloudless and cold and there was no wind. This was luck for the wild winds of winter, tearing the sand from the desert and grinding it against human flesh, torturing eyes and turnin hair and skin the color of dust, are calamity on a weddin day. James listened when he woke that morning and wa grateful for quiet. It was well past dawn, and were there to b wind it would have been already raging.

Instead it was a day of strange and even unusual peac The house was still and the Liangs slept late, for it was to b a holiday. Then they bestirred themselves and made ready fo the noon when the bride would come in her red sedan chai Uncle Tao was got up and ate and dressed in his best gar ments and every child was washed and given some new thin to wear. Since fresh garments had been prepared for the ne year, it was cheap enough to put them on a little early.

James rose late, too, and he took his breakfast with Che and Mary as usual. He had wondered how he would feel o his wedding day and was surprised that he felt nothing, neithe fear nor joy. This, he told himself, was because he had no seen the face of his bride. Other men had told in his hearin of their old-fashioned wives and how stupid they were an how shy upon their wedding nights, and how often they wep He would ask nothing of her tonight. He had already planne what he would say to her. "You and I have chosen one an other in the old way of our ancestors," he would tell her. "Y we are not as our ancestors were. We live in two worlds, th old and the new. Therefore let us be friends for a while, unt we know what we are. Then, after we are friends—" He did not believe that his mother would have chosen for him a woman too stupid to understand this.

After his breakfast he dressed himself carefully in his Chinese clothes. When she saw him it must be as a man of their people. He did not want to dismay her by looking foreign to her at first, for she would discover much that was strange to her in him as time went on.

In spite of all this determined calm, James felt his heart hurry its beat when noon came. He could not but realize, silently, that what he was about to do was unchangeable. Then he remembered how often in the centuries past men, his ancestors, had stood as ignorant as he of their fate. For them as for him marriage was not for individual pleasure. It was the unfolding of life itself. Man and woman, unknown before, took that step, each toward the other, and what had been separate became one. He must think of himself as man and of her as woman. Their life was only part of the whole of life.

In such spirit he waited in the main room of the Liang house with all the Liang family. Uncle Tao sat in the highest seat, dressed in his best robe of old-amber-hued satin and his leeved jacket of black cut velvet. Upon his head he wore his black satin cap with a red corded button. Each of the older male cousins, dressed in his best, sat in his proper seat, and the female cousins went out to welcome the bride and receive her into the house.

The red sedan wedding chair reached the gate an hour after noon. Half an hour later, while James still waited with Uncle Tao and the cousins in the big room, the doors were opened. James looked toward it. He saw Mary coming toward him, smiling and holding by the hand his bride. He saw a slender figure clothed from head to foot in scarlet satin. Her head was bent under its beaded veil, but through the strands he saw a grave good face, the eyelids dropped, the mouth firm and red.

Uncle Tao rose, and with him all the cousins. The wedding had begun.

When James entered his room that night and heard the door closed behind him, he knew that now the goodness of his life depended upon him and upon this unknown woman. She sat beside the table and her hands lay one upon the other on her lap. They were brown and not too small, and the nails were not painted. She still wore the beaded veil and her head was drooped as he had seen it and her eyelids were still downcast. She sat motionless, waiting, he knew, for him to lift the veil from her head. He went forward at once and putting his hand to the headdress he lifted it off and set it on the table.

He tried to make his voice pleasant, easy, something a woman need not fear.

"How heavy this is! I hope you have not a headache from wearing it all day."

At this she looked up quickly and then away again. "I have a little headache," she said, "but it will pass soon. I am very healthy."

He liked her plain voice, the accent rustic, yet clear. She was not pretty, but her face was good, the features straight and the skin smooth and brown as is common with country women. Her eyes were wide apart and large enough to look honest. The mouth was generous and it looked sweet tempered. For so much he could be grateful.

He sat down opposite her. "Tell me about your life," he said. "Then I will tell you about mine."

A mild look of surprise came on her face but after a few seconds she began without shyness. "What have I to tell? We are newcomers here and our ancestral home is some three hundred *li* away. I have no learning—and of this I am ashamed. But in a busy household on the land there is no time for a girl to go to school. My two younger brothers can read. We older ones had always to work. I am the middle child of my parents."

"It is easy to read," James said. "My sister will teach you if you wish."

"I do wish," she said. "That is, if you can spare the time for me to learn."

"There will be time," James said.

Then simply, so that it would not awe her, he told her of his own life and how it had been spent abroad and why he had wanted to come back to his own people. She listened, sitting motionless, her head inclined, not looking at him, and he found himself telling her more than he had planned. When he had finished she said in a grave quiet way which he already saw was natural to her, "Our country is now in bad times. There are those who go away in such times and those who come back. The good ones come back."

He was delighted with this. In so few words she had put what he had tried to tell himself often in many ways, but never so simply and clearly. Now he could make the proposal of friendship. "You are tired. Let me say what I have to say. You and I have chosen one another in the old way of our ancestors—"

He went on and she listened. When he had finished she gave a small quick nod of her head and for the first time she looked into his eyes. "Your mother told me you were a good man," she said. "Now I know you are."

After his wedding his life flowed on scarcely changed from what it had been. Within a few days Yumei had taken her place in the household. She was a quiet woman. Yet when they were alone James found an increasing pleasure in talking with her. She had a large mind, and her thoughts were fresh because they were her own. Since she had been always busy in her family of brothers no one had taken time to know her thoughts, and this treasure was his own now to discover. Soon she began to make small comfortable changes in their rooms and he found his food served hot and on time, at hours when he could most easily eat. When he came in at night there was always something light and hot to eat and he found he slept better for it.

And it was Yumei who first told him that Uncle Tao was frightened and in pain. "Please look at our Old Head," she said to him one morning. "Yesterday he was weeping behind his hand when he thought no one could see him. But I saw him and when the others left, I asked him to tell me what was wrong, and so I know that the knot in him weighs on his veins and he cannot sit or sleep."

"I have long told him that he should let me cut it out," James said to defend himself.

She sat down at a distance from him and folded her hands as she always did when she was about to talk with him. She spoke freely to him but she kept the little formalities she had been taught. "Please forgive me," she said. "You know everything better than I do, I think, but this one thing perhaps I know better—it is how people feel. The middle child, especially if she is a daughter, is the one who looks at both elder and younger and she is a bridge between them. Now Uncle Tao wants secretly to be rid of his knot, but he is afraid he will die if he is cut."

James was a little impatient with this. "I have told him he will die if he does not have it out."

"He told me you said so," she replied in the same quiet voice. "That is what makes him so afraid. He has no way to turn. Now let us tell him this way. Promise him that he will live if he has it cut out."

"But he might not live!" James exclaimed.

"Promise him he will live," she said coaxingly. She was looking at him now, her eyes bright and soft. "If he dies he will not know it. If he lives then you will be right. And if he believes he will live, it will give him strength not to die."

It was hard to refuse this shrewd persuasion. James sat silent for a while thinking it over. It happened to be true enough—the belief that he would live was more powerful than any medicine for a sick man.

"Surely life is the most precious thing," Yumei urged, when James did not speak.

Again it seemed to him that she was right. Men continued to kill each other as they had for centuries and for many reasons, not knowing that life was more precious than anything for which they died.

"I will do it, if Uncle Tao can be persuaded," he said at last.

"I will persuade him," she said.

What Yumei's persuasion was, none knew. But all knew that some sort of slow powerful gentle argument was going on between the old man and the young woman. She served him every day with a favorite food and she sat with him while he ate and when he had eaten she began her persuasion, urging him to life. For how would the Liang household continue without him, she asked. She pointed out that in such times as these the old and the wise were the only lamps to guide the feet of the people. She so persuaded Uncle Tao that he ceased to think of himself as an aging useless old man. She filled him with the necessity to live. It became his duty to live, and then she made him believe that he could live. When he had reached this place she went and told James.

All were astonished. Uncle Tao's sons were fearful but he himself put courage into them. The elder daughter-in-law was not too pleased at this success of a newcomer over the older ones who had failed, and Mary, who liked Yumei well, could not but wonder if Uncle Tao were worth so much trouble.

But James gave none of them time to think, either for or against. He knew that he must take this moment when Uncle Tao's courage was high. He prepared the next day to do the work, and he took no more patients that day and set himself to this one stupendous task. Did he fail with his own flesh and blood, did Uncle Tao die, no one in the ancestral village would believe in him again and he would have to move his hospital elsewhere. This monstrous knowledge was forced upon him by the excitement of the kinfolk in the house and by the villagers and by the men on the land, who came in when they heard what was about to happen, and to stay until they knew Uncle Tao had been cut and sewed up again safely.

Again luck was with James. There was no wind or sand the next day and the small operating room was clean. Early in the morning Uncle Tao was moved there upon a litter carried by his sons, and all the tenants who had spent the night in the courts rose while he passed and groaned in unison. Uncle Tao did not smile or speak. He kept his eyes shut and his lips set. When they lifted him upon the table he was inert. For him everything had begun. Only once did he speak after this. When he felt himself on the table he opened one eye. "Where is that young woman?" he asked.

"I am here," Yumei replied coming in at this moment. She looked at James with apology. "I had to tell him I would stay with him."

"Very well," James said.

Never had he undertaken so heavy a task and never had he been so afraid. Chen was with him and so was Rose, and she saw his hands tremble and she looked at Chen and saw that he saw it, too.

"Steady, Jim," Chen said in English. "We are here with you."

"Thanks," James said. But he knew that still he was alone. His was the hand that held the knife.

Rose put the ether cone over Uncle Tao's face and he kicked out his legs.

"Our good Old Head, I told you this would be done first," Yumei said in a quiet voice.

Uncle Tao shouted violently and then less violently and

then he gave out only a mumble and then a murmur, and then he was silent.

Now the eldest son of Uncle Tao had demanded to be in the room with his father to see that all went well. He stood against the door to let no one look through it, for the window was painted white, to keep out curious eyes, and he groaned when his father fell silent. "Is he not dying?" he asked.

"No," Yumei said, "I listen to the breathing."

James paid no heed to any of them. He had gone into that battlefield where he must make his solitary fight with the enemy who was Death. He must put out of his mind all else except victory. Chen had bared Uncle Tao's great belly and it was shaven and clean. Now with his knife James drew down a straight clean cut. The elder son moaned and fell to the floor and hid his face against the door. Yumei did not look but she stood by Uncle Tao's head, hearing his breathing. Once it faltered and she touched Rose's arm who spoke to Chen, who pressed a needle into Uncle Tao's arm.

The room was terrible in its silence. In the silence James worked swiftly. He was face to face with his enemy now, and time wa on the side of life. Chen was a matchless partner, standing at his side. Veins were clipped and held, and masses of old yellow fat were turned back. Working against time and the slowing breath, James lifted out at last the tumorous weight and threw it into the waste bucket. He did not look at Uncle Tao's face. Rose was watching that—Yumei, too, he remembered. Chen was handing him the veins, each to be put into place. His hands moved delicately, swiftly, and his courage soared. He had met his enemy and the victory was his. Uncle Tao would live.

Yet life after battle with death is a wary thing, poised always like a bird for flight. Uncle Tao had to be watched day and night, and Yumei never left him. She had some sort of life in herself which caught and held the life in Uncle Tao when it was about to escape. James with all his skill was not so alert as she to know when Uncle Tao needed food quickly or the needle thrust into his arm.

It was Yumei who did a thing at once absurd and yet of great comfort to Uncle Tao. She picked up the tumor from the waste and put it in a big glass bottle which had once held medicines. This bottle she filled with strong kaoliang wine, and she sealed it and put it in Uncle Tao's room. She knew it would give him pleasure to look at his tumor, even when he was too weak to speak.

He stared at it for a long time one day. Then he had asked, "Is that—it?"

She nodded. "That is what wanted your life, Uncle Tao," she replied. He lay looking at it often after that and to see it imprisoned and helpless made him feel strong. He knew himself saved.

"Who would have thought of doing such a thing except Yumei?" Mary cried when she heard of it.

"Yumei is close to people and to life," Chen said. To James, Chen began to speak of Yumei thus. "I begin to think your mother chose you a good woman."

"I begin to think so, too," James said. He was brusque because he did not want to speak of Yumei to anyone. Something as delicate as silver, as fine as a dew-laden cobweb, was beginning to be woven between him and his wife. It must not be touched.

When Uncle Tao was well enough to sit up he invited all his friends to come and see what had been taken out of him and he boasted of its size and color.

"I kept this thing in me for many years," he said, looking around on them all solemnly. "At first I was the stronger but it grew stronger than I. Then I said to my nephew, the doctor, 'Take it out of me.' He was afraid—eh, he was truly afraid! But I was not afraid. I lay down on the table and smelled his sleeping smell, and he cut me open. My elder son saw everything and he told me. My nephew lifted that knot out of me and my nephew's woman put it in the bottle. Now I am as good as new."

He was never weary of telling his story, and it must be said that no one was weary of hearing it. Even the kinfolk who heard the story every day or two were proud of Uncle Tao. Thereafter whenever someone complained of a pain in him somewhere Uncle Tao ordered him to come to the hospital where his nephew would cut it out and his nephew's wife would put it in a bottle. Thus it became a matter of some fashion to have tumors in bottles standing on the table in main rooms of houses, but Uncle Tao's was always the biggest and best of them all.

From now on James was Uncle Tao's favorite, and nothing

could be refused him. James was grateful for this, yet he saw very well that Uncle Tao had come out of the struggle with death as unrepentant as ever. He was still the same crafty bold old man and he kept his best friends among officials and secret police and tax gatherers. He still considered the tenants his possessions, and laughed when he heard of their small rebellions.

This troubled Yumei, who belonged to the people, and one night she told James of her fears. He listened, having soon learned to consider whatever she told him, for she did not talk idly.

"When that day comes and the people turn against the officials and the police and the tax gatherers," Yumei said, very troubled, "shall we be strong enough to save Uncle Tao?" She shook her head and broke off, not answering her own question.

"Can we save ourselves?" James asked.

"Our people do not kill those who serve them as you do," she replied. "We are safe enough."

He knew that it was she who kept them safe. He understood more clearly with every day that Yumei was the bridge he had needed to his own people. When they feared him and his foreign ways, they went to Yumei and she came to him. Through her he saw them and comprehended what he had not been able to know before. Thus through her he began to put down his roots into his ancestral land.

What is the end of a story? There is no end. Life folds into life, and the stream flows on.

No sudden love sprang up between James and his wife. He knew that she loved him before he loved her, and he was grateful for her patience with him. His love was to be the growth of years. But it seemed to him one day not too long after his wedding that a woman deserves to have children and so at last he became her husband. He was glad that he had not waited upon any dream of love. For after this Yumei took confidence as his wife, and she became a true part of all he did. It was she who stood beside women weeping in hard childbirth and she who held children in her arms when eyes had to be burned clean of trachoma, and she was not afraid to stay with one who had to die. She was no saint. Sometimes she grew weary and wanted to be alone and then he let her be. But she could always be called back when life was threatened. She had the gift of life.

And life, James knew, was what he wanted.